CW01080766

'Where Silence has Lease'

'…It's the great big, broad land 'way up yonder,
It's the forests where silence has lease…'
(Robert Service)

TRICIA A. BESSELL

'WHERE SILENCE HAS LEASE'

Published by Trishan Publications, 2014

Copyright © 2014 Tricia A. Bessell

ISBN: 978-1500469023

Tricia A Bessell asserts the moral right to
be identified as the author of this work

DEDICATION

To the First Nations people of the Yukon Territory, Canada

'WHERE SILENCE HAS LEASE'

'Where Silence has Lease'

Prologue
October 1964

The pilot announced the plane's approach to London airport. It had been a long, tiring flight and two year old Mary was tearful. She didn't like the roaring noise as the plane made its descent and her ears hurt.

'Are we there? I want Mommy.' She cried as she clung to the man next to her. The man took no notice of the little girl; instead he continued to look out of the window.

'The pressure on her ears is probably quite painful. Can I give her a sweet to suck?' asked John, a young man sitting next to Mary.

'If you like,' he muttered, without even turning around, 'anything to shut her up. She's whined like this since we left home.'

'Here you are little one. Have one of these fruity spangles. Suck it nice and slowly and it'll make you feel better.' John was from a big Irish family in Dublin, in Eire, and he was used to looking after his younger brothers, sisters and cousins. He felt sorry for this little girl. She had been tearful and anxious the whole time and this rude man, who was with her, didn't seem to want to be bothered with her.

'Are you taking her to her mother in England?' John asked.

'No. I'm stuck with her. She's a pain in the arse. I

know nothing about babies. I'm sick of it. Also, it's none of your business.' The man scowled.

'I'm not baby. I'm girl.' Mary pushed him away.

Once they got off the plane John walked with them in case this chap needed any help. He knew that Mary wouldn't cope with the long walk to the passport control and the baggage hall. She was very small and very tired. She clutched a little shopping bag which John could see contained a few clothes. Her hair hadn't been brushed and her face was wet and dirty from crying. Poor little waif, thought John. He considered his journey home. He had run out of money so he would have to hitch a ride to North Bucks where he had planned to stay with his sister for the night. Maybe she would lend him the money for the bus to Holyhead. Luckily he already had his ferry ticket back to Dun Laoghaire.

Just as he thought, after a few minutes of trying to keep up with Bob, Mary's little legs wouldn't take her any further. She sat down and refused to move. She sucked her thumb and stared at John. Bob kept on walking.

'Stay there then,' he shouted at her. 'See if I care.' Mary began to cry again.

John spotted an abandoned trolley and brought it over to where Mary was sitting.

'Here. I'll give you a ride and we'll catch up with your Daddy,' he said, sitting her next to his flight bag.

'He's not Daddy,' she said between sobs, 'he's Bob.'

They raced off down the corridor and found Bob in the queue.

'You can't just abandon a little kid. What sort of a man are you?'

'Well, she's not mine. She's my sister's kid. Take her

if you want. You know so much. Take her. You said you have big family. One more is nothing.'

'Don't be ridiculous.' John was horrified.

'Here, I give you some cash? You said you had no money. You take her then ... yeah?' They were now at the carousel waiting for their luggage.

John couldn't believe it. This man was trying to sell a child. He should really go to the police. However, he decided to take her to his sister. She would know what to do. He didn't trust this man. He was worried for the little girl's safety.

'Alright. I'll take her to my sister. *I* need the money and I don't think you'll look after her properly.'

Bob handed over some notes and told him her things were in her own bag. He picked up his suitcase and walked away without a word to Mary.

'What about her passport?' John shouted after him, but he had disappeared.

Somehow or other they managed to get to the arrivals hall without being stopped by a customs official. John began to panic. What had he done? Mary didn't seem to mind that Bob had disappeared, and she clung on to John's coat as though she knew he would take good care of her. They sat down in a cafe. John bought her a drink and a little cake. He realised that he had to explain to her what was about to happen and he didn't know how.

'Bob has to go to a meeting and so I'm going to take you to my sister's house. She has a little girl about your age and she will love you,' he said with a smile.

Mary was almost asleep. He lifted her back into the trolley and went in search of the Hertz Rentals desk. He had decided to hire a car. It would be easier, especially with a sleepy toddler to look after.

Once out on the road, Mary slept. John had put his coat underneath her head as she laid flat on the back seat. Strangely enough she seemed more relaxed than she had been on the plane. She seemed to trust John which made him feel guilty that he was about to lie to her again when they arrived in Buckinghamshire.

John headed out towards the motorway. When Mary woke up she needed the toilet and so he stopped at a motorway service station. He had to ask a mother with two young girls to take her in with them while he waited outside. He had a pressure headache. The seriousness of what he had done began to hit him. His sister would be cross with him and would make him take Mary to the police station. She was a single mother of two. Times were hard. There was no way she could raise three children on her own.

It was getting dark now and was starting to rain. The steady rhythmical movement of the windscreen wipers was making him feel dozy and he longed to be sitting in front of his sister's fire with a large glass of Bushmills. Mary was singing songs quietly to herself. He didn't know what they were but they sounded pretty. He couldn't believe how calm she was and how content she was in his company. As he made his way out towards his sister's village, he saw a sign ahead of him – all lit up against the night sky. It read: 'The Sacred Spirit Orphanage for Girls.' It seemed to beckon him. He drew up outside the wrought iron gates and switched off the engine.

'Are we there?' Mary asked as she gazed up at the big sign. John wrestled with his conscience. If he left Mary in the care of nuns then her future would be safe and assured, and he could avoid any contact with the police. He asked Mary if he could look in her bag for a moment to see if there was a letter or anything. She handed her little shopping bag to him.

'Here's a letter,' she said, clutching a grubby envelope with Mary written on it in big letters. It wasn't sealed. He opened it but there was no letter inside, just an old photo. He closed the envelope and added something on the front of it as Bob had requested back at the airport. He made a decision. He would take her to the front door, ring the bell and then hide so they couldn't see him. He hated himself but he knew she would be well looked after.

'We're here,' he said to Mary. 'Bring your bag with you. This is the sister I was telling you about. She'll meet you at the door and will take good care of you. She's a nun. Do you know what a nun is?'

Mary shook her head and looked anxious.

'You come too.'

'Yes, but I have to put my car away.' They walked towards the big house together. The moon cast eerie shadows across the drive in front of them and an owl hooted from the trees nearby. Mary was frightened and clung tightly to John's hand. In the distance, a lifelike statue of the Virgin Mary glowed in the moonlight. Mary put her arms up and asked to be carried, but John kept on walking. This is like a nightmare. Please let this be over soon, he thought.

'God forgive me' he said quietly as he made the sign of the cross. They stood in front of the double doors hand in hand. John rang the bell. He could hear some heavy bolts being pulled across on the other side. He stood rooted to the spot. When the door opened he couldn't move. A young woman, dressed simply in the black and white uniform of a novice, smiled down at Mary.

'Well now, who have we here?' she said to John.

'This here is Mary. She's about two or three years old I think. She was abandoned at London airport and was left with me. The man who was with her ran off. I'm on

5

my way back to Ireland and I didn't know what to do so when I saw your sign I brought her here. She's a dear little thing, so she is.'

'Have you anything more you can tell me about her? Who was the man that was with her? What is her surname? Where is she from?' John told her all that he knew and gave her the envelope.

'And who might you be?' She smiled at John. 'I think we had better discuss this matter with Mother Superior first, if you would like to come this way.' The young nun turned to lead Mary into the entrance hall and John used the opportunity whilst her back was to him. He panicked and ran off into the dark night.

Mary watched him go and began to cry.

'Where's John?'

'I'm not sure now Mary. You had better come with me and I'll make you a nice warm drink.'

Mary didn't like it in there. It smelt funny and it was dark. The floor was hard and cold through her little boots and there was that big lady again that didn't move. Another statue hung above her. The young novice took her to meet Mother Superior who frowned with annoyance at being disturbed so late in the evening.

'She'll have to go into the nursery and we'll find her a bed in the morning. She looks filthy so give her a bath and a hot drink and put her in a cot for tonight. May the saints preserve us,' she sighed.

Mary stared at the nun's wimple. She hadn't seen anything like it before. It fascinated her.

The 'nursery' was a small box room with nothing in it but four cots. Mary could see babies asleep in three of them.

'I'm not baby,' said Mary for the second time that day.

'I know, but for tonight you'll sleep here and we'll arrange something else for you tomorrow. Do you have a nightdress in your bag?'

'Don't know.' Mary was sucking her thumb.

'Take that out of your mouth child.' She pulled Mary's hand away. Mary began to cry again.

She was given a nightdress to wear. It felt rough and had a strange, sickly smell. She lay curled up in the cot with a single blanket over her and longed for her Mom to come and kiss her goodnight.

Chapter 1
Greenwich 1983

Mary arrived a few minutes late at the playgroup, but without four year old Alex. Her eyes were swollen from crying and streaks of mascara stained her cheeks. She clung to the gate as her friend Sally rushed through.

'Sal!' cried Mary. 'Help me. I don't know what to do.' Mary burst into tears and her legs gave way beneath her. Sally tried to catch her before she collapsed.

'God, Mary! I nearly ran past you. You look awful. What an earth has happened? Has something happened to Alex?' Sally noticed the large hold-all at Mary's feet, with her winter coat lying on top. It was mid-June and it was hot already.

'Alex is fine. It's me. I've walked out on my job. It's no good. I can't stay in the house with that man a minute longer. Oh Sal, I feel terrible about Alex. I've loved that little boy like my own and I didn't even say goodbye.'

Mary slumped down on her bag and wiped her eyes on the sleeve of her tee-shirt. All energy had drained out of her during the past few months.

Sally put her sunglasses in the pocket of her shorts and ran her hands through her thick blonde hair. She was already late for her tutorial and wasn't sure what to do either. She looked down at Mary's face, which was a picture of desolation. She realised that she had to stay with her.

'Wait there for a moment, Mary. I'll see if I can ring

the hospital from the office here and then we'll go somewhere quiet for a chat. I'll explain that I need compassionate leave for the day.'

Sally was in her final year of study for a Diploma in Occupational Therapy and she hoped to secure a job at the local Greenwich hospital as it would be really close to home and to her son's school in September.

Sally drove them up to Blackheath. Having parked the car, they chose a seat by the duck pond near the village. It was peaceful and watching the mallards, as they glided effortlessly around the pond, had a soothing effect upon Mary. They sat together in a comfortable silence for a few minutes.

'What's wrong with me Sal? Why do men feel they can use me for their own amusement. Am I giving off the wrong signals or something?'

'Are you talking about your employer – Gerard? I met him once when he brought Alex to the playgroup. He gave me the creeps. He seemed to undress me with his eyes. I loathe men like that.'

'He just won't leave me alone. I dread being in the house with him when his wife isn't there.'

'Has he always been like this? You never said anything before.'

'The first couple of years he was bearable, but once his wife became pregnant again he couldn't keep his hands off me. I guess he's not getting any from her. He's disgusting. I hate him!'

Mary began to sob quietly. Sally put her arm around her.

'It sounds like sexual harassment to me. Mary you could report him to the police for that.'

'I couldn't possibly talk about this to complete

strangers. I'd be embarrassed. Anyway, the police would probably blame me and say I encouraged him or something.'

'I guess you're right. It would be your word against his. So, what do you want to do now? Are those your only worldly possessions in the back of my car? Do you have any money?'

'Yes that's all I've got. Most of my clothes are what Teresa, Alex's mother has given me. I've saved up a little bit of cash but not enough for two month's rent anywhere, especially around here.'

'You can stay with us until you get yourself sorted, if you like.' Sally gave Mary another hug.

'If I like? Sally, that's fantastic. Of course I'd love to stay with you and William. What will William think? Will he mind? Oh Sal I was terrified that I might have to go back to sleeping rough again, like I did when I first came to London. I couldn't bear it!'

'No friend of mine will ever live on the streets. William knows you well Mary. He'll be pleased. It'll be someone new for him to play with or take him to the park. Come on. Let's go home and get some lunch. You haven't had any breakfast. You must be starving.'

Once in the car, Mary gazed across the heath towards Greenwich Park. When she first walked Alex up on to the heath in his push-chair three years ago, she had been amazed at the wonderful feeling of space everywhere even with the busy A2 road cutting across it on its way towards the city. Holiday-makers and people on their lunch-break were dotted all over the grass, enjoying the sun. Sea-gulls hovered above them, hoping for the odd stray crust. It had felt as though she was by the sea, somehow, although she had only seen the seaside in magazine pictures and films.

Sally and William lived in Greenwich, quite close to the hospital in Earlswood St. Mary hadn't been to their house before. She began to relax at the thought of her new home, however temporary it might be.

The next morning Mary lay in a warm lavender bath until the water was almost cold. She thought about her life and the things it had taught her during the past twenty years. She had learned more survival skills than anything. In the convent she had often wondered what it would be like to live with a family who loved her and encouraged her. She longed to find her own family one day. She needed to find out why, at the age of two, she had been dumped in a children's home. Why didn't my parents want me? Mary asked herself over and over again.

She studied herself in the mirror as she got dressed. Her dark olive skin, her jet black hair and her broad features told her that she was possibly of mixed race. As a school student she was tall and well developed for her age. She had looked older than her years. The other girls at high school had teased her about her dark skin, especially in the summer. The boys were constantly trying to date her. She hated school, except for hockey and music. She hated the convent. She hated her life most of the time and couldn't see that things would ever be any different.

That night, when William had gone to bed, Mary talked about this with Sally. She'd only known Sally for about a year and she hadn't really socialised with her, but from the very beginning, Mary was drawn to her, as though she had known her before somewhere. She believed they were soul mates. She felt that she could tell her anything and Sally would listen intently. She trusted her more than she had trusted anyone before.

'I feel ashamed. I've tried to change my life around this past three years. I had a respectable job as a nanny, had learnt to drive and was living with respectable people ... or so I thought and now this. Nothing seems to work out right for me. Why has my life been so awful Sal? Why am I being punished? What is it that I'm supposed to have done wrong?'

'Oh Mary! It's other people who have done things wrong, not you. You've done your best and look at you. You're lovely. A lot of girls would have become hard and bitter, maybe even entered a life of crime, after the childhood you've had. You're strong. You're a survivor. There are good things for you out there. I can feel it. You must believe in yourself.' Sally fetched two glasses from the kitchen and poured them both a glass of white wine.

'Here, get this down you. It'll help you to relax a little.'

'What shall I do? I'm definitely not working as a nanny anymore.'

'What would you like to do? Have you got any ideas? I'll help you.'

'I don't know. I'm not good at anything.'

'Yes you are. You'd make a great teacher. You could sing to your children. I've heard you singing to William. You've got a beautiful voice.'

'Sister Joseph told me that once when she stood next to me in church.' Mary blushed. 'Maybe I could get a job as a teacher's helper in a special needs class. I'd like that. Trouble is, I ran away to London before the school exams, so I don't have any qualifications. They'll think I've got special needs myself won't they?'

'Don't be silly, of course they won't. Why don't you go along to the college in New Cross and find out what classes you can take. I'll go with you, on Friday when William is with his father, if you like.'

'I'd better try to earn some money first. I'll go 'round all the shops in Greenwich and Blackheath this week and see if there are any vacancies. I don't mind what I do.' Mary reached across and hugged her friend. 'Thanks a lot for your support Sal. I'd be lost now without you.'

By the end of the summer, Mary was beginning to feel that life was worth living after all. She'd found a job in a small fashion boutique and the owner was good to her. She'd never been able to choose such trendy clothes before and as an employee she got a discount off the original price. Her boss looked at her one afternoon as she tried on a summer dress and encouraged her to think about a modelling course.

'You're beautiful, Mary. You're so tall and you have excellent posture. You could model my clothes for me.'

Mary was embarrassed and withdrew into the cubicle.

'I'd hate that. All those people staring at me. I'd like to work with children in a special school. I've signed on for a couple of evening classes at the local college.'

'Good for you. The children will be lucky to have you my dear.'

Mary enjoyed college. It wasn't like school. The tutors listened to what you had to say. She was mixing with young people like herself, many of whom had ambition and wanted to have a career but hadn't had the support or the opportunity at school. She could feel herself becoming a little more confident, although her tutors constantly told her to have more faith in her own ability. Several times she was asked out for a date with a young man in her class, but she always said 'No'.

'Why not say 'yes' for a change?' asked Sally. 'You never know, you might have a good time.'

'But how can you tell whether a bloke is genuine or

whether he's pretending to be nice?'

'Instinct, mainly, I suppose. You'll know when it feels right.'

'Oh I don't know. I don't think I will. Were you sure that you'd made the right choice when you married your husband? What exactly happened?'

'Yes of course I was, but I didn't anticipate that he'd then fall for someone else once I got pregnant. Still, that's a story for another time. William is due back any minute.'

Later that year, on a cold, wet November evening, Mary hurried in the direction of the college. She had missed the bus she wanted, so she had to walk quite a distance. It was raining hard and she'd forgotten her umbrella. Her long wet hair clung to the back of her neck as she ran and her right boot leaked. She was fed up. A car slowed down and the driver steered it close to where Mary was. God, that's all I need, she thought, 'a bloody kerb-crawler.'

'Get lost, you perve!' she called across to him.

'You're on the Health and Welfare Course aren't you? I've seen you there. I'm a student at the college too,' he persisted. 'Would you like a lift?'

'No. Leave me alone!' Mary shouted at him across the noise of the Friday night traffic.

'Here. Take my umbrella. You can return it to me when you see me.' He stuck the long black umbrella through the passenger window for her.

'I'll leave it at the office for you.' Mary grabbed the umbrella and carried on running along the New Cross Road.

'Press the button on the handle,' he shouted through the open window as he drove away.

The office was closed when she left her class and so

she took the umbrella home with her. She was glad of it. She studied it closely as she sat on the 'bus. It looked like a smart, businessman's umbrella. There was a tiny brass address label just below the handle. It read:

> Tom Selby-James,
> Flat 2, 8, Vanbrugh Gardens,
> Blackheath, London SE3.

She showed it to Sally when she got back and told her the story.

'It's a dumb thing to do, creeping up to a young girl in the dark. He's lucky he didn't get arrested,' said Sally, studying the address. 'This is a smart address alright. His name sounds posh as well. Did he seem nice? What did he look like?'

'He said he was a student at the college too. He sounded quite nice but that doesn't mean anything. I couldn't really see what he looked like. It was dark and pouring with rain.'

'Well, leave the umbrella in the office as you promised and if he's genuine he'll find you and apologise.'

The following week the secretary called her over and handed her a note. On the outside was written...

"The girl with my umbrella."

'A degree student called Tom asked me to give this to you. He described you to me and gave me the details of your course. Does this mean anything to you?' She said with a smile.

'Yes. Thank you.' Mary felt uncomfortable. 'I didn't

steal it ... honest. He lent it to me last week.' The secretary smiled.

'Of course, dear. Tom is one of my favourite students. Such a polite boy.'

Mary waited until she was in the classroom and then she opened the note. Mary's first thought was what beautiful handwriting he had.

Thanks for my umbrella. I'd like to apologise for frightening you last week. I was hoping you might recognise me. It was a stupid idea of mine. I first noticed you weeks ago and wanted to ask you out, but then I bottled it. I'm 23, single and hopeless at chatting up girls. I'm studying History at the college and I'd like to. take you for a drink sometime. Please say you'll come. I'll wait for you here after class next week. Tom S-J.

When she got home Sally also made a comment about the handwriting.

'It's unusual for a man. I wish I could decipher handwriting styles. Maybe he's a bit of a 'Mummy's boy'. I bet he's an only child and I bet he went to a public school.

Look at his hands when you meet him. You can tell a lot about a man by his hands.'

Mary was shocked by Sally's bluntness.

'That's terrible. How can you say that? He might not be any of those things. What do you think I should do?'

'Why don't you meet him outside the office? See how you feel when you've had a good look at him and chatted with him for a few minutes. If he gives you the creeps then catch the bus home and if he doesn't, go and have a drink with him and then catch the bus home.'

Mary laughed. She loved Sally's confident and practical way of dealing with difficult situations.

'What is your birth sign, Sally? I'm a Libran, I think.'

'Me too. That's why we get on so well. Mind you, at times I think you're more like a Gemini.'

The following week Mary carefully considered what she would wear for her class at college. She decided to look trendy, but smart. This would be her first proper date and if she liked him she wanted it to go well. After all, I must have looked like a drowned rat when he saw me two weeks ago, she thought. Christmas was in the air everywhere. The lights and the music were putting her in a party mood.

However, when the evening arrived, Mary sat in class feeling anxious and pre-occupied.

'What do you think this case might need first, Mary?'

The tutor asked her. Mary hadn't even heard any of the previous discussion.

'Oh, I'm not sure. Sorry.'

As she walked downstairs towards the front office, she could see him leaning against the window. His blonde hair was kept short. He was tall and well-built, like a sportsman. When he turned and saw her, he smiled. Lovely eyes, she thought. He has a kind smile. She liked him already.

'Hello Mary. I'm Tom. I'm so glad you've come. Have you forgiven me for scaring you the other week?'

'I don't know yet.' Mary smiled nervously.

'What would you like to do – go for a drink or a coffee somewhere? I know a pub with a log fire in Greenwich. It would be cosy on a night like this. What do you think?' Tom needed a beer.

'A coffee by the fire sounds good,' said Mary, 'and I live in Greenwich so your idea sounds fine.'

Tom walked with her to the students' car park and proudly indicated his white Triumph Herald.

'I love this car,' he said as she sat down next to him. He ran his fingers along the highly polished oak fittings. 'Look, it has a wooden dashboard and real leather seats. My dream is to own a Triumph Stag V8 one day – in either dark green or burgundy. They're really smart cars.'

'I'm sorry Tom. I don't know anything about cars. I passed my driving test, when I was a nanny, but I wouldn't know one car from another. If you asked me what kind of car my flat mate had I would say a little blue car.' They both laughed.

'Where are you from originally? That's not a London accent is it?' Tom asked her.

Mary went quiet. She wasn't sure how to answer him, because if she said that she didn't know, then the whole story would have to come out and it was much too soon for that.

'I don't know. I grew up in care, in a children's home in Buckinghamshire. It's a long story. I don't really want to talk about it, but one day I'll know the answer to that question. What about you? Do you come from London? Is Blackheath your home?'

'No. I'm from Suffolk in East Anglia. I moved to Blackheath in order to attend college here. I'm in my first year, reading history. Actually, the real reason I moved here was so that I could join the Blackheath rugby club,' he winked at her. 'Do you play any sports Mary?'

'I used to like hockey when I was in the high school. I was the top scorer one year. I'd really like to learn to swim sometime. We weren't allowed to do anything like that at the Convent.'

They talked and talked right through until 'last orders'. It was an easy and relaxed evening. Mary thought Tom was different from most men she'd met; he was a good listener and he made her feel that she was the only person in the room. He pulled a chair out for her to sit on in the pub ... and he helped her on with her coat. No man had ever done that for her before.

'Do you have to go to work tomorrow morning?' He asked her suddenly.

'Yes. I work in Blackheath village.'

Tom looked pleased.

'Maybe we could have lunch together in the village one day soon. I'd love to see you again.'

'I'd like that too. My lunch break is from one o'clock until two and my day off is Monday.'

'Right ... that's great. I'll check my timetable and then call in to see you. Now, give me some directions and I'll drop you home.'

Tom parked the car in the nearest available space in Sally's road and walked her to her door. They both stood shyly, facing one another.

'I've enjoyed this evening Tom. Thank you.'

'So am I forgiven?'

Mary nodded and smiled. Tom kissed her cheek, leapt over the brick wall and was gone.

Chapter 2
Christmas 1985

Mary stood at their bedroom window and studied the view across the heath. She loved her new home. It was one of those magical December days when the early morning sun lit up the hoar frost and made everything sparkle. Not a wisp of cloud was in the sky. Tom jumped out of bed and stood with his arms wrapped around her.

'Come back to bed darling. We've got hours yet before we have to leave.'

'I couldn't sleep. I keep thinking about meeting your family today. Are you sure it's not too soon? We've only been living together for three months. What have you told your parents about me?'

'I've told them how beautiful you are and that I love you. They will love you too, I'm sure. You worry too much.' Tom kissed her tenderly.

'Do they know that I've grown up in a children's home and that I work in a shop?'

'No. Not yet. But what does it matter what you do? You've got a new job now anyway. You must tell Mandy all about it. Your special school is probably similar to the one that she has just left.' Tom's sister was four years younger than him and had cerebral palsy.

Mary had just been offered a job as a teacher's assistant in a school for pupils with moderate learning disabilities. She had been too scared to ask Teresa for a reference, but her tutor at the college had spoken highly of her and the owner of the boutique had given her an excellent character reference. Mary was thrilled. It was the first time that anyone had written anything nice about her.

'Now, are you sure you've got everything?' Tom asked for the second time. 'We'd never have got all your stuff in the Triumph Herald. I'm glad I found a bigger car, even if it is an old banger.'

Half an hour earlier they had driven out on to the A2 and Mary had suddenly remembered that she hadn't packed any slippers. She had also left Tom's Christmas present in its special hiding place, so they had to turn around and go back. She felt a lot more nervous about this visit than she had about her job interview.

'Sorry love. My head is all over the place. I should have made a list like Sally always does. Will this make us late for dinner?'

'No. We've got lots of time. It's only a two hour journey and dinner at home is usually around seven o'clock; just as long as the bar is open when we get there.'

'They have a bar?' Mary couldn't imagine this country estate near Woodbridge. She had never seen one before.

'Only a small one in the library,' he grinned.

As Tom manoeuvred his Peugeot around the bend of a narrow country lane, Mary saw the sign above the wrought iron gates: 'The Selby Farm Estate.' As she stared at the gates, the drive and the big house, all floodlit for their benefit, she had a sinking feeling in her stomach. It could almost be another convent. Please let this be different, she said quietly to herself.

The front of the house was lined with Christmas trees which were covered in tiny white lights, and Tom's father had hung a huge cluster of mistletoe over the porch. He did this every Christmas. It all looked beautiful. Tom guided Mary towards the mistletoe and took her in his arms.

'Merry Christmas darling,' he said and kissed her. They didn't hear the front door open. Mary stood back and came face to face with Charlotte Selby-James who rushed past Mary without a word and threw herself at Tom.

'Oh my darling boy, it's wonderful to have you home. It's been ages. You never come to see us anymore.' Her loud voice filled the courtyard.

Meanwhile her husband, David, had quietly welcomed Mary and guided her into their imposing entrance hall. A ten foot Christmas tree stood at the bottom of a spiral staircase and the floor was piled high with exquisitely wrapped gifts. Mary stood like a small child and gazed in awe at her surroundings.

'Mother and Dad, I want you to meet my beautiful girlfriend. This is Mary. Mary Doyle.' Tom introduced her with pride. Charlotte offered her limp hand to Mary and gave her a brief 'air kiss'.

'Hello Mrs. Selby-James. I'm very pleased to meet you and thank you so much for inviting me.' Mary could feel her voice shaking slightly. David winked at her and smiled.

'You're very welcome dear. I hope your family are not cross with my son for luring you up here at Christmas time.'

'Oh no. I've been looking forward to meeting you all. Is Tom's sister, Mandy, here? I'd love to meet her and tell her all about my new job.'

'Oh really?' Charlotte sounded surprised. 'Yes, she's in the drawing room. Tom, do go through and see Amanda. She has been asking about you all day.'

Mandy sat in the corner of the settee, propped up with cushions. She had her father's auburn hair and her bright green eyes were focussed on Tom as the two of them entered the room. Tom bent down and gave her a big brotherly hug.

'Hello gorgeous,' he said.' You look lovely. Is that a new dress you're wearing?' Mandy shook with excitement. She just kept saying 'Tom' over and over again.

'Mandy, this is my girlfriend, Mary. She's going to be working in a school very like yours and she'd like to talk to you about it.'

'Tom's told me so much about you. It's lovely to meet you.' Mary took both of Mandy's hands in her own and smiled at her.

'Are you a teacher dear?' Charlotte gushed at the prospect of a professional daughter-in-law.

'No. I'll be a special support assistant with a Year 8 class in January.

'Oh, one of those...' Charlotte lost interest and took Tom through to the kitchen to show him the huge turkey they had bought for Christmas Day. David was opening a bottle of champagne. He came back into the room carrying a tray with four glasses.

'This is in honour of your visit,' he said, handing Mary a glass. He gave Mandy her own special glass and when the other two returned, he proposed a toast.

'Mary, you are welcome in our home. Let's drink to a very Happy Christmas together. Cheers!'

Mary noticed that Tom had stopped smiling and she could sense an atmosphere between him and his mother.

'Is everything alright?' she asked Tom as soon as they were alone on the top landing.

'I've had a bit of a show-down with Mother. She's

such a prude. She's put us in separate rooms. I told her that we've been sleeping together for three months now and she was most disapproving. She forgets that I'm twenty four years old and not a kid anymore.'

'Never mind love. We can always visit one another. Whose room is the furthest from theirs?' Mary sat on his knee and stroked the back of his neck. This usually calmed him.

'Yours.'

'Oh good.' They both laughed.

In the early hours of the morning, Tom was awoken by the sound of someone screaming. For a moment he didn't know where he was and he reached across the bed for Mary. Once he stepped on to the landing he knew that it was Mary's voice he could hear. He ran to her room and rushed in. Mary was sitting up in bed, wiping her eyes.

'Are you alright darling? Was it a nightmare or did something happen?' He sat on the bed and put his arm around her. David appeared at the door in his blue silk dressing gown. He had heard the scream too and he had a rifle in his hand.

'What happened? Have we got a burglar? Are you okay Mary?' He bent down towards her.

'Go back to bed Dad and put that gun away. Mary's fine. It was just a nightmare.'

'It wasn't just a nightmare Tom. It was terrifying,' said Mary, tucking her knees up to her chest and pulling the bedspread around her.

'Tell me about it. There's a lot you're not telling me.

How can I even try to understand?'

'Not now Tom. Not here. I'll never go back to sleep again. Stay with me 'til I doze off – please.'

As she awoke later that morning Mary could hear someone playing the piano. She thought she was dreaming at first but then thought it might be the radio. After all it was Christmas Day and she recognised the tune of her favourite carol – 'In the Bleak Mid-Winter'. Who was playing? Surely it wasn't Tom. He claimed to be completely non-musical. She quickly brushed her hair, put on her new satin dressing gown and crept downstairs. She followed the sounds of the music and could see David at the piano in the drawing room.. Mary sat down in a chair by the door and listened. David had seen her come in.

'Do you know any Christmas carols Mary?' he asked.

'O yes. I learnt a lot when I was a child. In fact you were just playing my most favourite carol. I sang it as a solo in high school when I was about twelve.'

'Then don't be shy. Come and sing it to me.' David turned back the pages of his book of carols. Mary stood behind him and sang all five verses. She hadn't sung for such a long time, not properly like this. It felt wonderful and David was such a good accompanist. He followed her voice as she sang.

'Good Heavens! What a beautiful voice you have. That was lovely. Now, would you please sing my favourite for me? It's 'Silent Night'. You sing it in English and I'll sing it in Welsh. The two of them were in a world of their own. They hadn't noticed Tom come in and sit down behind them. When they stopped, he clapped loudly, making them both jump.

'That sounded great. Darling, you sing like an angel.

I've never heard you sing like that before.'

'You never asked me to. Your father invited me to sing with him. Thank you,' she said to David. 'I haven't heard 'Silent Night' sung in Welsh before. What a musical language.'

This little impromptu concert set the scene for the day. Much to Tom's relief, everyone had a good time and even Charlotte was on her best behaviour. They went to church together and Mandy asked if Mary could push her wheelchair and then sit next to her in church. They opened presents, listened to the Queen's speech and ate the biggest Christmas dinner that Mary had ever seen. She couldn't believe that they had drunk a different kind of wine with every one of the four courses and then the men had brandy in the drawing-room afterwards. For Mary, this was a different world. Whilst she was helping Charlotte with the clearing-up, the telephone rang and David answered it.

'It's for you, Mary,' he said, handing her the receiver. It was Sally.

'Merry Christmas, Mary. Thanks for my perfume – you shouldn't have. Is everything okay? Here, William wants a word with you.' They chatted for a few minutes. Mary was glowing. It was the best day she had ever had. Everything was perfect and Tom's parents seemed to like her after all.

She said this to Tom as they parted on the landing. Tom was a little drunk and needed to lie down.

'I told you they would love you. Everybody loves you.' His speech was slurred.

'Tom, go to bed! Sleep well my love and thanks for the most brilliant day ever.'

Boxing Day was mostly spent walking off the excesses of the day before. It was cold and grey outside but it was dry. Mary and Tom took the two young border collies with them across the fields and around the edge of the town. Everyone was out walking their dogs and they exchanged Christmas greetings. Many of the local people seemed to know Tom. Mary loved the feeling of being a part of a close-knit community. In London, no-one really knew their neighbours. They were all too busy getting on with their lives.

After lunch, Mary and Tom sat with Mandy in the drawing room. Mary waited patiently for Mandy to control the spasms in her speech. Eventually, Mary found it easier to understand Mandy and Mandy told her bits about her school days. Charlotte and David came in with a tray of coffee.

'What about you Mary? Where did you grow up? What school did you go to?' Charlotte asked as she poured her a drink. Mary's colour drained from her cheeks and she glanced at Tom for support. She had been dreading this moment. Tom opened his mouth to speak but Mary raised her hand to silence him.

'Actually, I don't know anything about my family. I grew up in a Catholic children's home, in Buckinghamshire. Apparently someone placed me there when I was two years old, but the nuns had no idea who he was. He told them he had found me, abandoned at London airport. I left school when I was fifteen and I went to live in London. I want to try to find my family one day. I don't know how, but Tom said he would help me. The name Doyle is Irish so perhaps my father comes from Ireland.'

An uncomfortable silence descended upon the room after this brave little speech of Mary's. Both David and Charlotte looked very ill at ease.

'Oh dear, you poor child! If you were found at the airport you could come from anywhere in the world. Your colouring is very dark. Did they leave a letter or anything with you?' said Charlotte.

'No - nothing.'

'I suggested that we have a holiday in Ireland when Mary feels ready to pursue this, but she feels it's too soon at the moment,' said Tom.

'I'm only twenty-three and so many new things are happening to me. I don't think I could cope with the emotional upheaval just now. When I get back to London I'm going to have some counselling sessions with a woman that my best friend recommended. She might be able to help me interpret my nightmares.'

Tom couldn't believe what he was hearing. This secretive girlfriend of his was opening up to his mother of all people. He was proud of her. He hadn't realised that she was planning to arrange counselling sessions although he had suggested it to her many times. He studied his mother's expression. It was a look of disapproval, which he knew so well. It dawned on him that Mary's unfortunate background would not sit well in his mother's comfortable middle-class world.

'So what about job prospects, what do you want to be eventually?' David asked her.

'My friend Sally says I'd make a really good teacher.'

'There's no money to be made in teaching,' said David. 'You're worth more than that.'

'Hang on a minute. Teaching is what I would like to do once I've got my degree,' added Tom.

'What! You can't do that. I need you here to run this place for me when I retire.'

'Who's put that stupid idea into your head?' said Charlotte. She turned to Mary.

'I suppose it was you, was it?'

'No,' they both said together.

Mary was close to tears.

Mandy began to cry. She didn't like confrontations. They frightened her. David went to comfort Mandy and Mary rushed out of the room.

'Oh God! Now look what you've done. It's all money and status with you two isn't it?' Tom shouted back at his parents as he went in search of Mary.

'I want to go back to London; back to our home. Your mother doesn't want me here now that she knows about my background. I told you that would happen. I wish I'd let you speak first, now.'

'What about Dad. He seems to like you. He loved your singing yesterday.'

'Maybe, but singing doesn't compare with a degree and a 'proper job' does it?'

'Okay, we'll go back tomorrow. But you wait, they'll come round. Anyway, the most important thing is that I adore you ... and I do, even if you do hide secrets from me.'

'Tom I do tell you most things but some are just too painful still, which is why I've decided to go and see a counsellor. Sally told me about her. Her name is Karen and she sounds really nice.'

'Alright darling and, by the way, I'm sharing your bed tonight in case the armed invader returns.'

Chapter 3
October 1986

The marble tiles, in the hall outside her classroom, felt like ice through her thin gymslip. Her young, bony, knees pressed against the solid, unrelenting floor as she knelt in prayer. Seven year old Mary Doyle recited twenty 'Hail Marys' one after the other.

> *'Hail Mary full of grace. The Lord is with thee*
> *Blessed art thou among women .... .Amen'*

This was her punishment for not putting her hand up before answering a question. The giant shadow of Sister Francis towered above her on the wall and the featureless figure in a long black robe looked evil and foreboding. Mary shook with fear.
'Don't gabble, child. I can't hear a word you are saying. God will chastise you.'
Mary watched in tears as the nun's bamboo cane came down hard upon her clasped hands. The split ends of the cane pinched her skin and the force of the assault made her fall. As she fell she could feel her secret friend falling with her, but still she couldn't see her face.

A chilling scream rang through the flat in the stillness of the early hours. Mary sat up in bed, clutching the damp edge of the duvet. Her body trembled and her hands were cold – an icy cold as though the blood had drained from each finger.

'Who's screaming? Oh Tom, I feel sick,' sobbed Mary. 'You, darling. You were having another of your nightmares. Lie back. I'll make some tea.'

'No! Please don't leave me. Not yet. Not until I feel warm again.'

Tom held her, as he had done many times before when this happened, and he pulled the duvet around them both. He wanted so much to understand her suffering.

Mary curled against him and gradually the numbness left her fingers. The pain still persisted deep inside.

'I was dismissed from the Bible class. Sister Francis was bringing the cane down hard on my hands. They're hurting still.' Tom held her hands between his own and kissed them.

'What had you done wrong this time?'

'I'd spoken out of turn. She made me kneel on the cold marble floor at the end of the lesson and recite twenty 'Hail Mary's. That other girl was there again. She helped me.'

'Come on love. It's 2.30am. Let me make us a hot drink and then we must both get some sleep. It's Monday, so it's back to work for you.' He kissed her and reached for his dressing gown.

Mary rolled over to Tom's side of the bed and breathed in the familiar musky smell of him. Her life had changed so much since they met. Tom was her rock. He was patient and kind. She knew he would always protect her - though, from what, she wasn't sure.

'I want us to be together always,' she said, as Tom came back with the tea.

'Then marry me, sweetheart. Why won't you marry me?'

Tom sat facing her with that earnest and sensitive look that Mary knew so well. She studied the scar on his chin, and brushed a strand of blonde hair from his eyes.

'You know why. Before I become your wife or the mother of your children, I need to know who I am. I'm not the only one either. Your mother would like that too. She makes an effort now and pretends that she doesn't mind that I'm an orphan, but I know she does really. She doesn't think I am good enough for her only son.'

'Oh Mary, not that again. What mother thinks or wants is of no interest to me, you know that. When is your next session with Karen? You need to tell her about these bad dreams.'

'I have told her. She says that I must put a pen and paper by the side of my bed and record every detail before the dream fades.'

'Then do it. I'll get you a notebook from the College shop tomorrow. I've got a tutorial in the afternoon. Now let's try and get some sleep.'

'You're so good to me, Tom. I do love you.'

'Ditto.' Tom wrapped himself around her and held her tight.

Mary was thankful that she had an appointment with her counsellor the following afternoon. She enjoyed visiting Karen's apartment. It was on the first floor of a beautiful Regency house overlooking Greenwich Park, and right now the park wore its autumn 'cloak of many colours'. This was Mary's favourite time of the year. October was the month she celebrated her birthday, simply because that was the month she had arrived at the children's home. No-one knew when she had been born. She didn't feel like a Libran. One day I will know for sure, she promised herself. She just needed one clue to begin her search.

Karen's pathway was lined with potted plants which, even after months of hot dry weather, were still ablaze with the warm colours of summer. Mary pressed the buzzer next to the plaque which said:

'Karen Brooks – Counsellor/Hypnotist'

Some tiny bells tinkled above her head, and suddenly the tension of the day began to drift away. Karen always made her feel at peace. She was trying to teach her to meditate, but sometimes Mary found it hard to shut out all her worries and anxious moments.

She could see Karen's delicate frame through the glass in the front door. Her spectacles, as always, were on the top of her head, resting neatly amid thick brown curls. As the door opened a waft of lavender and frankincense aromas filled Mary's nostrils.

'Hello Mary. How lovely to see you.' Karen gave Mary a hug and ushered her into the spacious hallway. 'I love your hair. Have you just been to the hairdressers?'

'I went on Saturday. I've decided to wear it short for a while. Tom was disappointed. He prefers it long, but I wanted to try something different.'

Karen laughed. 'Well that's men for you. They always seem to prefer women with long hair, don't they?'

Mary's black hair used to be so long that it hung almost to her waist. It was the first thing that Tom had noticed about her, that and her huge brown eyes which, he said, always seemed to hold an expression of sadness. Her skin was even darker than it usually was, after the months of high temperatures. Tom was envious of her skin tone. Being blonde and fair-skinned himself, he burnt as soon as the first rays of the sun touched him.

Karen led Mary up the little winding staircase to the

first floor. Her door was open and Mary could hear the haunting strains of her relaxation music.

'Would you like to lie down or sit in your favourite chair?' Karen asked as she poured each of them a glass of elderflower cordial.

'If I lie down, I'll fall asleep. I had another disturbed night last night – Tom and I both did.'

'Where were you this time?' Karen sat opposite with pen and notebook at her side.

'I was kneeling on the tiled floor in the convent, being caned by Sister Francis. I can still smell the disinfectant and hear the rattle of rosary beads. I hated her so much. We all did. She was one of the worst. She enjoyed being cruel to us. You could see it in her eyes when she punished us.'

'How many years is it now since you left The Sacred Spirit, eight?'

'Eight years and five months. It was March 1978. I'll never forget that day. For years I had dreamt of running away, but I knew I'd be caught and brought back by the police.

I was only fifteen, but I looked older. I felt I could pass for seventeen.'

'Describe that day to me.'

'A girl, in my class at High School, had run away from home. She had hitch-hiked to London, so I thought I would do the same. I borrowed an atlas from the library and planned the route. A friend in school gave me a five pound note when she realized what I was planning to do. She came from a wealthy family – she always had loads of money on her. She offered me drugs more than once, but I was always too scared. I never ever did drugs except for the odd 'joint' or two.'

'So you decided to hitch-hike to London with only £5 in your pocket?'

'I took a few clothes from the laundry and put them in a plastic bag. I slept with it underneath my pillow that night. As soon as the first sign of light appeared between the wooden shutters of our dormitory I climbed through the laundry window and made my way towards the main road, hoping for a lift that would take me to the motorway. I was cold and hungry.'

Mary began to shake a little and she could feel the tears behind her eyes. She clutched her empty glass and stared out of the window. The pain deep inside was there again.

'Here, let me take your glass. Maybe that's enough for today. What do you think?

You look very tired. Let's try a brief meditation together.'

Karen lit a couple of candles. Together they visualized walking through a forest of bluebells on a warm Sunday afternoon in April. It was quiet except for the birdsong and the wind in the trees.

'Each time I visit you I feel refreshed and stronger. There are many deeply personal things about my past that I cannot talk to Tom about. He would be so upset and probably very angry. Thank you so much for helping me.' Just at that moment the door bell rang and Mary looked at her watch.

'Gosh, it's 5.30pm. That must be Tom. He's been at college all afternoon and said he would pick me up on the way home.' Mary followed Karen to the front door.

'Hello Tom. How are you?' Karen asked, offering her hand.

'Fine, thank you. I've just had a good tutorial, which has put me in a great mood. How are you?'

'Very good thanks. You must be in your final year now?'

'That's right. Only seven more months to go and then

I've got to do my teacher-training.

'Hey – are you alright darling? You look really tired.' Tom glanced at Mary as she rubbed her right eye.

'He's right. I always rub this eye when I am tired. He knows that, bless him. Thank you again, Karen. I'll see you next month,' said Mary as she reached for Tom's hand. 'Bye.'

'You know where I am if you need anything in the meantime. God Bless.'

'I bought you a notebook, this afternoon, to record your dreams,' said Tom.

'Thank you love, but before you ask, I don't want to talk about my session. I want to clear my mind of all that tonight. Let's go out for dinner and talk about your future.'

'Good Lord, you sounded just like my mother then.'

Mary laughed when she saw him frown.

'I know, I was meant to' she said.

As they drove up Maze Hill and along Westcombe Park Road, Mary felt, for the hundredth time, how lucky they were to have such a peaceful escape from the noise of the city. Living so close to the heath and the park was like living out in the countryside. She loved Tom's two-bedroom flat in Vanbrugh Gardens. His parents bought it for him when he began his degree course at university. When Mary first met Tom, three years before, he invited her to dinner, at his flat, one evening. She was shocked when she first saw it. It was a typical student flat, full of dirty socks, rugby kit and dishes from the previous five days piled in and around the sink. When she eventually moved in with him, a year later, Mary began the clean-up operation, scrubbing floors, cleaning cupboards and washing curtains.

Tom said he thought she had an obsessive compulsive disorder.

'Mandy's friend has that and she's autistic. What's your excuse?' He had said it jokingly but Mary was devastated.

'Sorry Tom. It's just that I had to do so much cleaning and washing during my years in the convent that it has become second nature to me now. If we didn't do it properly Sister Francis punished us. With rules like that you learn quickly,' said Mary.

It was then Tom's turn to feel mortified. They both ended up in tears.

Waving at a row of smiling faces, Mary watched the school bus pull away from the drive. She loved her job. She spotted Martha blowing her a kiss through the back window of the bus. Twelve year old Martha had Downs' Syndrome. She had had eight operations throughout her young life, and coped daily with her epilepsy, eczema, and poor circulation. Look at her, she is always so happy and loving thought Mary. As she walked to the 'bus stop in Greenwich she marvelled at the strength of these children to overcome so many hardships. They never complained or wished for a better life. They accepted, without question, all that had happened to them. She wished that she could do that. She was tired of sleepless nights spent trying to come to terms with her past.

A week later, Mary stood just outside the double doors at the front of the school. She could smell the damp chestnut leaves which had been piled up by the caretaker the day before. The taxis were arriving, one by one, and the students were being met by their new support assistants. Mary watched as fifteen year old Rick sped towards her in his electric wheelchair.

'Give me a high five,' he said, lifting his right hand in the air. Mary smiled as she slapped the palm of his hand. Somehow these students always managed to clear her mind of her own troubles.

'It's swimming this morning Mary. I've remembered my towels. Are you coming in with us today? Please say you will.'

'Not today Rick, I'm afraid. I have to help out in another class as someone is off sick. Come on love you're blocking the doorway, and we'll be late for registration.

Mary had been timetabled in the Further Education block for the day. The art teacher was new to the school and the first lesson was with a particularly challenging group of seventeen year olds. She asked Mary to get some materials from the store room, a small walk-in cupboard behind her desk. As soon as Mary turned her back on the class, one of the boys rushed up behind her and locked her in. He jumped around the room with the key in his hand, laughing loudly, and before anyone could stop him he had thrown the key out of the window and into a large evergreen shrub.

Inside the store cupboard Mary was shaking. The sweat stood out on her forehead and she could hardly breathe. It was dark and hot in the tiny cluttered space and she could hear the harsh tones of Sister Francis as the key turned in the lock. She began to scream. She banged the door with her fist.

'Please let me out. I feel ill. I promise I'll try harder,' she sobbed.

'I'm so sorry Mary,' said the teacher, shocked by

Mary's outburst. The students sat in silence.

'We've sent someone to the front office to ask for the master key. She'll only be a few minutes.'

Mary realised where she was and what had happened and suddenly felt very foolish. She hated confined spaces and being locked in the 'time out' room at the convent was one of the worst punishments.

When the door opened, Roy the headteacher stood

there. He saw Mary's white, tear-stained face and he took her hand, guiding her to a chair.

'What an awful experience for you, Mary. I get like that in lifts sometimes. Claustrophobia can be terrifying. Come to the staff room and get yourself a cup of tea. I've sent a replacement for you for the art class and the Head of F.E. has the boy in her room.' Roy knew Mary's background. It was one of the reasons he had given her the job. He admired her strength and her ability to overcome adversity.

Mary sat with her tea but she couldn't stop shaking. The minutes in that store cupboard had felt more like hours and she felt as though she was still in the convent and not in her workplace.

'I'd like to go home. I don't feel at all well,' Mary said to Roy. 'Could you telephone my boyfriend please? He could come and collect me. He's at home this morning.'

When Mary saw Tom at the front office she felt embarrassed about the disturbance she had caused. After all it had only been a boyish prank. The student hadn't meant any harm.

'When are the horrors of my childhood ever going to leave me?' Mary said to Tom when they were in the car. She explained to Tom exactly what had happened.

'Did you explain why you reacted as you did?' Tom asked. Mary shook her head.

'Is this why you don't want any locks on any of our doors and windows?' Mary nodded.

'Yes. I hear that sound of a key turning in the lock and I'm straight back in that cold, dark, 'time out' room. Oh Tom. I so wish it would all stop.' Mary burst into tears again. Tom reached for her hand.

'Will you be alright on your own this afternoon darling? I could stay with you if you like.'

'No Tom, you go. It's important. Maybe I'll see if

Karen has a space in her diary. I think maybe I'm ready for that hypnotherapy session now. Karen said that it might reveal the identity of the other girl in my nightmares. It might be my first clue.'

Chapter 4
February 1987

It was the half-term break from school and Mary decided to spend the morning in the college library whilst Tom was in a planning meeting for his summer placement. Ever since her outburst at school the previous term, Mary was even more determined to research the name Doyle and try to find out exactly what happened at London airport in 1964.

She easily found a book about the Doyles of Ireland and they could be traced back as far as the eleventh and twelfth centuries when their ancestors, the Vikings, arrived on their eastern shores. According to the book they could be found today living in and around Dublin, Wicklow and Wexford, all towns along the east coast. When Mary read that Doyle was one of the most popular Irish surnames in the Republic of Ireland, her heart sank. She realised it would be almost impossible for her to trace her family when there were so many Doyles living there. She read on and found that the Gaelic version of Doyle is "dubhgall" which means 'dark foreigner'. That's me, thought Mary, feeling a sudden link with her name. In the next book she scanned, Mary came across a chapter heading which caught her eye: "Who are the Black Irish?" Tom had said something about this when they were talking about their trip the other evening. They hadn't got very far because Tom had insisted that they needed a starting point, something to get her search in motion. Mary began to take down notes to show him what she had found. This was going to be such hard work. If only she could stumble across just one clue, however small. Still at least she now knew which part of Ireland they should visit. It was a start.

'How did you get on in the library this afternoon?' asked Tom as soon as they got home.

'I'm not sure that we'll find anything. Doyle is a popular name in Ireland and there are thousands of them everywhere, even in America, Canada and the U.K.'

'Did you find anything about the "Black Irish"?'

'Yes, but no-one is very sure what the term means. The "Black Irish" are thought to be descendants of either Spanish traders or Spanish sailors who were washed ashore after the Spanish Armada. They then married into the Irish Society, resulting in future generations that looked a bit like me. I don't think we'll hear the term used in Ireland. Their historical origins are never referred to today apparently.'

'I picked up a brochure and a map yesterday. There's no way we can tour the whole of Ireland in just ten days. According to the brochure there's a musical pub called Doyle's in Dublin, so I suggest we start there. They have the best Guinness in town and some good 'craic' apparently.' Tom grinned.

'What's 'crack'? You don't mean the drug surely!' exclaimed Mary.

'No, of course not.' Tom laughed. 'It's Gaelic. To have some good 'c-r-a-i-c' means to have some "fun company and a few laughs".'

'Dublin is a great idea. Sally had her 'hen party' there.' Mary told Tom everything that she had found at the library and where most of the Doyles could be found today. Tom opened out the map.

'We could fly to Dublin, hire a car, drive south to Wicklow and Wexford, then travel on to Waterford to buy my mother some Waterford crystal, and finally fly home from Cork. What do you think?'

'That sounds a very long trip. Will we have time to visit every one of those places do you think?' Mary was beginning to feel excited now, although she knew it wasn't going to be easy.

'It's not that far. It's only about 150 miles. So let's do it!'

'I must try to be optimistic. After all, I was found at the airport so I could have easily been brought over from Dublin. If I'm Irish, it would explain why I love singing and why I like the Irish folk-songs so much. The only Irish people I've known are the nuns and priests in the children's home so I need this trip to restore my faith in my Gaelic ancestors.'

'Just don't pin all your hopes on this. As you said, the Doyles are all over the place.

By the way, my final teaching practice placement is to be in a Deptford Primary School. I start straight after the Easter holiday. I'm quite pleased about that.'

'I'm sorry Tom. I've been so immersed in my own plans I forgot about yours. That's great news. It's so close to home.' Mary hugged him. 'I couldn't do any of this without you. I do love you so.'

As they stepped into the smoky bar in Doyle's of Dublin, Mary experienced a strange feeling of familiarity. Maybe it was just the sound of the Irish accents or maybe it was a feeling of connection with the pub's name, she wasn't sure. She looked across at Tom's broad shoulders as he leaned on the bar, chatting to the barmaid. What a good man he is, thought Mary. I'm so lucky.

'So you see,' said Tom to the barmaid, 'Mary wanted to come to Ireland to research her name and this seemed to be the obvious starting point, besides which I love the Guinness in Ireland, so it was an added incentive.' They both laughed.

'Well now, I wish you luck,' said the red-haired barmaid, known to her regulars as Foxy Flora. 'You should begin by visiting the National Archives. They have everything listed there.'

'Thanks.' Just as Tom sat down, some musicians arrived and set up their little stage quite close to where they were sitting. Mary studied the instruments and listened carefully as each one was introduced. There was a bodhran drum, the Uilleann pipes, a wooden flute, a penny whistle, and a guitar. They sang a lot of popular Irish songs and Mary joined in with the ones she knew. She was really enjoying it. The guitarist was studying her as she sang and much to Mary's surprise he invited her to come up to the microphone and sing to them. She sang 'Danny Boy' and the place erupted.

'More, more!!' They chanted and so Mary sang one of her favourites, 'Carrickfergus' which caused her to be quite emotional when she heard the flute and the pipes in the background.

During the break, the guitar player came over to them with a proposition. He asked Mary if she would like to audition for their group, as the lead singer. Mary laughed nervously and was embarrassed.

'My boyfriend and I are on holiday,' she said. 'We're only in Dublin for a few days, but thank you for asking me. I feel very flattered.' The young man took her hand and kissed it. As he left, a somewhat dishevelled, middle-aged man came up to Tom. He pulled up a stool and sat down opposite them.

'May I buy you both a drink?' he said. I have a

question to ask this beautiful lady.'

'Not a talent scout surely?' Tom winked at Mary.

'Please – sit down and join us.' Mary smiled at the man. She was intrigued.

'My name is Brendan Mahoney. I live here in Dublin. I was studying your girlfriend's lovely face as she was singing and there's something awful familiar about her. Tell me, are you from around here?'

'No,' said Mary. 'I don't really know where I come from. I've lived in England for most of my life though. Why do you ask?'

'Well now, my wife left me not long after we were married and she took my baby daughter Mary away with her. I've never seen either of them since. You look a lot like my Maureen. Seeing you brought tears to me eyes.'

Mary's face looked flushed and she couldn't believe what she was hearing. They had only been in Dublin for one day and she hadn't begun her search yet. Her heart was racing. She clutched Tom's hand.

'But my name is not Mahoney, it's Doyle – Mary Doyle.'

'My wife's name was Doyle. Maureen Doyle. She was beautiful just like yerself.'

Mary looked at this man. He wore a grubby flat cap and working boots. His hands were calloused and dirty. He didn't look as though he had enough money to be buying them drinks.

'Mary, the lady behind the bar is waving at you. I think she wants to speak to you,' said Tom.

She got up and walked over to the bar.

'Don't believe a word the old fella says to you,' she said to Mary. Benny's daughter died when she was a baby and the grief unbalanced his mind. He became a drunk and his wife left him. Every time a pretty girl comes into the bar he tells them the same story, and whatever surname she has, he says it was his wife's name. It's awful sad.' She noticed Mary's eyes fill with tears. 'I'm so sorry. He won't hurt you. Here, have these on us.' She pushed another round of drinks towards Mary. 'You have a beautiful voice, by the way.'

'Thank you.' Mary beckoned Tom over and burst into tears. The man at their table moved away quickly and disappeared. 'Oh Tom, you'll never believe this.'

Despite the upset of their first evening both Mary and Tom enjoyed their time in Dublin. They had photos taken by the statue of James Joyce, listened to the organ in the Christ Church Cathedral, visited the famous 'Temple Bar' and threw pennies in the River Liffey for 'good luck'. Most of their time though was spent in the National Archives, the National Library, and the Glasnevin Museum, but their search was in vain. There was a surprising number of Mary Doyles born in1962 and some of them came from the west of Ireland. Each time, Mary was advised that she needed more information – for example her place of birth or a parent's or a grandparent's name.

It was the same story everywhere they went, so they cancelled the search and became tourists. They visited the eighteenth century gardens in Enniskerry and drove into the heart of the Wicklow mountains. They enjoyed more music at 'Mooneys' in Wexford and drove across the Wexford Bridge, the longest bridge in the Irish Republic. They walked along one of the many beautiful deserted beaches and Mary took a crazy photo of Tom covered in bright golden seaweed, something she had never seen before. Tom bought his mother a crystal vase at the Waterford factory and Mary was fascinated by the glass-blowing. She was overwhelmed by the stunning scenery;

the mountains, the lush green fields and the quaint stone cottages everywhere. She took photographs of everything whenever the sun shone, which it did sometimes. She even sang again because a publican in Youghal locked the door of his pub one evening and said that no-one could leave unless they sang a song.

'That could only happen in Ireland,' laughed Tom who had drunkenly attempted to sing a rugby song, much to Mary's amusement.

However, by the time they reached Cork, Mary was ready to go home. Whilst the accents were fun in Dublin, after a while they reminded her too much of the convent and she felt sad. She didn't feel at home in any of the places they had visited and she could see that she would never be able to trace her family in Ireland.

'When all the paths are blocked and nothing works, it's a definite sign that I'm in the wrong place,' she told Tom on their last night in Cork. 'But thank you my love. We've seen some wonderful places, and had some fun moments. However, I've had enough now. I wasn't born in Ireland. Maybe my father was, but I wasn't. I just know it. I don't feel at home there!'

Back in Blackheath, Tom awoke with a start and a taste of blood on his lips. Mary was thrashing about next to him and had brought her hand down hard on his nose. He slipped out of bed and examined the damage. His nose was bleeding and felt sore. That was quite a punch, he thought. As soon as he could, Tom rushed back to see if Mary's nightmare had awoken her. It had. She was curled up in a ball on his side of the bed. She was shaking.

'Darling, I'm sorry that I wasn't there when you woke up. You have quite a strong right hook. I've had a nose-bleed.'

He smiled at her expression. She was staring, openmouthed at his red nose. 'Tom! How awful! Did I do that? You poor thing! I think I was throwing snowballs. I'm so sick of these nightmares Tom. Why do I have to re-live all of this? It's not fair.' Mary was tearful. Tom got back into bed and held her.

'I ran out of the school hall in a fit of temper and stood in the snow staring at the statue of the Virgin Mary. I kept thinking, if she's supposed to be so wonderful then why doesn't she protect me? I began to throw snowballs at her which is when I must have hit you. I'm really sorry love. I was so cold out there and Sister Francis wouldn't let me inside. That other girl was there and she helped me. Sister Joseph brought me in and was giving me a hot drink just as I woke up.'

'Why did you run out? What had upset you?' asked Tom.

'Sister Francis accused me of something I didn't do and she called me a sinner in front of the whole school. I hated her. She's evil. By the way, don't ever ask me to drink hot Bovril. I'd rather die of thirst than drink it, it's disgusting.'

'I've never heard of it. It sounds awful. I'll make us some hot chocolate instead.'

'The really odd thing was that the Virgin Mary's face was the face of the man in Doyle's pub – Brendan Mahoney.'

'Well, I know it wasn't his fault, but that was a mean trick he played on you.'

The next morning, Sally rang. It was her day off work. She was longing to hear about their trip.

'So how was it?' she asked. 'Did you find any clues or meet any Doyles?'

Mary began to tell her story, but Sally interrupted her. 'Why don't you come for lunch and then you can tell

William and me every little detail. See you around midday.'

It was a warm spring day and they all sat out in Sally's little garden after lunch. Mary told her all that had happened and also about her nightmare the previous night.

'What a sad story about the Irish chap, searching for his dead daughter all these years, and what a shock - having your hopes raised suddenly like that.'

'I felt like a child who had been given an ice-cream and then had it taken away before she even tasted it.' Six year old William looked horrified.

'Who do you think this other girl is in your nightmares? She always seems to be trying to help you doesn't she? What does she look like?' Sally poured them both a second cup of tea.

'Sometimes she suffers with me too. I don't know what she looks like. She has long hair, but I never get to see her face. She could be a sister or maybe I'm just imagining her. I wish I knew.'

'I have an imaginary friend,' said William who was playing with his cars nearby. 'His name is Josh. We play together and I help him a lot because he's smaller than me and can't always do things.'

'Good for you,' said Mary. 'I bet he enjoys that. It could be that this girl is an imaginary friend too, because at the time when all these things happened to me, I really needed help from someone.'

'Have you ever thought of going back to the convent to see if that nun you liked is still there? You never know, she might be able to help, as she knew you so well.'

'I don't know whether I could cope with that. I couldn't bear to come face to face with Sister Francis again. Just seeing the place and smelling the carbolic soap would make me feel ill.' Mary shuddered at the thought.

'Why don't you take your imaginary friend? She could help you,' said William.

'Or Tom,' said Sally. 'Tom won't let anyone upset you. He'll want to go with you, surely?'

'We could go before school starts, I suppose. Mind you, Tom's got teaching practice next week – his final placement. But thanks you two. I'll choose my moment and talk to him about it. Thanks Sal. What would I do without you?

Chapter 5
Summer 1987

'Tell me about hypnotherapy Karen. What will happen? Do you make me go to sleep?' Mary asked as she lay on Karen's couch listening to her music.

'Hypnosis first requires the relaxation of your body, through mental focus, and then of your mind. It can be used to bring back lost or vague memories so that you can move on from them if you need to. Tell me Mary, why do you feel that you need hypnotherapy?'

'I'm tired of these nightmares. I want to be able to leave my past behind me and move on from it. I need to know something about this girl who shares my pain and I need to find my family. At the moment I feel like a lost soul. Can I wake up whenever I need to?'

'You will not go to sleep, but you might be on a different level of consciousness. You come back when you are ready. Some people find it easier to relax than others and some people can go into a light trance more quickly and deeply than others.'

'Do you control my thoughts and my decisions?' Mary was apprehensive.

'Certainly not Mary. It's all about working together so that the client is empowered to make changes in her life. Maybe you should give yourself some time to think about what I have said.'

'Yes. Perhaps you're right.' Mary relaxed and felt relieved.

'You know Mary, I am wondering if it might be a good idea to actually face your demons and go back to the convent for a visit. You might find it surprisingly helpful. Don't go alone though. Ask Tom to go with you for support.'

'That's incredible! Sally said exactly the same thing to me yesterday, but for a different reason. She said I might learn something from Sister Joseph about my arrival at the convent, if she's still there. This isn't a coincidence. This is a sign that I must go. Thank you so much Karen. I'll book a hypnosis session with you as soon as I feel ready. Tom and I need to plan a trip to Buckinghamshire.'

'Take care,' said Karen and gave her a hug.

As Mary walked home she thought about the suggestion that she return to the convent. What if seeing it again re-awakened even more horrible memories? What if Sister Francis was still there and refused to talk to her; after all, she did run away and play truant for the rest of the term. What if the convent has been demolished and replaced by a supermarket? She didn't feel at all positive about this trip but she knew that she had to go. The signs were there.

As soon as they had eaten dinner and had a glass or two of wine, Mary told Tom about her visit with Karen. She tentatively mentioned that she would like to make a return visit to the convent.

'I know you have to get ready for your new job, but could we go together, maybe on Saturday? I just couldn't go alone.'

'I've got an important rugby match on Saturday darling, but I would be happy to take you on Friday. I wouldn't want you to go alone. You're very brave even to consider it. Do you think the children's home will still be there? I read somewhere that most of them had closed down by the late seventies,' said Tom.

'It might not be there at all. There might be a housing estate there instead, but both Karen and Sally have suggested this and I might learn something. I need this first clue if I'm ever going to solve this mystery.' Mary curled up against him on the settee. 'Tom, you're so good to me. I couldn't do any of this without you. I wouldn't even want to, love. How long would it take to get there?'

'A couple of hours maybe. The distance isn't a problem. This is an important trip. We must do it and if it's distressing for you it can't be any worse than these bad dreams you keep having. It might even stop them when you see the convent through adult eyes.'

'Goodness Tom, you sound like a psychologist. How do you know all these things?'

'Oh, it just comes naturally.' They both laughed.

Mary felt jittery all week. She couldn't properly put her mind to anything for long. She decided not to write to the Mother Superior at the convent, but simply turn up on the Friday. If the convent was closed she needed to see that for herself rather than have her letter go unanswered. Tom took her to the cinema on the Thursday night to distract her so that she could go to sleep thinking about the film and not about their trip. The film was 'Dirty Dancing', a new release from the USA. It wasn't Tom's choice but Mary loved it and consequently she enjoyed a good night's sleep.

She had always told herself that she would never ever go back to Buckinghamshire. As they left the motorway her mouth felt dry. Mary gave directions and they headed out towards the place that had dominated her dreams for almost ten years. She could see it in her mind's eye: the long drive, the religious statues, the bolted double doors to keep everyone inside the school and the grounds. She could smell the incense and hear the rustle of the nun's black habits. Her eyes filled with tears and she wanted to tell Tom to turn back. She wanted to tell him she had changed her mind.

'Are you alright darling? You're very quiet all of a sudden.'

'I'm terrified of seeing the place again. I didn't realise how much until we passed through these familiar villages. Part of me just wants to turn round and go back to London, but I can see that we're nearly there. Just turn this corner and you'll see the sign – 'The Sacred Spirit Orphanage for Girls',' Mary said as she wiped her eyes.

'Would you like me to stop for a moment before we do?' Tom asked, holding her hand.

'No. I'll be alright in a minute.'

The sign had changed. It now read – 'The Sacred Spirit Home for Retired Nuns'. Tom stopped the car in front of the wrought iron gates. Mary studied the drive, now lined with trees, and gazed up at the big house in the distance. Through her adult eyes, it looked very institutional.

'It all looks the same except the trees are bigger and the drive looks smarter,' said Mary.

'Is Sister Joseph likely to be there? She wouldn't be old enough to retire would she?' Tom had remembered Mary saying that she was one of the youngest nuns in the convent. He spotted a telecom system attached to the gate. He turned to Mary.

'I think we have to press the buzzer and announce our arrival. Would you like to do that?'

'No. Can you do it please? Don't say my name. Just say that I used to live at the convent ten years ago and have travelled from London especially to see Sister Joseph.'

Tom pressed the buzzer and a woman with a soft Irish

accent asked who was there. Tom did as he was asked and the big gates swung open. As they approached the main entrance a sign directed them to the visitors' car park. Tom took hold of Mary's hand which was cold and clammy.

'I feel as though I am just about to have an interview,' said Mary.

'Well I suppose, in a way, you are. You'll be fine darling.' He gave her a reassuring kiss.

They heard two large bolts being drawn back and Sister Joseph stood before them, smiling. Mary saw the freckles across her nose and the twinkly blue eyes and recognised her instantly. She had a much fuller figure but otherwise her appearance hadn't changed much. She recognised Mary as well.

'I don't believe it. Is it young Mary Doyle I am looking at? We often wondered what happened to you. You look well and so beautiful.'

'Thank you Sister. I am very well. I'd like you to meet my boyfriend, Tom Selby-James. We live in Blackheath in south-east London. Could you spare us a few moments of your time? I want to try to find my roots and I have one or two questions I would like to ask you.'

'Well now, why don't we sit in the gardens as it is such a lovely sunny day? We have worked hard on the gardens since you were here. You probably won't recognise them.'

They followed Sister Joseph along the path and sat down around a small table which stood on the veranda overlooking a tapestry of beautifully tended flower gardens. The statue of the Virgin Mary, that Mary knew so well, stood as a centre-piece and it seemed a lot smaller than she remembered. In fact everything seemed smaller except for the trees, of course.

'I have asked one of the sisters to bring out some tea

and biscuits for us. Do you both drink tea or would you prefer coffee?'

'Tea would be lovely. Thank you,' said Mary.

'Many of the nuns that you knew years ago have since died. Sister Francis passed away not long after you left us. My job now is to help to look after the older nuns who have retired and some of them have come here from other parts of the country, even from Ireland. You remember that our school closed in the early seventies and the orphanage closed at the end of the year that you left us, in1978. We don't often get a visit from any of our girls. How has life treated you since your hasty retreat?' She smiled.

Mary told her some of the events of the past ten years, but talked mostly about her work in the special school and about the love and support she had received from Tom. Once the tea arrived, Mary spoke about her need to find answers to certain questions and to discover her past.

'When I was brought to you by a man on that October night in 1964, did he give you his name? What kind of accent did he have? What did he look like? Did he look like me at all?'

Sister Joseph laughed.

'My goodness so many questions! I don't really remember what he looked like. It was dark and he hung his head as he spoke. He seemed a pleasant fellow and said you were a 'dear little thing'. He had an Irish accent; a southern Irish accent not a northern one. I do remember that. He said he had found you at London airport and that you had been abandoned.'

'Did he say where he had flown from? Did he say which terminal I was in? Why didn't he take me to the Information Desk or to the police or something?'

'We often wondered that ourselves. He didn't give us any details. In fact he didn't stay more than a couple of

job but at the same time his teaching career was real now and it would take up a great deal of his time.

'Then it will be my turn to feel nervous,' he added.

Chapter 6
1988

Another year had gone by since her visit to the convent and Mary had not had any further correspondence from Sister Joseph. She was finding it increasingly difficult to be patient. Karen was convinced that more clues would emerge, given time.

'That little package you received is a sign that there is more to come. I can feel it. You are meant to research your past. There is a young girl in your dreams waiting to be found. Try to be patient,' she had said during Mary's last session with her. Sally on the other hand had taken a more practical approach.

'Maybe you should be more proactive,' she suggested, 'rather than wait for something to arrive in the post. Why don't you go to the library again and look for some information about your little boots. There must be something about the people who wear them.'

'Tom says he saw boots similar to mine in Lapland when he went to see Father Christmas as a child. Maybe the type of animal skin used or the fur, around the top of them, would give me a clue as to where the boots come from. Tom told me that the boots in Lapland would have been made of reindeer skin. He thinks that mine are made of hide.

'Go to the library tomorrow morning and then meet us for a picnic in the park. You can tell us all about it then,' said Sally.

With the help of the librarian, Mary found a reference

book about the people of the Arctic regions. She made notes as she had done when researching her name. One article showed photographs of the different kinds of footwear. She photocopied these pictures, collected all her information together and set off towards Greenwich Park to show Sally and William.

As she strolled through the park, past the traditional band-stand, flower gardens and the family groups all enjoying the school holidays, it struck Mary that this same scene could easily be a hundred years ago. This is what she loved about the park, the sense that nothing much changes. She spotted Sally sitting beneath one of the enormous cedar trees which surely must have been there for hundreds of years. She had two boys with her and the tablecloth was set out ready for lunch.

'Hi Mary. You're just in time. I have two very hungry boys here. They've already eaten most of the crisps. Mary, have you met William's friend Brad?' Brad gave a shy smile.

'Hello everyone. What a great spread. I suddenly feel ravenous myself.'

'How did you get on? Did you find your boots in the library?' Sally asked.

'Yes I did. They're called "mukluks" apparently. The word comes from an Inuit word 'maklak' which means the bearded seal.'

'What's 'Inuit? Is it the name of a tribe?' asked Sally.

'It's the modern-day term for Eskimos. The Inuits were the first people to wear mukluks apparently. They were made from sealskin or reindeer skin gathered by the Arctic hunters.'

'Brad's uncle lives in Alaska you know, so Brad might be interested to see your little package.' Brad heard his name mentioned and watched as Mary produced her boots.

'I know what they are,' said Brad. 'They're mukluks. My uncle wears them in the winter. So do the dogs when they race. Yours look a bit like the dogs' mukluks. They're so little. Can I hold one please?' Mary handed him one of her boots and gave William one too.

'Dogs wear boots? That's crazy,' jeered William.

'He's absolutely right,' said Mary, 'and the reason they are small, though, is because I was two years old when I wore them. According to this article, my boots are made from moose hide. Here, look at these photographs.' Mary handed over her photocopy from the library. 'I think they look a lot like the ones in the north of Canada. Don't they look sweet?'

'The beadwork is similar and these have fur around the top like yours do,' said Sally.

'The First Nations people decorate their mukluks and their moccasins with pom poms and beadwork, and also use the fur of beaver or rabbit. I can't imagine walking on ice in these, but the ice is dry and the moose hide is good insulation, so the people don't get frostbite. It's clever isn't it?'

'My uncle is a dog racer. He's got an eight dog team and he's won lots of prizes. He lives in Fairbanks, Alaska. I want to go and race in 'The Yukon Quest' with him when I'm older.

'My goodness!' Mary stared at this young eight year old.' I wish I had shown you these a year ago. This is quite exciting. If I arrived from the Yukon or from Alaska I would have had an American accent wouldn't I? I knew that Lapland didn't sound right. I can't wait to tell all of this to Tom.'

The boys were silent as they ate their lunch and once they had eaten their share they ran off to play football nearby.

'Stay where I can see you, boys,' shouted Sally. She

turned to Mary. 'How's Tom these days? Is he enjoying teaching do you think?'

'He loves it. It's still an emotive subject in Woodbridge, but he has no intention of changing his plans. He's feeling hurt and rejected at the moment because I won't agree to get engaged. Sally, I can't can I? What if I do find my family and they live thousands of miles away. I'll want to spend time with them. Charlotte would be horrified if she heard I was from a primitive tribe somewhere. Mind you I'd love to see her face when Tom broke the news.'

'Yes, but you're not marrying Charlotte. Also indigenous tribes aren't necessarily primitive.'

'What about you Sal? Do you think you'll ever settle down with someone again?'

'I don't know. It would be good for William to have a good male role model at home though. His father is just the person who takes him to football matches and buys him expensive presents. I've been let down by two partners and I can't imagine trusting a man again. They both left me for someone else just when I thought I was in the middle of a happy and secure relationship.'

'I felt like that when I first went to live with you and William, didn't I? I remember telling you that I hated men and didn't ever want to get married … and then I met Tom, thanks to you.'

'Ah, but Tom is very special isn't he? Don't let him go whatever you do.'

When she got home, Mary shared all of her news with Tom, who agreed that Canada did seem a possible link. He became enthusiastic about the idea of a holiday there and suggested that Mary might like to do that sometime soon.

'I've never heard anything about the Yukon Territory. I didn't even realise that it was so close to Alaska. I bet it's wild country up there,' he said.

'It's moose and bear country and my boots are probably made of moose hide. I'd love to go to Canada but it's a long way to go with so little information.'

'Talking of holidays, mother has invited us to spend a few days with them during the half-term break. What do you think? There's lots we can do there. It's been a while since I last saw Mandy.'

'I'd like to see her too. Try to avoid the subject of work though. It always seems to cause trouble. Also I don't want to share my research with them, not at the moment anyway.'

'That doesn't leave us a lot to talk about,' laughed Tom.

A very peaceful scene greeted them when they arrived at the Selby Estate. It was unusually hot for early October. David was enjoying his favourite pastime, mowing the front lawns, and Mandy was sitting in the shade of an ancient oak tree watching him work. She waved and looked flushed with excitement when she saw Tom's car. She wore her sunhat and her sunglasses and Tom told her that she looked like a movie star. Charlotte was out shopping and wasn't due back until late afternoon. David stopped, jumped off his mower and disappeared into the house. He came out a few moments later with some iced drinks and brought them over to where they were all sitting.

'This is very pleasant,' said Tom. 'Mother will arrive soon and chaos will be resumed.'

'Now then son. Don't be unkind about your mother.' David tried to hide a mischievous smile.

'Where would you like to spend your birthday today?' asked Tom the next morning. Mary was standing by the bedroom window watching the early morning sunshine disperse the mist that hung over the fields.

'Let's take the dogs to Rendlesham Forest. I love walking through the woods in the autumn and it's going to be a gorgeous day out there.'

'We'll take a picnic and make a day of it. I'll borrow mother's hamper and raid her cupboard.'

They parked the car and walked deeper into the forest. The dogs loved it and sniffed endlessly amid the fallen leaves. They gave the dogs a good run and eventually found a quiet corner of the forest for their picnic.

'It seems strange, celebrating my birthday when I have absolutely no idea when I was born. October just doesn't feel right.'

'Well, we have to celebrate it sometime. 'Happy Birthday darling.' Tom produced a tiny gift, beautifully giftwrapped. Mary studied it. It has to be a ring or a pair of earrings, she thought. She gasped as she opened it. It was a ring; a round blue opal surrounded by tiny diamonds.

'Oh Tom. Thank you. It's really beautiful, but ...'

'It doesn't have to be an engagement ring. Wear it on your right hand. It's your birth stone.'

'Maybe it's my birth stone. I'm sorry I can't be more definite Tom. I have a long journey ahead of me and I could be anywhere this time next year. You know that.'

'Yes, I know darling. This ring is just a symbol of my love for you. Wear it and enjoy it. I had it specially made for you.'

Just at that moment, a blue van, with S.H.C.G.B. printed on the side, stopped on the road ahead of them and a man was running towards them. He barged into their space just as Tom placed the ring on Mary's finger.

'Hey, have you seen any signs for the Siberian Husky

Club competition? We haven't been here before and I think we've taken a wrong turning.'

'No, sorry,' said Tom. 'But I did notice a van like yours go past a little while ago. It turned left just a bit further ahead. What do the letters mean? Is there an event of some kind up there?'

'It's the Siberian Husky Club of Great Britain. We've got our dogs in the van. They're due to race in an hour's time.'

'You race Siberian huskies? That's incredible. Tom – can you believe that?'

'You can come along with me and the wife if you like,' he said noticing her enthusiasm. 'We have to hurry though. We're running late. I'm Rob Jamieson by the way.'

'We'd love to join you, wouldn't we Tom? It was only a matter of weeks ago that Sally and I were talking about the huskies in Alaska.' Mary was flushed with excitement.

'You were?' Rob looked amazed. 'Bring your dogs. They can sit behind the front seat. It'll be a bit of a squash, but hopefully it's not very much farther.'

'How can you race without any snow? Is it man-made snow or something?' Mary asked, as she packed up their picnic.

'No. Instead of a sled, we use racing rigs. They're made from bicycle parts,' he laughed at her innocence. 'This is my wife Wendy, by the way. You'll meet our family in a few moments, hopefully.'

As they turned left at the top of the road, they saw the sign and an arrow pointing straight ahead. A double row of vans and cars were parked either side of a dirt track and Mary could see groups of husky dogs resting under the trees. It seemed to be quite a big event. Mary couldn't contain her excitement.

'I won't be a moment. I have to go and sign in,' he said, jumping out of the van. 'You can wait here with Wendy and the dogs or you can wander around and get the feel of the place. There'll be people here from all over the country probably, if it's anything like competitions in Thetford Forest.'

'We'll wait,' said Mary. 'I'm anxious to see your dogs. How many do you have?' she asked Wendy.

'We have six and they're all Siberians. We love them. They're our children. We started out with two when we first got married and now we have six. Have you seen these dogs before?' Tom shook his head. Mary was staring at a group of them near the van in front.

'The ones with the steely blue eyes look familiar but I don't know why,' said Mary.

'You needn't be nervous of them. They're real softies – especially Simba, the lead dog.'

When Rob returned he unlocked the rear doors of the van. Each dog was in its own little cage. They immediately sensed what was happening and yelped with excitement. This startled other dogs around them and the noise was deafening. Mary and Tom helped as each dog, in turn, was put on a leash.

'We like to give them a little walk first so that they can do their business in the woods and not on the course,' explained Wendy. 'Would you like to take one each?'

Tom took the collies and Mary took Simba.

'Aren't they gorgeous? Look at the markings on this one, and his eyes – they seem to look right through you.'

'I'm impressed,' said Tom. 'That dog is fit and well cared for. He's lean and strong and his coat is so shiny.'

They watched as Rob and Wendy harnessed the dogs so that they were ready for their race. The three-wheeled rig looked surprisingly fragile. Tom put his feet on the two small foot-plates and grasped the handle-bars. He turned to Rob.

'How fast can you go with your team?'

'They can race up to 25 miles per hour and I tell you, that feels fast.' Now that Simba was harnessed he was anxious to get going. He yelped and jumped and pulled on the rope.

'That's our race. Come on let's go,' said Rob.

Tom put the collies back in the van and followed Mary and Wendy to the starting post.

'Once they set off we have to wait. It's a circular route so the finishing post is here too. If Rob's at the front we have to cheer like mad. It'll encourage the dogs if they're feeling tired,' said Wendy.

Around the bend came the winning team. Close behind it was Rob. Mary and Tom jumped up and down cheering loudly, but Rob and the dogs kept second place. The dogs were panting heavily and their long pink tongues lolled out of the side of their mouths. Wendy produced six individual bowls and filled them with water. She also had some chicken tit-bits as a reward for the team.

'We were so close. We were in the lead for a while and our time was good. Still we've not been here before. They're not used to this course.' When the times were announced, both Wendy and Rob felt pleased. It was a good competitive result. They were in The Final.

As the sun began to fade, the races came to an end and everyone was getting ready to go home. Mary spotted a beautifully marked husky sitting patiently whilst the rest of the dogs were being put in the van. It seemed much bigger and stronger than the other dogs. She asked its owner what breed it was. He explained that it was a malamute husky and that it was a working dog not a racer.

'He's very strong. He can pull some heavy loads, especially when we go camping', he said.

Rob and Wendy packed the van and offered them a lift back to the car park. 'We live near Bury St. Edmunds, just outside Thurston. Wendy, give Tom and Mary our card. Perhaps you'd like to join us for a training session in Thetford Forest, in the winter when we get some snow.'

'You mean if we get some snow. We don't get to use our sled very often,' added Wendy.

'Thanks. We'd love to.'

'It'll be an early start, of course, as we train them at first light, which in February could be around seven o'clock. Give me your details,' he said to Tom. 'We'll keep you posted.'

'Thanks for a brilliant afternoon. It's been fun', said Mary. They all shook hands and parted.

'Wow! That was a fantastic birthday, Tom. I felt so at home with those dogs. This was all predestined. I'm sure of it. Now I must start saving some money. Tom, how much is a return flight to the north of Canada likely to be?'

Chapter 7
1989

Mary couldn't stop thinking about their day with Rob and Wendy. She loved their husky dogs, especially the Siberians with the incredible eyes. She was puzzled as to why they seemed familiar and why she felt so at home with them. She and Tom had been over to visit their new friends a couple of times and they both enjoyed learning about the world of sled-dog racing, a relatively new sport in Britain.

'Why do you train them at first light?' asked Mary. 'You must have to get up incredibly early in the spring and summer.'

'These dogs are not bred to race in our climate,' said Rob. 'Their ancestors, in North America, were working dogs and they were used to much colder conditions. Our dream is to take the dogs to Alaska and Canada one year, for the 'Yukon Quest' race in February. We've opened a savings account. It'll cost us a fortune though. We hope to have eight dogs by then.

'You know I'd love to take up this sport one day. How do you teach the puppies to race then? How old are they when they first wear a harness and are attached to the rig?'

'That's Wendy's responsibility. She's the one who trains the pups.'

'We bring the puppies out with us every time we have a training session, which is four or five times a week during the racing season,' said Wendy. 'They soon get used to all the smells, the sounds and the routine of our session. When they're about one year old we pair them up with an experienced dog and give them short, trial runs so that they can become familiar with the commands and all the equipment. They learn very quickly. This one has only completed one season so far,' said Wendy stroking the youngest dog whose head was resting on her lap.

Rob managed to persuade Tom to try using the rig with four of the dogs. Tom loved it and did well, but Mary felt nervous of the rig and decided not to attempt it. She felt unsteady and was convinced that she would fall off.

'Wait until early next year,' Wendy had said. 'If there's enough snow we'll take you for a run with the sled. It's designed to take a passenger and you'll be well wrapped up. You must come and spend the previous night with us so that we can make an early start. We'll ring you.'

Mary watched the weather report every day throughout January and February. There had been several snow flurries in Suffolk and finally a week of heavy snow was forecast for the second week of February. Rob rang them and arranged for them to come over on the Friday night ready for a session the following morning. Mary was excited and prayed that they would be able to use the sled.

Just before 7.00am they followed the van through the heavy iron gates and into the heart of Thetford Forest. The light from an early morning crescent moon only just managed to splinter the darkness and a strange blue shadow flickered across the snow-covered track that lay ahead of them. The temperature on their porch thermometer had registered six degrees Celsius below zero. It was cold. Mary felt a fluttering inside her stomach. She was nervous of speed and wondered how it would feel travelling along the winding pathways of this pine forest at twenty-five miles per hour. She imagined it would feel very cold so she wore four layers of clothing, her warmest boots, a hat, scarf and gloves.

'We won't be travelling that fast today.' Rob reassured her. 'They need a straight run to go at that speed. You'll be fine.'

'Do the dogs wear mukluks in the snow Rob?' Mary was holding her camera.

'How do you know about mukluks?'

'I have a pair at home. I was wearing them when I arrived at the convent. Sister Joseph gave them to me quite recently and so I did some research at the library.' Rob fell silent so Mary turned to Wendy.

'I read that the huskies wear them too, when they take part in that famous race in the Yukon. I'm saving for a holiday up there. That's two people now who've mentioned the 'Yukon Quest' in the past few months. I can't ignore that. I believe it's a sign; a sign that I should research my family history up there in the Yukon.'

Rob looked tense and avoided eye contact with Mary. He kept his head down and concentrated upon unloading the sled, and the rest of the equipment. When Mary mentioned this to Tom later that day, he said he had sensed some tension too and wondered if Rob was jealous because he and Wendy couldn't afford to go to the Yukon just yet.

Tom offered to help Rob fix the tow lines and harness the huskies. He attached the stub line to the tree and settled the dogs, while Wendy showed Mary the sled. The dogs were excited and anxious to get going. A deafening chorus of whines, yaps and barks shattered the silence of the forest.

Wendy showed Mary the bag attached to the sled that

contained the passenger or the cargo.

'You'll be plenty warm enough. This is windproof and waterproof and just to make sure we can put a down-filled sleeping bag around you once you're inside. The only bit of you that's visible is your face and head and it's not cold enough for frostbite.' They both laughed.

When Mary was settled, the tow lines and the dogs were attached to the sled. The dogs at the front pawed the ground as they waited for Rob's command to be off. Rob stood behind Mary with his feet astride on the runners and his hands on the arched hand rail, which he called the 'handbow'.

'Wish me luck, love.' Mary looked across at Tom. Tom came over and kissed her.

'Don't worry. You'll love it. Just hang on to your hat,' he grinned.

'Okay!' Rob called, thus telling the lead dog to race straight ahead. Mary felt as though she had been catapulted on to the track. The icy wind stung her cheeks as they gathered speed. Freshly fallen snow caused some of the branches to hang low and Mary was caught unawares by a sudden snow shower. She pulled her hat down hard over her ears and stared ahead of her at the horizon. A watery sun was breaking through the blanket of whiteness and pink streaks lay like brush strokes across the sky. Just in time. Now she could really appreciate the beauty of her surroundings. The forest had opened out and thousands of new fir trees had been planted on both sides of the track.

'Look to your left. Can you see what's about to cross our path? It's a female white fallow deer. It's very rare that we ever see these. You're lucky. They are well camouflaged in the snow.'

Mary had never seen one before. Its thick white coat stood out boldly against the dark greens of the saplings. It leapt gracefully across their path and disappeared amongst the trees, clearly not wishing to confront their eager team.

'Ha, ha!' called Rob which instructed the dogs to turn left. Mary felt her body stiffen as they sped around the corner. She felt surprisingly safe and realised that she was starting to enjoy the speed.

'Gee, gee!' called Rob as they turned right, back into the heart of the forest again. The cold air was masking the smells of the woodland, but the crisp freshness of the breeze cleared her lungs and enflamed her cheeks. The adrenaline was pumping and Mary could see why so many people had decided to make this sport a life-time commitment. Rob and Wendy certainly had.

The final stretch of their two mile run lay ahead and they were out of the forest now and heading towards home base. Just as before, when they were at Rendlesham, Wendy handed out the water bowls to each of the dogs who were gasping for a drink as they collapsed in front of her. Once Mary stepped out of the sled she went to each dog in turn and thanked them for her exhilarating ride.

'Thanks Rob. Tom, that was fabulous,' she said as she hugged him. 'It was smooth and so peaceful. The only sound was the hypnotic swish of the runners against the frozen snow and the panting of the dogs. The sled was more comfy than I thought it would be and I was plenty warm enough, just as Wendy promised, except my nose is like a block of ice. We saw a white fallow deer. Imagine that!' Tom laughed at her enthusiasm, and handed her a mug of hot chocolate.

'It looked great. For a moment there I thought I was in Alaska. Very authentic! I can't wait for my turn, when the dogs have rested.'

Later that week, Mary had an appointment with Karen. She had booked a hypnotherapy session with her. The more she thought about it the more she hoped that something might be revealed about her early days before London airport. Mary needed to know who the faceless girl in her dreams was and why the huskies seemed so familiar. Was it a woman who abandoned her in the arrivals hall? Was she ill or in trouble? Just to know the number of the airport terminal would be helpful.

London had almost come to a standstill in the snow and as she trudged through the park, Mary smiled at the idea of being transported to Karen's flat by Rob's dog team.

'Hello Mary,' said Karen. 'I don't often see you in the morning during the week. Is your school closed today?'

'Yes. It's closed due to transport problems. The children come from quite a wide catchment area. Tom's gone to work though, as most of his children live within walking distance of the school.'

'It's good that we have more time, especially as this is your first session.'

Mary removed her shoes and lay down on the couch. The shutters were closed and the only light was from the fire and a row of tiny candles around the hearth. The whole room felt warm and safe and almost womb-like. Mary relaxed. She closed her eyes. Karen sat on a chair next to her and did some deep breathing exercises with her. As Mary's breathing became deeper, she quietly led her into a different level of consciousness.

'You want to open a door and go inside. Can you tell me why?' Karen asked her.

'A little girl is crying and calling for help.'

'Are you able to unlock the door?'

'It's not locked but there is a big key in the door.'

77

'Open it if you would like to, and tell me what you see.'

'The little girl is tied to a chair with a long scarf. They are cutting her long hair.'

'Can you see who is doing this to the little girl?'

'A white woman. She's scary and a big guy is helping her.'

'How old are you, Mary?'

'I don't know. The girl is little, like me. It's not allowed. Her hair must be long.'

Mary began to struggle. She became restless on the couch and shouted –

'Leave her alone. You're hurting her.'

Karen held Mary's hand. It was as cold as ice.

'I can hear the bells. He's coming. He'll help us. Don't lock the door. Help!'

Mary began to cry. She wiped her nose on her sleeve. She was distraught. Karen spoke to her and soothed her and gradually Mary relaxed again. Her tears stopped and her breathing was slower. Karen counted backwards from ten but continued to hold Mary's hand. Mary opened her eyes.

Karen smiled at her.

'How are you feeling Mary? You've just had a very upsetting experience. Do you remember any of it? You didn't tell me your age but I think you were very young.' Karen offered her a glass of water.

'I was trying to help a little girl. She was calling for my help. She didn't want them to cut off her long hair.'

'What happened next?'

'I went in. They locked us both in the room in the dark.' Mary was shaking and so Karen placed a fleece blanket around her.

'You said one or two interesting things while you

were in this dilemma. You said it was wrong for the girl to have her hair cut, you mentioned a 'white woman', and you referred to the man as 'a big guy'. Also why were you hearing bells do you think?'

'I don't know about the bells. The word 'guy' is a North American word and 'white woman' suggests that the little girl and me are not 'white'. This is another sign. What do you think Karen? I think I should definitely travel to Canada this summer. This has been really helpful.'

'I certainly do feel that there is a young girl out there somewhere who is longing to find you. I think you should follow your heart and your instinct. Don't go alone though.

Take Tom with you.'

'I can't do that Karen. This is my own personal quest. I must do it alone.'

'Is there someone you can spend the rest of the day with now?' Karen asked. It's been an emotional session for you. I'm concerned that you're now going home on your own.'

'As it's Monday, Sally has invited me to lunch and as you know, she only lives a ten minute walk from here. She doesn't work on a Monday, so the school closure worked out well for me.' Mary grinned. 'I feel really tired. I'll have a sleep there before Tom comes to collect me.'

'Don't make any decisions tonight. It's an important time for both of you. This could prove to be a painful search. It will affect both of you and you need to be ready for it.'

'You're right. Thanks. I'll see you again, before I buy my airline ticket.'

'Let me know what you decide to do. Don't forget – ask for guidance and help will come.'

Throughout the next few months, the dilemma of whether to embark upon this solo mission haunted Mary. She awoke thinking about it, she discussed it endlessly with Sally, and she even found herself sharing it with a couple of staff at school. She said very little about it to Tom as she knew that the final decision would spark an emotional scene. Sally was very supportive, as always, and she could see that Mary's search seemed to be leading her to Canada. She even offered to go with her rather than see her go alone. However, she was concerned about Tom's part in it all.

'Tom has been there for you in everything that you've wanted to do,' she said to Mary. 'He's been there through your nightmares, he's taken you to Ireland, and he was by your side when you went back to the convent. Mary, he loves you and he worries about you.'

'I know. The last thing I want is to do is to hurt him, but Sal, I've dreamt all my life of finding my family and it's a deeply personal thing. Also, I don't know what I'm going to find when I get there. If I enter a world that Tom would hate for some reason, it would spoil the moment for me. Tom's had quite a sheltered upbringing don't forget. He likes his comforts. He won't even go camping with me.'

'I must say, you're very brave. I'm not sure that I would want to travel so far into unknown territory on my own. You're a toughie that's for sure!'

'I've had to be, if you think about it Sal. When you live on the streets, you either sink or swim. Anyway, I'm only talking about going for two weeks.' Just at that moment William ran into the room.

'Are you going to see the husky racing in Canada? Can I come with you? It sounds wicked.'

'I expect you will come - one day.' Mary laughed.

Children find decision-making so much easier than

adults do, she thought. They don't see the pitfalls.

By the end of the summer term, Mary had made up her mind. She would fly to Whitehorse, the capital of the Yukon Territory and she would go for the last two weeks of August, so that she could have the first half of the holiday with Tom. How to tell this to Tom? That was her main concern.

She chose a Sunday while he was visiting Mandy for the day and she prepared all his favourite food. Mandy had moved out of the farm estate and was now in her own specially adapted flat with a personal carer. She was so much happier. Tom could enjoy their time together now without his mother trying to monopolise his attention all the time. Mary lit the candles the minute she heard his car.

'This looks very special darling,' he said as he came into the kitchen, 'and it smells wonderful. What's the occasion? Have you had some news?' Mary hugged him.

'I want to talk to you about my plans and I thought I would make the moment special for us. I've bought some oysters, I've cooked a rack of lamb the way you like it and I've made a sticky toffee pudding with custard, although the custard's a bit lumpy. It's all designed to go straight to your heart.'

'In more ways than one,' he said with a wry smile. Mary handed him a beer. 'Tell me about your day first. How is Mandy? Did you give her my love?'

'She's fine, much happier in her own little place. She said she missed you. We had a lovely day together and it gave her carer a break. Now darling, what's your news?'

'Tom, I've made a decision about the summer holidays. I want to fly to Whitehorse in the Yukon and I want to spend the last two weeks of the holiday there to see if I can research the name Doyle. Apparently the

Yukon is very sparsely populated so it should be much easier than it was in Ireland. I also want to get the feel of the place. I never did feel at home in Ireland, if you remember.'

'As you're saying 'I' rather than 'We', I'm assuming that you want to do this alone.' Tom sighed. He had guessed Mary would want to leave him behind. He finished his dessert in silence.

'Tom, talk to me, please. Let's take our drinks to the other room and relax.' They sat together, this time in an uncomfortable silence.

'It's not that I don't want you with me love. I'll miss you, I know. It's just that this is a very personal mission for me and I need to meet my family before I introduce them to you. Who knows, our meeting might turn out to be disastrous. They might make it clear that they don't want to find me. It does happen you know.'

'But surely you'll need some support if that does happen. I'd hate to think of you thousands of miles away in a state of unhappiness.' He put his arm around her.

'I'll come straight home if I'm not wanted. I promise.' Mary stroked the back of his neck.

'What will you do if it is a happy reunion? Will you stay longer?'

'No. I'll definitely be home in time for the beginning of term. I'd have to return to the Yukon, at some point though, if I do find my family there. Tom, we'll have three whole weeks to spend together before I go.'

'Darling, you're absolutely right. I'm being selfish. I just wish it wasn't such unknown territory where you're going. I'll worry about you. By the way, why have you chosen Whitehorse?'

'I've got to start somewhere. Whitehorse is where the Yukon Quest begins, and my mukluks looked like the ones in the Yukon and it's been the mention of the Yukon that has started all of this.'

'It's a crazy notion darling and it could be dangerous up there.'

'Not if I stay in a good hotel. Whitehorse is a capital city!

'Okay. You win. I'll pop into Blackheath Travel tomorrow to book a return flight and a hotel for you if you like. You'll have to fly to Vancouver first.'

'Oh Tom, you're wonderful.' She wrapped her arms around him. 'I knew you'd understand. It's only for two weeks ... not forever.' Tom managed a weak smile, but he felt near to tears.

When Sally and Karen heard that Mary was seriously planning a trip to the far north of Canada, they both warned her that this search might prove to be another big disappointment ... just as Ireland was. Although Tom had expected her to go ahead with this, knowing how much it meant to her, he was hurt that Mary would want to embark upon such an ambitious journey without him.

'The only two clues you have are a pair of tiny mukluks and the fact that two people have mentioned the "Yukon Quest" just recently,' Tom had said to her just before she left.

Mary accepted that everyone would think this, but the feeling of 'deja vu' she had experienced, when she met the huskies, had overwhelmed her and she regarded the Yukon race as more than just a coincidence. Besides which, Mary welcomed this little opportunity for her and Tom to have some time apart. Tension between them was growing and Mary needed her own space for a while.

'When something so unexpected appears suddenly in your life, twice within a month, I take that as a sign. Also, you've forgotten the third clue, my North American accent', she told Tom. Mary didn't believe there was such a thing as a coincidence. She believed that some things were destined to happen. The Yukon had entered into her vocabulary twice recently so Mary just knew that she had to go there. She didn't manage to convince Tom of this but nevertheless, he went into 'Blackheath Travel', the next day, and booked a return ticket to Whitehorse, via Vancouver. He also booked a deluxe room for her, at the High Country Inn in Whitehorse for two weeks.

Mary was delighted. She knew he would do anything for her. She was very lucky. She mustn't forget that, whatever happens.

Chapter 8
Canada – August 1989

As Mary boarded the Air Canada 747 to Whitehorse, in Vancouver, she was suddenly overcome by the feeling that there may be no turning back from this trip.

She found her seat by the window and looked out across the shiny black surface of the tarmac, which almost seemed to be melting under the intense heat of the afternoon sun. She was exhausted. It had been a long flight to Vancouver. She hadn't slept and now she had come to the final stage of her journey. Vancouver, a modern city, looked stunning from the air. Tom would love it, Mary thought. He would especially love all the water everywhere and the mountains. As the plane flew north and followed the coast Mary kept her face close to the window and looked down on the hundreds of islands that lay along the shores of British Columbia. Once the mountains came into view she gasped and began to wonder just where exactly she was going. It all looked stunning, but where were the towns and the villages? Her thoughts returned to that afternoon in Rendlesham Forest with Tom, which had started all of this.

'Hey, do you wanna drink?'

A young girl sitting next to her had her hand on Mary's arm and had made her jump. The flight attendant passed her an orange juice and a packet of nuts.

'Hi, my name is Julie,' the girl smiled as she studied Mary's warm clothing. Julie was dressed for the summer. Her long dark curls hung over her bare, suntanned shoulders and sunglasses still sat precariously on top of her head.

'Is this your first time in the Yukon?' she asked.

'Yes, it is. I've no idea what to expect. Will it be cold up there?

'It's usually still quite hot in the middle of August. Mom said that it's been the hottest July on record. Were you expecting snow?' she laughed. 'So many visitors to the Yukon seem to think that it snows all the year 'round.'

'No, not really, but I did expect it to be cold. Oh dear, you must think I haven't done my homework properly. My name is Mary Doyle, by the way. I've come from London. Actually, it was raining when I left home. I've never done a big trip on my own before. Do you live in Whitehorse?'

'Yeah. I was born there. We also have a cabin by the lake in Carcross, which is about forty-five miles from Whitehorse. It's a real small community, about four hundred people maybe. My Dads family live there. They're First Nations people. I'm at the U.B.C. in Vancouver. I can't wait to get home. I miss it when I'm Outside. It's been a tough couple of terms.' Julie chatted happily as though Mary was an old friend. Mary wondered why she had said 'outside' with such passion.

No-one had spoken to her on the flight from Heathrow. Most people slept or watched films. It was the longest flight that Mary had experienced. She had flown to Ireland, of course, and also to Corfu for a holiday with Tom once, but a night flight seems to go on forever, especially if you can't sleep. She hadn't dared to sleep in case she had any bad dreams. Mary spent most of the night thinking about her quest. If the Yukon was indeed the place of her birth, then surely her mother must be North American Indian? Julie had just used the term First

Nations. Rob told them that they are now called First Nation people, as they lived in Canada thousands of years before the white man. The book she borrowed from the library said there are many different tribes all over the Yukon, and each one has a different language and a different history. Her father must be from Ireland originally though, with a name like Doyle? She thought about her search in Ireland - so many Doyles everywhere; maybe even in the Yukon? Tom told her to go to the library in Whitehorse first to find out how she could research her family tree. However, all she had was her name and the year of her birth – 1962. This wasn't enough information in Ireland. They had needed her place of birth as well. This might be true in the Yukon too.

Mary gazed down at the splendour of the Coastal Mountains; the white-topped peaks glistening like royal-icing against a backcloth of blue. This country is so beautiful. According to the young man at the 'check-in' desk Whitehorse was about 2000 miles north of Vancouver. He thought Mary was very brave to venture so far on her own. He had never been further north than the 'Whistler Ski Resort' just north of Vancouver, he told her. She heard the pilot announce their arrival.

'Good, twenty-four degrees Celsius at 5.15pm,' said Julie, 'and there'll still be about five or six hours of daylight. It's warmer than it was Outside. Stick with me Mary. I'll show you where to go.'

Meanwhile in the airport Julie's mother, Annie, sat as close to the 'Arrivals' sign as she could and watched a little drama unfold in front of her. A group of American tourists had just arrived and someone had lost his luggage. Why do folks from Texas shout so loud? Annie wondered.

'Hi, Mrs. Hughes,' a familiar voice startled her. 'Are

you here to meet your daughter?' asked a tanned young man clutching an enormous back-pack. 'Is Julie home for the summer vacation?'

'Hi Greg. You're right on both counts. She'll come through those doors any minute now. Why don't you stop and say 'Hi'. She'll be pleased to see you I know.' Greg flushed a little.

'Gee, I'd like to, but Dad is bringing the truck 'round, so I'd best get out there. We'll drive down to Carcross for a visit sometime. See ya.'

Annie watched as he moved quickly towards the automatic doors, marvelling at the way his heavy burden didn't slow him down in the slightest.

Two arms came around her neck from behind and warm hands covered her eyes. Annie had missed that special moment when her little girl bounced towards her.

'Hi Mom, you're gazing at the wrong doors! Gosh, it's good to be back, and you look great,' laughed Julie as she gave her mother a hug.

'Did you bring Honey? I can't wait to see her!'

'Yep, she's in the van. You're looking mighty thin. Don't they feed you down there?'

'Mom, look who I found on the plane. Her name is Mary Doyle and she's never been to the Yukon before. Can we give her a ride into town?' Mary stepped forward to shake hands with Annie, who smiled a greeting.

'Sure, as long as you don't mind being covered in dogs' hair. Welcome to Whitehorse, Mary.'

Annie led them over to the carousel. She had collected a trolley as she guessed that her daughter would have a lot of luggage, a pile of dirty washing for one thing. Julie had carried her guitar on the plane with her. Mary had been intrigued when she spotted the guitar, and wondered if Julie, like herself, enjoyed singing?

As they drove on to the Alaska Highway, Mary looked for signs of the city, but apart from a couple of hotels and garages there didn't appear to be very much. There was no skyline in the distance, so she decided that the airport must be a long way from the capital city, just as Heathrow Airport is a long way from London. The windows of the van were open and Mary was struck by the purity of the air, so different from back home. Even walking across the heath at home you're aware of the pollution, she thought. There didn't seem to be very much traffic coming towards them either. Mary commented upon this to Annie, and asked her where Whitehorse was.

'All will soon be revealed,' laughed Julie.

'I hope you don't mind me being nosey, but what has brought you up here, alone and so far from home?' asked Annie as they approached the Two Mile Hill.

'It's a very long story, but I have been searching for my roots, for the past few years and something has led me here. I grew up in a convent, a Catholic children's home in the south of England. There's no paper-work, only two tiny clues so far ... oh, and my dreams, of course.'

'Where are you staying while you're here?' asked Annie.

'My boyfriend, Tom, has reserved a room at the High Country Inn on Fourth Avenue. Do you know it?'

'Gee, very nice. Yeah I know it. Your boyfriend is looking after you well. It's quite close to the river and you'll have a good view of the S.S. Klondike, one of the last remaining paddle-wheelers in the Yukon. There used to be 250 of them on the river a hundred years ago, you know. They were our only means of transport from Whitehorse to Dawson City.'

Mary caught sight of the city then as they approached the bottom of the hill. It appeared to have been slotted comfortably between some very high clay cliffs on the right and the banks of the Yukon River on the left. No wonder she couldn't see it from the airport. They made their way towards the centre and crossed over Main Street. This seemed, at first glance, like a small town. Many of the buildings were made of wood, and were only two or three storeys high. Again, Mary was struck by how empty the streets were, for a Friday evening.

'It's so quiet. Back home, Greenwich would be buzzing on a Friday night,' she said.

'A lot of people will be out in their cabins, as it's the start of the weekend,' said Annie. Our summer is so short that we make the best of it while we can.'

They stopped outside of the hotel and Julie helped Mary with her luggage, just the one suitcase and a small flight bag.

'As Julie has got to know you a little, I wondered if you'd like to join us for supper tomorrow night. We eat around six o'clock, so I'll pick you up from here around five-thirty. Will you have rested enough by then?

'Oh yes! Thank you very much. I'll look forward to that.'

Julie surprised her, by giving her a hug. 'See ya tomorrow then. Bye.'

Mary looked up at the front of this smart hotel. The statue of a Canadian 'Mountie', as tall as the roof, peered down at her. Mary immediately wondered how much Tom must have paid for this. It must be the largest hotel in Whitehorse! Mary glanced at her watch. It was six o'clock. The time in England was eight hours ahead so it would be the early hours, but she had promised Tom she would call him, whatever the hour, as soon as she arrived at the hotel. He would worry otherwise. Her room on the second floor was lovely and she could see the boat in the distance.

'Hello love. It's me.' Tom groaned. He sounded sleepy.

'Did I wake you?'

'Darling, I'm missing you already! How was your trip? What's the hotel like? Is Whitehorse amazing? Did you meet anyone?'

Mary laughed. 'Hold on. Not so fast - one at a time please.'

Mary tried as best as she could, to reassure Tom that all was well, that everyone had been very kind and helpful and that her arrival in the Yukon had been better than she could have imagined.

'What were the Air Canada flights like? Were they comfortable?'

'They were fine. I met a really friendly student, on the flight to Whitehorse, who introduced me to her mother at the airport. She looks of mixed race, like me. Her mother is white but I think her father is from a native village called Carcross. They have invited me for a family supper in Whitehorse, tomorrow evening. Isn't that great? My first point of contact! The hotel is gorgeous. Thank you love, but I need food and then bed right now.'

As Mary climbed in between the cool, crisp, sheets of a queen-size bed an hour later, she thought for a moment about Tom's last question: 'Did you meet anyone?' She could hear in his voice that he was so afraid of losing her to this mission. She had tried hard to explain exactly why she needed to make this trip alone and yet Tom had still felt she had rejected him. She decided to call him every day with a progress report. In seconds she was asleep.

Mary felt his hot beery breath on the back of her neck and his sweaty hand grabbing her right breast. She felt sick. 'Ugh! Get out. I'll scree ...' Just as she tried to scream his other hand came around from behind and covered her mouth. She could hear Mother Superior's voice outside - shouting: 'You're late again Mary Doyle. God will punish you!'

'Shut up! There's no point in screaming. No-one will hear you.'

Her own face appeared before her. She was crying. 'Here hold my hand,' it said. 'We must escape.'

She drew her knees up to her chest and tried to roll away from the monster, but his strength overpowered her. He was naked and in a state of frenzy. He flung her back on the bed and forced himself upon her, groaning and straining on top of her. The pain shot though her. He had his hand over her mouth once more. In minutes he was done. The girl facing her grabbed her hand and they struggled away from him as he slept. They locked themselves in the bathroom across the hall. Mary felt bruised dirty and ashamed.

'Come out Mary Doyle or you'll be sorry,' shouted one of the nuns. Mary wept silently ...

The cold wet pillow and her muffled cries woke Mary and she hurriedly looked around her to re-assure herself of her safe surroundings. She missed Tom so much at that moment and regretted that she had left him behind. She knew he would hold her and comfort her. She felt exhausted and yet she needed to get out of the bed. Bright sunshine squeezed through the heavy drapes and Mary assumed it was time to get up. She decided to have a warm, soapy bath, and then go for a walk by the river before breakfast to clear her mind of these vile memories. The warmth of the water and the aromatic oils soothed her.

The breeze was cool and clear as it wafted across the river towards her. It was peaceful and the only people on the highway were eager travellers, keen to get as much out of their day as possible. The snow had gone from the mountains, after the heat of the previous month. Fading wild flowers, some pink and some blue, lined the shore, and the river glistened in the early morning sun. Patches of brown were scattered around the lawns, a reminder that the summer had been hotter than usual so far. Mary stood by the water's edge and studied the bow of the S.S. Klondike. She tried to imagine how this scene would look, with the boats departing for Dawson, loaded with passengers and cargo. 'A hundred years ago,' Annie had said. It didn't seem so long ago, somehow. A majestic bald eagle rested for a moment on top of one of the smokestacks, and surveyed its territory. Mary let out a deep sigh and realised that she was breathing more slowly. She felt cleansed after her restless night. She just knew that the beauty of her new surroundings would help to clear some of the past. The magic of the Yukon was working already.

Chapter 9
Whitehorse

There was lightness in Mary's step as she walked along Fourth Avenue towards the centre of town. She hadn't been on holiday without Tom before, during the five years and nine months they had been together. Everyone at home was worrying about her but she knew she would be fine. If she could survive a childhood in the convent and then thirteen months living amongst the homeless in London, she could survive anything. Mary rarely ever thought about that latter part of her life and she had never shared it with Tom. She felt too ashamed and was afraid he would think less of her.

Mary was happy to be on this adventure alone and the small, remote city of Whitehorse wrapped itself around her, helping her to feel safe. She studied the little map that she had found in her room. Her map-reading skills had improved a lot since she started to navigate for Tom. He found it difficult to do two or three things all at once and so he preferred that Mary study the signs and follow the map.

She turned right on to Main Street. She studied the colourful wooden buildings: the hotels, shops, banks, drug stores, travel agencies and coffee bars. Not everywhere had opened to greet the late-summer visitors. Mary thought it resembled a film set, and she half expected the sheriff to ride into town and tie up his horse outside the Goldrush Hotel. The thought made her smile. Maybe Julie might like to go shopping with her one afternoon or go for a coffee together sometime. As she arrived at Second Avenue, she noticed the White Pass train station. She decided to enquire about getting a train to Carcross during the week but everywhere looked closed. She would ask Annie later. Mary crossed over to the look-out platform by the river and studied a lone kayaker as he paddled expertly downstream. Tom would enjoy doing that, she thought. Mind you, the glacial water was probably very cold.

She followed the path along by the river and soon realised she was standing in the grounds of the Government buildings, and just behind these was the public library. Mary froze for a moment when she considered what she was about to do. What if they find her name right away? What if her parents really are here? What if the person in her dreams is her sister after all? She stood motionless for a moment at the entrance and then realised that someone was patiently holding the door open for her. 'Thanks' she said.

The library looked new and more comfy-looking than their local library back home. People sat in armchairs, reading or glancing at the weekend newspaper. Tom had told her to look for the 'Genealogy' section. Mary noticed that a woman behind the desk was smiling at her.

'You look lost,' she said.

'Excuse me, but I've come from England because I believe that I may have been born here in 1962. My name is Mary Doyle.' Mary told the woman about her search so far. 'I think one of my parents might come from one of the First Nation villages here. Can you help me please?' The librarian studied Mary for a moment as though she was trying to recognise her.

'Do you have any more information? For example, do you know where in the Yukon you might have been born or how you arrived in England?' Mary's heart sank, just as it had done in Ireland, over and over again.

'No, I don't know either of those things. In October 1964, I was abandoned at London Airport. An Irish man found me and took me to a children's home in England. I was two years old. There was no letter, just an envelope containing a photograph with my name written on it.' Mary placed this on the desk in front of the librarian, who stared at the creased photograph of a pianist sitting at his piano in a bar, with his back to the camera.

'That looks very like one of the bars in Dawson City,' she said. 'Mind you, the hotel bars up here all tend to look very similar.'

'That's fantastic!' said Mary. 'Where is Dawson City? Can I get there by bus or by train?'

'Yes, there are coach trips to Dawson, but first, you need to check out the 1962 birth registry for your name. I suggest you try the Archives or the Vital Statistics Department on Monday. We don't have a genealogy section here in the library, I'm afraid.' The woman saw Mary's face and gave her hand a friendly pat. 'Good Luck,' she said.

Mary's eyes filled with tears, knowing she would find it really hard to wait for two whole days.

'Thank you,' said Mary 'Can you recommend a place nearby where I could get some lunch?'

'Sure, Tim Horton's, two blocks down towards Main Street. They do soup, salads, filled rolls, and doughnuts. Their iced coffee is real good.'

Mary sat by the window and studied the variety of people wandering back and forth. There were several people who, from their appearance, could be of mixed race like herself. She studied their black hair, olive skin and high cheekbones. The tourists were easy to spot. She watched a group of holiday-makers amble past clutching ice-creams and wished in a way that she could treat this venture merely as fun trip. A back-packer went by, no doubt looking for a budget hostel. She had noticed several tourist 'buses parked around town, many of them going to or from Alaska.

'Hi there, I haven't seen you for months!' A middle-aged woman standing in the doorway called to her. She was clutching the hand of a small child. 'Someone said you'd been ill. Are you better now?' Mary was so surprised by this greeting that she jumped and spilt her coffee.

'I'm sorry, but I don't know you. I arrived in Whitehorse yesterday. I'm a visitor from England.'

'That's incredible,' said the woman, noticing Mary's British accent. 'You look just like a girl I know called Josie. She must be your double. They say we all have one somewhere. Sorry. Bye.'

She pushed open the door and was gone. In a daze Mary mopped up her coffee. She suddenly realised what this encounter could mean. It's another clue! She left the remainder of her lunch unfinished and ran out into the street, hoping to find the woman somewhere nearby, but she and the little boy had vanished.

'Shit!' Mary cursed quietly to herself. Why hadn't she reacted sooner? Why didn't she ask who this Josie was? She walked aimlessly around the streets for nearly an hour, but there was no sign of the woman anywhere. In her heart, she knew the chances of seeing her again were slim. They might even have come from out of town. Mary was tired, emotionally tired. She made her way back to the hotel and set her alarm clock for half-past four. Jet-lag had caught up with her. The minute she lay down on her bed, Mary was asleep and this time she slept peacefully.

Annie and Julie arrived at exactly half-past five, just as Mary walked through the glass doors at the front of the hotel. Julie waved to her as she jumped down from the van. She gave Mary a big hug. Everyone hugs a lot here, thought Mary, something that she would have to get used to. The British are more reserved, generally, and Mary had not been used to displays of affection from anyone over the years, except from Tom and her best friend, Sally. Tom's mother usually kissed the air rather than her, and certainly never touched her. But then Mary knew that Charlotte didn't really like her.

'Hi there Mary! What great weather! We've decided to have a barbeque. I hope you like sockeye salmon, or if not you could always have a steak with my brother, Jake. I don't eat red meat anymore.'

'She's become a fussy eater ever since she went to Vancouver,' said Annie. 'Come on Mary, jump up here with me. Julie is fine in the back with Honey.'

They headed through town and up the Two Mile Hill to the Alaska Highway to go to Porter Creek, a suburb of Whitehorse. They travelled north for a couple of miles and Mary regaled them with all she had done during the day. Julie was very excited about the incident in Tim Horton's.

'Gee! That could have been a real clue. She might even have been a relative of yours. Awesome! Was she a First Nations woman?' asked Julie.

'No. She was white. The little boy who was with her looked either native or of mixed race though,' said Mary.

Annie told Julie to calm down and stop raising Mary's hopes too soon.

'This whole process of trying to trace your family could take a long time,' she warned Mary. 'You must try to be patient. Don't forget, the name Doyle could have been your mother's name, and if your parents weren't married you probably wouldn't have been given your father's name. We're almost home now; this is our road.'

'Oh no! I hadn't thought of that!' Mary said this quietly to herself as they parked on the driveway. 'If that's the case it will change everything,' she said out loud to Annie.

The houses in Annie's road looked really smart and each one had so much land around it. The roads seemed huge, much wider than in any housing estate at home. Annie's was a large two-storey detached house, made mostly of wood. In front, the lawns were wide and spacious, and were ornamented with shrubs and flowers. A beautiful blue spruce tree stood in the middle of one lawn just in front of what Mary assumed might be the living room. At the side of the house was a double garage which was big enough for the camper van and also a large black vehicle.

'The Suburban truck belongs to my son Jake. He works for White Pass, and lives in Carcross during the week. He'll be driving back there later tonight I expect. Sometimes he takes Honey with him, but not this time. Julie is home. She would never forgive him.'

'If he works for White Pass he'll be able to tell me whether I can get a train to Carcross and also to Dawson City from here,' said Mary.

Annie shook her head. 'No – to both of those, I'm afraid. There are no longer any passenger trains to Carcross and there never was a train to Dawson.' This was disappointing news for Mary but before she could say any more, chaos erupted inside the garage. Jake had come from the house, and Honey was jumping all over him as though she had not seen him for months.

Mary was introduced to Jake and soon everyone was sitting around the kitchen table. Mary was asked if she would like an Arctic Red beer or a Caesar cocktail. She didn't know what either of them was so she asked for some orange juice with ice. Julie put it all in the blender, and called it an 'orange frappe'. Mary had never tasted anything so cold. It burned her lips. Jake noticed her struggling and gave her another juice, this time with two cubes of ice in it. Mary watched Jake as he chatted easily to his mother and his sister. He was a handsome man and had a Mexican-style moustache which she normally didn't like on a man. He was tanned and his long black hair was tied back from his face in a pony-tail. She noticed his hands, brown, strong and dependable. She always noticed men's hands. Tom had lovely hands – his nails always nicely manicured. She could never date a man with limp, pink, hands like the priests in the convent. Ugh! Mary shuddered at the thought of it. Jake noticed this and asked if she was cold. Maybe she would like a hot drink? Mary was embarrassed, when she realised that he had been watching *her* too.

'Oh no! Juice is fine, thank you. Sorry, I was miles away for a moment.'

The barbeque was a great success. Jake relished every moment of being in charge of the food and being able to help their new guest. Mary couldn't decide between steak and salmon and so she tried a little of each. They sat out on the deck until quite late. Sunset wasn't until 10.30pm.

'Give us a song Julie,' said Annie. 'You know how I love to hear you sing. Go and get your guitar. Do you play a musical instrument, Mary?'

'No, but I quite like singing. My friend Sally and I used to sing together sometimes at home. We mostly used to sing nursery rhymes though, when her son was younger.'

Julie sat comfortably with her guitar and everyone sang a medley of popular songs, most of which Mary had not heard before. Suddenly, Julie struck up with 'Puff the Magic Dragon' which Mary did know and she sang the harmony to Julie's tune. She glanced around and saw that Annie and Jake had stopped singing. They were listening, instead, to the two of them. Mary blushed.

'You have a beautiful voice,' said Annie, 'and your voice blends real well with Julie's. Why don't you come to Carcross with us next Friday? You could sing with us around the campfire. We thought we'd go for a long weekend. You could meet some of my husband's family too. His mother is Tlingit and comes from Tagish and his father is from Dawson City. You never know, they might be able to help you.'

'That's very kind of you. I'd love to visit Carcross. Does your husband work there too?' asked Mary. Everyone looked at one another.

'Didn't Julie tell you? My George died two years ago. He was trying to save a woman, from Carcross, who had fallen from the bridge into the partly frozen lake. It was the hypothermia that killed him, but she survived. He was a section foreman for White Pass. He was a wonderful man. We miss him every day. He would have loved to have heard you and Julie singing just now.'

'I'm so sorry. I shouldn't have asked. He was very brave to do what he did. I'm always asking my boyfriend, Tom, to teach me to swim. We've been together for almost six years and I still can't swim. This is the first time I've been away from him for more than a weekend in all that time,' said Mary. 'I'll call him later tonight and tell him about this evening.'

Mary thought she could detect a slight look of sadness in Jake's eyes when she said this, but surely not? No, he was probably still thinking about his father.

'Thank you very much. It's been lovely, but I am feeling quite tired. I think I had better go soon.'

'Would you like me to come to the Archives with you on Wednesday?' asked Julie. 'We could also go for a coffee at Tim Horton's and see if that woman comes back.'

'That's a great idea! Where shall we meet?'

'Mom, could I use your van on Wednesday so that I can pick Mary up from the hotel?'

'Sure. Jake will run you back now on his way to Carcross. It's time he was on his way anyway. He's got an early start tomorrow. We'll get in touch with you about the weekend. It'll be fun.' Annie gave Mary a hug. Jake didn't need any persuading. He grabbed his bags and led Mary through to his truck.

'See you guys on Friday then,' he called out from the garage. Mary looked back and waved.

Jake drove into the hotel car park and turned off the engine. Talking to Jake was easy. Mary found herself describing one of her dreams to him, something she would never do with a stranger at home. She told him of the return visit to the children's home, a year ago with Tom, and of her unhappiness there as a child. She mentioned the other person who kept appearing in her dreams.

'This person shares my suffering and cries with me sometimes. It's very strange.'

'What does she look like?' asked Jake.

'Most of the time I can't see her face, although once she was like a mirror-image of me. Usually I just hear her voice – a loud sobbing or a scream.' Mary was astonished. This was easier, even, than talking to Karen.

'Why the Yukon though? Most people don't know about us up here. Is this where you had come from when that man found you in the airport?' Mary shook her head.

'No, I have no idea where I came from that day.' Mary explained a little about the package from Sister Joseph and also told him about her friendship with Rob and Wendy Jamieson. She described the feelings she had when she saw the huskies racing for the first time.

Jake spoke about his father's First Nations family and told her a little about their history.

'The Indian word 'Tlingit' means 'human'. Our people have been de-humanized in so many ways up until the 1980s when life started to improve for us all and people began to claim their land back. You wait until you meet Grandpa Joe and Grandma Nora. My grandmother is an Elder of the Carcross/ Tagish Tlingits and Grandpa's family is Tr'ondek from Dawson. Gee they can tell some stories! People say I'm a lot like my Grandpa,' he said smiling with pride. Mary looked at her watch in the half-light.

'Goodness, we've been talking for hours. It's past midnight and you've got to get back to Carcross. I've been chattering away without thinking about the time. You're such a good listener. Thank you, Jake. I'll see you on Friday. Drive carefully. Goodnight.'

Jake waited until Mary was safely inside the hotel. As she turned back to wave to him, she could see that he was smiling. It had been a great evening in more ways than one.

Chapter 10
London/Suffolk

This was Tom's first weekend without Mary so he planned to take the opportunity to visit his parents alone and have a good talk with them. He planned to have an honest discussion with them about all the grievances that had been building up inside him lately. They clearly didn't approve of any of his life choices so far and his mother's coldness towards the woman he loved had gone on long enough. After all, Mary was going to be the mother of their grandchildren in the near future, so they must start to accept her as a part of their family.

Tom talked this through with Ted, the manager of his rugby club – an older man whom Tom admired and often confided in. Their Saturday morning game on the heath had ended in victory and the rest of the chaps had gone off to the 'Princess of Wales' to celebrate.

'I need to tell them exactly how I feel about everything. I'm sick of my mother's attitude towards Mary, for one thing, and also her refusal to accept my choice of career. She and my father are such snobs! How dare they? I'm bloody-well going to have it out with them this time,' Tom said, feeling the sweat break out on his forehead.

'It isn't as though you're both eighteen,' Ted replied, as he locked the club house after the game. 'What you do with your life at your age has nothing to do with your parents. I told my wife this, when our daughter emigrated to Canada and married a chap from Calgary.'

'Exactly!' said Tom, encouraged by his words. Nevertheless, Tom knew it wouldn't be easy. He declined Ted's offer of a pint and decided to get going straight away. 'I've missed mother's birthday and the sooner I go, the sooner the weekend will be over. Thanks, anyway.'

Tom left the M25 and struggled through the road-works on the A12 towards Chelmsford and Ipswich. He could feel his body becoming tense and the pulse in the side of his head beating faster as it often did when he was agitated. He had not slept well; he never did just before visiting his parents. It was a warm August morning and the air already smelled fresher. Suffolk was a beautiful county. There was nothing dramatic about it, but the countryside was quaint and peaceful. Parts of his mother's mansion dated back to the sixteenth century and the two hundred acres of land had been farmed by her family for generations. Charlotte had told him that her dream was for Tom to take over the running of the farm and the estate once his father tired of it all and that could be any day now.

Tom had warned his parents for years that he had no intention of doing this, but they just wouldn't listen. Money wasn't the driving force behind Tom's future ambitions, as it was for his parents. He wanted to work with disadvantaged children and try to make a difference in their lives. He had tried a privileged lifestyle. He didn't need it. It wasn't for him. He needed to live and work amongst people who cared – whose lives were enriched because they made the best of their difficult circumstances. He admired the way Mary had come through an abusive and neglectful childhood and yet never let bitterness destroy her ability to care for others. His mother just didn't see it. He would love to live in Suffolk with Mary though, in a modern property which they could design themselves, but Mary was against the idea. Suffolk, to Mary, represented grandeur and Tom's mother. She was fond of Rendlesham Forest and their Sunday walks, but they could do that on a weekend visit, Mary had said and that's what it would have to be! Tom planned his speech carefully.

Two hours later, he steered his old Peugeot down the tree-lined road that led towards the imposing gates of the Selby Farm estate. He noticed that the leaves of the chestnut trees were already beginning to change colour and his heart sank. It's too soon for autumn – the summer holidays have only just begun. Autumn meant changes, changes for both of them. This trip of Mary's could alter their lives completely. Tom hastily pushed this thought to the back of his mind.

David Selby-James was gliding happily around the front lawns on his 'sit-on mower' – his favourite activity. Charlotte had refused to lose her family name when they married so hence the hyphened surname. It sounded imposing. Tom knew that his mother loved it.

'I'm not sure my Welsh parents would have agreed with you,' David had apparently said just before their wedding, but Tom knew that secretly his father was happy with his new name too. Tom studied his father. The sight of this distinguished-looking man in a Stetson hat and plus-fours, made him smile. David's dress sense was eccentric to say the least. His mother would go mad when she noticed that he hadn't changed into his gardening trousers. David waved as he saw Tom get out of the car.

'Darling!' gushed Charlotte as she ran towards him. 'How lovely, that you've come on your own.' Tom winced. Not a good start, he thought.

'Come and see what David and Amanda have bought me for my birthday. Fortunately not everyone forgot.

Really, Tom, you are shocking. Why doesn't that girl of yours remind you? Most women are good at these things.' Charlotte ushered him into the dining-room.

Tom immediately sprung into attack. 'First of all mother, Mary has been away in Canada for the past week and secondly, she has never had a family and so these things don't come naturally.' He had told himself that he must try not to react to his mother's rudeness and yet he had done so in the first five minutes.

Tom stood by the grand piano in the drawing room and looked around him. Nothing really stood out as being anything new or impressive. His face remained blank.

'Look,' Charlotte breathed excitedly, 'a set of original Constable sketches. David went to the auction at Sotheby's in London, and he bid for it. Isn't he clever?'

'Very nice.' It was yet another status symbol. The house was full of them. Tom made the excuse that he had to park his car in the garage and bring his bag upstairs. He decided to go out and help his father. Maybe they could slip out for a pre-dinner drink at his father's favourite local. At least with his father, the talk would be mostly about rugby or the latest progress report concerning the farm. David would be seventy-one in November and although he looked good for his age, he was showing signs of wanting to hand over all the responsibilities to someone younger. Tom knew his father wanted him to take over the estate but at least he didn't put pressure on him and go on about it all the time. What they must do, was to stay off the subject of teaching. David had hated his school days and had left at the age of fourteen during the 'Depression' in South Wales.

'You don't have to ponce about in a University in order to be successful. Look at me,' he would say, 'I did alright. There's no money to be made in teaching and most of the kids today don't want to learn today anyway.

I suppose you just want the long holidays.' Tom had heard it all before and decided not to mention his new job unless he was asked directly.

After the meal they all withdrew into the lounge for an after dinner cognac.

'Amanda is coming home for Sunday lunch tomorrow. You will stay won't you? She is longing to see you,' Charlotte announced.

'Oh great! It will be lovely to see her too.' He must embark upon his discussion tonight rather than tomorrow in front of Mandy. He knew that his mother would not react well to what he had to say and that would upset his sister.

'I wanted to talk to you both about my future with Mary. So far, she has refused my proposals of marriage because she needs to know who she is first, but as soon as her search is over I intend to marry her and start a family with her. We've talked about it a lot.' Tom saw his mother's expression change to one of horror and so before she could retaliate, he continued:

'I adore Mary and I know she loves me, and there is no-one else I want to spend the rest of my life with. I want to make it clear that if you reject Mary then you'll lose both of us and also any future grandchildren.' Tom poured himself another brandy. He was feeling much stronger all of a sudden.

'This is ridiculous. You can't marry her. She hasn't had any proper schooling. She probably comes from some primitive native background, and you know how we feel about the Irish – half of them are unemployed and drink too much.' Charlotte shook as she gulped the last of her gin and tonic.

'Why don't you find someone of your own kind? She is just not one of us!' Charlotte grabbed her husband's newspaper. 'David – say something. Don't just sit there.'

'Tom is twenty-nine years old dear. He'll do what he wants to do. I like Mary, and anyway she might discover that she is from an interesting and creative family. You never know there might have been an excellent reason why she was taken into care.'

Tom was speechless. Where had all of that come from, so suddenly?

Charlotte frowned and clenched her fists. The colour had drained from her face and matched her cream Jaeger trouser suit. She was breathing heavily as she tried to regain control of the situation.

'If you marry this girl, I will simply strike you from my will, and you can make your way on your own,' she said mixing herself another drink.

'You married Father, and he didn't have much schooling,' shouted Tom.

'No, but he did have money - and money changes everything!'

'I've had enough of this. I'll leave after breakfast, visit Mandy and then head home. Mandy and I will go out for lunch.' Tom knew that he couldn't pursue this discussion any further and he left the room. He rang Mandy's carer and explained that there was a change of plan. He would collect Mandy at 12.00 tomorrow and take her out for lunch - somewhere peaceful where they could sit outside by the river and enjoy the sunshine. His sister would love that. Charlotte always spoke to Mandy as though she didn't have a brain in her head, and would even reduce her to tears sometimes. Tom had always known how to understand Mandy's efforts at conversation and how to encourage certain responses from her. Mary did too. Mandy loved Mary and she would be thrilled with Tom's announcement, although Tom felt he should wait until an engagement actually happened first.

On his way back to London the next day, Tom decided that he would pay Karen a visit, not for a counselling session, but merely for some advice. She had become a good friend to them both over the past couple of years.

Karen was pleased to see Tom. She had been wondering how Mary's 'voyage of discovery' was going? She was surprised to hear Tom say that they would marry as soon as Mary had found her family. She had not gathered this impression from Mary herself but, being the consummate professional, Karen didn't say anything. They had a cup of tea together and Tom told her of the row with his parents. Karen was interested in his father's comment that Mary's family might be 'interesting and creative people'.

'It sounds as though your father has got to know and understand Mary a little. It might be worth meeting your father on neutral ground somewhere away from your mother. How much influence does he have over her?' asked Karen.

'On the surface, none but underneath the surface, she does listen to him. She would be lost without him, in fact.'

Karen nodded in agreement. This was so often the case with dominant women and their husbands, she thought.

'He'll be pleased that you have confided in him and could help you more than you realise.'

'A good idea. Why didn't I think of that? I'll arrange to meet him in Colchester at his team's next away match and then have lunch with him afterwards.'

'You know, you should do that more often.' Karen said as she walked with him to the car.

Driving through the Park, Tom felt like a lost soul. An

uneventful week stretched ahead of him - no Mary, no school work to do, no rugby training. He was like his father ... couldn't function properly without his lady by his side. Greenwich Park was full of tourists and families, all enjoying the freedom of the weekend – children feeding the ducks, teenagers playing tennis, and skateboarders taking advantage of the hills. His thoughts returned to Suffolk, and as he drove up on to the heath and turned on to the A2, he decided to drive to Thurston to visit Rob and Wendy. Maybe he could help exercise the dogs? He felt sure that Rob would be pleased to hear that Mary had gone to the Yukon. They could talk about the Yukon Quest race when she got back.

Tom parked in front of their rambling property on the edge of the village, and as he walked towards the front door, he could hear the dogs. He couldn't see Rob's Land Rover though.

Wendy came to the door.

'Hello Tom. Have you come to see Rob? He's at work until late tonight. He's doing a double shift to help out a mate. Did you ring me, only I was out the back feeding the dogs? Come in.'

Tom felt a little uncomfortable on his own with Wendy. What would they talk about? Wendy didn't appear to notice. She chatted on quite happily – mostly about the factory and the staffing problems that Rob was having, as company foreman.

'A man died last week,' she said. 'He fell into one of the big vats. The ladder had collapsed. It's been awful. Everyone's worried now that the maintenance men aren't doing their job properly. Rob reckons they might get the union involved.' She poured them both a mug of tea and produced some home-made scones.

'Here, help yourself,' she said. 'Where's Mary today?'

Tom told her the story, and how Mary had made her decision to travel to the Yukon based on two small clues. Wendy just laughed when Tom explained that two quite separate friends had mentioned the 'Yukon Quest' within a couple of weeks of each other, causing Mary to regard this as a 'sign'.

'Mary believes in fate,' said Tom. 'Meeting you and the huskies has had quite an impact on her. '

'I don't believe in things like that. I must say she's very brave. I wouldn't want to go all that way on my own. There are bears and wolves in the Yukon. I'd be scared.' Tom hadn't given much thought to the wildlife up there.

'How did you and Rob first get into husky-racing? How did you find out about it?' asked Tom, trying to steer the conversation away from Mary.

'I met Rob at the factory in 1984 when we worked together. We were both trying to get over a failed relationship at the time. His boss had four Siberian huskies that he raced in Thetford Forest and we went along to one of the competitions, to watch him race. Well that was it. Rob bought two puppies, which two years later produced four pups of their own. It's been wonderful. We really enjoy the sport. Dog people are the best, you know. We'll get to the Yukon, or Alaska, one winter. Rob is determined. I don't know how I feel about it though. All that snow! Brrrrh.'

'I hope you don't mind me asking this, but Mary wondered if Rob might be of mixed race, like herself? Where does he come from originally?'

'I know nothing about his life before we met, because he won't talk about it. The only thing he has told me is that he has been searching for his father for twenty-five years.

Apparently he disappeared from his workplace in

suspicious circumstances and hasn't been seen since. I keep telling him he might be dead by now. But he won't accept it. He's searched all over. He's been to London, to Wales, to Spain. I feel sorry for him. He needs to give up after all these years.'

Wendy chatted away.

'Why did he go to Wales?'

'Because his father is from there,' she said. 'Why do you ask?'

'Oh, just interested because my father is from there too.'

Tom couldn't believe what he was hearing - Rob searching for his father, Mary searching for her parents. What's going on here? I need to speak to Rob thought Tom. He thanked Wendy for the tea and said they would be in touch when Mary got home.

Chapter 11
Whitehorse

Mary sat by the phone, waiting for the agreed time to call Tom – 4.30pm. Only another fifteen minutes. She was beginning to feel very despondent about this trip. No-one seemed to know anything about the name Doyle. Maybe Tom and Karen were right; maybe this search would bring even more heartbreak for her.

She and Julie had been to the Yukon Archives as planned but nothing had been found under the name of Doyle in 1962. Julie then drove Mary up to the Vital Statistics Department but once again, they needed to know her place of birth, as well as the name of her community if she was part First Nations. Mary just did not have enough information. Even their lunchstop at Tim Horton's proved unsuccessful. There had been no sign of the woman that she had met earlier in the week, although Mary had not really expected to see her again.

As soon as she heard Tom's voice she felt the tears come. She was cross with herself. He would now worry. 'I need another clue. I need someone else to recognize me.' Her voice shook a little.

Tom tried to raise her hopes a little. 'Don't get upset, Darling. You knew it was going to be a 'shot in the dark'. You've got another week yet. There is still time. It'll be interesting to see what happens when you meet the First Nations family in Carcross this weekend. They might be able to help. Don't forget to show them the photograph.'

Mary felt calmer. Part of her problem was that she was trying to cope with this without him.

'I'm wondering if I should go to Dawson City, as the photograph might have been taken in one of the bars there. It's a long trip though. I don't know whether I want to go into any bars on my own.' She had come all the way from London and yet, for some reason, she felt daunted by the thought of Dawson. It was the fear of yet another closed door with noone there to comfort her, she decided. Maybe she should ask Jake to go with her? No! That would be too risky at the moment, the way she felt in his company.

'Are you still there, Darling?' asked Tom.

'Oh yes – sorry. I was thinking. Tom, I must go. We'll talk tomorrow. I'll try to call you from Annie's cabin, but I don't know what the reception will be like out there. Apparently the village is quite remote. Sleep well love. I do miss you. 'Bye.'

Mary went to bed early but she couldn't sleep. She tossed and turned for a while and then got up to make some tea. The drink didn't help. She felt anxious and couldn't stop going over everything in her mind. Finally she switched on the T.V. and fell asleep watching a movie.

Her head was spinning; too much bourbon. Gerard was leering at her from the bar. Four guys playing pool flirted with her and offered to give her a good time. Mary was flying.

She danced around the guys lifting her skirt as she did so, taunting them. Where was Tom? What was she doing here in this sleazy bar? Gerard was dancing with her, his hand inside her blouse. Suddenly she was surrounded.

The four guys had pushed Gerard out of the way, and were playing with her. Why didn't anyone do anything? The barman was enjoying the scene. One of the guys lifted her on to the pool table and ripped her clothes.

'Me first! You hold her down,' said one of them, as he undid his jeans. 'There's plenty more where this came from.' He laughed through her screams. 'Who's next?' All four of them had their turn. Gerard cheered them on.

Mary awoke in a foetal position. Her pillow was soaking wet. She sobbed hysterically. Her duvet was on the floor. She could hear someone knocking gently outside. She froze.

'Who is it?' she cried.

'Are you alright?' a female voice spoke through the closed door. We heard you screaming and we thought we should check on you. Do you need any help?'

Mary grabbed her dressing-gown, turned the key and opened the door.

'I'm alright, thank you. I had a really frightening nightmare. It's my fault. I watched a film last night called 'The Accused'. I shouldn't watch films like that late at night. They always give me bad dreams,' said Mary.

'Is that the movie with Jodie Foster? She's my favourite actress,' said the young girl. 'Would you like some breakfast in your room this morning?'

'No, I'll be okay. I'll have a bath and then come down. I would prefer the company. I'm going to Carcross with friends later in the morning. Thank you for your concern.'

Mary relaxed in the bath and thought about the trip with Julie and Annie. Julie told her that Carcross is really beautiful and that their cabin is on the beach by Lake Bennett. Mary tried to imagine it all and felt calmer. The thought suddenly struck her that the other girl hadn't been there to share her nightmare this time. Did that mean she was getting close to her family? Was it a sign? Mary was excited about the coming weekend - her first contact with a First Nations family.

Around mid-day Mary waited outside the hotel with her flight bag and jacket.

'No-one dresses up in Carcross.' Annie had said. 'Wear something comfortable and take a sweater or a vest for the evenings.'

'Will there be mosquitoes by the lake?' asked Mary as she climbed into the front of the van. She hated bugs of any description and always reacted badly to insect bites, at home.

'Probably, but we've got stuff,' said Julie. Annie and Julie had been to the store that morning to stock up on supplies.

'There isn't a proper food store in the village. In fact, Whitehorse is the nearest place and we're forty-five miles away. So if you run out of something, you just have to do without.'

'Good Heavens!' said Mary. 'Then Carcross really is in the wilderness then!'

Annie laughed when she saw Mary's surprised expression.

'The 'wilderness' isn't really a Yukon word. We tend to say 'the bush' up here.'

Annie continued south, past the S.S. Klondike, along the Robert Service highway and then turned off towards Miles Canyon.

'I thought I'd take you along the scenic route,' Annie said as she parked the van by a look-out point. Mary had to smile at this because she felt sure that the whole trip would be a 'scenic route'. They stood and looked down upon a narrow strip of the Yukon River surrounded by a warm summer patchwork of light and dark greens – the pines and the aspens and the birch trees.

'It's beautiful,' said Mary. She reached in her pocket for her camera.

'The lake we just passed is called Schwatka Lake. Miles Canyon used to be the infamous Whitehorse Rapids before the dam was built in the '50s,' explained Annie. 'That's where the name Whitehorse came from – from the frothy 'white horses' on the rapids. Years ago, these rapids used to be so hazardous for anyone trying to navigate the river that they had to build a wooden tram-way on both banks in order to by-pass this section of the river. Have you heard of Jack London?'

'Did he write 'The Call of the Wild'? I saw that film once on the television.'

'Well he spent a few weeks hauling people through the rapids, in those days, to earn some money. A dangerous sport, that's for sure.'

'Who needs a Tour Guide with Mom around eh?! You can tell she's a teacher. Come on you guys. You'll no doubt want to stop by Emerald Lake as well, and I'm starving.'

Julie ushered Mary back in the van. 'Mary doesn't have to see everything on this trip. There will be other times.'

Mary wondered if this was true. She'd be flying home next Thursday. Annie had warned her that the roads might be busy seeing as how the weather was good and it was Friday.

Mary wondered what she would think about the M25 on a Friday at this time. Annie had always wanted to go to Europe, but George wasn't a traveller. He hated to leave the Yukon, even to go to Vancouver.

They soon arrived at the turn-off to the South Klondike Highway – the Carcross Road. A driver about a hundred metres in front of them braked suddenly as a young deer jumped out of the bushes and ran across the road in front of his car.

'This can be quite a problem on the highways,' continued Annie, the tour guide. 'We are in moose and bear country, and if you collide with either of those when they are fully grown, you are in big trouble, especially a bull moose or a male grizzly.'

'I'd love to see some though,' Mary reached for her camera again just in case. She gazed ahead at the mountains, which increased in size the nearer they got to Carcross. They were dramatic from a distance with their jagged peaks clearly defined, as there were no trees on the top. Their slopes bore streaks of grey and brown and green, almost as though they'd been painted. They were a tempting backcloth to their final destination. Mary thought she would love to see them in the winter-time or in the spring when they were covered with ice and snow.

'Goodness. Look at that lake. It's stunning,' exclaimed Mary. 'The water is the most beautiful shade of green I've ever seen, especially with the sun on the water. Could we stop for a photograph?' asked Mary. Annie drove off the highway and parked the van.

'I knew it!' moaned Julie. 'This is Emerald Lake,' she said to Mary. 'The First Nations people call it 'Rainbow Lake' because it has lots of other colours in it too.'

'Is it safe to get out of the van?' Mary was thinking of the bears. Everyone laughed.

'The next beauty spot that will tempt you is the Carcross Desert – just before we reach Carcross,' said Annie, 'but we'll visit that on Monday, on the way back to Whitehorse, otherwise 'madam' here will moan some more! It's the world's smallest desert, they say.'

'Mom, I haven't seen the cabin for months. Anyway, Honey's getting restless!'

They drove past the little desert, past two more beautiful lakes, and finally turned right into the village. Mary had not seen any photos of Carcross and so had been unable to create any picture in her mind as to what it might look like. The leaflet in the hotel had said that it is the most photographed place in the Yukon, and that thousands of tourists pass through it every year. A village in Suffolk might bring to mind thatched, Suffolk pink cottages, a fifteenth century pub and probably a twelfth century church surrounded by farmland. This village was unlike anything that Mary had ever seen before. It had a beauty all of its own. The mountains stood on guard around it and the lakes created a feeling of tranquillity. They crossed over the little railway line, past the one hotel and Matthew Watson's General Store and on to Bennett Avenue, the street that ran along the shoreline of the lake. The feeling of space was the thing that struck Mary: wide roads, no traffic, and a big sky! The avenue was lined on both sides with log cabins and wooden houses of varying colours, shapes and age.

Annie's place wasn't so much a cabin but a three bedroom log house, which Annie explained they had bought from a friend of George's just after Julie was born.

'We've done quite a lot to it. We've even got a new bathroom,' she said proudly.

'There is also the outhouse, of course, if you fancy the rustic life-style.' She pointed to a tiny log building with net curtains at the window above the door.

'It looks very smart, smarter than some of the ones in our English campsites,' said Mary. She loved camping, but Tom wasn't keen. It always rained and he liked his comforts.

'You'll be sharing a room with Julie – hope that's okay?'

'Correction ... with Julie and Honey,' added Julie. 'She always sleeps with me.'

The next morning, Mary woke early. There were no curtains or blinds to shut out the view and so the room had been filled with sunlight for hours. She had slept peacefully the night before and felt sure that she would do so while she was in Carcross. She dressed quickly, in sundress and sandals, and slipped out of the house with Honey close at her heels. They ran down on to the beach. It was surprisingly warm and the air smelt perfumed. She sat on an abandoned log and listened ... complete silence. How soothing that was. The colours of the lake seemed to be layered; from dark to light blue. Nothing stirred. She felt safe and comforted by the mountains which seemed to circle protectively around her. She kicked off her sandals and the soft sand felt warm between her toes. I could live here, Mary thought. As if to remind her that there was life out there, a huge crow, or maybe it was a raven, flew across her line of vision and perched on a nearby television aerial. It felt right. There was something very healing about this beautiful place ... nothing tangible, it just felt right.

Without warning, Honey barked and then began to wag her tail. Mary jumped. She had been in a safe little world of her own. She didn't hear the rustle of the bushes as Honey had done.

'Hiya. How did you sleep?' Jake appeared, wearing summer shorts and a vest. His rich brown skin was even more tanned by the warm summer sun and his well-developed body, made Mary catch her breath for a moment. He stood with his hands on his hips, smiling down at her. She asked him if he was about to dive into the lake.

'Not likely!' said Jake. 'It's a glacial lake; the water is much too cold. Maybe I'll swim later - towards the end of August. Mom usually has an annual dip around that time. Mary, I was thinking. I could take you across the bridge after breakfast, to meet my grandparents if you would like that. They would like to meet you. I've told them all about your search.'

'Thank you. I was hoping that you would suggest that,' said Mary. 'Can you show me around the village too? You won't believe how different all of this is from anything I have seen back at home. I would like to take some photographs to show Tom, Sally and Karen.'

'All in good time,' Jake laughed.' He held out his hand to her to help her get up. 'Come on, Mom has a basket of freshly made muffins waiting for us.' Mary grasped his hand and jumped to her feet. Yes - it felt right. It definitely felt right.

After breakfast the two of them stood together, in silence for a moment, on the highway bridge and studied the village. The short river between the two lakes made it seem as though the lake narrowed in readiness for the bridge. Mary studied houses and cabins on both sides of the water. Children were fishing from the railway bridge in the distance. An older couple crossed the footbridge hand in hand.

'Years ago, said Jake, the First Nations people lived on this side of the water and the white people mostly lived on the other side. It was like that everywhere, but things are different now. This is an important time for us. The First Nation people are claiming their land back and their traditions are returning. My grandparents will tell you that it's been a long time coming.'

They crossed the bridge and followed the road past the cemetery. Jake explained that the First Nations people were not allowed to have their own burial ground for many years, but since the1970s this cemetery had been set aside for the local First Nations people.

'My Uncle Joey is buried there. He died in 1976. He was only thirty years old.'

'Why did he die so young?' asked Mary.

'It was the booze that killed him. It's a common problem here. My Uncle Sammy is also an alcoholic. He's in a clinic in Whitehorse at the moment. My father didn't drink and neither does Mom. They've seen too many people die.'

Jake looked sad. He stopped and his eyes followed the path of an eagle which took flight from a nearby spruce tree. Mary took more photos of the village.

'Tell me some more. This is so interesting,' said Mary.

'Grandpa has had a tough life, growing up in Dawson in the 1920s. Some of that time was spent away from home in a residential school. He doesn't like to talk about it. Grandma Nora grew up in Tagish, the next community and she went to school here in Carcross too. She's an Elder of the Tlingit Deisheetan clan and she's a story-teller. She's a good one too. Everyone knows her around here. She has fostered several children as well as having four of her own. You'll probably meet my Aunt Amy. She lives nearby too.' He explained that he and Julie were part Tlingit because they follow the line of the women in the family. This is the First Nations tradition. He added that his mother, when she married his father had all the same rights as his First Nations family, but if it had been the other way around, she would have lost them all.

'My generation is not so strict about mixed marriages, thankfully. When a couple married in Grandma's day, the man usually moved to live near his wife's family. So Grandpa left his family in Dawson and came here. Their language and their traditions are different from ours. I expect Grandma will be happy to explain it to you when you meet her.'

Mary listened intently, as Jake talked with great pride about his First Nations roots. He spoke with such a depth of understanding. She tried to imagine Tom talking about his family in this way. It was a very different world, she realised. What was it that Tom's mother had said to him last weekend? 'Money changes everything!' Tom had been appalled. She could hear it in his voice on the phone.

'Julie and I feel differently about all of this. I'd like to learn the Tlingit language. I'm a drummer and am learning some of the ceremonial songs. Julie isn't so interested. She loves her family, but she doesn't feel their spirit, as I do. I guess she takes after Mom's side of the family. They're from Alberta.'

'What kind of drum do you play?'

'I haven't got my own drum yet. I'd like to have a Tlingit drum made for me one day.' Jake described the drum he would like and specified that it must have a beautiful twin-tailed beaver printed on its skin – the symbol of the Deisheetan Tlingits. 'Here we are,' said Jake, pointing to a wooden house, painted white, with lots of vehicles and old appliances standing around it in the yard.

'Grandpa fixes things,' said Jake as though he had read Mary's thoughts.

Chapter 12

Jake led Mary into the kitchen. Grandma Nora was sitting in her rocking chair surrounded by pieces of tanned hide, bundles of brown fur and boxes of tiny coloured beads. She was making a pair of slippers. She looked up and smiled at her favourite grandson.

'Hi, Grandma. I've brought Mary to see you,' he said as he gave her a hug. 'I'm showing her around Carcross and she said she'd like to meet you both. Where's Grandpa?'

'Where d'ya think? Round the back, with Amy, fixing her bike. Young Danny borrowed it. Bent the back wheel. Coffee's fresh. Help yourself. Got to finish this today.' Nora's weathered hands expertly embroidered the head of a red rose on to the hide, ready for the next slipper.

Mary gazed around her. Every wall was lined with framed family photos. The house was cluttered, with piles of clothes, papers and toys on most of the furniture. Despite the disarray, the house felt cosy and welcoming. Mary and Jake pulled up two dining chairs and sat near Nora – awaiting her stories. Jake had told Mary there would be plenty of them. Nora was beautiful. She looked younger than her seventy eight years. Her black hair had lightened over the years and was now streaked with grey. She wore it short, framing her face which was almost free of lines. She peered over her glasses, which were on the end of her nose, studied Mary for a moment and smiled.

Mary picked up one of the finished slippers, to feel the

fur against her cheek. The smoky smell of the leather tickled her nostrils. 'Those moccasins are really pretty. I love the bead-work. Is that moose hide and what kind of fur is that?'

'This is moose hide. Fur is beaver. Sometimes I use rabbit. I make slippers, gloves, mukluks for family and friends long time. My mother teach me. She sew lots. She make good money when American Army was here building Alaska Highway in the '40s. Later she make them for tourists.'

'Have you lived here in Carcross since you were first married?' asked Mary.

'I grew up in Tagish. Went to Mission School here. Met Jake's Grandpa at mission school. Joe come from Dawson - was away from home ten months every year. Jake's Uncle Albie come from Carmacks. It's hard away from family.'

'Goodness me. Dawson is such a long way away. They must have been very homesick.'

'Government, they take Indian kids from across Yukon. White man's rules not our rules. School life tough long ago. Teachers tell us: "Don't talk Indian.". Kids who broke rules got strap. Teacher told Joe he worth nothing, broke his spirit. He just a boy ... bad times. Joe and Albie, they don't talk about it. Albie, he has bad dreams. Many changes now. Everyone in same school. Jake excused himself and went outside to join his grandfather and his Aunt Amy.

'When were you able to attend the state schools, I mean public schools?' asked Mary, trying to keep away from the stories of abuse for the moment.

'1960s or so. Some kids still leave families, go to hostel in Whitehorse. Some hostels they bad too like mission school. That's why George and Annie they move to Whitehorse.'

Mary sighed deeply. She was finding this subject painful, not just for Nora and Joe, but also for herself. She wasn't quite ready for all this detail. A cloud of melancholy descended upon her. These stories were important to this family. If Mary really did have roots in the Yukon she needed to hear them. Maybe her mother had gone through all this too? Poor Albie! He must have the same kind of dreams as me, thought Mary.

'Did you hunt for all your own food and clothing, in those days?' she asked.

'Our families had trap lines. We set snares, catch rabbit, squirrel, muskrat, catch fish at fish camp. My mother she taught me. We pick berries. Still do. Joe always hunt moose, caribou, mountain sheep with our sons. Too old now.' Nora joked, with a twinkle in her eye. They both saw Grandpa Joe coming into the kitchen. He had heard her.

'Hey - who's too old?' shouted Joe from the doorway. 'Not me. I'm never too old for nothin'. He grabbed some soap and a towel and ran over to the sink. Jake laughed.

'That's true. Mary, this is my Grandpa, and here's my Aunt Amy and Uncle Albie. Aunt Amy is my Dad's sister. Uncle Albie and me work together at White Pass.'

'Hi. What brings you all the way from England?' said Uncle Albie. We've never had an English girl visit us before.' He limped across the floor to where Mary was sitting, hung his stick on the back of her chair and sat down next to her. Mary recounted the short version of her story to him, and added that all she had with her, from the time when she arrived at the convent, were two little mukluks and a photograph.

'What's your last name?' asked Grandpa Joe. 'Maybe I know your folks.'

'It's Doyle - D-O-Y-L-E. It was written on the envelope that contained the photo. It's a popular name in

Ireland, so maybe my father is Irish? I'm assuming it's my father's name.' said Mary, handing the photo to Grandpa Joe who stared hard at it, but shook his head. Albie asked to see the photograph.

'Who's this?' he asked, 'and when was it taken?'

'I don't know. I was hoping to find that out during my visit to the Yukon.'

'Hey Joe, look at this. Don't you think it looks like the Downtown bar in Dawson? I don't know the guy though. Do you?' Joe shook his head.

Mary felt flushed with excitement. That's what the woman in the library in Whitehorse had said. Now two people had said it. There must be some truth in it.

'Joe comes from Dawson City. We know it well. We could take you up there, if you like, although it can't be until next Saturday. I have a real busy week ahead, at work,' Albie added.

Mary's face fell. 'That's kind of you, but my flight home is on Thursday. It does look as though I have to visit Dawson though, doesn't it? Maybe I'll come back with my boyfriend or with my friend, Sally, and we'll spend some time up there.'

Amy's expression looked wistful and she clearly wasn't listening to their discussion. She'd been studying Mary's face, whilst Mary had been talking to Albie.

'Mom, don't you think Mary has a look about her of Joanna, especially when she smiles?'

'Yeah. Thought that soon as she come in,' said Nora.

'Who's Joanna?' Where was this going to lead?

'Joanna was my little sister, who died. She was only three. She had very dark hair and a smile similar to yours', said Jake.

'She was such a pretty little girl. She died of meningitis,' said Amy.

'Oh, how sad!' Mary's eyes filled with tears.

'So what's Mom been telling you – not life in the mission school, I hope?' said Amy changing the subject.

'Albie and my Dad don't like to talk about it.'

'I was just about to ask about the fish camp. What exactly is it?'

'You'd love Mom and Dad's fish camp. It's just a few miles up the highway on the way to Skagway. We have a great time. For generations families have come together to camp, relax, fish, hunt and pick berries and talk about the winter.

This mostly happens in the summer now, when the kids are home from school.

'Do the children fish too?' asked Mary.

'Of course. We've started to teach our children traditional ways, which have long been forgotten: skills such as using a bow and arrow, recognising animal tracks, fishing, building shelters and lots more. Everyone gathers, while the salmon are spawning, to catch and clean the fish ready for winter storage. You're welcome to join us. We'll be down there until Monday, won't we Albie?' said Amy. Albie had closed his eyes for a moment and he almost jumped out of his chair at the sound of his name.

'Yeah, the fish camp was the best time of the year for my brother and me when we were kids,' said Albie. 'It meant we could stay at home in Carmacks for six weeks and be with our family. We used to have feasts around the camp fire and listen to the Elders tell their stories. We set snares, and played games, and there was always plenty to eat.'

'It must have been wonderful to be back with your family and to share your meals with them,' said Mary 'which reminds me, Jake we should get back for our lunch soon.'

Albie was determined to finish his story.

'Sometimes, someone would kill a moose. It would be skinned and divided up amongst all the family. We were brought up to share everything. It was special. We never wanted to go back to school ... no way! We always tried to hide when the boat arrived. That place killed my little brother, I reckon. He got sick a lot. It was so cold and damp, especially in the winter and the work was hard. He missed Mom a lot. We both did.'

Amy put a finger to her lips and nodded towards Jake who immediately glanced at the clock.

Annie would be lighting the barbeque ready for lunch. Also, Aunt Amy and Uncle Albie would be off to Whitehorse, to stock up on supplies.

'Thank you very much,' said Mary. 'It's been great to meet you all. Maybe I'll see you at the fish camp if either Jake or Annie is planning to visit you?'

'You betcha!' said Amy.

Later that night, exhausted from their shopping expedition to Whitehorse, Albie had the worse night's sleep that he had had for years. It was all that talk of the mission school days. Amy knew he didn't like to think about it. It always caused him to have bad dreams. Sometimes the dream was so real that he felt he really was that homesick boy again, and he would wake up in tears. There he was ... right back in the year of 1946, the year their Mom died, the year that changed everything.

Chapter 13
Anglican Mission School 1946

The War in Europe was over and bit by bit the young soldiers, who enlisted from the Yukon Territory, were returning to their families. They were the lucky ones. They had survived to tell their tale. However, they had seen another life beyond the Canadian shores and, for the First Nations men especially, it was hard to adjust to the old ways. Some arrived home only to discover that their children or their younger siblings were missing. They had been taken away to residential schools or hostels. Families were fragmented and those who were still at home were depressed about the way the changes were affecting their livelihood. Without their children they were unable to run their trap-lines. Food was scarce. White folks had moved on to their land. Many of the First Nation families were living in fragile accommodation, in shacks that couldn't keep out the summer breeze let alone the winter blizzard. Staying in one place was not their custom. They were used to following the source of the food. The winters were severe and without the children to help with the chores, it was hard. Diseases such as T.B. and smallpox had been brought in from Outside and many people got sick and died.

Charlie Luke hadn't enlisted as his brother had done, because his wife was ill and his boys needed him. He managed to get a job helping out at the Trading Post in Carmacks. Others weren't so lucky and had to rely upon the allowance that was given to them by the Government as long as their children attended school.

Eight year old Albie Luke stood hand-in-hand with his little brother Dougie, who was just seven. It was a warm autumn morning in early September. The boys' faces were white and tear-stained and Dougie was whimpering quietly. Their great uncle, the shaman, had sat with their mother for many nights. The doctor had wanted her to go to the hospital in Whitehorse, but she was too ill to be moved and finally the pneumonia claimed her. Charlie sat by the stove in the kitchen, with his head in his hands, listening to two government officials as they quoted the white man's rules to him.

'The law states that all children above the age of six must attend school. Both of your children are eligible for schooling and as there isn't a school in Carmacks they must be sent to a residential school. There is one in Carcross which provides an excellent education for all Indian children.' The man in the grey suit announced this as though he was offering Charlie a prize of some kind.

'You will be given an allowance of $20 per month as long as these children continue with their education. You have one week to prepare them for the trip. The boat will arrive from Dawson around mid-day next Tuesday. Good-day to you.'

Without even looking towards the boys or speaking to them, the men walked out.

That week, Albie and Dougie were both given new clothes and shoes. They didn't know why they were suddenly getting all these gifts, but it made them happy.

'Dad what did the white man mean 'bout the boat picking us up?' Albie asked his father that weekend.

'Don't worry yourself. You boys are going on boat trip to Carcross.'

'You coming too Dad?' Albie sensed that there was something missing, something that his father wasn't telling him. Maybe it was a special surprise for him and Dougie. He didn't know where Carcross was. He wished he could talk to his Mom or his Grandma about it all. His father didn't explain things like his Mom always did. Albie had never been on a steamboat before. He wanted to work on one when he was older.

'Can't do that son. Have to work. You know that.'

For Charlie, a proud Northern Tutchone trapper from a long line of trappers and traders, to see his family disappear before his very eyes was like having an arrow pierce his heart.

So many families had already lost their traditional lifestyle and Charlie couldn't see how he could continue with his trap lines without help. He didn't want anything from the government. He wanted to work. He would go into the bush for some of the time. His sons would be home next summer. He would make sure of that, even if he had to go and get them himself.

The boys leaned against the white railings of the S.S Klondike, clutching their burlap bags with their clothes in them. Their father was on the river bank waving his hat. His sad face was trying to smile. Albie couldn't understand why he couldn't come with them, and then when he saw other children with luggage saying goodbye to their families he knew. They were all being sent away. Tears filled his eyes. He mustn't cry. He must be strong for Dougie.

The boys arrived at Carcross and were lifted on to the back of an open truck with other Indian children. They were exhausted and hungry. Both boys had been sick on the boat and there was no food on the train from Whitehorse to Carcross, only water. Albie kept his young brother close to him. He was determined not to let him out of his sight.

Dougie had always been a fragile child. He was often sick, with asthma in the summer and bronchitis in the winter. He had pneumonia once when he was very little but luckily their great uncle cured him.

'Anymore for Chooutla ?' shouted the driver of the truck.

'What's Shutela?' Albie asked an older boy standing next to him.

'It's a mission school. We have to live there and get our schooling until next June. I warn you, it's tough. Don't get caught speaking Indian,' said the boy trying to sound grownup.

Albie's heart filled with dread. He tried to explain this to Dougie, but he didn't mention how long they were to stay away from home or how tough it was going to be. He would find out soon enough. Two dejected little souls stood before the school principal and his deputy, a big, fierce-looking woman.

All the boys were taken down to the basement of what looked like a huge barn. They were lined up according to their size and they all had their hair cut short. To an Indian, that was a physical assault. The scissors kept snagging their hair and it hurt. The man was rough and the younger boys were crying. Albie had seen a photograph of his grandfather when he was a grown man. His hair had hung down almost to his waist. His granddad told him once:

'We had long hair in long ago time. With long hair, you'd be strong hunter. Never cut hair.'

Supper was fish soup and rice pudding. It didn't taste of anything and the pudding looked like a pile of white mush. Dougie said he felt sick.

A group of boys were deloused with a sharp comb and something that smelt bad, and then they were all showered together. Once they were in their pyjamas they were put in different dormitories according to their age. The younger ones were taken upstairs. Dougie screamed and clung to Albie, asking for help in Tutchone.

'No Indian!' shouted the deputy principal. The woman towered over them all. Dougie was taken away without a word. Just before getting into bed, they were all made to kneel by their beds to pray. There were about twenty beds arranged in rows each side of the dormitory with no more than a thin mattress and a blanket on each of them. Albie listened to the other boys and pretended to join in. He didn't know who he was praying to. His Mom had never taken them to the church. That night he hid under the blanket and cried himself to sleep. He missed his brother and his Mom and his Dad. He missed his life already.

The next three or four years that followed were tough for Albie and Dougie. They didn't often get to see each other. It wasn't encouraged in case they talked in their own language and made each other too homesick. The original school had burned down ten years before in 1939. The temporary living accommodation and schoolrooms, mostly barns and shacks, were cold and uncomfortable for most of the year. Everyone had chores to do. They had to carry wood and water, clean the toilets and the floors, collect and prepare the vegetables and care for the animals. If jobs were not done properly they had to be done again or else they would get the strap, usually on the hand, but sometimes on the bare bottom. Albie thought the food was weird. It was stuff he had never tasted before, like porridge and rice. Even the white fish was boiled so much it was tasteless. Dougie got lots of colds and Albie was depressed and homesick. Albie felt like he did when his Mom got sick, close to tears all the time and he couldn't sleep. He never laughed any more.

Every year he dreamed of running away and making his way back to Carmacks, but the other kids told him it was too far and too risky. Two boys had tried to do that in the winter. Their bodies were found; they had died of exposure. Punishment was severe for anyone trying to break the rules. One teacher was kind, Mrs Cardle, their house-mother. Everyone liked her. She comforted Albie sometimes, knowing that he didn't have a mother, and she would occasionally sneak written messages to and from his brother for him and put them under their pillows at night.

One afternoon Albie and his buddy from Carmacks, Bobby James, were chatting quietly about their lessons in the schoolroom.

'How come we go to mission school? We learn nothing. I don't know Tutchone language no more,' said Albie as they played their secret 'stick game', an Indian game his father had taught him.

'We should learn from Elders, the skills of our people. We'll never know about trap lines or hunting or living in the bush. My Grandpa Tommy Black says I've forgotten everything,' said Bobby.

At the school they learned how to do chores and how to hide their feelings. There wasn't time for much schoolwork. There were too many jobs to do.

Albie's two friends at Chooutla were Peter, from Whitehorse and Bobby from Carmacks. One year in early summer, when they were twelve, all three of them got together in the dormitory and planned to make a run for it once the ice began to clear. They would hide their coats in one of the outbuildings and then they'd escape from their work out in the fields. Albie wanted Dougie to be included, but Bobby was against the idea. He said he was too young and sickly and wouldn't be strong enough to cope with the journey. Albie said he would think about it.

'Let's go to Whitehorse,' said Peter. 'My family live in Whiskey Flats. My Dad can help. He has big van.'

The boys all agreed to try. None of them stopped to consider how far it would be to Whitehorse by foot or where they would sleep at night or what they would eat or drink.

They had forgotten most of their survival skills for life in the bush. They had one thought only. They had to get back home.

'Bears wake up soon. They'll be hungry,' said Albie, 'We gotta be careful.'

The three boys spent the next few days dreaming about their escape, and whispering in corners about it when no-one was looking. They knew what would happen if they were caught, so everything had to be carefully planned. Albie was worried that he might be expecting too much of his brother.

'Dougie might get sick or die on road to Whitehorse,' Albie said. 'If he has bad asthma, I can't help. Don't know how. You're right Bobby. We'll leave him here. I'll tell my Dad and say Dougie's sick. He'll come and get him. When Dad knows 'bout this place, he'll keep us home for sure.

The day finally arrived. They spread themselves far apart on the edge of the ploughed field and one by one they made their way to the outbuildings. Albie's heart was racing with fear and excitement.

'Hide,' said Bobby, 'keep to bush, not open road.'

Darkness fell quickly, but luckily there was a full moon.

Albie's father had told his two boys never to wander off into the bush alone, but to always go with an adult who carried a gun and could protect them. This time they had no choice.

They stopped by a little creek where they could hear the trickling sound of a fresh water spring. They were very thirsty so they drank deeply even though it was icy and burned their throats.

'I'm cold like ice,' said Peter.' Where we gonna sleep? I'm tired. I need my bed.'

'We might find empty trapper's shack,' said Albie, 'or we can make shelter with dry pine branches. We sleep close and keep warm.'

'What if bear finds us?' Peter had never seen a bear up close.

'We look dead and hope it's not hungry grizzly,' Bobby grinned at Albie. 'Just don't make noise. Now stop bellyaching! Some Indian!'

The temperature had dropped to below zero, and the boys were tired and hungry. Even the disgusting food that was dished up at the school seemed tempting as they struggled on. Albie had promised to try to steal a few scraps of food for their journey but he didn't have a safe opportunity to do it. He couldn't get to see Dougie either, but their Dad would come back and get him. The main road wasn't very far and yet it felt as though they had been trudging through the snow for hours. The boys were cold and hungry. Between the trees, Bobby could see the roof of a building in the half light. He couldn't see any wood smoke though. 'Hey, look! A cabin. Maybe someone lives there.'

'Could be trapper's place.' Albie had also spotted it

'Looks good. I hate the wind. My fingers and toes are dead. I could get frostbite,' said Peter, their weary friend. 'Let's go. No bears can get at us in there.' He ran towards cabin.

The shack was derelict and was leaning badly, but it was dry and a protection against the wind. The boys curled up together in the far corner away from the door and tried to sleep. The wind sounded eerie as it whistled amongst the trees, and the tired boards of the old shack creaked and moaned. Albie kept listening for the unwanted sound of a hungry bear, but very soon he too was asleep.

All three of them sat up with a start at the sound of dogs barking just outside the door. The R.C.M.P had been searching for them through the night. The boys knew what that meant. They would be taking them back to Chooutla.

'The bush is a pretty stupid place to hide. You guys could die out here – lots have,' said the older of the two policemen. 'It's a hell of a long way to Whitehorse if that's where you were heading. You're real lucky we found you.'

The boys followed the policemen out on to the highway and climbed into the back of the van with the dogs. Peter was relieved that they had been discovered. He'd hated it out there in the cold and the dark. Albie's heart sank at the thought of three more years in their 'prison' so far from home. He would never attempt to escape again though. There was no point. Besides which the punishment for running away was severe. Everyone dreaded the beatings.

Albie decided that he would never return to Carcross again once he left school ... but then sometimes life has other plans.

Chapter 14
Carcross

Everyone was up early the next morning ... early for a Sunday that is. Even Julie was up before Mary and there were sounds of activity coming from the kitchen. Ruby, one of Annie's neighbours, had a family christening in St. Saviours, the little wooden Anglican Church that Mary had noticed on the way into the village. Annie had offered to host the reception after the service. Jake had boasted that this was typical of his Mom because she was always hosting something for someone in Carcross or in Whitehorse. This was Annie's church and it meant a lot to her. Mary slipped on a simple summer dress and went down to join the others. Annie, the matriarch, was there in the midst of things – giving instructions. Her sleeves were rolled up above her elbow, she wore a large white apron, patterned with photos of Alaska, over her Sunday clothes, and her face was flushed as red as the beef tomatoes waiting to be sliced for the burgers. The morning sun was pouring through the huge picture windows. It was hot. Jake was in charge of the barbeque again and had also stacked the logs by the side of the stove.

'Where's Julie gone now, just when I need her?' Annie sounded flustered, which was unusual. 'I want to get all of this done so that we can all go to church. I promised Ruby we'd all be there.' Julie and Honey came in just at that moment.

'What time is the service, Mom?'

'It's at 11 o'clock – that's if we're ready on time. By

the way, I forgot to give you and Mary a message from Ruby last night. She's says that there is no-one to play the organ and would you girls lead the singing with the guitar. I told her how good you two sound when you sing together.'

'Oh Mom! I couldn't do that. What – sing in church, in front of everyone? I don't think so.' squealed Julie. 'What about you Mary?'

'It depends what they want us to sing. It would have to be something that I know. I learnt lots of hymns as a child. Also we sing them at school in Assembly twice a week. How about if I sing and you play the guitar?' Mary suggested. 'Maybe you'll get brave by the second verse and join in with me.'

'Ruby suggested 'All Things Bright and Beautiful', said Annie 'and also 'Jesus Wants Me for a Sunbeam'. She gave me the sheet music for both of those. Julie – you know them.' Julie groaned. 'Go off somewhere and have a little practice,' said Annie.

They did a fine job, and everyone said they should be on the T.V. Once everyone, including the minister, had tucked into Annie's splendid lunch, they decided to pile down on to the beach with iced drinks to enjoy the sunshine.

Jake was very proud of his girls, but he'd had enough now of the party chatter. He wanted some time alone with Mary. He was confused about his feelings for her and was anxious that she might be coming back with her boyfriend next time. He didn't know what to do. Things were going well right now. He didn't want to spoil that .He looked across to Mary as she chatted easily with Ruby and her daughter, with the baby. She looked happy and relaxed. She looks as though she belongs here, not in London, he thought, studying her freshly tanned skin and her long black hair.

Mary was keen to see the rest of the village. She and Jake walked down to the lake with Honey close at their heels. They kept near the edge where the sand was wet and firm, while Honey splashed in and out of the water. It was cooler by the water and there was just enough breeze to make it enjoyable. Jake took his cap out of his back pocket and offered it to Mary, but she said it looked so much better on him. She had never liked baseball caps. They just didn't suit her. Within minutes they were the only people on the beach as they strolled west in the direction of the Watson River.

'It was lovely meeting your Dad's family yesterday,' said Mary. 'Why does Uncle Albie walk with a stick?'

'His leg was badly mauled by a young grizzly when he was out hunting once. Grandpa Joe fired his rifle and frightened the animal off. Uncle Albie was real lucky.'

'Do bears come close to the village?' Mary decided that she didn't want to see a grizzly after all.

'Occasionally, but it's mostly black bears that come. They won't eat us, they're vegetarians, but they'll attack sometimes, especially if they're hungry or if they have their young with them. Don't ever run from a bear or go close to one if you've got food with you.' Mary promised she never would.

'Why is the beach so deserted?' Mary asked. 'A really beautiful beach like this, at home, would be crowded on a day like today.'

'It's because quite a few of the cabins are only used at weekends and during the holidays. We're lucky today. August is usually the busiest month if the weather is good,' said Jake.

After a while Jake suggested that they sit for a few minutes and enjoy the view before climbing up towards the back of the village. They sat side by side and looked out towards the mountains that framed the lake. The sun was high and cast a pathway of gold across the surface of the water.

'It's so peaceful. We could be the only people on the planet right now,' said Mary. She could feel the warmth of his body through her summer dress. It was comforting. Jake was feeling nervous and unsure of himself.

'When might you come back here with your boyfriend?' He tried to sound casual.

'I don't know. Tom is a teacher and his first main holidays will be at Christmas and at Easter. I don't know whether I can wait that long. I might bring my best friend, Sally, instead, if she is able to get her parents to look after her son William. I'll feel guilty about leaving Tom again, of course, but I know he'll understand. He's good like that.'

'You're wearing a ring,' said Jake, touching her right hand. 'Does that mean you're engaged?'

'No. It's a friendship ring. Tom continually asks me to marry him, but I need to find out who I am, first, before I take on someone else's name, which is why I am here.'

'He must hate being apart from you.' Jake said this with passion in his voice as he took her hand in his. 'I know I would.'

Mary had dreaded something like this happening once they were alone. It frightened her that she was so attracted to him. Jake leaned forward to kiss her, but she stood up suddenly.

'Jake, I can't do this. Please don't ask me to. I love Tom. I do enjoy your company though. Can we just be friends? Come on. Let's see some more of the village. You promised me a tour.'

'Okay. Sorry.' Jake was embarrassed and jumped away from her. He should have known it would be like this. 'Let's just walk to the end of the beach. You never know, we might be lucky enough to see a moose down by the river. Mom and Julie saw a female with her two young ones earlier this year. Have you got your camera?'

Mary nodded. 'It's always with me,' she said. They walked in silence and withdrew into their own thoughts. It was a comfortable silence. Mary was grateful for that. Honey raced ahead – glad to be moving again. Within minutes, they could hear her barking.

'Oh shit!' said Jake, and ran up a winding path that led through the trees overlooking the river. His heart was beating fast. He hoped that Honey had not come across a bear. Honey was standing at the edge of the hill, tail wagging furiously, and down below Jake could just make out the ungainly gait of a young female moose as she staggered out of sight. Mary reached them a moment too late. She had climbed the path quite cautiously, not knowing what she might find.

'What did she see down there?' said Mary.

'Just a young moose. If Honey had found a bear, it could have been disastrous, especially if it had been a grizzly. They're carnivorous and they're huge. When a fully grown male grizzly stands on his hind legs he's about nine feet tall.'

'Stop it, Jake, you're scaring me.' Jake laughed and took Mary's hand to help her up the slope.

They made their way back to Bennett Avenue and did a circular tour through the village, past the two gift shops and past the train which had just released its eager tourists travelling from Skagway in Alaska. Most of Annie's visitors had left when they got back to the cabin. When they recounted their little adventure, about Honey, to Annie, she simply looked straight at Jake and said,

'Son, you should have known better. Now can you please collect all the chairs from the beach and bring them inside. There's a gathering at Nora's Fish Camp tonight, so we're all going. If you haven't eaten salmon which has been caught in the morning and cooked over a campfire, then you're in for a real treat.' Annie said to Mary. 'Don't forget to bring a sweater with you and your bug spray.'

'Will there be any bears?' Mary asked.

'No. You'll be fine. Bears don't like fires, or singing, and Julie will be taking her guitar.'

Annie and Mary sat out on the deck with their coffee, enjoying the early Monday morning sun. Mary studied the small Balm of Gilead trees that offered protection from the icy breezes off the lake in the spring and now provided a welcome barrier between them and the tourists. Two robins had found shade amongst their shiny leaves. She was surprised by their size; they were so much bigger than the English robins – more like the size of a blackbird. It was peaceful. Jake had reluctantly gone to work and Julie had taken Honey for a good long walk to wear her out before the trip back to Whitehorse. Mary had felt relaxed all weekend and she hadn't had any bad dreams since they arrived in Carcross.

'You have that far away look again,' said Annie. 'Are you thinking of home and that boyfriend of yours? You must be missing him?'

'Actually, I was watching those two robins and thinking how relaxed I've been since I came here. There's something about this village. I can't describe it – it's a special feeling,' said Mary.

'I always feel that too,' said Annie, 'that's why I come down almost every weekend in the spring and summer.' Annie tied her light brown hair back from her face. She was wearing a sun dress today. Mary had not seen her wear a dress before. It made her look younger.

145

'Last night was fun, wasn't it? Everyone loved your singing. We'll have to get the two of you on our local radio station sometime.' Annie smiled. 'I love it when the family get together, although it's the time when I miss my George the most.'

'The food was delicious. I'm not sure the local beer suited me though. I only had one, but I'm not used to it. I don't drink much alcohol anymore at home.'

'Why not?' Annie was about to hear yet another alcohol story.

'When I worked as a nanny in London – before I met Tom – my employer was a heavy drinker. When he was sober he was charming, but when he was drunk he was horrid. He disgusted me and I was afraid of him when he was like that. He assaulted me once. I walked out and never went back. It broke my heart to leave their little boy. Alcohol changes people. It takes away their self-control,' said Mary. 'I'd rather do without it. Tom doesn't drink a lot, except if his team wins a rugby match.'

'George would agree with you if he were here. It's a big problem, although there's a lot more help for everyone now. Folks drink, to shut out bad memories. George lost a brother and an uncle to the dreaded booze, and his youngest brother, Sammy, is in the clinic in Whitehorse at the moment. He's in and out of there all the time. It's very sad.'

'What about your family, Annie? Were you born in Whitehorse?' Mary had often wondered why she never heard Annie talk about any member of her own family.

'My parents were from Alberta. Mom was from Edmonton and Dad from Calgary. They brought me up to Whitehorse when I was thirteen. I found it hard at first – leaving all my friends behind.'

'Why did they decide to come so far north?'

'Dad had always wanted to experience life in the

North. He was a carpenter and his ambition was to set up his own business here, making furniture and also children's toys.

Mom wasn't strong enough for life up here in those days. She hated the cold, dark winters,' said Annie.

'Did you have any brothers or sisters?'

'No. Mom had been ill with her heart for quite a few years so she couldn't have any more children after me. She died just after Julie was born. As soon as Dad got to be sixty five he moved back to Calgary. I always knew he would.'

'Do you get to see him sometimes? Does he come back for a visit?'

'No. Dad never approved of me marrying into George's family. He always reckoned that people should stick to their own kind and he never accepted or befriended any First Nations people. Dad hasn't been back since – even to visit Julie or Jake. We send each other Christmas cards and that's about it. I don't miss him. Julie keeps in touch with him and says she'd like to find work in Calgary when she's done with UBC. I'm a Yukoner now and George's folks are my family. Anyway, that's enough about me. What about you? What's your story? Why do you think that your family might be here in the Yukon?'

When she heard the abridged version of Mary's life story so far, it struck Annie that Mary's childhood story could belong to almost anyone in the village – anyone over forty, that is. She decided that this young woman was a lot stronger than she pretended to be. All these panics about bears and mosquitoes! She'd survived some really tough times and as far as Annie could see, Mary seemed fairly unaffected by it all. She didn't, of course, know about her nightmares and her years of counselling. That belonged to the full version of her story

147

'You're a pretty amazing gal,' said Annie, impressed by her strength of will.

'There have been a few people along the way who have liked me and supported me. From that point of view I've been lucky. Tom is wonderful. He's been my rock,' she said. 'You might get to meet him some time soon. He's keen to join me up here when he gets a holiday from school.'

Mary was reluctant to leave Carcross. This weekend had been like jumping off the world for a little while; no stress, no bad dreams, no responsibilities. It was like being on holiday by the seaside ... only much better. She wanted to ask Annie if Jake would be at the airport to see her off on Thursday, but she didn't think that this was quite the right time to ask.

He surprised her later by coming back to the cabin just as they were loading up the van. When he discovered that her flight to Vancouver was at five o'clock on the Thursday he gave everyone a hug and said he would be at the airport to say 'Bon Voyage'.

Everyone was quiet and thoughtful on the way back to Whitehorse; so much so that when one of Mary's little wishes came true, she didn't have her camera close to her. It was in the back of the van. They had only just left the village and were on the main highway, when a black bear and her two little cubs came out from the bushes. They crossed the road ahead of them and the cubs were struggling to keep their mother's pace. Their little legs kept tripping them up. It was a touching sight. Annie stopped the van so that they could watch from a distance.

'Would you believe it – the one time I haven't got my camera in my pocket,' sighed Mary.

'They look really sweet. You can't imagine that cuddlylooking bear hurting anyone can you?'

'You'd soon find out if you went anywhere near those cubs.' said Julie. 'There are some gruesome bear stories up here – especially involving tourists. They're awesome.'

The little family disappeared amongst the bushes on the other side of the highway.

'I don't think we want to hear any of those just now, thank you. Julie has always loved the horror stories a lot more than her brother,' Annie explained to Mary. 'Jake is too sensitive. That's why he doesn't like to go hunting with his uncle.'

Julie laughed. 'Some Indian eh? Uncle Albie says he's letting down the family tradition.'

Mary considered that Jake's sensitive nature was one of the reasons she liked him so much.

Chapter 15

Back in the hotel, Mary sat waiting for Tom's call. It seemed ages since she had talked comfortably with him. The reception in Carcross wasn't good and there was always someone around. Tom had sounded a little depressed during their last call.

'You sound different my love. Are you alright or has something happened?'

'Oh I'm okay really. It's just that nothing has gone right this past week. My visit to Woodbridge was difficult, as usual, I can't seem to track down Rob, I haven't been picked for the first team, and I'm having strange dreams about teaching. Most of all, I'm missing you, darling. The flat is so quiet. How was your weekend?'

Mary told him everything that had happened during her four days in Carcross, especially the visit to Julie's grandparents and their reaction to her photograph.

'Are you planning to go to Dawson to take a look at this bar?'

'No, it's a long way from here and there is no-one free to go with me. Anyway, there isn't enough time. I'll need more clues before I come all this way again. Annie's father-in-law recognised the bar in the photo but not the piano player. The woman at the Archives needs a place name or the name of someone in my family. The name Doyle isn't known here. It'll soon be Thursday. So it won't be long now, love. Only two more days and we'll be together. You must come with me next time – if there is a next time.'

Mary was glad that no-one was sitting next to her on the flight to Vancouver. Her departure from the Yukon and from Annie, Julie and Jake, had been a sad one and she needed to think about the way she was feeling. She knew she should feel excited at this point because she would see Tom and her friends soon, but Blackheath and her school in Greenwich seemed a million miles away from where she really wanted to be. At the airport Annie had said that everyone wants to return to the Yukon once they have experienced it. How true that was. Jake's sorrowful expression remained in the fore-front of her mind. He'd arrived late due to the pressure of work and so he had stood outside the windows of the departure lounge and waved. Mary felt a lump in her throat. Her cheeks were wet. Her silent tears reminded her of her solitude. She needed to be home now, with Tom. Being in the air between the two places was hard.

It was clear to everyone that Tom was very happy to have her home. He didn't leave her side for the first two days. He bought her flowers, booked a table at her favourite restaurant, brought her breakfast in bed and even got tickets for her favourite musical in the West End – 'Les Miserables'. Mary knew all the songs from the show and Tom loved to hear her sing them.

'I could get used to this.' Mary laughed. 'But honestly Tom, enough is enough. Let's start saving for our trip to the Yukon. You do want to go don't you?'

'Of course, but I can't think about holidays at the moment, with a new job starting in a couple of weeks time. A lot depends upon when you want to go,' he said. Next week would be good, she thought, and then changed the subject.

'So why can't you get in touch with Rob and Wendy?

They can't have gone far with six huskies. Maybe they're away at some major dog-racing competition somewhere?' Mary was as puzzled as Tom was. This had never happened before.

'Not for ten days. Anyway, the last time I called to see them I had arranged it with Wendy. I could hear the dogs, but nobody seemed to be around. It's quite a mystery.'

'We'll drive over there together early next week. They are bound to be there then.'

'Come on love let's go to bed early. It's been a long two weeks. I've missed you.'

Mary sat up in bed and shouted through the stillness of the early hours.

'Turn the light on ... please!'

Tom turned on the bedside light and threw his dressing gown around her trembling shoulders. He held her as she sobbed and waited silently until she had stopped shaking.

'Oh Tom. I didn't have any of these nightmares during the second week in the Yukon. That little village by the lake seemed to banish all my demons. I'm so sorry.'

'You have nothing to apologise for. It must be so frightening for you. Why don't you have a session with Karen this week? She's longing to hear about your trip.' Tom gently eased her back under the duvet and wrapped his arms around her. With her head on his chest she was asleep in minutes, so he left the light on.

'So why do you think your nightmares stopped in Carcross?' Karen asked. 'How did you feel when you were there in that little village? How was it different?' Mary lay on Karen's couch and imagined she was back on the beach with Jake.

'I'd like to think it was a sign – a sign that I was close to finding my family, but at the same time, the beauty and the feeling of peace that surrounds you in that place would soothe any troubled soul,' said Mary.

'Tell me about your visit to the First Nations family. How did it make you feel?'

'I felt very comfortable with them and I felt as though we would always be friends, but I didn't think for one moment that I was with anyone who could be family. Does that sound strange to you?' Mary asked. She hadn't thought about this before, but it was true. 'There is something else. I met a young man in Whitehorse. He is part First Nations and his name is Jake.'

Karen noticed Mary's expression soften at the mention of his name. She said nothing.

Mary knew that anything she shared with Karen would be kept in confidence. She'd said very little about Jake to Tom, just that he was Julie's brother who worked long hours. Tom knew that Annie and Julie and Honey had taken her to the airport to see her off.

'Jake is a special person,' began Mary. 'When we are together it feels as though we've always known one another. I can tell him anything. I feel comfortable and safe with him.'

'You've said all these things to me about Tom over the years,' said Karen. 'How is this different?'

'Jake shakes my world. My heart races when I see him. My body trembles when he touches me, and yet we have never kissed or had a passionate embrace or anything. He held my hand once and tried to kiss me but I told him to stop. I told him I loved Tom.'

'And do you?'

'Yes, I do, but the way I feel about Jake is different somehow. I can't stop thinking about him. I still want Tom to come with me to Whitehorse next time, but I don't think he'll be able to – not until next spring anyway. Karen, I don't think I can wait that long.'

'The important thing is finding that thing that will truly put your heart at rest.'

Karen came across the room and gave Mary a hug. 'Listen to your heart – it will guide you. Now, let's finish with a meditation together.' Karen lit the candles. Mary closed her eyes.

There was just one more week before the beginning of term. Mary had almost made a decision. She would arrange to have a chat with her headteacher, Roy Bentley, and see how he would feel about her taking a week without pay just after the half-term break. Sally was very keen to come with her to Whitehorse as long as her parents agreed to have William for two weeks. They had done it before when she was in hospital. They were very good with him, and they only lived a short distance away in Lee Green. The hardest part would be explaining to Tom that she couldn't wait until he was free. Mary raised the subject in the car as they drove to Thurston to visit Rob and Wendy. She thought that this would be a good time to explain her plans as there would be a distraction at the other end.

'I never dreamed you would want to go back so soon. You said you needed more clues. You know that the best time for me is next Easter when we have a two week holiday. I want to do this with you this time. I don't need this right now Mary. You know I'm anxious about my new job. Anyway, what if Roy says 'No'? Will you resign from your job?' Tom was desperate now.

'No, of course not. I'll wait until next year, but can you imagine how hard it'll be, to be so close to finding my family and then to have to wait for six months?'

They had arrived at Rob and Wendy's ramshackle

property and Rob's Land Rover stood on the front drive. Tom drew up alongside it. This was a good sign. They would finally get to see him and bring him up-to-date with everything. Mary was relieved the discussion couldn't continue. It wasn't getting anywhere and she hated it when they were at odds with one another.

Mary clutched some flowers for Wendy, and Tom had a six-pack of lager for Rob.

They rang the ship's bell that hung at the side of the front door. It was loud enough to wake the neighbourhood. The dogs started barking.

'It looks like we've struck gold this time.' laughed Tom, feeling calmer. But nothing stirred.

'That's strange. They must be there. They wouldn't leave the dogs on their own for long. Maybe they have music on in the house or something?' Tom gave the rope another pull. He stood back away from the door and looked up at the windows. Wendy was a net curtains type of person so it was impossible to see anything.

'What do you think? Should I go around the back?'

'I'm not sure that's a good idea. You might upset the dogs and someone might think you're trespassing,' said Mary, staring at the closed side gate. She had a strange feeling about this. With all this noise, they must realise that they had visitors if they were home.

'Maybe they don't want to see us for some reason? Maybe they're hiding up?'

'That's crazy,' said Tom. 'What could be their reason for doing that? The last time we saw them was when we told them about your trip to the Yukon. They seemed really excited for you.'

'Wendy was, but I seem to remember that Rob didn't say much. I think he was jealous. Have you seen him since that visit?'

'No. I saw Wendy and had tea with her, but Rob was

at work,' said Tom. 'I'll try the bell one more time and if no-one comes, I suggest we leave,' said Tom. He cursed and tugged at the bell rope

Some minutes later as Tom was about to drive away, Mary turned and glanced back at the house. Her eyes were drawn to one of the upstairs windows. The net curtains immediately moved back into place.

Chapter 16
Dublin

John Doyle stood on the Ha'penny Bridge watching some children throw pennies into the Liffey for good luck. He had just spent the morning with his little grand-daughter, Brigit, in Castlerock on the north side of Dublin. He was in need of a quiet drink in his favourite pub – the pub with his name – 'Doyles' on College Green. He looked forward to meeting a few friends in there and enjoying some 'good craic'. He didn't have the energy for two year olds these days. They wanted to do something different every ten minutes it seemed to John. Mind you, the two boys wore him out more than this little angel. Saturday morning in early September was the best time of the year in Dublin. Most of the tourists had left, it was still mild and the autumn colours warmed his heart. Only one thought spoilt his day.

Earlier that morning, John and Brigit were building their new house with her Lego. They sat on the floor of his daughter's front room together. It was peaceful. His daughter was shopping in town and the boys were back at school. Brigit looked up and smiled at her grand-dad.

'Will we make a garage for your new car, Dada?' she asked.

'Oh I think we should.' Her smile moved him. He looked into her bright blue eyes and tugged one of her dark brown curls playfully. The years suddenly melted away and for a moment he was standing at the door of

'The Sacred Spirit' with a very similar little girl in his arms. How could he have done it? He asked himself for the hundredth time. 'How could he have placed such a beautiful and vulnerable little soul - somebody's little grand-daughter - into the hands of complete strangers? Without warning, the tears streamed down his face and settled in his thick grey beard.

'Are you sad Dada? Don't be sad.' Brigit put her arms around his neck.

'Don't worry mauvereen. Dada just has a bit of a cold that's all.'

The guilt he felt on that October night, twenty-five years ago, stayed with him continually, especially at special moments such as the birth of his daughter and his granddaughter. He wished he had told his wife what had happened, but he felt too ashamed. He spent hours lately thinking about the girl, wondering if the man on the plane had tried to find her? He hoped she had been well looked after by the nuns. The young nun he had spoken to that night seemed very nice. In his heart he wanted to go back to the orphanage and find out what happened to her. Maybe then he would sleep at night. He was tired of carrying this secret.

John sat at the bar and talked this through with the barmaid. It was quiet and John was making his pint of Caffreys last as long as possible. He had told this story to Kelly, behind the bar, once before.

'Now why don't you tell all this to your wife? Isn't it time that you shared this problem and explained your nightmares? You'll need to have a reason for going back to England, sure you will. Now me – I can't keep a secret for nothing.'

'I've heard some of them places are hard,' said John. 'I may get an awful shock and hear somethin' I don't want to hear. Then I'd have worse nightmares would I not?' John stared at his empty glass whilst she served another customer.

'Are you hoping the glass will just fill itself?' She took it from him, with a smile.

'Not just now darlin'. I think you're right. I think it's time. Have one for yerself and thanks for listening.' John paid for the drinks.

Later that day John and his wife Breda sat down for supper. She made the best Irish stew this side of the city.

'This is very good Breda. Now listen up. I have somethin' that I need to get off me chest – somethin' that will explain those restless nights I have,' he said, with his head down.

'I've kept it inside me long enough. I can't keep it from you another minute.'

'Is this goin' to be somethin' awful? Will I not like it?' She poured them both a cup of tea and sat down. John told her the story of that night in 1964 – the year before they met and two years before they got married. Breda was shocked and said nothing at first. They sat in silence drinking their tea.

'When you found her sitting there, why didn't you hand her over to the Information Desk or to an airline official? Her mother might have been close by. She might have thought you kidnapped her.' Breda couldn't believe what she was hearing.

'The little girl said she had no mother. She'd obviously been abandoned. We sat together for half an hour. I bought her a drink and something to eat. Surely someone would have claimed her?'

'How old was she? Was she upset?'

'The same age as our little Brigit, and no, she seemed more frightened than anythin'. Anyway, the young nun at the orphanage was very kind, and I couldn't bring her to Ireland with me now could I?'

159

'No, but you could have taken her with you to your sisters. Colleen would have known what to do. Did you tell her about this at the time?'

'No.' John wished he hadn't said anything. He knew it would be like this.

'Well, who knows, that little girl may have had a far worse time with whoever left her there than with the nuns looking after her. Poor little soul! She'll be the same age as our Sheena, now. I wonder what happened to her.'

'Well I need to find out,' said John. 'I've decided to go back to the orphanage to see if I can trace her. I need to make it right with her. I need to put this thing to rest.' John put his head in his hands to hide the tears. 'I did a terrible thing and God is punishing me for it.' Even now, he couldn't bring himself to tell the truth. How could he tell Breda that he had done it for the money, money which bought him a ticket back to Dublin?

John flew to London and then hired a car. As he approached the M1, he felt butterflies in his stomach. He realised that the convent could have closed down years ago. If this turned out to be the case, he decided that he would contact the Missing Persons Bureau. After all she might have kept the name he gave her that day.

He hadn't seen this place in the daylight before, but he recognised it straight away. He studied the sign over the wrought iron gates. It read: 'The Sacred Spirit Home for Retired Nuns.'

His heart sank. He should have guessed that this would have happened after so many years. He pressed the buzzer and announced himself anyway. After a few moments a soft Irish voice spoke to him from the intercom: 'Good day to you. Who is it please?'

'I've come to see a nun who received Mary Doyle into the convent in October 1964. I'm the man who delivered the little girl. The nun might remember me. I think she was a novice at the time.' John spoke loudly and clearly as though he was speaking directly to her up the long drive.

'Just a minute please,' said the voice.

As he studied the gates, they swung open, silently acknowledging that he was able visit. He put his car in the visitor's car park and could see someone standing at the open door waiting to invite him in. He didn't recognise her at first, not until she smiled.

'Well now, it has been a long time, and I don't even know your name. I'm Sister Joseph. Yes, I do remember you. Please do come in.' She was dressed quite simply in a black skirt and cardigan with a white blouse, and she had a heavy silver crucifix resting on her ample bosom. She looked too young to be in retirement though, even after twenty-five years.

'Good afternoon. My name is John Doyle and before you say anything further, I am here to tell you the full story and to ask about the little girl that I left with you.' John took off his cap and followed the nun into a large sitting room which was sparsely furnished. An elderly nun struggled in with a tray of tea and a plate of digestive biscuits. She laid it down in front of them. She then went to sit by the window and picked up her knitting. A witness, thought John.

'Thank you,' said Sister Joseph. 'Now, Mr. Doyle, explain yourself if you will.' John told his story, without alterations this time. He told her that the man who was travelling with Mary was called Bob James and that they were both from the Yukon Territory in Canada. He thought the man was a North American Indian, but he wasn't sure.

'I bitterly regret that I was tempted by the offer of money, but I needed to get back to Dublin and I was skint,' said John.

'The devil was on your shoulder,' said Sister Joseph as she poured another cup.

'Are you still in touch with this girl? How is she? Where is she now?'

'As it happened, Mary came to see us a short while ago.

We hadn't seen her or heard from her for years. She is now a beautiful young woman and is in the process of searching for her roots. She is well, and is working in London. Your information will be a great help to her. She is finding it difficult.'

'Then could you please give me a contact telephone number or an address if you have one? I would like to tell her my story,' John twisted his cap in his hand, nervously.

'I regret to say that I am not able to do that due to our rules about confidentiality. However, with your permission, I will write to her myself and explain this latest clue to the mystery. Please be re-assured that she was well-cared for here at 'The Sacred Spirit' and that she is well and happy in her life now. I have never forgotten her you know. There was something about her ... she was a very musical child. Thank you for your honesty Mr. Doyle.'

'When you write to her could you please let her know how very sorry I am and that I wish her well for the future? Please do not mention the exchange of money – I beg you.'

'Repent of your sins, and God will forgive you. Goodbye Mr. Doyle.'

John felt justly chastised and left hoping that life would be easier for him from now on.

The following day in Blackheath Tom collected the

morning post and took breakfast for them both up to the bedroom. He was determined to enjoy these last few days before the start of term. He guessed that there wouldn't be many more of them once his new job was up and running.

'You're popular today,' said Tom, giving Mary a nudge, 'a letter and a postcard. All I've got is bills. The card is from the Yukon.' Mary sat up instantly and studied it.

'It's from Annie and family. She hopes I had a good trip back. I must write to her and thank her for everything. She must think I'm terrible.' Mary rarely wrote to anyone. She sipped her coffee and reached for a croissant.

'Don't forget your letter. It might be something important.' Mary opened the crisp, white, hand-written envelope. Her face flushed, her breathing became more rapid and her eyes opened wide.

'What is it darling? Is it good news?' Mary handed him the letter.

The Sacred Spirit
4.9.90

My Dear Mary,

Two days ago I had a surprise visit from the man who delivered you to us in 1964 - an Irish man from Dublin called - Mr. John Doyle. He said he had been carrying a secret around with him all these years and could bear the burden no longer. He came to explain the full story of what happened all those years ago.

He explained that the man who was travelling with you on the plane was a Canadian called Bob James and that the two of you had come from the Yukon Territory in Canada. He didn't really know anything about this man

163

except that he wanted to try to find his father who had been missing for five years. Mr. Doyle thought he might have been a native Canadian but he wasn't sure. He asked if we had seen you and he asked how you were. He wanted your address or telephone number, but of course, that would have gone against our rules of confidentiality. Mr. Doyle admitted to me that he had added his own name to the name on the envelope which simply said Mary. He specifically requested that I tell you how very sorry he is for not referring you to the appropriate authorities. He said that you had been abandoned and so he did what he thought was best for you at the time. I reassured him that you are now well and happy. He did seem genuinely pleased to hear this and hoped that this new information would help you in your search for your birth family. You may, of course, have already discovered your roots during your recent trip to Canada.

I wish you every success with your mission.

May God bless you.

Kind Regards,

Sister Joseph.

'Good Lord!' exclaimed Tom.

'Exactly,' said Mary, smiling at his choice of words. This unexpected news left her feeling very confused. Part of her was excited that she now had a name of a real person in the Yukon and part of her was feeling distraught because she had been abandoned so young by someone who might turn out to be a close relative.

'Don't you think it's a strange coincidence that this man Bob has your surname, or at least, part of it?' Mary was sidetracked for a moment, wondering if this could be another sign of some sort.

'If you're thinking that these are more signs – forget it. The name James is very common,' said Tom. 'Surely you should be focussing upon the fact that you now have something real and tangible to work with when you return to the Yukon? There must be a record of this man, Bob James, somewhere up there.'

'I don't know whether I ever want to meet this man. How could he abandon a two year old child? What reason could he possibly have for being so heartless?'

'It could be anything,' said Tom. 'The man may not even be alive now. You have to be prepared for that. You have no idea how old he was when he brought you over. No-one said that this search was going to be easy, darling.' He put his arm around her and kissed her.

'Now let's try to enjoy our last weekend together before school starts next Tuesday. Actually, I'll have to go in on Monday to set up my classroom and meet some of the staff.'

'Are you nervous about it?' She must put her own adventures to one side for the next week. She could see that Tom would need her support. However, she still planned to book an appointment with her Headteacher. Returning to the Yukon was even more important now. She would also go and see Sally, maybe on Monday while Tom was in school.

Mary put the letter in her bag and made her way down Vanbrugh Hill towards the hospital. Sally and William lived in a two bedroom garden flat just off the Greenwich High Rd. She was very creative and had transformed the place since they moved in. She had never received any financial support from Will's father, so everything had to be done with as little money as possible. She was brilliant at spotting bargains and all her blinds and curtains had come from local charity shops. Now that William was in full-time schooling, Sally had gone back to her old job four days per week, working as an occupational therapist at the hospital. She loved it.

'Wow! That's amazing news!' said Sally, when Mary showed her the letter. 'What a bastard – abandoning a two year old in a strange country like that! I wonder who he was. He wouldn't have been your father surely; at least I hope he wasn't.' Mary couldn't help smiling at her friend's blunt response.

'I wonder what your name is really. What are you going to do now?' Sally asked.

'What I'd like to do and what I should do are two quite different things. What I should do is delay my return to the Yukon until Easter when Tom can come with me, but honestly Sal I can't wait that long. It's over half a year away.'

'Surely you are also back at work tomorrow, anyway, aren't you? I hope you're not thinking of quitting your job yet? You'd be taking a huge risk if you did.'

'No. I'll wait until the new term is up and running, maybe next week, and then I'll go and see Roy. I want to ask him if he'll agree to me taking a week off school without pay. After all they are extreme circumstances, don't you think? Would you like to come with me?'

'I don't mean to pry but how can you afford all these trips to the Yukon? Would we stay in a hotel when we get there?' asked Sally.

'Tom paid for my last trip but I will pay for this one out of my savings. I'm fairly sure that we'll be able to stay with Annie, either in Carcross or Whitehorse. I hope so, anyway.

Roy suggested that they have a chat at the end of the staff training day.

'Hello Mary. Come and sit down. How was your summer holiday? Did you and Tom go away anywhere interesting?' Mary laughed and felt sure that he wouldn't believe her at first, if she simply said – The Yukon

Territory in Canada. None of the staff had heard of it. Strangely enough, Roy knew quite a lot about it, because his nephew had been on an arctic expedition with a group of university friends one summer.

'Alistair loved it up there. His photographs were fantastic.' said Roy. 'Did you enjoy it?

Mary recounted her story and added that she had received a letter from the convent giving her the name of the man who had brought her from the Yukon to England years ago.

'So you see,' Mary explained, 'I now have a chance to trace my family. Even if this man is not a relative, someone will know him if he comes from the Yukon. The total population is very small.

'That's wonderful Mary. I'm pleased for you.'

'I'd like to go back to Whitehorse as soon as possible. I feel I am now quite near to the end of my search. Would you agree to me taking a week without pay, either before or after the half-term break? I can't go all that way just for one week. It's about 9,000 miles away.' Mary had her fingers crossed beneath the lip of his desk. Roy considered this for a moment. He picked up the office diary and turned the pages slowly.

'It would have to be the week after half-term, as your students are only now getting used to all the changes. Rehearsals for the Christmas concert begin on November 9th and you'd be back by then. Yes, I'm sure that'll be fine. I'll inform the governors and ask one of our relief staff to come in that week. Are you going back with Tom this time?'

'No. He has just started his first teaching post in Deptford. He'll be disappointed that he can't join me. I haven't told him yet as I wanted to see you first. I'm hoping that my friend, Sally, will come. Thank you so much for this opportunity. I really appreciate it.' Mary uncrossed her fingers. She was thrilled. Now she had to break the news to Tom, of course. She would have to choose her moment carefully. She would wait until the weekend.

It was Saturday. Mary had purposely kept off the subject of the Yukon until the weekend when she knew that Tom would be more relaxed. They got up late and had a leisurely brunch before Tom's afternoon rugby match. Tom sipped his coffee without looking at her.

He was devastated by Mary's news. He knew that she was planning to ask for an extended half-term break, but he didn't think her Head would let her go. At his school, the only two occasions when teachers were granted leave of absence was in the event of a family bereavement or a house-move. He had already spoken to his Deputy Head about this in case he needed extra time next Easter.

'You know that I really wanted to go with you this time. Isn't it important to you that I share the discovery of your family with you? Hopefully, they will be my family too one day?' Mary could sense his anger. He was almost shouting at her. 'How can you share such an important trip with Sally? She'll have met your parents before I do. If it was the other way around, I would hate to go without you. Also, this is an important time for me at the moment. So where's your support for me?'

'Tom, I can't wait until next Easter. I thought you'd understand that. I'll only be away for two weeks. You could go off on a ski-ing trip with one of your friends during the school holiday. The time would go very quickly. Anyway, this Bob James might not be a Yukoner, so I might not be able to trace him. Why are you so upset about this? Are you afraid I won't come back or something?'

'Yes.' Tom slumped back on to his chair and looked

dejected. Mary sat on his knee and held him for a moment.

'Oh Tom, of course I'll come back. I'll be longing to tell you all my news - that's if there is any. Don't you trust me? Please don't make this any more difficult than it already is, love. I'll be here for you during your first half-term and then back again two weeks later. By the way, I'm paying for this trip out of my savings this time. Sally is doing the same thing.' She slipped her hand inside his shirt. 'Now, let's go back to bed. The match isn't for another two hours.'

Chapter 17
Whitehorse

As the aircraft made its descent to Whitehorse, Sally fixed her eyes on the sunset as it cast a pink glow over the snow-capped mountains.

'This is gorgeous,' enthused Sally. 'Poor Tom! I feel so guilty that I'm enjoying all of this whilst Tom is still in Blackheath. He looked so sad at the airport. Do you miss him already?'

'I will do, I expect, once the initial excitement has died down.'

'But maybe it won't die down. Who knows what will happen?'

Sally stepped on to the tarmac. It had snowed earlier in the day, and it felt cold and crisp. She was glad she had worn boots; the ones without high heels. Everyone around her had dressed for Arctic weather. She threw her day-sack over her shoulder and ran to catch up with Mary who was rushing towards the main building.

Mary could see Annie and Jake waving at her as soon as she approached the double doors. Julie was back at the U.B.C. Jake was smiling. She was thrilled to see him again. She had not mentioned her feelings for Jake to Sally just yet, but she guessed that she would have to very soon.

Annie had her arms open wide, ready for a hug.

'Hi there, Mary. It's good to see you so soon. Now this must be Sally. Welcome to Whitehorse Sally. Mary has told us a lot about you.'

'I've heard plenty about you,' said Sally 'and it was all good too.

Annie laughed. Jake hovered awkwardly behind his mother. Needing something to do, he took the trolley over to the carousel and waited for their luggage.

'Hello Jake. How are you?' Mary put a hand on his arm. 'This is my friend, Sally. Annie, I was thrilled to get your invitation for Sally and me to stay with you for two weeks. It's really good of you, especially as you'll be at work and we'll be on holiday,' Mary said as they walked towards the car park. She turned to Sally. 'Annie is a teacher and they don't have a half-term break here in the Yukon.'

'We're pleased to have you stay with us. Mary, you can have Julie's room and Sally can have our spare room in the basement. It's real cosy down there.'

As they drove out on to the highway, Sally studied the white world around her. It was still very autumnal at home, but here it was definitely the winter already.

'My son, William, would be so excited if he saw the snow. There must be so many opportunities to enjoy it here. We sometimes get snow in February but it doesn't last long. In London it's mostly a muddy slush.'

'Glad to see you girls have brought winter clothes with you. It'll get colder and darker from now on. I won't be spending so much time down in Carcross soon, and Jake will stay down there some weekends.' Annie saw Mary's expression. 'Don't worry. I'll take you girls down though. The family will want to see you again. We're anxious to hear about this important news of yours.'

By the time they reached Porter Creek it was quite dark.

The next morning they all sat around the kitchen table and discussed what should be the first step of Mary's search. Mary wasn't sure whether to go straight to Dawson, with her photograph, or visit the Yukon Archives with the name Bob or Robert James. Maybe the man in the photo is Bob James, she thought. Everyone voted for a visit to the Archives first, before making any trips.

'If this man is a Yukoner, then he can be found in the Yukon Directory,' said Annie. 'His place of birth should also be there, which means you would be able to trace his family. If he's from Dawson, you'll still need to look for him in the Archives. Dawson was our capital until 1953.'

'This is quite exciting,' said Sally.

'I'm feeling quite nervous again,' said Mary. 'What if he can't be traced? What then?'

As soon as they walked in, Mary recognised the clerk who was there when Mary and Julie visited just two months earlier. She recognised Mary too and smiled.

'Well 'Hi' again. How did you get on? Did you manage to trace a member of your family in the summer?'

'Not during that first visit,' Mary explained, 'but since then I've learned the name of the man who took me to England in 1964. It was Bob James. Could you look this up for me please?'

'Let's hope we can help you this time. Why don't you and your friends have a seat and wait in comfort. We'll try not to keep you waiting long.'

What seemed like an eternity, to Mary, as she flicked through the pages of the Whitehorse Star, was actually less than twenty minutes. The clerk called them over to the desk.

'We've found a Robert James, born in Carmacks in August 1940. His mother is listed as Sara Black, also of Carmacks, but there is no mention of his father. Do you think that this could be the man you're looking for?'

'He'd be nearly fifty years old now,' Sally spoke out loud what everyone else was thinking. 'He could easily be your father.'

Jake reminded Mary that his Uncle Albie came from Carmacks.

'He's around the same age as this man, so he'll know him. We must talk to him.'

Mary was in shock. All these years she had longed to know something about her background and now the real search was about to begin.

The woman continued:

'Sara Black is a member of the Little Salmon Carmacks First Nation and possibly her son will be too. They are Northern Tutchone-speaking people. There's no mention of her death so she's probably still there. You should be able to find her easily. Good luck with your search,' she said.

When they got outside Annie agreed with Jake that they should contact Albie.

'Jake's Uncle Albie is married to my husband's sister. He and Amy live in Carcross.' Annie explained this to Sally. 'We'll have some lunch in town and then we must call Albie before we make any more plans. Meanwhile, who's for fish and chips at the 'Rib and Salmon' – my treat?'

Sally laughed. 'Fish and chips? It's just like being back in Greenwich.'

Albie did know Bob James, although he hadn't seen him for years. They were at Chooutla around the same time and they hung out together in the village during the summer vacation, as kids.

'His mother, Sara Black, is still in the village and also her brother, Freddie. Do you want me to take the girls up to Carmacks? Someone should be with them. '

'Thanks Albie, but I think we're all going up tomorrow. Mary is anxious to get going,' said Annie, 'and we've all got work on Monday.'

Carmacks was north of Whitehorse and was a two hour drive away. Jake offered to do the driving and he suggested that they set off as early as possible. They didn't know how much time they would need before it got dark again. It hadn't snowed overnight. It was cold and the sky was grey. They headed out on to the Alaska Highway and very soon turned off in the direction of Dawson and Carmacks on the North Klondike Highway. Sally couldn't believe how few people lived in this stretch of the Yukon. Apart from the occasional lodge or cabin it seemed to her to be pure wilderness. They drove past forests and streams, past Fox Lake and Lake Laberge. In the shaded October daylight the scenery took on a beauty all of its own.

'I don't think I'd want to break down if I was driving on this road,' said Sally. 'You could wait for hours for anyone to help you.'

'There is an unwritten law of the highway in the north that if you meet anyone who is in trouble you must always stop and offer to help. People take this quite seriously,' said Jake.

At Annie's request, Mary and Sally provided some entertainment to while away the time. They sang one or two 1980s hits and also a couple of folksongs. They sang John Denver's 'Annie's Song' for their hostess. The journey went very quickly and soon they were parking the van outside the Carmacks Hotel, the only hotel in the village. Annie offered to walk over to the General Stores to see if anyone knew Sara Black and could direct them to her house.

She spotted a woman about her own age in the bakery section. She didn't look like a tourist.

'Hi,' Annie said, 'do you live here?' The woman nodded. 'Can you tell me if Sara Black lives here?'

'Who wants to know?' The woman asked, cautiously. A visiting white woman could mean trouble, especially if she was official.

'My name is Annie Hughes. I'm here on behalf of my husband who knew Sara years ago. His sister married Albie Luke who was born in Carmacks.'

'Not George Hughes? I remember him. Someone said that he died a couple of years back. Albie used to go fishing with Bob and me in the summer vacation. I'm Sylvia Black. The woman you are looking for is my aunt, my Dad's sister. She's outside in Vancouver just now. She's had an operation. We are hoping she'll be home by the middle of this week.'

'Oh dear,' said Annie. 'Perhaps you can help us? I have a visitor from England staying with me who has reason to believe that she might be related to someone in Carmacks. She was told to contact Sara Black for further information. Could you have a chat with my young friend?'

'I suppose you could bring her to my house, but it can't be for at least an hour because my old man is asleep and then he has to go to work. I'll meet you the other side of the bridge in an hour. I'll be in our red truck.'

'Thanks.' Annie ran back to the van to tell the others what she had arranged.

'I can't believe that you chose to ask the one woman in the shop who happened to be Sara's niece. We're meant to do this. I can feel it,' said Mary.

'Meanwhile can we grab some lunch? Breakfast was hours ago and I'm starving. There's a restaurant across there,' said Jake.

Feeling revived, an hour later, they drove out on to the main road and turned left across the bridge that lay across the Yukon River. The river was covered with a thin layer of ice which, according to Jake, would be thick enough to drive a truck across in a few weeks time. They parked just the other side of the bridge as arranged and pulled off the road. There was no sign of Sylvia, even though they were about ten minutes late. There wasn't a lot to see ahead of them. The houses were hidden amongst the trees and the bushes for protection against the wind from the north. Everyone sat in a world of their own thoughts. This village was very small and quite remote. Mary wondered how she would feel about living in a place like this after twelve years in London. Her thoughts raced ahead. I mustn't do this, she thought. It's too early.

By now, it was half an hour past the time they had agreed to meet Sylvia.

'Maybe she's thought better of it and decided not to come,' said Annie.

'Or maybe she doesn't want to meet me after all.'

Sally put her arm around Mary's shoulders.

'Don't worry. I'm sure we'll find her. If not we can hire a car and come up again,' she said.

'I think we should drive around the village to see if we can see a red truck parked anywhere,' suggested Jake. He started the engine. They turned left and studied each house in turn. Most of the front yards had a variety of vehicles, but there was no sign of a red truck.

As they turned a corner, Mary shouted –

'Look, there's one over there. That must be Sylvia Black's house.'

Jake parked a short distance beyond their driveway. He turned to Mary and said:

'I think you girls should stay in the van with Honey. Annie and I will call at the house. After all, we don't know if it's the right place, and also we don't know what dogs they might have.'

He locked the van and followed Annie up the drive. They stepped on to the veranda and Jake knocked on the door. Just as he did so they heard a scream coming from inside and a man's voice raised in temper. This was followed by the sound of glass being smashed.

'I don't want any white strangers snooping around my house,' the man yelled.

'But the older lady is George Hughes' wife and they know Albie Luke. They're not strangers, or at least she isn't.'

'Shut up woman and get out of here. Talk to them somewhere else. I wanna sleep.'

The door burst open and Sylvia was pushed out on to the veranda. She landed at Annie's feet.

Her face was bleeding, and she lay in a crumpled heap. She had no coat and she was crying.

'Let me help you,' Annie half lifted the woman on to her feet and gave her a Kleenex.

'I'm alright,' said Sylvia, 'I'm used to it. He's always like this when he's drunk. I'll go to my friends' house next door. She understands. She wiped the blood off of her face and struggled across to the neighbour's house leaving Annie and Jake staring at her in silence.

'It's best if you talk to Aunt Sara when she gets back,' Sylvia shouted over her shoulder.

'I'm glad the girls didn't see that,' said Jake as they made their way back to the van. 'Do you think they need to be told exactly what happened?'

'No. We don't even know if Bob James is related to Mary yet, do we?' said Annie. 'There's time enough for her to see scenes like that one.'

She explained to Mary that, unfortunately, Sylvia was unable to talk to them as she was in the middle of a family crisis. The upset had caused her to forget their arranged meeting.

'It looks as though you'll have to come back. Maybe Albie will come with you next time. He knows the village and he knows the family. It would be better for everyone.'

Somehow the drive back to Whitehorse had temporarily lost its magic, and both girls dozed for most of the trip. Annie and Jake were concerned about the scene they had witnessed; concerned mostly for Mary.

'You know, Mom, I think I'll take some holiday from work next week – they owe me some.' Jake said quietly. 'If Uncle Albie is free then we could both go back to Carmacks with Mary and Sally and maybe even to Dawson as well. What do you think?'

'What will your boss say? You're not giving him much notice.'

'He'll be okay. I never take sick days and I'm always doing overtime, as you know.' He had already made his decision. Annie could see that.

The following morning, Jake announced that they couldn't go straight back to Carmacks as Sara wasn't due home until Tuesday or Wednesday. He came up with a plan which he shared with everyone over breakfast.

'I could drive the girls to Carcross and go into work for a day and a half. This would be an opportunity for Sally to meet the family. Then we could drive back to Whitehorse with Uncle Albie on the Wednesday night and all go to Carmacks together on the Thursday. What do you think?'

'What if Sara Black isn't home yet?' asked Mary.

'You could call her before you leave. Albie has found

Sara's number,' said Annie.

Annie had asked Amy to go over to her house, to light the stove and replenish the log pile, so it would be warm when they arrived. Whilst Jake had topped up the gas in his suburban, the girls had been shopping for some supplies as there was no grocery store in Carcross. It was a much nicer day for travelling and another light snowfall had come during the night making everywhere look clean and whitewashed again.

'It's beautiful,' breathed Sally. 'I can't stop taking photographs. I must get a shot of that amazing green lake that Mary took photos of in the summer.'

'Let's hope we've caught it before it freezes over. It'll have to be a quick stop anyway. I said I'd report for work as soon as we arrive. Aunt Amy and Uncle Albie said they would come over in the afternoon, for a visit, so you won't be on your own.' Mary could see that he had thought of everything.

'He's almost as thoughtful as your Tom,' Sally said to Mary. 'Why can't I find a man like that ... or maybe I just have?' Sally smiled at Jake, who shifted uncomfortably in his seat as he stared straight ahead.

Chapter 18

When Jake and the girls drew up outside the house in Carcross, Amy and her elderly malamute husky were just coming towards them on Bennett Avenue.

'Where's Uncle Albie?' Jake called through the open window of his suburban.

'He's inside, in his favourite chair no doubt.' Amy shouted back. 'He's waiting for you.'

Jake helped the girls unload the groceries and then introduced Sally to his uncle. Albie was sitting in a large, cosy armchair which was positioned close to the stove. From there he could look out towards the lake and watch the last few fluttering leaves of the balsam poplars drift on to the beach.

'Hi Uncle Albie. This is Mary's friend, Sally, from London. I'm going to leave the girls with you. I said I'd report for duty at work. So, see you guys later. 'Bye.'

Sally was intrigued by her surroundings. She sat and studied the size of the huge logs in the walls, the local pictures and artefacts all over the kitchen/diner, the woodpile by the side of the stove and most of all - the view!

'Wow! This is awesome,' said Sally, trying to sound Canadian.

'Sally, meet Jake's Aunt Amy and her dog Trixie. They live across the bridge,' said Mary.

'What a treat,' laughed Amy, 'two English visitors in one year.'

Trixie put her head on Sally's knee and wagged her

tail. She clearly sensed that Sally had a dog at home. Sally buried her hands in Trixie's thick fur and tickled her.

'She's an old lady now,' said Amy. 'A short walk up the road and back is all she can manage.'

Later that afternoon, once Jake was back from work, they all sat down together for a supper of barbequed moose steaks, salad and baked potatoes with soured cream. They brought Amy and Albert up-to-date with their visit to Carmacks. It got Albie thinking about the long ago time again. He reminisced about his fishing trips with Bob and Sylvia, and his time round at Grandma Sara's house.

'Grandma Sara was strict. We all had to do chores, even me who was a visitor. She said we learned nothing at 'that school' and it upset her that we'd forgotten the traditional ways. She taught us to set snares and find food in the bush. She taught Bob how to fire a rifle. Me, I already knew 'cause my Dad had shown me.'

'What about Bob's father,' said Mary. 'Did she ever talk about Bob's father?'

'No. She never mentioned him. Folks say that he disappeared from the Yukon years ago and that he's wanted by the cops. He stole a pile of money they say. Grandma Sara told Sylvia that she believes he went back to live in Britain.

'Did you ever meet him?' Sally asked.

'No. The family was living in Dawson when he took off. Sara's Mom died at the same time, so she moved back to Carmacks with the two kids, to be close to her father and her two brothers. Sara's father, old Tommy Black, still lives in the village. He must be well into his nineties by now. He understands English, but rarely speaks it. He's one of the few Elders left who still prefers to speak Tutchone.'

Mary didn't want the evening to end. She wanted to know something about Bob James, the man, but Albie hadn't seen him for years.

Amy, Albie and Trixie went home leaving the young ones to sort themselves out. The girls said 'Goodnight' and left Jake to clean up the barbeque and replenish the woodpile. Mary would have loved to have had some time on her own with him, but it was too soon, and also it was Sally's first night in Carcross. They shared Julie's room and gossiped until they fell asleep.

It seemed strange to Mary, waking up in Annie's house without her. Jake had gone to work quite early. He had moved around very quietly so as not to disturb them. It was Trixie who woke them up. She made straight for Sally and licked her face. 'Come on you two. There's no point in spending the day in bed – its way past nine-thirty,' called Amy. 'Get yourselves dressed. Nora is inviting you over for bacon and pancakes.'

Most of the snow had gone and it was a beautiful autumn morning. Splashes of yellow and orange daubed the hillsides and the sky was a clear blue. It felt surprisingly warm in the sunshine for late October. Sally gazed around her in silence.

They walked over the wooden footbridge and as they approached Nora and Joe's house, Mary could see Jake's grandfather working outside.

'There's Grandpa Joe, Sally. He's probably trying to repair something. It's his hobby.' She smiled as she remembered Jake's words. Once Sally had been introduced and Mary had hugged everyone, the family sat down to a good breakfast of eggs, bacon, pancakes, maple syrup and a continual supply of coffee. Amy and Albie had passed on all of Mary's latest news to Nora.

'Albie say you might come from Carmacks Mary?' Nora peered at her over her glasses.

'I still don't know what First Nation blood I have in me or where I was born. Apparently this man, Bob James, brought me to England from the Yukon in 1964 and that is all I know, so far. The lady in the Yukon Archives found his name, place and date of birth for me but I don't know for sure that it is the right Bob James. Is it a common name in the Yukon?' Mary asked Nora.

'James as first and last name is common. We hoped that you come from Carcross.' Nora smiled but there was disappointment in her voice. 'The Inland Tlingits have fine tradition and big history.'

'Actually, Robert and James are also very popular British names, so this man's father could be British I suppose.' said Mary.

'These names come from outsiders, long ago. Some chose their 'white man's last name' from a man they respect, like Danny Johns. When my parents were young in long ago time, they used First Nation names, but they had to be earned. Many people want to return to that. If you want Tlingit name we need to know about you, your strengths, who is your family. You're a singer; it would be part of your name. A boy in Albie's village, called Jack, was fine swimmer. He stay under water for long time, so his First Nation name was 'Jackfish'. Is Bob James, your father?'

'I hope not. He abandoned me at the airport when I was only two years old. He sounds heartless.'

'That's fascinating about the First Nations names,' said Sally. 'I've never heard anything like that before. I wonder what my name would be.'

'You're very creative and are brilliant at sewing. Those skills would be considered I expect,' said Mary.

'So what is the Tlingit philosophy of life, Nora?'

Albie and Amy had gone outside to help Grandpa, so Nora had the girls' undivided attention.

'We believe in the 'medicine wheel'. The number 'four' tells us many things:

- four stages of life: life as child – as adult – in middle age – and as Elder.

- four parts of a person: body, feelings, beliefs and what we know,

- four rooms in the heart,

- four limbs and four fingers on each hand,

Our beliefs are in our stories and history of Inland Tlingits. We learn from grandparents and all Elders in our community.

'Could you tell us one of your stories?' Sally would tell it to William when she got home.

'The crest of my clan, the 'Deisheetan Clan' is twintailed beaver. The legend says that once, long ago, someone speak with anger to beaver. Beaver flapped his strong tail and he made a big wave which washed away the whole town. From this we learn to think before we speak and so speak wisely.'

'My mother reads stories called Aesops Fables to my little boy, and there's a moral to every story just like in your stories.' Sally had managed to take everyone off the subject of Mary's family history.

Mary's thoughts were beginning to stray. In her heart she did not feel that she would find her family in Carcross, and she was impatient to return to Carmacks and to meet Sara Black, the mother of Bob James. Albie, Joe and Amy came in asking about lunch, and Mary was surprised at how quickly the morning had gone. She wondered if the people of Carmacks believed in the same stories. Albie came in looking pleased with himself.

'I've just called Carmacks,' he announced, 'and Sara returned home, from Vancouver, yesterday. Apparently she's doing well and is willing to see you tomorrow as long as you don't stay too long. She didn't seem surprised and said she knows why you want to see her.' Mary felt that this was a good sign.

'So, would you like me to drive you girls to Carmacks? It's about a three hour drive from here so we'd have to set off real early. Jake is planning to come too isn't he? I hope he's cleared it with his boss?' Amy and Mary both nodded.

'Actually, could I possibly stay back in Whitehorse with Annie and Honey?' Everyone stared at Sally in surprise. 'Only I haven't really explored Whitehorse yet and I'd like a couple of days without any travelling. Also, this bit is Mary's personal quest and I'd feel in the way.'

'Sure,' said Albert. 'We'd have probably had a coffee stop in Whitehorse, anyway.'

'Will you be alright wandering around Whitehorse on your own?' Mary felt as though she was abandoning her.

'Of course I will. You did it.' Sally laughed.

Later that evening, whilst Sally was in the shower, Mary and Jake sat on the couch by the stove and shared a beer. They hadn't been alone since their afternoon on the beach in the summer.

'Do you mind if I come to Carmacks with you and Uncle Albie? I don't want to crash in on something which is personal to you though?' Jake felt he had no more right to be with her than Sally did.

'No, of course I don't mind. I'd like you to come.' Mary suddenly felt shy. 'I feel safe when you are with me and I can tell you what is in my heart. I wouldn't be able to do that with Uncle Albie now would I?' Jake took her hand and kissed it. His lips felt warm. He held her gaze for a moment and she began to shake very slightly. Before she knew what she was doing, she had her arms around his neck and was kissing him passionately. Everything else left her mind. That was what she had wanted to do since forever it seemed. As they pulled apart Mary's eyes filled with tears. Jake looked elated and slightly stunned.

'Oh Jake, this is so difficult for me. I'm sorry. I shouldn't lead you on like this,' she said softly.

'I wish things were different. I think about you all the time. Please don't tell me to pretend that this never happened because it did and it was wonderful,' said Jake reaching for her hand once more.

'I know. I think about you too even when I'm with ...

'Hey, you two, what's happened, why the tears Mary?'

Sally burst into the kitchen in her dressing gown. She noticed that Mary and Jake were holding hands.

'Oh, it's this search for my family – it's getting to me now.' Mary was feeling flustered. 'Jake asked how I would feel if the search didn't reveal anything, and I just got upset.'

'Well, this time tomorrow you'll know one way or the other, hopefully.' Sally gave Mary a sideways hug. 'Would you like me to come with you after all?'

'No. You enjoy a quiet couple of days. Albie and Jake will take good care of me.'

'The shower is all yours. I love the hour-glass timer so you don't use too much water. What a great idea. I guess water is a special commodity way out here.'

'It sure is.' said Jake. 'Everyone has water delivered by huge trucks each month. It has to be used sparingly.'

Sally glanced towards the empty beer bottle. 'Is there

any more where that comes from? I'm parched.' Sally and Jake split a beer this time. Mary wasn't able to finish hers. She needed some space to think about what had just happened with Jake.

An hour later, Sally got into bed and settled down for a nightly gossip.

'You know, I reckon that Jake has got the hots for you Mary. Did you see the way he was looking at you? Is there anything going on that I should know about?' asked Sally.

'Straight to the point as usual I see, love. I'm trying not to let anything happen, but yes, I am aware of Jake's feelings for me. He told me in the summer and asked me if I was engaged to Tom.'

'God! Poor Tom! You haven't told him have you?'

'No. Why would I? There's nothing to tell. I love Tom. I don't want to talk about it just before I go to sleep Sal. I'll have one of my bad dreams.'

'I'm wondering if I'm doing the right thing letting you two to go off to Carmacks without me. Still, you have a chaperone, I suppose,' Sally said with a grin.

Mary had a restless night, not because of any nightmares but because she felt so guilty and so torn between her deep love for Tom and her passionate feelings towards Jake. She had never felt on fire with Tom like she did with Jake. She decided that she must keep her head in charge of her heart, and yet Karen had advised her to 'follow her heart'.

She heard footsteps downstairs. She looked at her travel alarm clock - 02.35. Jake must be having a disturbed night too.

The next morning they all had coffee and doughnuts

together in Whitehorse and then Sally set off on a walking tour of the town. Albie called after her:

'Don't forget Sally, Annie will meet you after school outside Tim Horton's on Second Avenue. She'll see you around four, so you've got a whole day of shopping and sightseeing ahead of you.

'Have you got a street map?' asked Jake.

'I have. I've got Mary's map with all her little notes on it. Have a good trip you guys. Good luck Mary. 'Bye.'

Albie drove Jake's suburban as it was more reliable than his truck, but he paid for the gas. Mary had offered to pay for it but he wouldn't hear of it.

'I haven't been back to Carmacks for ages,' he said, 'not since my Dad died in fact, and that was a couple of years ago now. I'm looking forward to it. I bet nothing has changed.'

'No. You're right,' said Jake. 'The people are changing, though. Some are more open and less wary of white folks, although Bob's cousin, Sylvia Black, was careful what she said to Mom until she knew who she was apparently.'

'Well, we've got an Indian and two 'half-breeds' here,' joked Albie, 'so we should be alright.'

Chapter 19

It was now mid-morning and the bright sunshine transformed their journey. Everywhere looked clean and shiny, as though spring-cleaning had begun early. The lakes sparkled and the blues and greens of the glacial water looked almost creamy where the ice was becoming thicker.

'Do you have any days in the winter without snow or ice?' Mary asked Jake.

'No,' said Jake. 'Once the snow arrives, it stays with us right through to the spring. When I was a boy, I remember it snowed as late as June one year.'

Mary shuddered. 'Gosh! I don't think I'd like that.'

Albie drove faster than Jake had done. He knew the road so well. As they passed through 'Elk country', Mary clutched her camera, but the wildlife was staying well hidden.

Very soon, they were pulling off the road into the gas station, in Carmacks, to top up before their return journey, which would probably be after dark. Both Albie and Jake knew that if Bob James was connected to Mary in some way, then she must be prepared for a long story. They drove across the bridge and then turned into Sara's road. Albie knew exactly where he was going. He knew nearly everyone in this tiny community. As they parked amongst the vehicles on the drive, Mary spotted the red truck.

'It looks as though Sylvia is here too,' said Mary.

'She'll be Sara's main carer for a while, I expect; until Sara has fully recovered, anyway,' explained Albie. 'She doesn't have a daughter or grand-daughter to look after her.'

'I suddenly feel really nervous again,' whispered Mary to Jake. 'In fact I feel a little sick.'

'It's only natural. After all, you don't know what you're about to find, do you?' Jake squeezed her hand. 'I'm sure it'll be fine, you'll see.'

Albie knocked on the side door, and Sylvia answered.

'Hi Albie – haven't seen you for ages.' Much to Albie's surprise, she gave him a warm hug.

'Auntie will be pleased to see you.' Albie introduced Jake and Mary as they all took off their boots by the door.

'I haven't seen you since you were a boy,' Sylvia said to Jake, 'when Albie and your Dad used to bring you to see Uncle Tommy years ago.'

'Sorry Sylvia. For a minute there, I didn't recognise you. It's been quite a few years,' said Jake.

As they entered the main room, Mary's eyes went straight to Sara who was staring at the door in anticipation of her visit. When she saw Mary, she gasped out loud and put her hand on her heart as though it was in danger of stopping. Albie opened his mouth to introduce Mary, but Sara silenced him.

'I know who she is,' said Sara. 'Come here girl. Give your grandmother a hug,' she blurted out.

Everyone froze, including Mary who simply stared at the old lady's stern face. She couldn't speak. No words would come. Sara sat on the sofa, wrapped in blankets. She wore a knitted bed-jacket over a thick wool jumper and had a blanket over her knees. She looked frail, but her voice had the tone of someone in charge. She acknowledged Albie and Jake with a nod, but it was Mary she wanted to speak to. Mary was shaking. She looked at Jake who smiled and nodded towards Sara.

'I've waited for this day for long time. Bobbie never told me about you but he's brought you to me. Come...' She beckoned to Mary.

Mary walked across the room and gave Sara a tentative hug. She smiled at Sara and sat down next to her. 'Grandmother?' was the only word that Mary could manage.

'It's long story and sad story. Sylvia will make coffee and then we sit down and talk of your life. I have many questions and you must have many questions too.' Sara smiled for the first time as she studied Mary's very familiar face.

'When did you come to Yukon?' Sara asked.

'Just a few days ago, but this is my second visit this year. I came in the summer for two weeks, but I'd been led to believe that my name was Doyle, so I couldn't trace anyone. I, too, have waited many years for this day; twenty seven years in fact.'

Mary's bottom lip trembled and her hands shook. It was going to be quite difficult for Mary to explain the events of the past few months to this lady who was claiming to be her grandmother.

'How is Bob James connected to me?'

'He's my son. Your mother was my daughter, Jeannie James.'

'Was your daughter? Does that mean that my mother is dead?' Sara nodded.

Mary's eyes filled with tears. She had tried to picture her mother so many times in her dreams and the most important part of her search was to find and embrace her own mother for the first time. Now, it wasn't to be.

'How do you know that I am the same Mary that you remember from years ago? I don't even know what my surname is. I must look very different from the two year old child that you knew. Why did you recognise me immediately?'

'I know because you look same as your twin. When she's well, you two look same person.' Sara said this without emotion, which, in a strange way, made it easier for Mary to digest it.

'You say I have a twin sister and you say she's not well? What's her name, where does she live? Can I see her? What's wrong with her?' The questions poured out of her. Sylvia and Jake came in with the coffee and some freshly baked bran muffins. Sara remained quiet whilst everyone claimed their refreshments. Jake noticed Mary's tear-stained cheeks and pulled up a chair next to her to support her.

'Her name is Josie Quinn. She's in 'Crossroads Centre' in Whitehorse. They help her to get off drink and drugs,' said Sara, again without emotion in her voice.

'So my name is Mary Quinn. That's an Irish name. Is my father from Ireland? Is he still alive?'

'Yes. I begin this story at beginning. This is hard for me. I live with guilt all these years and you make me face this.'

'When you've heard this story I may have to ask you to leave,' warned Sylvia. 'Auntie tires easily and has been told to have plenty of rest.'

'Jeannie was a bad child. After residential school she got into big trouble. She was seventeen when she met Jack Quinn, your father. He was miner, good-looking guy, older than her. She shack up with him. I never like him. He was a boozer and he got Jeannie drinking too. She thought he was big man and would jump in half frozen river, if he told her to. Well, she got pregnant straight away. He didn't want to know ... not until he knew that she would have twin babies.'

'Why did the idea of twins change his mind?'

'His mother was a twin, in Ireland. He said this was special. My mother, Granny Edith said 'No!' In long ago time some Indians believed that twins bring bad luck to family. Twins must not stay together. Jeannie chose you. I took Josie.'

'My mother chose me?' Mary clung to these words for a moment. Whatever else she heard she would always keep these words in her heart.

'When pregnant, she quit the booze. It made her sick, but she start again after you were born. Sometime she'd forget to feed you or change you. There was a fire, otherwise Welfare would come and take you.' Sara was beginning to tire. She looked at Sylvia, who took over the story from this point.

'Jeannie was drunk and she left a cigarette burning .It set light to the drapes, and in minutes the whole place was on fire. Jack was outdoors at the time. He rushed in and grabbed you and then went back for Jeannie, but it was too late. The smoke had killed her.'

Mary found herself reaching for Jake's hand. Tears were streaming down her face. Again, she made no attempt to stop them.

'Jack never got over that night. The mine had closed and he was earning beer money in the bars in Whitehorse by singing and telling stories. He couldn't have looked after you ... no way,' said Sylvia.

'Didn't my father want to look after me?'

'Yeah he did, but he was too drunk most of time. You'd have to go with Welfare.' Sara stared straight ahead rather than witness Mary's tears. Her eyes narrowed as though she was trying to shut out the past. Mary waited.

'That's why I said Bob must take you to England. He'd saved up money to find his father who'd run away from Dawson in 1959 when we lived there. I say he went back to Britain.'

'Is my grandfather English?'

'No. He's Welsh. Maybe he's not alive now. It's been long time. I believe you grow up with your uncle and your grandfather.' Sara gave a deep sigh and rested her head on the back of the sofa. Before Mary could say anything more, Sylvia spoke up:

'Auntie is tired now. She needs to rest. I think you should go.'

Mary was devastated that she had to leave now. She had so many more questions about her father and her sister. She needed to find them more than anything, but most of all she needed time to try to piece this incredible jigsaw together in her mind.

Albie spoke up on Mary's behalf.

'Sara, could we come back tomorrow when you've rested? Mary has heard only half the story and she'll want to see her father if he's still up here. It's been a lot for her to take in.' Sara nodded.

'Could you do that?' asked Sylvia. 'It's a lot of driving.'

'Don't worry about that. Mary has waited for this day all of her life. We can't leave now.'

'Come back around noon. I'm staying with Auntie until she feels stronger,' said Sylvia 'Maybe you could get a couple of rooms at the hotel for the night.'

Everyone said their 'goodbyes'. Mary gave Sara's arm a gentle squeeze, but didn't hug her this time. She had felt so little warmth from her. So, this was her longed-for grandmother. She couldn't even use the term to her. Not yet anyway.

'Goodbye for now,' she said to Sara. 'Have a restful evening. We'll see you tomorrow. Sylvia, thank you for the lovely coffee and cake. I guess you must be my auntie then? I'm having a job to get my head round all of this.' Mary managed a weak smile.

'I'm not surprised. See you tomorrow. 'Bye.'

They walked back to the suburban in silence. Jake put his arm around Mary and gave her a hug when Albie's back was turned.

As Jake drove them back across the bridge, Albie turned to Mary.

'What d'ya think about all that? What a sad story. I can't imagine how I'd have felt if I'd been you. You're a tough one that's for sure. I'd have been in pieces,' he said to her. Jake had warned Mary that Albie could be very outspoken at times.

'That's exactly how I do feel. It's not at all the story I wanted to hear. Maybe we could talk about this later. Did I hear right? Are we staying in the hotel tonight?' Mary hadn't expected this.

'I think we should, don't you Jake? I don't really wanna drive to Whitehorse now only to come back again early tomorrow morning. You can share a room with me, can't you boy?'

'Sure. There are bound to be rooms. Its way past the tourist season,' said Jake.

They stopped outside the hotel and Albie went in to find out what was available. He booked a twin room for him and Jake, and a double room for Mary. They didn't have any single rooms. Jake was hungry. They had missed lunch and the mid-morning muffins were hours away. Mary wasn't hungry, and needed to have some time alone. Albie showed her to her room and they agreed to meet in the bar in about an hour.

It was late afternoon and the bar was deserted, except for a couple of inebriated locals propping up the bar. The air smelled of stale cigarette smoke and the room was dimly lit.

Mary chose a table in the far corner, and Albie ordered some food. Mary wanted a cup of tea more than anything, so Jake paid for two beers and a pot of tea. They chatted about their visit with Sara.

'Was that anything like what you were expecting? How do you feel?' Albie asked Mary.

'No. Of course not. I didn't know what to expect. My grandmother sent me away when I was two years old, my mother was drunk when she died, my father is an alcoholic and so is my twin sister. It's what they'd call in England, a very dysfunctional family. How do you think I feel?' There was anger in her voice. Mary looked Albie straight in the eye and challenged him to say anything more.

'You must be in a state of shock. Mary, what's the first thing you'd like to do tomorrow?' asked Jake, embarrassed by his uncle's lack of tact.

She didn't hesitate. 'Find my father – find Jack Quinn.' They talked about the events of the afternoon so much over dinner that Mary was convinced that she wouldn't be able to sleep. Everything was going round and round in her head and the knowledge that her mother was dead was the worst discovery of all. She would now grieve for someone she had never known. Sara's coldness towards her had been hard too. She had dreamed of this happy, exciting, reunion with her family, and so far it wasn't happening. How could she tell Tom? He would want her to come home immediately. He had warned her that this might happen. She had hoped to call him later that evening, from Whitehorse, but she would have to postpone the call until they got back. She needed to know the whole story before she spoke to him. She was much too emotional at the moment.

The bar was getting busy and noisy. It was late, but there was no sign of 'last orders'. Albie was exhausted and he suggested that they all get some rest. He decided to do one more thing. He made enquiries about Jack Quinn from the woman serving behind the bar.

'He's a sad case these days,' she said. 'He comes into town to get supplies. He's half-cut most of the time. You wouldn't recognise him: long hair, long beard, thin. He used to be a big strong fella. The 'Mighty Quinn' we used to call him, but the drink has changed him. He lives alone out in the bush. He likes it that way.'

'Where is he living?'

'If you take the river road and head out towards Grandma Sara's Fish Camp, he lives in an old miner's shack just past the camp. You can't miss it. It's just off the road and has a sod roof. You'll see his rusty old blue Chevy. How long has it been since you last saw him?' she asked.

'I don't really know him, but I have someone with me who needs to find him - his daughter.'

'Christ! You'd better warn her then. Good luck.' She turned to another customer.

Albie decided to keep this close to his chest until the morning. Mary had had enough for one day.

'Come on boy, let's get some rest. Got a lot to do tomorrow,' he said to Jake.

'Will you be okay? Jake asked Mary as he walked her to the door of her room.

'I'll be fine Jake, thank you.' Mary stepped back. 'I know where you are if I need anything.'

Jake stepped towards her and held her for a moment. Mary weakened and collapsed against him allowing her tears to moistened his shirt.

'Would you like me to stay with you for a while longer?'

'No Jake. I wouldn't want you to leave,' she whispered.

'I never want to leave you – ever.' His eyes were full of tenderness and longing.

'I know. Jake please let's say goodnight. Uncle Albie will wonder where you are, and I must try to get some sleep before tomorrow.' She kissed him on the cheek.

'Dear dear Jake. I, too, wish things were different. Sleep well my love.'

Mary quickly withdrew into her room, leaving Jake to join his uncle at the end of the hall. She felt more relaxed after a hot bath. She curled up in bed and tried to focus on Tom and her life in London rather than all that had happened during the day, but she couldn't. Jake filled her every waking moment. She pictured his crumpled face as she left him. She had wanted so much for him to stay with her. She was trying to be strong for Tom, but it was becoming more and more difficult every day. Sleep just wouldn't come. She tossed and turned, and, after an hour, she switched on the light, put on the robe she had found in the closet and made some tea. She had an aching deep inside her, a feeling of emptiness that was unfamiliar to her. She hadn't felt anything like this while she was away from Tom. She heard a gentle knock on the door and looked at her clock. It was 1.30am. She knew it must be Jake. Her heart raced and her body felt on fire. She jumped off the bed and flung open the door. Jake stood there, in his shirt and summer shorts, unsmiling as though he expected to be sent away. Before he could say anything Mary grabbed his hand and pulled him into the room.

'Mary,' he whispered, holding her and pushing his face into her silky black hair. His warm hands slipped inside her robe and gently caressed the slight hollow in her lower back. He pulled her close to him, breathing in the warmth of her perfumed skin. Mary began to unfasten each of his shirt buttons, gently kissing his smooth tanned chest as she did so. As she threw his shirt to one side, he kissed her hungrily and she felt the power surging within them both. He let his shorts drop to the floor and slipped the robe from her shoulders. His eyes moved down from her lips to her breasts and then downwards to the tops of her thighs.

'Oh Mary, you're so beautiful. I want you so much. Are you sure you won't regret this?' he breathed against her ear as he carried her over to the bed. She kissed him deeply.

'Jake, I've been secretly longing for this moment.'

He eased himself down on top of her. Mary had never known anything like this. It was if they were one person, joined forever together, on a wave of high emotion. She cried out and clung to him, her fingers digging deep into the small of his back.

As they lay curled up inside one another some while later it seemed to Mary that the world had suddenly changed. She felt she could face anything now and she wasn't afraid anymore. She knew that she didn't want to be parted from Jake ever again however difficult that might seem at that moment. Her life was going to be full of heartache and turmoil for a while and yet, with Jake, she knew it would be alright in the end.

'I've never felt so complete,' whispered Mary. 'I feel as though my future is right here in this room. I need you Jake.'

'I do love you, and I want you to be with me always, but what about Tom?' asked Jake.

She turned round and faced him.

'I know. I can't think about Tom now. Tonight is our time,' she said reaching out for him once again.

They finally slept, but not for long. Jake awoke to the sounds of life returning to the hotel, and he slipped back quietly to his room so that his uncle wouldn't wake and see that he was missing. As he entered the room Albie stared straight at him. He was dressed and watching the T.V.

'And where have you just spent the night?' He said with raised eyebrows and a knowing smile.

'I love her Uncle Albie. I really do.' Jake hung his head. He felt guilty that his uncle now knew.

'She already has a boyfriend who adores her,' said Albie.

'We both know that. We'll work this out together somehow. We've got to.'

Chapter 20

Albie sat at an empty table in the restaurant waiting for Jake and Mary. He and Jake had agreed to make an early start to try to find Jack Quinn. More snow had been forecast and he didn't want to get stuck out in the 'boonies'. Jake had called for Mary on the way downstairs and they hadn't appeared yet. Finally, they came towards him looking a little sheepish. Albie looked at his watch and frowned.

'Come on you two. We've got a lot to do and I'd like to get back to Whitehorse today, not tomorrow.' Albie's empty breakfast plate said it all. He was just finishing his third mug of coffee and he was ready to begin his day.

'Sorry, Uncle Albie,' said Mary, 'and thank you for finding out where my father lives.' She said the word 'father' as though she had just learnt a new word. Part of her still did not truly believe all that had happened. Sara didn't seem like her grandmother at all. She felt closer to Jake's grandmother, Nora, than she did to this rather cold and distant person. What if Jack Quinn refused to accept her as his daughter? What would she do then? This trip was getting more painful by the minute.

They followed the road that ran alongside the river. The sky looked grey and heavy with snow, the wind was icy and Mary couldn't imagine living rough in the bush in weather like this. The barmaid had described an old cabin with a sod roof. It sounded terrible to Mary. It would probably be dirty, damp and cold. She shuddered, and

Jake immediately put his arm around her shoulders for warmth, ignoring his uncle's disapproving glance. They turned off the main road and followed the unpaved track close to the river. Albie spotted the blue Chevy which was parked at a precarious angle with its nose pointing towards the river bank. The cabin looked derelict. There was no sign of life; no smoke, no light, no movement. Mary felt slightly sick again. The colour left her face and she caught her breath as she stared at the tired old shack. She was glad that it was Jake at her side and not Tom. Tom would be horrified by all of this. Albie parked off the road and knocked on the cabin door. There was no sound. He knocked again and called out Jack's name. Mary was shaking. She reached for Jake's hand.

'Why don't we see if the door is unlocked, and then go in. If he's not there, at least there might be some evidence as to Mary's connection with this man,' said Jake.

'He also might be in there with a rifle pointing towards the door,' said Albie. He peered through a dusty window at the side of the cabin. 'Can't see damn all.'

'I don't reckon he's there. I should try the door.' Jake had stood still long enough.

'Hey Jack,' Albie shouted. 'It's Albie Luke from the village. I need to see you. I have a surprise for you.' He pushed the door and it opened easily. No dog greeted them, nothing stirred and it was dark. The cabin smelt of fish and wood smoke and stale beer. Mary struggled to adjust her eyes to the lack of daylight.

'Oh my God,' she gasped, her eyes filling with tears. 'He's dead!'

Jack lay on a mattress next to a cold and unrelenting wood stove. His mouth was open, his hair was a long, grey, tangled mass and he lay in his coat and boots as though he had collapsed on arriving home. Jake touched his hands and his face. They were as cold as the ice on the inside of the windows.

'No. He's alive and in a drunken stupor,' said Albie. 'God knows how long he's been lying like this. Jake, let's get the fire going. Quick, bring some firewood in boy.' Albert and Jake lit the stove, stacked fresh firewood in the corner and then filled two old buckets with water from a nearby stream.

'Mary, there are a couple of blankets in the truck,' said Jake. 'Go get them for me will you?'

Mary collected the blankets and piled them on top of the sleeping stranger, tucking him in as though he was a small child. She knelt beside him and stared at his face in repose. His mouth turned up at one corner in a kind of wry smile. She saw vulnerability in his face and she felt drawn to him. She wanted to wake him and see his expression when he saw her. He'd probably think he was dreaming, thought Mary. The fire in the stove crackled and hissed, and the candles that Mary had lit and placed around the cabin created a warm glow. The cabin gradually came to life. Jake found a coffee pot and made coffee for them all. There were only two tin mugs so he gave them to Mary and Jack.

'Why doesn't he wake up?' Mary asked. 'All this movement plus the light and the warmth and he hasn't stirred.' Just as she said this, Jack coughed and opened his eyes. Albie knelt down and gently shook him.

'Hey, old man, wake up. It's Albie from Carcross. You've got visitors. Here – have some coffee.'

With Albie's help, Jack sat up and pulled the bedding around him. He sat cross-legged on the mattress, wrapped in the blankets as though he was an old Indian Chief, from another century, about to give counsel. Jack's hands were too stiff and cold to grasp the mug so Albie fed him the drink with great care. Mary was impressed by this sudden display of gentleness. She hadn't witnessed this side of Uncle Albie before. She wanted to say something to Jack and to move towards this sad and lonely man, but instead she waited for a sign from Albie. Everyone sat in silence in a circle around the bed. The cabin was sparsely furnished and was dirty, but the candlelight and the warmth from the stove made it bearable.

Jack suddenly caught sight of Mary.

'Josie. What you doing here? Where's the little guy?'

Again, Albie spoke up for Mary. 'Jack, this is Mary, your other daughter. She's come all the way from England to try to find you.'

Jack's rheumy eyes stared at Mary. He wiped them on his sleeve and held out his hand to her. Mary crept closer to him and held his rough, calloused hand in hers.

'What! Sara told me you were dead. How is this happening? Am I dreaming this?' His face had the expression of a small child who had just woken up from a strange dream. There was something warm and comforting about this tired old miner which stirred Mary. She hugged him, breathing in the earthy, smoky, beery, smell of him as she did so. She wanted to take care of him. After all he had saved her from the fire and had tried to save her mother. He must have loved them both. Jack's eyes focussed upon Albie.

'Albie Luke. What has all of this got to do with you?' This was said without malice. 'I haven't seen you since you were a boy. Not since before I took up with my Jeannie. How is it you know my girl when I haven't seen her since she was a baby?'

'It's a long story Jack and we haven't got time to explain it all now. We promised to visit Sara and Sylvia this afternoon. We'll come back to see you in a couple of hours. We'll bring you some food. Meanwhile, you've now got some water, some firewood and a fire, so don't let the fire go out,' said Albie.

'Can you bring me some beers as well?' asked Jack. Albie grunted.

'I want to hear all about your life and I want to know as much as possible about my mother,' said Mary. 'I've got lots to tell you too.'

'Go and see old Tommy Black. He'll tell you all about Jeannie. He adored her. I can't talk about her, even after all these years.' Jack hung his head.

Mary didn't want to leave him. She wanted to sit with this man who was her father and get to know him. She was suddenly aware of the small amount of time that she had set aside for this expedition, only a few days left and so much still to do. What was she thinking of, allowing just two weeks for finding her long-lost family and forming a link with them all? She might have to change the date of her return flight and stay in the Yukon for the time being.

'You're very quiet,' said Jake as they made their way back to the truck. 'Are you alright? Seeing your father living like that must have been a huge shock for you, although it's more common than you think up here.' He reached for her hand and helped her into the front seat. Mary felt the tears come again. She quickly wiped them away and swallowed hard. There was more still to come, and she didn't want to be an emotional wreck in front of everyone – not yet, anyway.

'Don't be too nice to me Jake. I have to stay strong. Meeting my father is only the beginning. Now I have to hear about the rest of my family.'

'We should go straight to Sara's house now. We're running late already. Lunch will have to wait I'm afraid. We'll get coffee at Sara's, for sure.' No lunch again! Albie ignored Jake's raised eyebrows.

In no time at all, it seemed, they parked next to

Sylvia's truck. Sylvia had seen them arrive and was waiting by the open door. Mary noticed that Sylvia's left eye and cheek were both slightly swollen, and her face looked grey.

'Oh Sylvia, what's happened? Have you had an accident?' asked Mary.

Sylvia took a step backwards and mumbled that she had walked into a cupboard door, when she popped home to cook her husband's supper for him. As Sylvia walked ahead of them, Albie looked at Mary and put his finger to his lips to silence her. Mary blushed, not knowing what she had done wrong.

'Auntie seems a lot brighter today,' said Sylvia. 'She'll soon be chopping wood again. She's looking forward to your visit. Would you all like some coffee?'

'Yeah. Thanks. Coffee would be good,' said Albie.

Mary gave Sara a tentative hug and sat down next to her on the sofa.

'Hello Grandma. I hear you're feeling a little better today. That's good news.'

'It's good thing. There are many things to talk about.' Much to Mary's surprise, Sara took her hand and held it for a moment. Her hands were surprisingly big and strong for such a little woman. The sign of a tough character, of a survivor, thought Mary.

'Where to begin?' Sara's smile was warm.

'I've just met my father, Jack Quinn,' said Mary. 'How long has he lived like that? He was drunk and the cabin was dark and cold. He could die out there and no-one would know.'

'Sometime, I'll tell you why many people here have addiction to alcohol. It's same story all over in Yukon ... our family too. Jack, Josie, Uncle Freddie, and Sylvia's husband, all have drink problems. It's ruined their lives. It's sad. Josie gets help now because she has child. Not enough help for all people, except if you have money and go Outside.'

'But I need you to tell me Grandma. Please tell me, why has this happened to so many people?'

'First Nation people have been depressed for long time. We lost our traditions, our language. No pride now ... everything gone. In early 1960s when Indians could go into bars, alcohol drowned people's sadness. It was way out. Jack always liked beer. Jeannie's death killed his spirit. He was angry when I sent you to England. But I thought it was best thing. Later, the mine closed, Josie lived in Whitehorse hostel to be near school. He said he'd lost everything and he blame me.'

'Poor man! It must have been awful for him.' Sylvia came in with coffee and buns for them all. Mary was grateful for the interruption, so that she could wipe her eyes and let this painful news sink in.

'Jack earned some money by entertaining in the bars around town,' said Sylvia, 'but most of it went on beer. He was lonely. Auntie believes that he would have gone back to live in Ireland if he'd had the money. She did her best for Josie when she came home for weekends and holidays, but Josie was a wilful and rebellious teenager. It was hard for her. She's not young anymore.' Sara smiled at Sylvia on hearing these words of support.

'You seem different,' said Sara. She stared straight at Mary. Mary blushed again and chose not to acknowledge this last comment.

'You said that Josie has a child. Is the child with her in the Rehab. Centre? How old is the child? Is it a boy or a girl?' Mary's family was growing by the minute.

'Mikey is nine now. He's with white foster family in Whitehorse. He has F.A.S.D and needs special help.'

'F.A.S.D. is everywhere in the Yukon,' added Jake, 'several people in Carcross are still having help for it. It's been like a national epidemic.'

Mary stared at them both. 'What exactly is it?

'It means 'Foetal Alcohol Spectrum Disorder', said Jake.

'Mikey has it because Josie drank when she was pregnant. He has slight brain damage,' explained Sara. 'Mikey is slow learner and has bad temper sometimes.'

'He has problems with concentration and also his memory. He can't play on his own or do anything by himself. He gets very frustrated. We all have to be patient with him.' Sylvia glanced at Sara as she said this. 'He's a very handsome little boy though.'

'I think I might have seen him, briefly,' said Mary. She recounted the story of her first day in Whitehorse, in Tim Hortons, when a woman with a small child called her Josie and made her jump.

'If that was Mikey, he would be with foster mother or the Welfare,' said Sara. 'Was the woman white? Why she not give you her name?'

'Yes, she was. The whole thing took me by surprise and I knocked over my coffee. By the time I pushed back my chair, they had both gone. I wish I'd known then what I know now. I'll go and see Josie as soon as we get back to Whitehorse. Do you have a photo of Josie and the little boy that I could see please?'

Sylvia went to the far end of the room and took a small photo frame down from the dresser. Josie and Mikey stood hand in hand by the river and Mary recognised them both instantly. Josie looked so like herself, only thinner. She looked happy though.

'It was taken the summer before last,' said Sylvia. 'Josie was off the booze for a while.'

'I work with children in London who have learning disabilities, and I've never come across this condition in our school. Maybe it's called something different at home or just brain damage? I know that smoking during pregnancy can affect the unborn child of course.'

'Well, your sister does that too. We all tell her it's bad, for baby, to drink booze and smoke. Josie wouldn't listen, even my father, Tommy, and she always listen to him.' Sara sighed deeply. Sylvia came to her rescue again.

'Grandpa Tommy is still here in Carmacks. He's ninety four and still fishes for the whole village when he can. You must meet him,' said Sara. 'He's a man of action not words. He doesn't speak much English. He prefers Northern Tutchone. I will take you up there. We go every week.'

Mary's head was buzzing. She had been given so much information in the past twenty-four hours. She didn't know whether she could take in much more. She suddenly noticed that Uncle Albie wasn't in the room. Jake explained that his uncle had gone to Sylvia's house to get supper for her old man, to save risking any further trouble for Sylvia.

'He'll be back soon because we'll have to get back to Whitehorse in a little while. I know he doesn't want to be too late.' Jake could see that Mary looked puzzled but he gave no further explanation.

Mary turned her attention back to her grandmother, who was beginning to look weary.

'All this must be very exhausting for you,' said Mary. 'As you heard, we'll be going soon, but could I just ask some more about Bob James? Has he kept in touch with you over the years?'

'Only twice; once to say he'd arrived in London and next time to say he had got married to some English woman named Wendy. He said they race Siberian huskies in forest. That sound wrong to me; huskies in England? No way!'

Mary gasped and her brain began to work overtime.

Sara stopped and waited but, as Mary said nothing, Sara continued with her story. She clearly hadn't noticed the colour drain from Mary's face.

'He never tell me about you. I believe you grow up with your Grandpa and Bobbie. He never even tell me about his father. That was main reason he went there ... to find *him*.' Sara drank the last drop of her coffee which must have been cold by now. She smiled at Mary. 'I'm tired now. Just tell me short story of your life in England. Is your Grandpa still alive?'

Mary told Sarah an abridged version of her life story from the beginning, stressing only the main people and events in her life so far. When she referred to Bob's behaviour at the airport and her harsh treatment by the nuns in the convent, Sara burst into tears and covered her face with her hands.

'I feel ashamed,' sobbed Sara, 'you and Josie, hurt by people who should help you. You're lucky to have good boyfriend – not like Josie. When will this man come to Yukon?'

Mary froze and for a moment she didn't know what to say. She looked at Jake who was staring at the floor. The tension between them almost screamed out loud and yet Sara didn't appear to notice.

'As soon as he has a holiday from school and that probably won't be until Easter, next year.'

There was a sudden rush of cold air, and Albie burst into the room, followed by Sylvia who had been clearing up in the kitchen.

'Come on you guys, it's time we went back to see Jack. I don't want to be driving on icy highways.' Mary heaved a sigh of relief that she didn't have to talk about Tom anymore.

Sylvia went towards Sara and took her hand.

'Auntie, have you been crying? Are you alright?'

'Don't fuss girl. I'm fine, just tired.'

'I've just told her a short version of my own story, and it upset her.' Mary put on her coat and scarf as she said this. She gave Sara a warm hug this time and promised to come back to see her soon.

It was dark and a bitter wind burned their cheeks. They stopped at the store and Mary bought food supplies for Jack. She also bought a couple of blankets and some candles. As Albie had stayed in the truck, Mary asked Jake to get some beer for Jack from the hotel bar.

'Uncle Albie will probably disapprove of you doing this,' said Jake.

'I know, but Jack will need it anyway and this way it saves him having to come out tonight.'

Mary didn't know what to call Jack, not yet anyway. This time, it was the wood smoke and the patterns of light in the window which told them they had arrived at the cabin. Mary knocked on the door.

'Who's there?' Jack shouted. 'What d'ya want?'

'It's Albie Luke with your visitors,' called Albie.

The door opened and Jack stood there with a rifle in his hand. His eyes squinted against the dark and he stared straight at Mary.

'Bloody Hell, Josie! What brings you here after all these years?' He clearly did not remember their earlier visit.

'Well let us in, you old codger, and we'll tell you,' said Albie, who was not one to waste words.

They all entered the cabin and Mary was relieved to find that it felt warm and dry this time.

'I had a weird dream that you visited me, but it was the other girl, Mary,' said Jack, closing the door and placing his rifle in the corner of the cabin.

'It wasn't a dream. We came to see you this morning, but you were still drunk. This here is Mary. She's come from England to try to find you,' sighed Albie, annoyed at having to repeat himself.

'Good God! I thought you were dead. I can't believe this.' He shook his head and gazed at Mary who was smiling at him. Both of them were near to tears. Mary stepped forward and hugged him gently. She was shaking and Jack put an arm around her to steady her.

'How did you manage to find me way up here?' Jack was in a state of shock and reached for a chair. Mary pulled one across for him and one for her too.

'I finally traced you through Bob James, whose name was given to me very recently,' said Mary. 'I've been searching for you for years.' She didn't really know where to begin.

Jack looked up at Albie and Jake who were still standing by the door.

'Albie Luke. God – you're a face from the past. Who's he?' Jack nodded towards Jake.

'Jake is my nephew. It's a long story,' said Albie.
'We've brought some food, so why don't Jake and me cook something for us all, while Mary gives you all her news. The boy is starving.'

Jake laughed. 'I'm always hungry.'

'Have you got any beer?' Jack asked, studying the bags. Sure,' said Jake, handing over his parcel. Albie raised his eyebrows and frowned at Jake. He was about to say something, but Jack was already gulping down his first beer.

When Jack heard that Bob had handed Mary over to a complete stranger at the airport, he exploded in temper. He banged his fist down hard on the table and he cried out, the tears filling his shaggy grey beard.

'How dare he! He had no right – no right at all! When I think that I begged to keep you meself, but Sara said I was a drunk. She said the Welfare wouldn't let me raise a young child.' Jack hung his head. 'Maybe I did drink a lot, but I'd have quit the booze if I could have had you back. Sara said Bob had told her that you had died in an accident. I tell you, that son of hers has a lot to answer for.' Jack held Mary's hand. Mary decided to say very little about her life in the convent at this stage, as Jack was already in a very emotional state. She simply told him that she ran away to find work in London when she was sixteen, which, apparently, is exactly what Jack, himself, had done when he lived in Ireland.

'Have you seen Josie yet? Is she still living in Whitehorse?'

Mary shook her head. 'No, I haven't met her yet and yes, she is still in Whitehorse. I hope to visit her tomorrow, at the Crossroads Centre, if I can.'

'I haven't seen her since she was a teenager you know. Folks say she's had a tough time these past few years. She has a kid, I'm told, a boy who has F.A.S.D. Mind you, half the town has got it I reckon. My Jeannie was a bit of a drinker, but she never touched a drop when she was pregnant with you two.' Jack was beginning to ramble on a bit, as the beer loosened his tongue and gave him courage. 'I could never get close to Josie. She blamed me for not being a proper father to her; but what could I do? Sara had no time for me. This stuff has taken everything from me,' he said, opening another beer, 'your mother, my home, my children, even my work, I guess. I could never keep a job once the drinking started. Christ, that food smells good!'

'Maybe I could arrange for us all to get together – you, Josie, Mikey and me?' Mary decided that her main task, from now onwards, must be to bring the broken fragments of her family back together again. However she realised that this would be an impossible task just now, with only a few days left of her holiday.

'Oh, I don't know. Josie won't want to come and see me. When do you have to go back to England?'

'I'm not sure. I might have to extend my trip.' Jake caught Mary's eye as she said this, and he gave her the 'thumbs up' sign. 'I'd have to resign from my job, but give a months' notice,' said Mary.

'Albie came over to the table with plates of food all of which had been cooked in a large cast iron frying pan over the stove: sausages, bacon, tomatoes, eggs, grits and a large packet of bagels. Jake put two mugs of coffee in front of Mary and Jack.

'Thank you, that looks wonderful. I should have bought some more mugs,' said Mary. 'I didn't think.'

There were also only two chairs, so Albie and Jake sat cross-legged on Jack's mattress and ate their food. Everyone ate in silence, savouring the taste and smell of their first meal of the day.

'Jack, what shall I call you from now onwards? What does Josie call you?' Mary asked, finally.

'I've no idea what Josie calls me – a 'drunken bastard' probably. She used to call me 'Pa' when she was little. You can call me 'Dad' if you like. 'Dad' sounds good to me.' His smile was tender.

Albie had been keeping an eye on the time as usual, and he came over to the table.

'It's getting late now and I reckon we should get going soon. I should have called Annie from the hotel. She'll be getting worried. Maybe we should do that on our way out.'

'Sorry Uncle Albie. This must be so boring for you. Of course we must go.' Mary turned to Jake.

'Jake could you give Jack your Whitehorse phone number in case he wants to call me?'

'Dad, I'll come to see you again as soon as I can and I'll tell you what I've decided to do once I've seen Josie.' She and Jack held one another for a moment. Jack was reluctant to let her go.

'Promise you really will come back,' he said.

'I promise, and you have two witnesses,' she said, looking towards Albie and Jake. 'Meanwhile, Dad, don't let the fire go out and make sure you eat regularly. I want my new father alive not dead.'

'Stay off the liquor!' Albert called from the doorway. Mary mouthed the word 'sorry' to Jack, as she followed the others out to the truck.

It was a peaceful drive back to Whitehorse and Mary was content to go through in her mind all that had happened during one short visit to Carmacks. Today had been good. She felt she had bonded with both her father and her grandmother and she knew that she wanted to see a lot more of them. She would have liked to have heard more about her mother, but sadly, Jack refused to discuss her. She must meet Sara's father, Tommy Black, next time and hopefully he would talk about her mother. Mary had also forgotten, for the second time, to show the photograph, so the identity of the piano player was still unknown. The biggest mystery of all, however, must be left for Tom to solve. Who, or where, in England, is Bob James? Is he who she thinks he is? She needed to talk to Tom as soon as possible.

Chapter 21

As soon as they had arrived back in Porter Creek, Mary asked if she could call Tom. She had so much to tell him, but most of all she wanted to share her thoughts about Bob James with him. It was mid-day in London, so she hoped Tom would be having breakfast. She couldn't bear it if he wasn't there.

'I'll give you all the news once I've spoken to Tom,' Mary said to Annie and Sally.

'Darling, it seems ages. Are you alright? I was beginning to get worried about you, but I wasn't sure exactly where you were.'

'I'm so sorry Tom. A lot has happened here. I've been up in a native village north of here, with members of my family, for two days.' She told Tom all that had happened and she listed the family members she had met so far, talking mainly about her father, Jack Quinn.

'God, you've discovered a lot in less than two days and all because you had the name of one man. I can't imagine that being so easy in London. So who is Bob James?' asked Tom.

'He is my mother's brother – my uncle. It's a long and complicated story, but listen to this. Bob's mother – my grandmother – told me that Bob is married to an English woman called Wendy and they have Siberian huskies which they race in a nearby forest. Now who do you think that might be? She also added that he went to the U.K. to search for his father who is Welsh. Now think of those two names. Maybe Rob changed his name to hide his identity. Maybe that's why he's gone missing now? Maybe he has just realised who I am. What do you think? Surely they have to be the same man?

'If they aren't, then it's a huge coincidence. If you think about it, Rob did disappear once he knew that you were planning to go to the Yukon', said Tom. 'He was obviously afraid of being found out. Did you tell your grandmother this?'

'I haven't said much about my life to her yet as she's still weak from a recent operation. Tom, could you visit Robs home again, or go to Rendlesham Forest – anything to try to find this man for me? Maybe you could trick him into revealing his story. I need to know.'

'You'll be home soon, darling. We could do this together. It could be risky.'

Mary fell silent for a moment and Tom thought the line had gone dead.

'Mary? Have I lost you? Are you there?' Tom raised his voice a little.

'I'm here. Please don't be cross love, but I may have to extend my stay up here. I haven't even met my twin sister or several other family members yet. This trip is the climax of my search. I now have a family for the first time in my life. It was stupid of me to think that two weeks would be enough for this. I can't walk out on them yet. I don't want to. I'm sure you understand that?'

'I see. What will you do about school? There are only a few days left. Will Sally come home as planned? Is there anything you're not telling me?' Tom sounded despondent. Mary knew this would be difficult. She wasn't ready to tell him about Jake, certainly not over the phone.

'I'll call Roy tomorrow. Yes of course Sally will go back. She has Will to think about. I promise to call you as soon as I've talked to everyone here. I just need a bit more time.'

'Alright darling. Meanwhile I'll do my best to find Rob and Wendy.'

That night Mary sat on Sally's bed down in the basement and talked until the early hours. She told Sally everything that had happened in Carmacks. Sally could hardly believe Mary's description of Jack's cabin and the sorrowful state in which she had found her father. She thought of her own father and mother in their smart three bed semi in Lee Green. This was a different world altogether. The hardest thing for Sally to accept was the fact that Mary had slept with Jake and was in love with him. Sally could see that her best friend's life was about to turn upside down.

'What about Tom? You always said you were madly in love with him and he worships you. He's planning his future with you – even talks about starting a family. Does he even know that Jake exists?'

Mary shook her head. She had anticipated this reaction from Sally. Karen would probably react the same way. They had only ever known Mary with Tom at her side. 'Her rock', Mary had called him.

'I know. I thought I was until I met Jake. Tom was the first man to show me kindness and genuine affection, and I do love him, but I realise now that I have not been 'in love' with him.'

'What's missing?' Sally asked.

'Passion is missing and also being with a man who understands me completely. I feel as if I have always known Jake. It feels right for us to be together.'

They talked long into the night and Mary explained that she planned to extend her stay. Someone had told her that for $100 she could change the date of her return flight, so she intended to do so. Sally was okay about flying home alone, but she asked if Tom could still meet her plane.

'If you're not too cross with me I'd love you to come with me to meet my twin sister, Josie, tomorrow. She's having help for her drink/drug dependency so I'm not sure what we'll find. You've seen this at the hospital with your work. Please say you'll come.'

Sally gave her a hug. 'Of course I will, but right now we must both get some sleep.'

The next morning Mary detected an atmosphere, a slight tension between them all, as they had breakfast together. Annie banged two waffles down onto Jakes' plate. Her body language said it all. She was cross with him about something. Albie rarely ever spoke when he ate anyway. He loved his food too much. Honey sat with her head on Mary's lap. She certainly sensed something was wrong.

'When are you going back to Carcross Uncle Albie?' Mary attempted some conversation.

'Jake and I are leaving now, as soon as I finish this coffee. We both want to check in at work this afternoon. Come on boy, get your things together.'

Mary and Sally stood by the front porch in their coats so they could see them off. More snow had fallen during the night and Albie had already cleared the drive for Annie. It was cold. Jake came over to Mary as if he was about to take her in his arms right in front of everyone, but fortunately, for Mary, he didn't. Instead he gave each of the girls a quick brotherly hug and said he would try to see them off at the airport. He looked so sad, and Mary was close to tears.

'*I* leave at 5.00pm on Thursday,' said Sally. Jake winked at Mary.

'Thank you so much Uncle Albie for taking me to

Carmacks and helping me to find everyone. I couldn't have done that trip without you.' Mary smiled at Uncle Albie.

'Just make sure you think real hard before you make your life plans from here on,' said Albie as he drove away from the house.

'I echo that,' said Annie. 'Come on in you too. It's too cold to stand around.'

'Annie, are you angry with Jake? Did he tell you about our overnight stay?' Mary needed to face this at last.

'Yes he did. Albie, Jake and me stayed up talking for a while last night. Mind you I'm not sure that Jake would have said much if Albie hadn't blurted it out. Jake shouldn't have taken advantage of you like that. He knew you were missing Tom. I'm shocked. He's usually so considerate.'

'He didn't do anything wrong. Annie, I'm in love with Jake. I've tried to fight it and so has he, but now we both know more than ever how we feel.'

'I think it's best that we don't discuss this at the moment. You have more family to meet and more heartache to face and a nice boyfriend at home who loves you. Any decisions about your future should be made when you have seen everyone and when you truly understand what life up here in the Yukon is all about. Trust me - I know. I told you - moving up here with my father ruined my parents' marriage and ultimately killed my mother. It's not something you can take lightly. There's no rush. Jake isn't going anywhere. Now, if you girls are going into town you'd better get organised. I'll give you a ride to 'Crossroads' and then I must come back and do some school work.

'Thanks, Annie. That's kind of you.' Mary was stuck for words after that little speech of Annie's, and she suddenly felt like a teenager again.

'What exactly is Crossroads? Is it a rehabilitation clinic?' Mary asked, as they drove into town. She was anxious to dispel the tension that had built up between herself and Annie.

'Yes. It's a treatment centre offering both counselling and spiritual support for the First Nations population of The Yukon. George's brother, Sam, is also there at least he was the last time I asked about him. It's helped him a lot. The staff members are mostly ex-alcoholics themselves so they understand the needs of their clients.'

'Do people live there until they are well enough to cope on their own?' Mary wondered how long Josie would be there.

'They are given a bed for short periods whilst they detox and receive counselling, and then it's up to them to keep the appointments that are made once they leave. Also, a support worker might visit your sister in Carmacks. I suspect that Josie is trying to get clean so that she can claim her son back. It could be a long wait. It depends upon how long she has been having the support. Does she know you are here?' Mary shook her head.

'Then my advice is – tread carefully. Don't go barging in. This could be your biggest challenge yet. Do you want me to come in with you? I know a couple of the staff in there.'

'Thank you. Just an introduction to someone would be helpful.' Mary felt the butterflies in her stomach.

'Hi Annie,' said a friendly, middle-aged male member of staff as they approached the main office. 'Are you here to see Sam?'

'No,' said Annie. 'I've brought a surprise visitor for Josie Quinn – her long-lost sister Mary. Tell me, is Josie well enough to cope with this news? It'll be a huge shock if no-one has warned her. Maybe one of you could try and talk to her first?'

'She has someone with her just at the moment.' He turned to greet Mary. 'Good Lord! I can see who you are. You look so much like her, you could be twins.'

'We are,' laughed Mary.

'My name is Don. If you wait here, in reception, I'll let you know when her visitor leaves and then we'll decide what to do.'

'In that case, do you two mind if I head back home now?' said Annie. 'Good luck. I hope it all goes well. 'Bye Don.'

Just as Annie and Don left through their respective doors, a white woman came up the stairs ahead of them. Mary instantly recognised her. It was the woman she had seen in the coffee shop in town during the summer.

'Excuse me,' said Mary. The woman stared at her in disbelief. 'Do you remember me? We met briefly in Tim Hortons in August. I'm Mary, Josie Quinn's twin sister. Have you just been to see her?'

The woman gasped and then smiled at Mary. She sat down in the chair next to her.

'Hello again. I talked about you to Josie shortly after our little meeting and I said at the time that you looked like her twin sister, but Josie said you were dead. Why didn't you say who you were?'

'I'd spilt my coffee everywhere and by the time I was able to chase after you, you'd disappeared. Anyway, I hadn't found my family at that stage. I was still searching for them.'

'I'm Betty Turner, Mikey's foster mother. Mikey is Josie's son.'

'Yes, I know. My grandmother told me that Josie had a little boy.' Mary introduced Sally. 'We're on a mission from England – a mission to find my family. I can't wait to meet Josie. I've dreamed about her for years. How is she?' Don had re-appeared when he heard Betty's voice.

'Hi Betty. You've met our surprise visitor, I see. Mary is concerned that her unexpected arrival will prove to be too big a shock for Josie. What do you think? I feel that I should have a chat with her first. Would you like to come down with me? You seem to get on really well with her,' he said to Betty.

'Sure. Mary, is Josie likely to know about your arrival in the Yukon?'

'Not unless her Auntie Sylvia from Carmacks has visited her in the past few days. Could you explain to Josie that I've been trying to trace my family for years and that this is my second visit to Whitehorse, from England, in the past three months? The first person I met, just last week, was Sara Black, our grandmother. I have also met our father, Jack Quinn.'

'Gee, what a story,' said Don. 'We'll do our best to give you a good introduction, although you must understand, Josie has had a tough time and we have a way to go yet. She's been in and out of here for two or three years, but just lately she has decided that she wants to win her son back. The power of the incentive is wonderful and she's trying real hard this time.'

'How did she seem to you just now?' Mary asked Betty.

'She talked a lot about Mikey, which hasn't always been the case. She didn't sleep too well last night due to some disturbance involving one of the male clients, so she might seem tired. Just give her time.'

'Come on Betty. I have a meeting in thirty minutes.' Betty and Don disappeared down the stairs to the residential quarters in the basement, leaving Mary and Sally staring silently after them.

'Are you feeling okay?' Sally asked. 'Do you really

want me to come in with you? It might be easier for your sister if you go in alone. It sounds as though she is still quite fragile.'

'Yes please, Sally, I need you to observe our meeting and talk to me about it afterwards. Put your 'work cap' on. This could either be painful or joyous for both me and Josie. I know which one I want it to be. She's always been there for me in my dreams. That has to mean something.'

They sat in a world of their own thoughts and observed the comings and goings of the staff. It was quiet except for the tap tap of the secretary's typewriter and the constant ringing of her telephone.

'It must be tough being a member of staff here, don't you think?' said Sally. 'They must have to deal with all kinds of challenging situations, especially in the winter.'

'According to Annie they understand the problems of addiction from first-hand experience and they'll all have followed a course of training, I expect. I can't imagine any client accepting help from staff who haven't been down that path themselves,' said Mary. She wondered about Josie's temperament.

Betty suddenly re-appeared.

'Josie has asked if Don could come with you and stay for a few minutes. She already knows about you and isn't convinced it's really you. She's quite anxious so don't visit for too long,' said Betty.

'She's not the only one,' laughed Mary. 'I must go - lots to do before the end of the school day. It's been good to meet you properly this time. You must come and meet Mikey. After all, he is your nephew.'

The girls followed Don downstairs and knocked on Josie's door. Mary took a deep breath.

'Yeah?' Josie sounded weary. Mary pushed open the

door slowly and peered into the room, smiling nervously. Josie was sitting on her bed. The two girls stared at one another, both lost for words in the emotion of the moment. Don broke the silence.

'As you can see, Josie, this is your twin sister Mary, and with her is her friend Sally from London, England. Here girls, have a seat.' He pulled two chairs across for them. Would you all like some coffee?' he said to all three of them.

'Yeah. Thanks. The coffee here tastes like shit, but it's better than nothing, I guess,' Josie spoke in a whisper. Don disappeared, ignoring the criticism. He heard it from everyone.

Mary walked over to the bed and sat down next to Josie. She took her hand, but Josie pulled it away, and moved along the bed. Sally sat facing them both, intrigued by the similarity of their physical appearance. She said nothing.

'Josie, I've longed for this moment all my life. I've tried to picture how it would be and where it would happen. I suspected that it was you who constantly appeared in my dreams and now I know it was you. I have so much to tell you. Where would you like me to begin?'

'How do I *really* know that you are who you say you are? Grandma Sara told me you died when I was a child. She said Uncle Bob told her. What did she tell you about me? Nothing nice, I bet.' Josie hung her head and picked at her nails. Her hair was the same colour as Mary's but it was much shorter and had lost its shine. Josie was dressed in black. She sat cross-legged on the bed, protecting her personal space.

'You seem too posh to be one of us.' Josie rubbed her right eye, something that Mary always did when she was tired. 'How did you find us? Who is she?' She said, as an afterthought, pointing at Sally.

'Hello Josie. I hope you don't mind me being here. Mary and I have been friends for a long time and I've heard such a lot about her search for her family. Mary's boyfriend couldn't come with her so she asked me to come instead. This is an amazing place – the Yukon I mean. My little boy would love it.'

'I've got a boy too. He don't live with me though.' She turned to Mary. 'You got a boyfriend? What's he like? Does he beat you?' The question came as a shock to Mary and luckily Don re-appeared with 3 mugs of coffee which provided a welcome distraction.

'I've gotta go Josie – everything okay?' Josie nodded and Don left the room. She reached for her jacket and took out a cigarette. 'I can't have coffee without a smoke. I bet you don't smoke or drink or do drugs or anything, do you?' She stared straight at Mary.

'I used to, before I met Tom. As soon as I escaped from the children's home I tried everything that was wrong for me. Sally knew me when I was smoking, even the odd spliff or two, didn't you Sal?'

As they sipped their coffee Mary attempted to put Josie's mind at rest by telling her story.

Mary had repeated this abbreviated version of her life story so many times that she was almost word perfect when she told it. She said more about her childhood than she had done to Sara though.

'Shit, you had it almost as bad as me,' said Josie. 'So, if Uncle Bob dumped you at the airport and never saw you again, how did you find him?'

'I didn't. I went back to the convent and the man who'd taken me there in 1964 had been to see the nuns, the month before, to try to find me. He explained the true story but he only knew Bob's name and the fact that we were travelling from the Yukon. The library gave me

Sara's name and Sara explained my connection with Bob James. I need to find this man in England. I wondered, at the time, if it might have been my father. I'm glad it wasn't.'

'Christ! What a low life, dumping a little kid on a stranger like that. Was he drunk?'

'I don't know. Maybe he was.' Alcohol and violence clearly still played a big part in Josie's world. She wondered if she should ask her any questions about her life, but then decided to let Josie tell her when she was ready to share it with her. She didn't seem ready at the moment. Instead she said, 'I'd like to come and see you again. I'd dearly love for us to get to know one another. Do you know whether you'll be here for the rest of the week?'

Josie smiled for the first time. 'Yeah. I'd like that too. I ain't going nowhere just yet.' She looked so sad that Mary leaned over and hugged her. Josie felt tense. She wasn't used to hugs, but she didn't attempt to pull away.

'Tell me, did you ever dream about me?' said Mary

'Yeah. I thought you were the ghost of my dead sister come to help me out. Hey, you'd better go. I'm feeling twitchy which means the medication is wearing off. You can come again if you like.'

'Sally goes back to England on Thursday, but I'll be here again soon.'

'Cheerio, Josie,' said Sally. 'It's been great to meet you. Could I take a photo of you two, with Mary's camera before I go? You can see how alike you are. No-one could doubt that you're sisters.'

Mary sat back down on the bed next to Josie and put an arm lightly around her shoulders. They both smiled at the camera. This will definitely be one for the mantelpiece, thought Mary. She would treasure it. She rested her face next to Josie's for a moment.

'I'll come to see you on Friday if that's okay?' Mary got up and followed Sally to the door.

'You won't like me when you've heard my story though,' said Josie.

'You haven't heard all of mine yet either,' said Mary.

'Take care love. 'Bye.'

'God,' said Sally when they got outside the building. 'I wonder what Josie meant by that. How much do you know already about her life so far?'

'She's had a tough childhood ... bit like me, I think.'

'How many of your family have you found now?

Maybe you should write out a family tree for the ones you've found so far.'

'That's a great idea Sal. I don't know about the whole family yet. I found it confusing when I tried to explain it all to Tom. Let's go and sit by the river and see if we can sort it all out.'

'I've got a pen and also my journal – we can write in that,' said Sally.

'Oh, I knew you would. You're always so organised,' laughed Mary.

They made their way back into town to a seat by the library and put together Mary's family so far.

'Goodness Mary, you've found ten members of your family already ... fifteen when you find the five missing names,' said Sally, giving Mary a hug. 'That's amazing!'

'I still can't believe it. How many more, I wonder.'

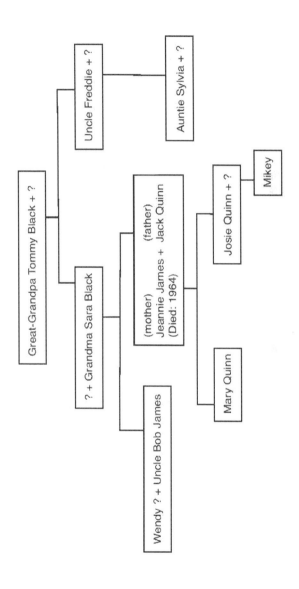

Chapter 22
Carmacks 1973

Eleven year old Josie crouched inside a felt-leaved willow bush at the back of their yard in Carmacks. She clutched some cold toast which she was eating when the school bus arrived. She wasn't going back to that hostel in Whitehorse. No way! They were cruel to her there. She hated it. She wanted to stay in Carmacks. Even Grandma Sara was better than that stinking place. Why would no-one believe her? She pulled her jacket around her and waited. The neighbour's four year old son had spotted her.

'Hey, Josie, you playing hide 'n seek?'' He crawled inside the bush with her, smiling excitedly.

'Shhh, big mouth,' whispered Josie, putting a finger to her lips. 'It's not a game. I'm running away.'

'Where you hiding, you horrible child? I know you out there somewhere. The bus don't wait for bad kids.' Sara's voice rang out across the yard. 'Hurry! Josie - come NOW.' Her voice was louder. She sounded really angry. 'In here, in here' chanted the little boy, convinced that this was a game. Josie slapped him hard. He began to wail. 'Help! Josie hurt me.'

'Come out, child. Get on that bus. They call you a truant and then I get no money. You know the rules.' Sara pulled her roughly through the front of the bush.

'Don't make me Grandma. I hate that place. They beat me,' sobbed Josie.

'Well you're a bad child. Take your bag, and your

lunch. Now go.' She pushed Josie on to the bus, turned her back, and walked away without a wave or a smile.

Josie pressed her tear-stained face against the window and stared back at her home as the bus drove across the bridge.

'Hey cry-baby, you'll have worse to cry about soon,' jeered a boy from Pelly. He was older than Josie. He was known by everyone as a bully.

'I get my Dad on to you,' said Josie, trying to sound tough.

'Your Dad's a no-good drunk.' The boy laughed and Josie cried some more.

'Quiet back there,' shouted the driver.

Josie moved into the front seat behind the driver and thought about her lovely teacher, Mrs.Morely. She really liked her. She was the only one who listened to her and believed in her. Their class was a special class. Someone said it was for stupid kids. They even had their own playground in case they got bullied during recess. I'm not stupid, Josie mumbled to herself. I know lots of things. My Grandpa Tommy teach me. I fish real good and snare rabbits. See me swim. Grandpa Tommy say I'm fast like beaver in the water. He's proud of me.

'Josie's talking to herself again,' said a girl sitting in the seat behind her. Everyone sniggered.

'Cover your ears, she'll be singing soon,' said a boy opposite.

Josie loved to sing when she was on her own or with her dog. She made up her own songs. Her teacher said she had a beautiful voice and let her sing her songs to the class sometimes.

As they stepped off the bus a couple of hours later and hurried towards the school gates, Josie kicked the boy from Pelly hard on his left ankle. The boy yelled but could do nothing as the teacher on duty was watching everyone line up in their class groups. 'Wait 'til tonight,' he hissed, rubbing his leg.

Later that afternoon, Josie's heart sank as the school bus stopped outside the hostel entrance. The place smelled of cabbage and wee and the food was disgusting. They had boiled fish and cabbage and a hot drink that didn't taste of anything, just coloured water. As they sat in rows either side of the trestle table, the boy from Pelly came over from the other end of the hall. He tipped up Josie's plate with a flick of his wrist as he passed her. Her supper fell on the floor and some of it splashed on to the girl sitting next to her. The boy grinned and slipped quietly back into his place with the rest of the boys, whilst a fight broke out between the two girls. Josie got the blame of course. She always got the blame.

That night, Josie was sent to bed in the isolation room without any supper. The tiny room was no bigger than a cupboard. It was cold and dark. She lay curled up in a ball beneath a single stained blanket, terrified that anyone would come and mess with her like last time. She was wide awake. She listened to the familiar sounds of voices and tea cups and tears, dreading that any minute the handle of the door would rattle and 'Handy' Tandy would creep in. Everyone called him that because he couldn't keep his filthy hands to himself.

She must have fallen asleep, because she awoke suddenly and felt H.T's onion breath on her face. His hand was stroking her thigh beneath her nightdress.

'I've brought you another blanket to keep you warm,' he said in his sleazy friendly voice. His hand was now stroking her between her legs and he tried to get her to play with his big thing. It frightened her and she felt sick.

'You're such a sweet child. So developed for a little kid,' he crooned as his right hand fondled her budding breasts.

'You dirty bugger. I'll scream.' He slapped her hard across her mouth.

'Get off me.' She scratched his face.

'Why, you little vixen! No point in screaming. They'll punish you even more.'

Before she knew what was happening he had forced his ugly thing up inside her with his hand clamped firmly over her mouth. The pain was like a knife tearing into her flesh. He pulled back from her. She was sticky and sore and humiliated. Her tears streamed silently on to the mattress as she curled herself into a tight ball again away from him.

'No-one will be any the wiser and you won't say anything to anyone.' His voice was harsh and threatening. The door clicked shut. Josie wished she could die right there in that hell hole.

The next morning she felt ill and in pain. It hurt just to walk a few steps. She kept apart from the other girls in the communal shower in case anyone noticed anything. One of the laundry staff caught her trying to wash her nightdress.

'Have you wet the bed again?' The woman frowned at her.

'Sorry Miss. I didn't get to bathroom in time,' said Josie.

'Put it in the laundry basket. I'll see to it. You'll miss your breakfast.' Josie sighed with relief and hurried as fast as she was able in case she was late and had to go hungry again.

She felt so poorly when she arrived at school that she disobeyed the rules and made her way up the stairs to the classroom before the bell sounded. She knew that Mrs. Morely would be there, sitting at her desk. Josie was in a state of collapse as she entered the room and she fell in a heap at her teacher's feet.

'What's happened to you Josie?'Mrs. Morely helped her to her feet and held her for a moment. You look as though you're in pain. Has someone hurt you or are you ill?'

Josie sat down at her own desk. 'Please Miss, I can't say. I talk to you alone later, okay?

'Of course you can. Meanwhile, tell me if you feel any worse during the morning.'

Mrs. Morely smiled at her. No-one ever did that. It felt good. Josie tried to smile back.

It was hard for Josie to talk about herself. She didn't know all the words and she worried that her teacher might not believe her. She felt embarrassed and her face kept going red. She stared at the floor whilst she told her teacher what happened the night before.

Mrs. Morely was disturbed by Josie's story and did not doubt that this distraught child was telling the truth. Josie was in pain both physically and emotionally.

'Josie, I'll have to tell the principal, the school counsellor and your community worker about this, to make sure that it doesn't happen again.'

'They'll beat me like Grandma Sara. They think I tell lies?'

'No, of course they won't, but they will have to ask you some questions.' She held Josie's hand and smiled at her.

'You be there too?' Mrs. Morely nodded and gave her a reassuring sideways hug.

'I wish you were my mother.' Josie envied her teacher's three children who could have hugs whenever they liked.

'Will you tell your grandmother about this when you go home to Carmacks?'

'No. Grandma says I deserve it. She says I'm bad.

She'll say I'm lying and send me to bed early.'

'Be a good girl and stay away from that bully in case he lands you in more trouble.'

'Thank you Miss.'

Mrs. Morely kept her promise and sat with Josie while the school professionals questioned her about her ordeal in the hostel. The community worker had dealt with a number of similar cases before and she told them she was doubtful that anything would come of Josie's disclosure.

'They cover up for each other at that place and think of us as second class citizens,' said the community worker, an Indian woman from Josie's own village.

That is exactly what happened. According to the member of staff concerned, Mr Tandy, he had delivered an extra blanket to Josie out of kindness. He thought she might be cold. Josie was accused of lying and was sent to bed without supper again, this time to her own bed in the dormitory.

'Handy Tandy' continued his unwelcome night-time visits whenever Josie found herself in the isolation room. She did try to keep out of trouble, but her quick temper and her strong sense of fair play kept letting her down.

'Everyone hate me,' she said to her school counsellor one day. 'Everyone 'cept Grandpa Tommy and my teacher. If not for them I'd kill myself.'

Chapter 23
London

Tom had set his alarm clock for 5.00am. It was Friday so the M25 would be full of rush hour traffic. Sally couldn't have chosen a worse time and day to arrive at Heathrow Airport. Besides which he had taken a sick day which made him feel very guilty, so soon after going back to school. He was really looking forward to seeing her though. She would be his first contact with Mary since all the excitement and she could bring him up-to-date with everything. He liked Sally. Both her confidence and her directness were good for Mary. He had only really seen them together, so he planned to treat Sally to a late breakfast somewhere so that they could enjoy a good chat before she met up with her family.

Tom managed to find a space in the short term car park at Terminal 3. Sally's plane had landed when he arrived but she hadn't come through yet. He usually enjoyed watching the arrivals at an airport but this time he couldn't help wishing that it was Mary was coming home. Sally must have read his mind.

'Sorry it's just me Tom. I'm sure you must wish that it was Mary instead?'

'Hi Sally. Don't be daft. It's good to see you.' He gave her a quick hug and took her suitcase. 'I thought we could stop off for breakfast somewhere before I take you home. I need to hear all the news. Can you bear another hour away from William?'

'Yes of course. What a good idea. I've got lots to tell

you,' said Sally. 'It was quite a trip.'

'How is Mary? Is she thrilled to have found some of her family? Is she missing me yet? I wish I could join her. It's frustrating being tied to term dates. What did Roy say about her staying up there?'

'My goodness – so many questions - all in good time,' laughed Sally.

The arrivals hall, at Heathrow, was strangely quiet. Sally had never seen it like that before. Tom took over the trolley and they made their way to the lift. Once he had paid the parking ticket and stowed away the luggage in the boot, they headed out towards the motorway. Rush hour would be over soon and Tom wanted to get going while the traffic was moving.

They decided to eat in a cafe in Greenwich so that Sally would be close to home. Tom chose a table in the corner by the window.

'It's been a very emotional couple of weeks for Mary, and her head is buzzing. Meeting her father and her sister has been the most important thing for her, of course, although both of them have a serious alcohol dependency and live in conditions which neither you nor I could possibly imagine,' said Sally.

'God! Mary didn't mention the living conditions. I need to hear about the family first though.'

'As you know, the first person she met was her Indian grandmother, Sara Black, but she's wary of her at the moment. She was quite cold and distant towards Mary at first apparently. Her sister, Josie, was too, whereas her father bonded with her instantly. He sounded quite a sweetie, I thought. Mary says he still has an Irish accent after all these years of living in the Yukon.'

Tom was shocked. 'Heavens! She's taking on a hell of a lot of problems, by the sound of it.'

Sally gave Tom a lot more detail than Mary had done

over the 'phone, although she said nothing about Jake. She mainly talked about Annie, Uncle Albie and Mary's family.

'Her main concern at the moment is finding Bob James.

She seems to think that he and Rob Jamieson are the same person. Has she asked you to try to find him?'

'Yes, she has, and I must say I feel apprehensive about this. If she's right, then Rob has been desperate to hide his true identity, maybe even from his wife. I could be opening a can of worms here.'

'I agree Tom, but Bob James is her uncle and so Mary has to know whether Rob is the man who dumped her at the airport. Also, Sara will need to know that her son's been found.' Sally drank the last of her coffee and looked at her watch.

They could have talked like this for the rest of the day, but Sally was anxious to see her son. She rang her parents and announced her arrival, and then Tom drove her home.

'I won't intrude upon your home-coming, Sally, but I'd like to meet up with you again, if that's okay. I have to go in search of Rob and Wendy this weekend and it would be great to share any further news with you. I also have to break Mary's news to my parents. I'm not looking forward to that.'

'Thank you so much for meeting me Tom and thanks for breakfast,' said Sally as they parked outside her house. 'I realise that this isn't easy for you, so take care.' Sally kissed him on the cheek. Tom carried her luggage to the front door. 'You've got my number. Please ring me.'

'Don't worry Sally. I will. See ya.' Tom decided to head back to school for the afternoon. It might help to take his mind off things.

He didn't sleep much that night. He saw every hour from 2.00am onwards and couldn't stop thinking about all that Sally had said. He wanted so much to join Mary and to be a part of her world. He was anxious about seeing Rob and Wendy again. If Rob really was trying to hide his identity from Mary then there could be an ugly scene, and Tom didn't like confrontations. He had enough of those with his mother. He decided to make out that it was just a social call and then test the waters.

He had an early breakfast, for a Saturday morning, and set off along the A2. He had only got the morning, as he was playing rugby as usual in the afternoon; his first match in the 1st team.

He loved driving alone. It gave him time to think and to plan what he was going to say or do.

As he entered Rob's front drive Tom could see that the Land Rover was missing. Maybe he was doing some overtime at work again or maybe they were away racing somewhere. As he got out of the car, he heard the dogs, and this time Wendy came to the door.

'Hello Tom. Rob isn't here. He's at work until four o'clock this afternoon, I'm afraid.'

'I haven't seen you both for ages and so while Mary is in Canada I thought I'd call on the off-chance that you might be around. Mary and I came to see you at the end of the summer but you must have gone for a walk or something,' said Tom feeling decidedly uncomfortable talking on the doorstep.

'Do you want to come in? I've just made some tea. It's good to see you.' Wendy seemed just like her old self as she bustled about in the kitchen and chatted to Tom.

'Is Mary enjoying her time in Canada? You must miss her. When is she coming home?'

'She's staying for a while longer because she's managed to track down some members of her family. She's due to meet her twin sister soon and is very excited about that.'

239

'I expect you'd like to be there too wouldn't you?'

'Yes, of course, but I'm a full-time teacher now so my next holiday isn't until the third week of December. I really miss the freedom I had as a university student.' Tom decided to change the subject while he planned how to go about this. 'How are the dogs? Have you won any races since I last saw you?'

'Actually, the racing season has only just begun and tomorrow is our first race in Rendlesham Forest. Rob can't wait to get started again. He misses it terribly during the summer.' Wendy brought a pot of tea and a plate of biscuits over to the table. Theirs was a real farmhouse kitchen and all visitors were entertained around the scrubbed antique pine table in the middle of the room.

'Wendy, do you remember, when I had tea with you before, you said that you didn't know much about Rob's life before you met? Have you ever asked him about his background since then?'

'No not really. I asked about his family once and he said he didn't have any family. Neither of us do which is why we are good for one another. The dogs are our family now. Why?'

'Well a very strange thing has happened to Mary since I last saw you both. She received a letter from the convent to say that a man from Ireland had been to see the nuns with the story of how she arrived at the convent in 1964. She said a man named Bob James brought her from the Yukon. Through this man Mary has been able to trace her father, her grandmother and her sister, who live in a native village north of Whitehorse. She has learned that Bob James is her uncle who still lives in England with his wife Wendy, and their Siberian huskies, which they race in a nearby forest.'

Wendy looked blank. There was no sign of guilt in her face and Tom's guess was that she had not heard the name Bob James before. She raised her eyebrows and exhaled loudly.

'Phew! That's quite a coincidence. Is Mary suggesting that this man is my Rob and that Rob changed his name? Why would he do a thing like that?' Wendy looked puzzled.

'To conceal his identity, I expect. Don't get me wrong, Wendy. I'm not saying that Rob is this man. I'm simply sharing the story with you to see what you think.' Tom literally held his breath.

'People change their name because they're hiding from the police. My Rob wouldn't do anything like that. He's an honest, hard-working bloke,' said Wendy defensively. 'Are you planning to go to the race tomorrow, because if you are you could ask him yourself?'

'No,' Tom lied 'I have to spend the day with my parents tomorrow, so that I can tell them Mary's news about her family. I'm not looking forward to it. They won't like what I have to tell them I'm afraid. Anyway, I'm sorry if I upset you. I wasn't accusing Rob of anything. I just thought it was an amazing coincidence. Mary would like to find this Bob James because well ... he is her uncle.'

Tom thanked Wendy for the tea and left while the friendly atmosphere was still intact. Either Wendy was being truthful when she said she knew nothing of Rob's early life, or she was an extremely good actress. He decided to drive straight to Woodbridge and stay overnight with his parents. That way he could go to Rendlesham Forest on Sunday morning. He would miss his rugby match and would let the team down, but this stuff was more important right now. He would stop off for lunch at 'The Dog' in Grundisburgh and ring both his mother and his team manager, Ted, from there. Ted wasn't too pleased with his news but Charlotte was thrilled with hers.

'I'll have my darling boy all to myself again. How lovely!'

'Oh how absolutely ghastly!' shrieked Charlotte a few moments later. 'It's even worse than I thought it would be. David, are you listening to this? Mary is an Indian half breed and she was born on a reservation – ugh!' Charlotte screamed as Tom attempted to explain Mary's news. David said nothing, and, ignoring his wife's hysteria, he continued to read the Saturday Guardian.

'Mother you're living in the dark ages. Such racist talk! I'm ashamed of you. Mary is of mixed race. You've always known that. She's discovered that her Irish father was a miner before he retired, and her First Nations mother died in a fire when Mary was just two years old. Her father, her maternal grandmother and her twin sister all live in small village called Carmacks. She has a family for the first time in her life. You should be pleased for her.' At the mention of Carmacks, David put down his paper and listened.

'Pleased? It's all too horrid. How can you think about marrying someone with a family background like that? And where will you both live? Surely she won't expect you to live up there in the frozen North. You would hate it. The people will be wild and uncultured.'

'Oh mother, for God's sake! Sit down and stop pacing about the room. I need a drink.' Tom marched across the room to their drinks cabinet and poured himself a scotch.

David's voice took them both by surprise. 'Not necessarily Charlotte. The First Nations are very creative and spiritual people.'

Charlotte glared at him. 'Don't be silly. How would you know anything about it?'

'I've read about them and I saw an exhibition of their art in London once, before I met you.' David remained unruffled and went back to his reading. Tom decided not to mention Bob James. He felt it would only make things worse, if it could be any worse. He sat down opposite his parents.

'Mary has extended her stay in the Yukon, so that she can meet her whole family. If she's still there at the end of term I intend to join her and return with her in the New Year. After all, her family will be my family eventually. I reminded you of that the last time I was here.'

Charlotte poured herself a large G&T and slumped back into her chair. She began to cry. 'I will keep to my word. If you marry this girl, you won't get a penny from me and I certainly won't dance at your wedding. Why couldn't you have found an educated girl, someone with breeding, someone like us? Surely you could have had your pick of anyone when you were at university?'

'Maybe I'll emigrate and get a teaching post in the Yukon and then we can get married up there.' Charlotte screamed again.

Tom had had enough. His mother's prejudice was bound to drive him away from them eventually, and this was the last straw. David peered at Tom over his reading glasses and then stood up.

'It might be best if you leave this discussion for now, son. Everyone is saying things they don't mean. Leave your mother to me. Isn't there someone you can go and have a pint with? We'll see you later.'

Tom left the room with a sigh of relief. He would miss his old man if he went to live abroad.

The next morning his mother gave him the silent treatment over breakfast, which suited Tom. He didn't have anything more to say to her anyway and his father had his head in the newspaper as usual.

It was a glorious autumn morning and if it wasn't for the underlying reason for his drive out to Rendlesham Forest, Tom would be really looking forward to kicking up the leaves and breathing in the crisp clear air which he missed so much when he was in London. But then he thought about the prospect of finding Rob and his heart sank. He felt sure that Wendy would have told Rob about his visit yesterday. As he walked along the familiar track, he thought of Mary. If only she was here with him for this. He knew he was close to the racing as he could see a long line of trucks and vans stretching ahead of him either side of the track. Also, the noise from the excited dogs was deafening. He pulled the hood of his parka over his head and kept a low profile. It could be a long wait. Owners' dogs sat contentedly amongst the trees, waiting for their turn to race. He knew he wouldn't be able to recognise Rob's team, even if they lay in front of him. He walked deeper into the forest and tried to observe from a distance. It wasn't easy. One minute he thought he had spotted Rob and then the next minute he realised that it was someone else. Each time this happened his knees felt weak and his heartbeat quickened.

Someone called across to him: 'Hey, mate, are you lost? Has one of your dogs gone missing?' Tom gave a wave and shouted back that he was fine. 'Dog people' are good people. Any one of them would help him to track down Rob if he asked them, thought Tom. He was getting restless. Time was dragging and the past hour had seemed like the whole morning. He was hungry and cold from staying out of the sunshine. He saw a woman recording the results, so he approached her.

'Is Rob Jamieson's team racing today?' She checked her list.

'Yes it is, but not until two o'clock. Are you a friend

of Rob's?' She said with a smile.

'I know both Rob and his wife. They introduced me to this sport. I'll catch them later,' said Tom.

'Theirs is probably one of the last vans in the line up. If not then they should be here quite soon.'

Tom looked at his watch: 12.15pm. He decided to retrace his steps back to the parked vehicles. He crouched down behind one of the trees and watched. A blue van had just arrived and was parking some distance from the others. As the driver jumped out, he could see that it was Rob. He realised that he had to move fast before they got the dogs out of the back of the van. He didn't want to be mauled to death in the event of any heated discussion. Tom stood up and ran towards them. Rob saw him and instantly ran off into the trees. Wendy had obviously forewarned him. Tom was a fast runner, thanks to the rugby. He sprinted hard, keeping Rob in sight. He caught up with him easily and rugby tackled him to the ground.

'What's the problem, buddy, you got a guilty conscience?' asked Tom as he held on to him. 'Why have you been avoiding us? Is it because you're not who you say you are? Does your wife know who you are? You've got some explaining to do.'

'Well get off me, you fucking idiot, and I'll tell you.' The two men stood up and faced one another. Tom noticed that Rob's forehead was bleeding. He must have hit something hard when he fell.

'I could charge you with assault,' said Rob, wiping the blood from his face.

'But you won't.' Tom said. 'What you did to Mary all those years ago is far worse than any minor assault. Is that why you changed your name, so Mary couldn't trace you? What a bastard! She was two years old and her mother had just died. What have you got to say for yourself?'

Rob looked pale and sat down on a nearby log. He put his head in his hands and said nothing for a moment. All the fight had gone out of him and he seemed to be near to tears.

'I know. No-one hates me more than I do, for what I did to her. It was Sara, my mother. She said that if I didn't take her to England with me, Mary would go into care. She said she couldn't look after both of the girls because they were twins and Granny Edith insisted that it would bring bad luck and poor health for the family if she did. What could I do?'

'Who's Granny Edith? I haven't heard about her,' asked Tom.

'My grandmother, one of the old timers, who must have died by now,' said Rob, trying to stand up. 'Hey, I've gotta get the dogs ready. We race soon. Wendy can't manage them without me.'

'You're not going anywhere. I need the whole story. Mary needs to know all of this.' Tom pushed him back down on the log. 'What about her father? Did anyone ask him what he wanted?'

'He was a drunk and spent all his time in the bars. The welfare would have taken her from him.'

'But Mary ended up in care anyway, in a foreign country, with no hope of going home.'

'I didn't know that. The guy on the plane talked about his family in Ireland. They sounded a real nice family. I thought he was going to take Mary with him and give her a new life. I needed to find my father. I hadn't seen him for five years, since he ran off with a fortune. Sara said I'd find him over here.' Rob wiped his forehead which had started to bleed again. The fight had left him. He looked a sorry sight.

'Did you find him?' asked Tom.

'No. It's impossible. The name James is all over this

country and Wales too. Some years later I even went to Ireland and tried to find the guy, John Doyle, in the hope of finding Mary, but it was the same problem, there are thousands of Doyles in Ireland.'

Tom nodded. 'Don't I know it? How did you find out about Mary's childhood?'

'Mary had confided in Wendy. She told her she'd been put in a convent, in the 1960s, when she was two years old. Then I guessed who she was. There was always something about the girl that seemed familiar to me so when you said she was going to the Yukon, I panicked. I've carried this guilt for years. It's haunted me. I guess Mary hates me. What will she do now?'

'I've no idea, until I talk to her. You realise that Sara will know this story very soon, don't you? Mary will almost certainly give her your contact details. She's your mother, for God's sake, and she's not well at the moment.' Tom was exhausted. A weekend in Suffolk was supposed to be relaxing.

'Does Wendy know all about this? Does she even know your real name?' Tom was angry now.

'No. She thinks that I don't have a family. I'd lived here, as Rob Jamieson, for twenty years when I met Wendy. She didn't need to know any of this. I guess she'll have to know now. She'll probably hate me too, for what I've done.' Rob put his head in his hands again and sighed deeply. 'Will you tell her?'

'Of course not! That's your job. You made your bed and now you can bloody well lie in it. Our lives are connected now, through Mary, and she'll want to see you when she comes home, but for the moment I've had enough. After all, I'm only the messenger.' Tom turned abruptly and walked, away from him, towards the visitors' car park, leaving him in a crumpled heap on the log. All these secrets: John Doyle, Bob James ... suddenly his own family seemed quite ordinary compared to Mary's. Even so, Tom couldn't face another session with his mother. He decided to call his sisters' carer and have a peaceful visit with Mandy before heading back to London. Mandy always cheered him up.

Chapter 24
Whitehorse 1989

Mary sat in Annie's kitchen, sharing her breakfast with Honey who sat next to her, eagerly awaiting the next morsel of food. Annie was in school and Jake was in Carcross, so she was relishing the chance to think, in solitude, about the events of the past week. She had called her headteacher after Sally left for Vancouver to see what he wanted her to do. She didn't really want to fly home for a month and then have to come back again. He had been great about the whole thing. He had accepted Mary's verbal resignation over the phone and even gave her the option of re-applying should she return to England. Mary was so relieved. She wondered how Tom had got on. She hadn't spoken to him all week, although he did leave a message to say that he would meet Sally as promised. The phone rang and made her jump. Annie had told her to answer the phone and take a message any time. It was Tom.

'Hello love,' said Mary. 'I was just thinking about you. I'm off into town to see Josie in a minute. How did you get on?'

'Hello darling. It's been a busy week. I took a sick day to meet Sally this morning. She arrived on time and we had breakfast together so she could tell me all your news. She said that your father sounds a really nice chap and that your sister looks a lot like you. She loved the Yukon.'

'Tom, I'll talk about that with you in a minute. I'm dying to know. Did you manage to find Rob?'

Tom told her the whole story. He gave her a dramatic version of their chase in Rendlesham Forest. Mary was very impressed, especially with the rugby tackle.

'Well done love. You were so brave. I'm proud of you. So he is my uncle? Rob really is Bob James, the swine who abandoned me all those years ago. Still, at least he did try to find me ... once. I can't believe he wanted you to tell his wife. I wonder what Grandma Sara will say. I reckon she'll be angry and embarrassed. She's already beginning to feel guilty every time she sees me. Tom, have you been to see your parents? Was your mother horrified when she heard my news?'

'Well I didn't expect her to be thrilled. She was more upset about the possibility of me going to live in Canada than anything. Dad took me by surprise though and was really supportive of the First Nations culture. He even used the term First Nations and not Red Indians as my mother had done.'

'It does seem strange, but maybe he just hates your mother's prejudice. Tom, I must go. I promised Josie that I would spend some time with her today. She thinks I'm posh. She was quite wary of me last time and she kept her distance from me. I haven't had a chance yet to say anything about my life to her - not in any detail anyway.

'Do you think you'll stay up there until Christmas now? Maybe I'll fly out and join you in the school holidays. Would you like that?'

'Oh Tom, I just don't know at the moment. It's too early to say. We'll discuss it another time. Must go. Take care love. 'Bye.'

Mary took the bus into town. She was getting to know her way around Whitehorse quite well now and was thinking that she could easily drive in these half empty streets. She took a box of chocolates, from home, with her which she had bought for Annie not realising that she was a diabetic. If Josie is anything like me, she'll love these thought Mary.

As she entered the Crossroads lobby, there was a little drama unfolding in the office. The secretary had been hit by one of the residents and had banged her head on a cupboard as she fell. Two male members of staff were insisting that she go to hospital in case she had concussion. The door was open so Mary introduced herself.

'Hi. My name is Mary Quinn. Is it okay if I visit my sister, Josie?' She spoke to all three of them.

Everything went quiet and they stared at Mary in disbelief. She had not seen any of them during her last visit and by the looks of it, no-one had told them about her either. One of the men finally spoke up and stepped forward to take a closer look at her.

'Bloody Hell! I thought I was hallucinating,' he said, smiling at Mary. He closed the office door behind him and sat down with her in the lobby.

'I didn't know Josie had a sister. Is that an English accent I hear?'

Mary explained that she was here from London to try to find her long lost family.

'Don took me to meet Josie last time I visited. Is he on duty today?' Mary asked.

'No. It's his day off. My name is Brian and I'm working with Josie today.' His voice softened. 'I'm afraid she's had a bad night. She's only just been given her medication. Have you any experience of anyone in a detox unit or of anyone who has a drink/drug problem?' He studied Mary's neat, groomed, appearance. Her reply surprised him.

'Yes. When I was younger and homeless for a while in London,' said Mary in a matter of fact voice. She disliked people who judged others by their appearance. 'Poor Josie. She must feel terrible. Can I see her? Maybe I could try to comfort her.'

'As you no doubt heard, it was Josie who just hit our secretary and knocked her over, so you must be careful. Do you mind if I come with you?' His manner was ingratiating.

They went downstairs together and Brian knocked on Josie's door. Mary could hear someone singing. It sounded plaintiff but beautiful.

'That's Josie,' said Brian. 'She sings when she's unhappy. She has a lovely voice.'

'What song is she singing? I love it,' said Mary.

'One of her protest songs I expect. She writes most of them herself. Not this one though. I've heard it before.'

He opened her door slowly and let Mary go in first. Josie sat curled up in the far corner of her room, on the floor, and was rocking back and forth to the rhythm of her song.

>"No more silence. No more silence.
>We will shout it out. No more silence."

Josie looked up and could see that Mary's eyes had filled with tears. 'I don't need you or anyone to feel sorry for me. Get out and leave me alone! Josie shouted at her.

'I'm moved by your powerful song and by your incredible voice,' said Mary. 'Beautiful music always makes me cry.'

Josie stopped rocking and stared at Mary. Brian stepped back and left the room, leaving the door slightly ajar. Mary's heart lurched at the sight of her sister's suffering. Josie looked so ill. Her hair was a tangled damp mass and she had big dark circles under her eyes. She was wearing a short sleeved teeshirt and for the first time Mary noticed that her arms were each lined with thin scars from the wrist to the elbow. Mary had seen this many times before when she was homeless and she knew that these were due to self-harming. She threw her bag to one side and sat down next to Josie on the cold lino floor.

'I love to sing too and when I was in the children's home I sang when I was unhappy, which was most of the time. It always helped,' she said.

'Where were you in a children's home?' Josie asked after a moment of silence.

'In England. It was a Catholic convent. I was there from the age of two to sixteen. Then I escaped and ran away to London. That convent was a horrid place. I hated it. The nuns were cruel and the priests were perves.' Mary said, not looking at Josie and using a word she hadn't used for a long time.

'I ran away when I was sixteen too,' said Josie. 'I went to Vancouver with this English guy I'd met, but he dumped me after a week. Where did you live, in London?'

'I lived on the streets for over a year. Then the Salvation Army took me in and helped me find a job. I lied about my age and said I was almost eighteen.'

'Did you do drugs or go on the game?' Josie asked.

'No, just 'grass', but I drank a lot. It always made me sick though especially the cider. Yes, I slept around a bit to get money for food and booze.' Mary hadn't talked about any of this for years, and she had never ever told Tom about those early years in London. She needed to talk about it now though, with her sister.

'The 'Sally-Ann' found me too. Someone out of uniform – a really neat guy – saw the sign I was holding and helped me get back to Whitehorse. I'd been away for three years. I lived on the street and in crack houses. I'm an addict and an alchie. You don't want to know me. Look at you ...'

Josie began to shake violently, crying with pain. Mary was distraught.

'What can I do?' Mary wanted to hold her.

'Hold me 'til I stop shaking. My medication hasn't kicked in yet.' She yelled out once more. Mary held her and Josie clung to her. It was as if the two of them had fused into one, just as they used to in Mary's nightmares.

'That's enough,' said Josie when the tremors stopped. She pushed Mary away, but Mary continued to stay on the floor beside her.

'What sign were you holding?' Mary asked, deciding to ignore Josie's withdrawal symptoms.

'What? Oh that. I lied about my age too. I was nineteen and needed to come home. I wrote: –

"I'm 16 and pregnant. Please help me."

To this day I don't know who put me on that C.P. Air flight to Whitehorse. I guess I must have been ill or drunk or both.'

'Were you really pregnant?' Mary wondered if this was when she was carrying Mikey.

'Yeah, I told you. I have a boy who is in foster care with Betty and Jim right now. I'm going to get him back one day when I can stay clean and sober. I'm off the booze at the moment anyway, thanks to those people at the A.A.' Josie stood up and went over to the bed.

'Could you get me some of that shit coffee they serve here? I need caffeine,' said Josie.' Just follow the smell of food to the dining-room. It'll be lunchtime soon.' Mary picked up her handbag.

'Don't worry, I won't nick anything, not from you

anyway,' said Josie. Mary blushed.

'I thought I might need money for the coffee,' she said, feeling ashamed for no reason.

'It's free. No-one would pay for that muck.' Josie lay down on her bed.

This reunion with her sister was going to be a lot harder than she thought. They had made a good start though and Josie had opened up a little just now. When she got back to the room some minutes later, clutching two mugs of coffee, she heard voices inside. She knocked on the door with her foot and a middle-aged native woman stood before her. She could see Josie in the background, sitting cross-legged on the bed and smoking.

'Come in Mary. I'm Grace, Josie's community support worker. It's lovely to meet you. She's just been telling me about you. How wonderful that you two have found one another after all these years. Did you think that your sister was dead too?'

'No. I didn't know anything about my family background until earlier this year,' said Mary as she handed Josie her coffee.

'I have to take Josie to the hospital for a check-up and then she has a counselling session. Could I meet you for lunch somewhere? I'd love to have a chat with you. I know the rest of Josie's family. How about Starbucks, on Main Street, in an hour's time?'

'That's fine with me.' Mary looked across at Josie. 'Josie, can I come back later for a while?'

'If you want. I might be tired though – didn't sleep much last night. What about tomorrow?'

'Okay. I'll come in the morning again.' She gave Josie a hug and Josie gave her a tired smile.

Mary bought a hot chocolate and waited at a table by the window, in Starbucks, so that she could let Grace know she was there. It was really busy. She was lucky to find two empty seats.

'Sorry to keep you waiting Mary,' said Grace as she bustled in with a large file tucked under her arm. 'The visit to the hospital took longer than I thought. Would you like some soup or a sandwich or anything? I'm going to have both.'

'Thank you, that sounds good,' said Mary handing her a $20 bill.

'No, you keep your money. I'll take it out of expenses.' She laughed at Mary's worried expression.

As Grace brought the food over to their table, Mary realised she was hungry.

'Now tell me all about yourself. This is very exciting for Josie, to have found the twin sister she thought had died years ago. It's exciting for both of you of course. There's no mistaking who you are. You look very alike and I've noticed a few similar mannerisms already too.'

Mary laughed. 'It's amazing. Our early lives have been quite similar, so we have a lot in common. I've been lucky in that I've met one or two strong, dependable people who have supported me and cared for me, such as my boyfriend, Tom, my best friend Sally and my counsellor, Karen. I wouldn't be here talking to you today if it wasn't for them. I think Josie's had a much tougher time than I have. She looks so poorly.' Mary had been shocked to see the state her sister was in earlier. 'How can I help her?' She asked Grace.

That's a very difficult question to answer.' Grace sat quietly for a moment, trying to collect her thoughts. 'Josie has never ever known any real warmth in her life. She has been badly abused and neglected by a number of adults, especially by the staff in the hostel in Whitehorse where she lived as a child. The only two people she has any affection for are her son and her Great-Grandpa Tommy who is 94-years-old and still living in Carmacks.

It was your Great- Granny Edith, who died a few years back, who insisted that you girls be split up in the first place. She was a real old timer and kept to some of the traditional beliefs of her people. She believed that twins brought bad luck to the family. Old Tommy Black seems to love Josie and he never judges her. That's so important, don't you think?'

Mary nodded. 'Grandma Sara told me about Granny Edith and about Josie and me being separated. She said that my mother kept me. I would have loved to have known her,' said Mary.

Grace reached across the table and patted Mary's hand. For Grace, this was such a familiar story and a very sad one.

'I must warn you that Josie doesn't trust anyone. Why should she when so many people have let her down? She has some very strong views about the future of the First Nations and deep down she has a sensitive and creative spirit. You can tell that by the songs she sings.'

Grace smiled at Mary. 'So don't be put off if Josie pushes you away to begin with. The best thing you can do for her is to love her and support her in what she is trying to do, which is to get better. Her loyalty is to the First Nations half of her and I believe that her voice will be an important one once she gets well again.'

I must introduce her to Jake, thought Mary.

'She hasn't mentioned our father to me at all and yet they have lived in the same village for years.'

'You'll need to talk to her about that yourself Mary. I don't want to put words into her mouth. Have you met the whole family yet?'

'No. I haven't met Great-Grandpa Tommy or Sylvia's father, Uncle Freddie, and also I believe that the mysterious ex-husband of Sara might still be in England somewhere?'

'I don't know anything about him,' said Grace, 'long before my time. Now, I'm afraid I have to leave you as I have another meeting to go to. I'll give you my telephone number, so please call me if I can help in any way. I used to live in Carmacks, but I live here in Whitehorse with my family now.'

'Thank you and thank you for my lunch. It was good to meet you.'

'It was good to meet you too. I have a feeling that you are just what Josie needs right now, but you have to be strong.' With a smile and a wave, Grace disappeared up Main Street in search of her car.

'There is no way I can go back to England to live. My family need me here,' said Mary to Annie later that afternoon. 'If Tom still wants to be with me after all that's happened, then he'll have to live up here too.'

'Have you told Tom about the night that you and Jake spent together?' Annie asked.

'No, I haven't. It would hurt him terribly. He is talking about coming up in the Christmas holidays and that will be a time of major decisions. Annie, I love Tom, but I am in love with Jake. Can you understand that? I don't know what to do. I feel I've come home. It's tearing me apart.'

'I don't know. You're asking the wrong person. I met my George when I was sixteen and he was eighteen. He was my world. We adored one another. I never went out with anyone else. You're a grown woman with a lot of life experience behind you. Only you can make that kind of decision,' she said.

Mary realised that Annie still wasn't on her side over this. She sighed. Yet another potential mother-in-law who disapproves of me, thought Mary. She needed to see Jake. Where was he? He was due back in Porter Creek hours before.

Chapter 25
Carcross 1989

Jake had decided to stay back in Carcross for the weekend. The only way he could keep away from Mary was to not see her at all. He was tired of his mother's disapproving looks. Amy and Trixie were sitting either side of the stove with him in Annie's house on Bennett Avenue. There was more snow around the Southern Lakes than in Whitehorse and much of it was virgin snow. He loved it when it was like this. Everywhere looked beautiful and he could follow the tracks of the local wildlife. They sipped their coffee and ate the butter tarts that Amy had brought him.

'I don't know what to do,' Jake confided in his aunt. 'I've never felt like this before, about anyone. I love Mary and I want to be with her all the time. I'm nearly twenty-six for goodness sake. It's none of Mum's business what I do or who I choose to fall in love with.'

'Your mother is probably trying to protect you,' said Amy. 'Mary could go back to England at Christmas and marry her English boyfriend and then where would you be? Here with a broken heart.'

'Mary feels the same as me. She plans to explain all this to her boyfriend next time she sees him. She won't want to leave the Yukon now that she has found her family. She's thrilled to have met her father and her sister. Mind you, I think her father's a bit of a hopeless case.' Jake told Amy his first impressions when they visited Jack Quinn in the bush.

'Exactly, Albie told me all about it. He says it's too late. He believes that Jack could never manage to be a father to those two girls now, let alone be a grandfather to Josie's son. It might all prove to be too much for Mary.'

'I know. Her whole family have got big problems. Mind you who hasn't 'round here?' Jake said. 'I'd like Mary to live here in Carcross with me. She loves it here.'

'Then be careful. You might be hoping for the moon,' warned Amy. 'You're doing the right thing at the moment. Just lie low for a while and see what happens.'

Trixie licked Jake's hand as though she was trying to comfort him. How do dogs sense these things, Jake wondered, as he tickled Trixie's ears.

'Did you just hear a car drive up and stop outside the house?' said Jake.

'Surprise!' called Mary as she burst into the kitchen jangling her car keys. Jake and Amy stared at her, openmouthed, and glanced behind her to see who was with her. Mary laughed and enjoyed the shocked expression on their faces. 'You both look as though you've seen a ghost,' she said.

'Well – haven't we? Who's brought you here?' Amy stared some more.

'Have you just driven from Whitehorse on your own? Whose car are you driving? Surely Mom hasn't let you drive hers?' Jake didn't even know that Mary could drive.

'I've just rented it for a couple of weeks so I can visit Carmacks and Carcross whenever I like. It's great driving in the Yukon.' Mary rambled on excitedly. 'There's hardly any traffic on the roads and the highway is kept really clear. Not like at home. It's mad in London and if we had this much snow the city would be at a standstill.'

'But it's Sunday. I'm back to work tomorrow morning,' said Jake, looking disappointed.

'I know that. I thought you'd be pleased. I've come for the day. I have to see Josie again on Monday and then I'm going up to Carmacks,' said Mary glaring at Jake.

'Your big surprise has obviously back-fired. You youngsters are crazy,' laughed Amy. 'Your first day of driving in the Yukon and you choose to come all this way.'

'I'll have to get used to these long trips if I'm driving to and from Carmacks between now and Christmas,' said Mary, cheering up a little and feeling very pleased with herself.

'I'll call in on Nora and Joe and let them know you're here. Maybe we could all have supper together. Do you like pot roast?' Amy asked Mary.

'That would be lovely, wouldn't it Jake?' said Mary.

Jake grunted. He had hoped to have Mary all to himself now that she was here.

As soon as Amy had gone, Jake rushed to Mary, wrapped his arms around her and kissed her until they were both gasping for air.

'I've missed you so much, Mary,' Jake breathed in her ear. 'I think about you all the time.'

'Me too,' said Mary, kissing him some more.

'Come on. Let's go upstairs,' said Jake throwing his sweatshirt over his head and sweeping Mary off her feet. 'I need you. I need all of you.' They both laughed as Jake kicked open the door of his room.

As Mary lay secure in Jake's arms a while later, neither of them had any idea how much time had passed. The room was dark and her nose felt frozen.

'Hey you two, don't you figure on eating anything today? I assume you're up there somewhere. Everyone's expecting you across the bridge. You've got ten minutes.' Amy's voice brought them back down to earth. All the lights came on downstairs.

'Be right down,' called Jake.

Mary had a quick shower and twenty minutes later they were climbing into Albie's truck.

'Sorry Aunt Amy. It's good of you to come and get us.

We lost track of the time,' said Jake, hurriedly putting his sweatshirt back on.

'Obviously!'

Mary was relieved to notice that Amy was smiling. At least someone is on our side she thought.

It was a happy family gathering. Everyone was in good spirits. Amy and Albie's two boys were there, and also Amy's brother, Sam, who was home from Crossroads. Mary noticed that he was drinking orange juice and was impressed.

'It won't last long,' whispered Amy. 'He's always on his best behaviour when he first comes home.'

Mary brought everyone up-to-date with her news. They were thrilled for her that she had met up with her sister. Sam knew Josie, of course and clearly understood her struggle. He said he had often listened to her singing in her room.

'So, your sister sing like you Mary, and both have lovely voices. Maybe you sing together one day on the wireless,' said Nora.

'We have quite a lot in common,' said Mary.

'Who was the guy in the photo?' Grandpa Joe called across from his reclining chair.

'I don't know yet. I keep forgetting to show it to anyone. I'll definitely take it to Grandma Sara this week when I go to Carmacks. She'll probably know who it is. Anyway, thank you for a wonderful supper but I have to get back now. I promised Annie that I wouldn't be too late. She seemed quite worried about me coming down here on my own.'

'I'm not surprised,' said Jake. 'I'll follow you back just to make sure you're okay.'

Nora shook her head in disbelief. She wouldn't want to go anywhere in the dark at this time of night in November. She glanced at Amy.

'Don't look at me. Jake's a grown man. It's up to him what he does. Come on you two. I'll run you back to the house.'

Mary got up early so that she could have breakfast with Annie before Annie went off to school.

'This is nice,' said Annie. 'Are you going up to Carmacks today?'

'No. I'll go tomorrow. Today, I want to see Josie again. She was so poorly the last time I visited that I feel that she needs my support now. Also, she was starting to open up to me a little.'

'So, why the early start?'

'I wanted to ask you something. I've made the decision to stay in Whitehorse for the time being and I don't want to take advantage of your kindness. You've been wonderful and I really appreciate it. Annie I was wondering if I could be a paying guest and rent your basement suite while I'm here?'

'I've loved having you stay. I get lonely sometimes when Julie's away in Vancouver and Jake's in Carcross, especially if Jake takes Honey with him. You're welcome to stay with us and if you insist on paying then can I suggest that we eat our meals together. I hate eating alone and one more doesn't make any difference to the cost or the preparation.' She smiled.

'I'd never have done all this without you and your family. Thank you so much,' Mary gave Annie a hug. I was meant to meet this family thought Mary. It seems almost as though they were waiting for me to come.

'Annie, do you believe that we're meant to cross paths with certain people in our lives? Is it all a part of a 'life pattern' do you think?'

'Yes I do believe that. If you think about it, life is like a school. We have lessons which we must learn and we find significant people in our lives to help us with these. Some have it easier than others, of course, because they are old souls and have the spirits of their ancestors to guide them. You ought to talk to Nora about this. Anyway, talking of school, I must go. Have a good visit with Josie. Maybe you could go for a walk with her this time – get away from the Centre – if she's in a good space.'

Mary drove downtown later that morning and thought about Annie's words. It made her wonder why she and Josie had had such a difficult start in life. They obviously both had a lot to learn according to Annie's philosophy.

When she entered Crossroads it seemed unusually quiet. Even the office was empty. The smell of food wafted up the stairs so something was happening. She decided to make her own way to Josie's room. She knocked but there was no reply. She tried the door, but it was locked. She suddenly felt cold. Where was she? What if there had been an accident? What if Josie had been taken to the hospital? Something was very wrong. She made her way to the dining room and the secretary, whom Josie had hit last Friday, was there talking to one of the female staff and showing them her bruised face.

'Hello. Do you remember me? I'm Josie Quinn's sister. Do you know where she is? Is she okay?' Mary was dreading that it was going to be bad news.

'Yes she's had quite a good weekend compared to some. Grace, her support worker called for her and has taken her to see her son in Porter Creek. Apparently he's not very well.' The secretary's mind seemed to be elsewhere as she was recounting this piece of news.

This was a good opportunity to see her nephew with everyone together. 'Could you call Mikey's foster mother please to see if I could visit them? I have a car now so I could drive up there.'

'I can give them a call. It mainly depends upon whether Josie can cope with you being there. She gets very anxious about her son.' They walked back to the office together. Mary watched the secretary as she dialled Betty's number. It looked as though Betty was fine about it and the 'phone was being handed to Josie.

'They are not due to be there for too much longer but Josie says she would like Mikey to meet you. She has told him about you apparently. I'll give you their address,' she said in an official tone of voice. She clearly didn't get involved in the personal lives of the residents.

Mary studied her map of Porter Creek and was surprised to notice that Mikey lived just three blocks from Annie. She took this as another sign that all of this was meant to happen.

'Hi Mary. Come on in. Mikey had the chance to see his mom this morning, so I've kept him off school. She's been too ill to see him for a while now and he misses her. I'll send him back this afternoon though,' she added as though she expected Mary to disapprove.

As they entered the living-room, Josie looked up and smiled, but Mikey was pretending to be engrossed in the transformer toy he was playing with. He and Josie were sitting together on the floor. Josie looked relaxed. Mikey was small for a nine year old. Mary had thought he was much younger when she had seen him in Tim Hortons that day in the summer.

'Mary, would you like some coffee?' Betty asked. Mary noticed the empty coffee cups and remembered they were leaving soon.

'No thanks. I'm fine.' Mary sat down next to Josie and waited for Mikey to notice her. He looked up and studied them sitting side by side. His big brown eyes opened wide and he stared at Mary.

'You look like my mom,' he said pointing at Mary.

'Mikey, this is your Auntie Mary. She's my sister. She's come all the way from England, in an aeroplane, to meet us,' said Josie, putting her arm around Mikey's shoulders.

'What's England?' Mikey asked.

'It's a country a lot smaller than Canada,' replied Mary.

'It's a very long way away from here.'

Mikey continued to stare. He was indeed a handsome child. His skin was darker than theirs, but he had their same black hair and long eye-lashes.

'I want you to play with me,' he said to Mary eventually.

The three of them played contentedly together for a few minutes whilst Betty and Grace chatted quietly in the kitchen, then Betty returned and reminded Mikey that it was lunchtime. Everyone got up to go.

When they got to the cars Grace excused herself and said she had a meeting to go to. She said she was already twenty minutes late so she left them with a wave and a 'See you soon.'

'Is this yours?' Josie asked as she sat in the passenger seat of Mary's rented Subaru.

'No I've just rented it for a couple of weeks, so I can travel about without relying on anyone to drive me. I've just thought, do you have to get back to the centre or shall I make us some lunch at Annie's, where I'm staying. She only lives three blocks away. Annie's at work but she won't mind. The only thing is, you can't smoke in her house,' Mary said, noticing Josie light up. 'You'll have to go out in the yard.'

'I haven't got long. I have to get back for my medication, but that would be okay.' Josie agreed.

As they ate their lunch Mary told Josie that she was planning to go up to Carmacks the next day to see Jack, Sara and Grandpa Tommy.

'I might even stay overnight there if Grandma Sara lets me sleep on her sofa. When was the last time that you saw our father?' Josie turned her head away.

'Before Mikey was born, before I ran away to Vancouver.'

'Gosh. That's twelve years ago,' said Mary. 'Have you seen Grandpa Tommy since then?'

'Yeah. He's a good guy. He accepts me as I am. I lived with him and Granny when Mikey was born. Jack and Sara don't like me. They never have. It became really hard after Granny died.'

'I'm not sure how Sara feels about me either. She was quite cold towards me when we first met. I kept telling myself it was because she wasn't well. She'd just been to Vancouver for an operation.'

'She's hard. She's had a tough life, I guess. Like we all have. When I'm well I want to get a job where I can do something to help the First Nations. We've had a shit time for generations and we want our lives back. I've heard the Elders talk. It's not enough just to give us money or land. It's our self-respect that's been taken away and the booze is killing everyone. Grandpa Tommy still speaks our native language. He's about the only Indian in the village who does. He tried to teach me when I was a kid.' Josies' eyes sparkled with surprising passion.

'You must meet Annie's son Jake. He's a couple of years younger than us. His father and grandmother are Tlingit – from Carcross and Tagish. He's part First Nation too and he is very proud of his First Nations roots. He speaks very much as you do. He says it's up to the young now to make the changes.'

As soon as Josie had finished her lunch she became anxious about getting back to the centre, so Mary drove her downtown.

They hugged one another outside the office and said their goodbyes.

Just as Josie was about to head downstairs she turned to Mary and asked –

'By the way, did Uncle Bob ever find Grandpa Davey in England do you know?'

'No. He's given up the search. Josie, I keep forgetting to ask you - when is our birthday?'

'May 28th. See ya.' Josie disappeared down the stairs.
So I am a Gemini, not a Libran, thought Mary and my grandfather's name is David James.

'Oh my God!' She said out loud as she got into the car.

Chapter 26

Mary hardly slept that night; there was so much to think about. She tossed and turned and kept waking up feeling anxious about the secrets surrounding the names. It was spooky. So many secrets ... She got out of bed and searched for her photo of the piano player. She couldn't see enough of the man to know whether she recognised him or not. It was an old photograph and she could only see the back of him.

Her mind was racing. She debated whether to go downstairs and call Tom. She glanced at the clock. It was midnight, so Tom might have left for school already at 8.00am in London. She decided against the idea; no point in upsetting Tom at the start of his school day when nothing had been confirmed yet. She would show the photo to Jack and to Sara tomorrow. Surely one of them would know who it was? Sara had probably given the photo to Bob in the first place.

The next morning Mary slept later than usual. She had finally fallen asleep when everyone else was just getting up to go to work. Annie had gone off to school a couple of hours before. Mary was awoken by the sound of the telephone in Annie's bedroom. It was Jack, calling from the Carmacks Hotel.

'Is that you Mary? It's Jack. I was wondering when you were coming up here again. It seems so long since your visit that I'm beginning to wonder if I dreamt it.' Jack sounded quite sober and it was ten o'clock in the morning. Mary was really pleased.

'Hello Jack – oops, sorry Dad. I can't get used to using that word after all of these years.'

'Me neither. It's good though,' said Jack.

'You sound great. What are you doing in the hotel at this time in the morning? Are you alright?'

'I was on a bit of a bender yesterday and they let me sleep here last night. I've had lots of coffee. I feel good. When are you coming up again?'

'You must have read my mind. I'm leaving here very soon and will probably be with you around mid-day. I've rented a car so I'll be on my own this time. Make sure the cabin is warm won't you?'

'That's good news. I thought you'd forgotten about me, like your sister has done. Drive carefully now and don't give anyone a ride – any strangers that is.' The line went dead. Mary assumed he'd run out of money for the pay phone.

She left a note for Annie explaining her plans and packed an overnight bag just in case she stayed with Sara. She drove into town first to get some gas and also to stock up with some groceries for Jack. She was enjoying her newly-found independence, although it was proving to be expensive. She might have to find some work if she stayed in the Yukon until Tom's visit, whenever that was likely to be. Her savings were beginning to disappear fast. Some back pay from school had just gone into the bank so that would help a little, but she was paying for her car, for gas and for her accommodation now. Maybe she could find a job as a teaching assistant? She would ask Annie.

Mary remembered the route to Jack's place and kept an eye open for his blue chevy. The first thing she noticed was that he had cleared some of the land around the cabin and had built a sort of lean-to on one side. He had filled this with freshly chopped firewood, almost enough for the winter. The place looked more cared for. She parked the car and knocked on the door.

'Come in,' called Jack.

Mary stood in the open doorway and gazed at the scene in front of her. Jack had cleaned up the cabin too. He sat at the table, drinking coffee and reading a newspaper. The place smelt of wood smoke and fresh coffee instead of beer and fish, and it was warm. She put the box of groceries on the table and gave Jack a hug.

'This place looks great Dad. You've been working hard. I wish Jake and Uncle Albie could see this. They'd be really impressed. You've got four chairs now and four mugs too,' she laughed as she spotted three matching coffee mugs hanging from one of the shelves. 'So you're ready for visitors.'

'I wondered if you might bring Josie along with you. Where is she, do you know?'

'She's in Crossroads in town. Where's that coffee? I've got lots to tell you.'

As they sat at the table together, drinking coffee, Mary thought this would be a good opportunity to produce the photograph. She reminded Jack of the day she was taken to the convent in 1964 and also of the parcel that Sister Joseph had given her many years later.

'This is all I had to help me, when I began my search, as well as my name, of course, which I thought was Mary Doyle. I wondered if the photograph might be of a member of my family. Dad, do you know this man?' Mary handed over her battered old photo of the piano player.

Jack studied it for a few minutes.

'That bar looks very like 'The Downtown' in Dawson City, but I don't recognise the guy. Maybe I would if I could see his face, although I did most of my drinking in the Westminster. Do you know when it was taken?' Jack asked, handing the photo back to her.

'No. I've no idea. I don't know anything about the photo except that it was in a white envelope with my name written on the outside. Actually, the two names, Mary and Doyle, are written in two different styles of handwriting which puzzled me in the beginning. I know the answer to that now.'

'What does it mean?' Jack stared at the envelope. 'Bob James gave me away at the airport to an Irish man named John Doyle, in exchange for cash, and this man added his surname to my name on the envelope before handing me over to Sister Joseph at the convent. Mind you, I don't know why he did that unless Bob told him to. I know now that Bob James is Sara's son and my uncle, but I don't ever want to see him again,' said Mary angrily. 'He destroyed my childhood and deprived me of a family.' Mary wiped the tears from her face. Jack held her hand. His eyes had misted over too.

'You wait 'til I see him,' said Jack, 'he'll wish he'd never been born.'

'I don't think he'll ever return to the Yukon now. He won't dare to show his face. I don't know how I'm going to say this to Grandma Sara. She's thrilled to be in touch with him after all these years.' Mary told Jack about Tom tracking Bob down in Rendlesham Forest in England, and about Bob's new name so that he couldn't be traced. Jack laughed when Mary described the rugby tackle.

'Good for Tom. He must love you a lot to do that for you,' said Jack with a twinkle in his eye.

'So, would you like to hear something about Josie?' Mary carefully avoided any further talk about Tom for now. 'How about a top up for my coffee first though?'

Jack got up and went over to the stove for the coffee

pot. He produced a packet of jam doughnuts from a plastic bag on the floor and handed them to Mary. 'Here, I guessed you might be hungry,' he said.

'Oh thanks.' Mary smiled at him. 'It looks as though you've thought of everything. You know, it broke my heart when I heard Josie's story. You were right when you said she's had a tough time. She looks so ill and is so mistrustful of everyone. I asked her to come with me today but she seems to think that you've never liked her, Dad. I'm sure that's not true.'

'No. That's not right at all. I loved her, but because of my drinking Sara wouldn't ever let me see her or spend time with her. Josie got it into her head that I didn't want her and so she turned against me. Sara was hard on her. I heard stories from the village folk. She couldn't handle her during the teenage years. I guess that's why she ran away to Vancouver with that English tourist. I haven't seen her since then. Is she getting some good help in Whitehorse? Some people go in and out of that Centre for years; mostly for a bed and some food they say. What are they doing for her?'

'She's determined to get better so that she can have her son, Mikey, back. She's off the alcohol, at least she says she is, thanks to the A.A. meetings that her support worker has been taking her to for over a year now. She has counselling with someone at the Centre, and is on medication for her drug addiction. She still smokes dope though. She's smoked since she was a child, I think. It's really sad,' said Mary. 'I'm going to see a lot of her while I'm here and I'll try to help her if I can ... and you Dad as well. Have you ever tried those A.A. meetings?'

'No. I had no way of getting to Whitehorse. I don't drink as much as I used to. I just go on benders, especially in the winter. Christ - all this talk of booze. I need a beer,' said Jack suddenly. 'Come on, let's go to the hotel. I'll buy you a drink.'

'Only if you promise to eat as well,' said Mary. 'Will you come with me to meet Grandpa Tommy after we've eaten? I also want to see Sara of course.'

'No. You have to do those two visits on your own. Neither of them have any time for me; too much has happened over the years. Sara can take you up there. She visits Tommy a couple of times a week.'

Once in the hotel bar, Jack had drunk two beers before the food arrived. Mary guessed that he would drink several more after she left him.

'Dad, I could take you to the A.A. every week, if you were willing to go. I don't want to lose you to the drink when I've only just found you. I'm sure I could stay with Grandma Sara overnight.'

'We'll see,' said Jack. 'You've got to get yourself sorted out first. It must be costing you plenty to pay for all these trips as it is.'

Once they finished their steak and French fries, Jack walked out to the car with Mary.

'Do you want a lift back to the cabin, Dad?' Mary said as she hugged him.

Jack shook his head and gave her a guilty smile. 'No thanks - just one more for the road.'

There was no sign of Sylvia's truck as she drove into Sara's yard. She realised that she should have called Sara before she left Whitehorse as she might not be there either. As she got out of the car she could see that a light was on in the kitchen and Sara was sitting by the window staring straight at her. Mary waved. She opened the door slowly and called out to her.

'Hi Grandma. It's me, Mary.'

'Come,' said Sara. 'I've just made tea.' Sara was

standing by the kettle.

'You look really well Grandma. Have you fully recovered now?' Mary hugged her.

'Almost. The doctor say I mustn't chop wood yet or lift heavy things.' She smiled.

As Mary sat down opposite her grandmother with a mug in her hand it felt as though she was in the midst of an 'action replay', especially when she took the photograph out of her bag.

'Grandma, I've just shown this old photograph to Jack, but he didn't know the man in the picture. He thought it looked like the Downtown Bar in Dawson, but then everyone has said that. I meant to show it to you last time I was here, but I forgot. Do you know who this is?' Mary handed over the photo. She watched Sara's face. Her expression had changed and her mouth was in a tight, straight line.

'This is your grandfather – Davey James,' she said between clenched teeth. 'It is the Downtown Bar. Davey work there every night. He play the piano and sing. Jack never met him. Davey left Yukon before Jack take up with Jeannie. Who gave you this?'

The colour drained from Mary's face and her heart was pounding.

'Are you ill?' Sara looked concerned. 'What d'ya know about this picture? Did you see Davey?'

'I had this in my coat pocket when I arrived at the children's home in 1964. Grandma, do you have any other photos of this man? I need to see his face,' said Mary. She was silently praying that her fears were unfounded.

'I might have one someplace ... an old one. Haven't seen him for thirty years.' Sara got up and walked into her bedroom. She came out carrying a small wooden box and put it on the table in front of Mary. She turned it upside down and a small pile of old photographs scattered everywhere. She handed two of them to Mary.

'This is you and Josie when you were first born. That's my mother with you. Here's one of Jeannie. She was fifteen or sixteen. She was beautiful, with hair black like raven – like you.' She smiled at Mary.

The tears were streaming down Mary's flushed face. She couldn't believe it, a photograph of her mother at long last, and she looked just like her. She stared at it as though she was willing the image of her mother to come alive.

'Do you have any more of my mum? I've longed for this all of my life. I now know what she looked like. She looks lovely. I'd like to get a copy of this one,' she said clutching the photograph firmly as though she didn't want to let it go.

'That's the last picture. She met Jack then. Here's one of Davey near our house in Dawson and that's Bobbie when he was six. It's years ago. I didn't see this box for long time.' Sara handed Mary the photo.

There was no doubt; my worst fears have been confirmed, thought Mary. Something snapped inside her and she sobbed and sobbed. She had tried to stay strong through all of the shocks and disappointments, but this was heartbreaking for both herself and for dear Tom. Sara placed a box of Kleenex and a glass of water in front of Mary. She looked concerned but clearly didn't know what else to do to help her.

'I don't understand. Why tears? You don't even know him,' said Sara nodding towards the photo in front of Mary.

'Oh yes I do,' said Mary and then burst into tears again. Sara said nothing. She just waited until the storm had subsided. Finally, Mary dried her eyes and told her grandmother about Tom's parents in Suffolk. It was

Sara's turn to look shocked and upset.

'What year was your Tom born?' was Sara's first question.

'He was twenty-nine in September, so it would be 1960.Why?'

'Davey left Yukon in 1959. So he married the rich woman soon when he got to England. He stole money from hotel in Dawson. That explain why he can live in big house now, I reckon. The dirty thief! My mother told me 'never trust white folks. What's he like? He must be old man now. He was same age like me. We must tell R.C.M.P. about this, soon. '

'His wife, Charlotte, is the main land-owner. The estate, where they live, has belonged to her family for generations. Tom told me that his father has made a lot of changes to the big house though. Her family name is Selby so their married name is Selby-James. They have a daughter too. Amanda has cerebral palsy and is four years younger than Tom.'

Sara stared into space and seemed to be trying to make sense of Mary's story. She frowned and suddenly banged her hand down hard on the edge of the table.

'What a bastard! He wouldn't marry me. I wasn't rich like this woman. All those years he forget me and his children, and marry white woman with money.'

'Actually, I quite like Tom's father. He's quiet and easygoing. He lets his bossy wife make all the decisions. Surely he must have recognised me as I look so much like my mother. It must have been obvious, especially when he heard that I was from the Yukon.'

'He'd be too scared. He'd have to tell you whole story.'

'He never ever gave a sign that he knew, except he does seem to like me, whereas Charlotte hates me and doesn't want me to marry Tom. Well, I won't be able to now, will I? All this time that we've been together I've been living in sin with my step-uncle.' Mary began to cry again. 'What will Tom say?' She was heart-broken.

Sara simply did not know what to say to comfort Mary. A moment of silence fell between them.

'How much time d'ya have?' Sara said at last. 'This might be good time for you to meet Tommy Black. my father, to clear your mind. Josie loves him. Jeannie did too. Come with me. I'll drive you there. He lives outside the community, in big house.'

'That's a good idea Grandma. Thank you. Could I please stay here tonight? Maybe I could sleep on your sofa? Then I'll have plenty of time to visit Grandpa Tommy.'

'You can sleep in Josie's room.' Sara actually seemed pleased.

'Does Josie stay with you when she comes out of Crossroads?' Mary asked.

'No. She like to stay with Tommy. He and Edith, look after her when Mikey was born. My father is patient, not like me.' Mary was thinking that her grandmother had poor relationships with almost everyone in the family. She wondered how she'd be with Grandpa Tommy.

Mary offered to drive, as Sara was still convalescing. Sara looked very small and fragile as she sat in the passenger seat next to Mary. In the house she had seemed much bigger and stronger. Mary realised that it was her strong character and stern ways which made others feel smaller. Sara directed her around this corner and that corner and up this lane and along that track so that Mary had no idea where they were going. Grandpa Tommy lived on the edge of the village in a quiet plot away from everybody.

'He likes it that way,' said Sara. 'He used to have

many dogs and needed space. He was champion musher long ago and won the big races. He's good trapper too. When we were kids and heard dogs' bells in the winter, we knew lots of food was coming to us. You must hear his stories of long ago times.' Sara spoke with such pride that Mary was quite surprised. At last, someone Sara obviously loved and was proud of.

'Josie told me that he doesn't speak much English. Do you speak the Tutchone language with him? Will he understand me?' Mary longed to talk to him.

'I know what it means, but don't speak it. When we were kids in Mission school the white teachers tell us 'Don't speak Indian'. If we did, we got the strap. Only old timers who speak Tutchone. Listen good to Tommy when he speak English words. He mumbles. Soon, you get used to it,' she said.

Mary was quite surprised when she saw his house. It looked fairly modern and was made of wood and brick. Next to it was a large, derelict, wooden cabin which was leaning badly. It was a big plot and Mary was concerned that it appeared to be quite isolated. She said this to Sara as they parked the car.

'He's used to it. I come and see him all the time. That shack next to his house was our family home. There were six then; my parents, three kids and my grandmother. It began to fall down so my brother Freddie and his friends built him new house. Tommy wouldn't move for long time but he's proud of his new home now.' Some dogs began to bark, when they heard the car.

Mary drew back behind Sara. She liked dogs but she was used to Honey and Trixie who were gentle old dogs; these sounded young and energetic.

'Will they jump up?' she asked warily.

'Don't worry. It's only two Siberian huskies. They're tied up and live outside. You'll be fine.' Sara opened the front door and announced their arrival.

Tommy was sitting in his rocking chair by the stove. He seemed to be busy with his hands but Mary couldn't see what he was doing. He didn't look up but greeted Sara with a wave of his hand.

'Look at the mess you make,' accused Sara. 'Wood shavings everywhere.'

Tommy grunted. He was carving a small figure from a lump of wood, his gnarled, weathered hands working with surprising dexterity. He mumbled something in his own language.

Sara replied: 'And I suppose you want me to do the clearing up as usual? Pa, I've brought someone to see you. Put that thing down for a minute. You'll need to listen to this.' Tommy looked up and saw Mary for the first time. His rheumy old eyes opened wide and he stared at her.

'This here is Josie's sister, Mary, from England. Bobbie told us she died in accident. She didn't, he lied. Mary has come to find us. Sara pulled Mary forward as though she was a young child. Mary lifted a chair over to the stove and sat next to her great-grandfather. She smiled at him and took his bony hand in hers. He looked confused and said something which Mary couldn't understand. She looked at Sara for an interpretation.

'He said why didn't you come before now?'

'Hello Grandpa. It's a long story which I'll tell you another time,' said Mary, speaking slowly to him. 'Bob left me when I was two years old and I've just discovered that my family are here in the Yukon. So far I've met my father, Jack, and my sister Josie. I've also met Sylvia and Grandma, of course, and now you. It's very exciting.'

'Albie Luke brought her here. Remember Albie? Mary met George Hughes wife, Annie and lives with her in town.' Sara called from the kitchen where she was busy making some tea.

'Your carving looks beautiful. May I have a closer look?' Mary asked. She studied her great-grandfather's face. It was a face full of character and was deeply lined, displaying the marks of a hard life in the bush for ninety-four years. She longed to hear his stories. Tommy handed her his carved figure. It was of a wolf with a small creature in its mouth like a rabbit or a ferret. Mary wasn't sure what it was. It had been lovingly crafted, right down to the last detail.

'I love it,' enthused Mary. 'I'd love to be able to do something like this, but I'm not very artistic. Will you show me one day?' Tommy was smiling at her enthusiasm.

'Keep it. I make more. Polish it good,' he said. He picked up an old cloth and showed her how. 'This is muskrat,' he added pointing to the unfortunate creature in the wolf's mouth.

They drank their tea and ate the biscuits which Sara had made.

'These are only cookies he can eat. Not many teeth left now.' laughed Sara.

It was very peaceful sitting by the stove in Tommy's neat and tidy living-room which Sylvia kept clean for him. Mary could see why Josie liked to stay there when she was in Carmacks. It felt like a proper home. Karen would tell her that it is the people that make a house a home and how true that was in this case. Grandpa Tommy didn't say much but somehow Mary just knew that he would take good care of her.

'Where's my Josie? I miss her,' Tommy said suddenly.

I'll bring her with me next time I come. She's still having treatment in Whitehorse just now.'

Tommy grunted. 'I'm getting old. My heart is heavy.

She must come soon.'

After a while, Sara and Mary said their goodbyes.

'I made a stew. Don't forget to eat it,' Sara said to him. 'It's on top of the stove.' She turned away from him and headed towards the door. Tommy continued to gaze at his young visitor and he kissed her hand. Mary smiled and held both of his hands in hers.

'It's been great to meet you at last Grandpa. Next time I come I'll bring Josie with me,' she said.

'Come soon,' he sighed. 'Not many winters left now.'

'We will ... I promise.'

That evening, Mary asked Sara if she could telephone Tom using her international phone card. She felt that she had to let him know this awful news about his father. She was almost afraid to tell him. She just knew how desperately upset he would be. For him, it would be the end of their future life together.

It was past midnight and Sara had gone to bed, so it was quiet. She rang Sally first and left her a message to say that she was about to give Tom some awful news. She asked Sally if she would keep an eye on him for her. Mary said simply that Tom's father is her own grandfather, that she and Tom are now related and that she is devastated. 'I know ... it's horrid!' she said when she heard Sally gasp. 'I can't say anymore right now. I need my phone card for Tom. I'll call soon. 'Bye.' She put the phone down.

Mary just hoped that Tom would be still at home. She dialled their home number. Her hand was shaking.

'Hello darling? You're up late tonight. How are you?' His warm, comforting voice brought no comfort this time. She was about to hurt him very deeply.

'Hello love. I'm in a state of shock and so will you be, so sit down while I explain what's happened.' Mary told him the whole story, even the bit about David embezzling a fortune from the hotel in Dawson City and escaping to Britain in 1959.

'So you and I are related to each other. You're my step-uncle,' said Mary and then began to cry.

The line was silent. Tom wasn't saying anything.

'Tom, are you there. Are you alright?'

'Of course I'm not alright.' He snapped. 'How does Sara know it was Dad? Without seeing his face, it could have been anyone, surely.'

'She showed me a photograph of him, taken forty years ago. It was obviously a picture of your father as a young man. He had six year old Bob James in the photo with him. I'll get a copy done for you so you can see for yourself.'

'Oh Mary, I feel as though I've just been given a death sentence. We'll never be able to marry now. Oh God, this is horrible.' Mary could hear the tears in his voice. 'I'll get a flight straight away. I need to be with you. I can't cope with this 'bombshell' on my own. I'll never sleep at night. '

'But Tom, the first thing you have to do is to visit your parents and face them with this. Surely your mother doesn't know about her husband's background. She'd never have married him if she did. Your father must have known who I was all along. That's why he was always saying positive things about First Nations people I suppose. I've seen a picture of my mother, his daughter, and I look just like her.'

'Why don't you come home? We need to be together. I'll pay for your flight,' Tom begged.

'Just imagine it. Your mother hates me. It'll be a very emotional visit. I'm feeling too raw myself to cope with that at the moment. You must face your family on your own and then you could come up here at the end of term. It's not long now. What do you think?' Mary hoped he would agree. 'Go and share this news with Sally. Go today. You'll go mad if you don't tell someone.'

'Oh Mary!' Tom cried out again. 'Shit! What a mess. I wish there was some way that Sara could be proved wrong. Christ! How am I going to face my parents with this? I've been sleeping with my niece for six years. I feel sick, just thinking about it .Thank God we've found out about this now and not after the birth of our children,' said Tom, taking Mary by surprise.

'I wasn't expecting that.' In a strange way, this practical comment of Tom's made her feel a little stronger about the whole dilemma. He had actually pin-pointed something positive in the midst of this appalling news. The beeps told her she had run out of time.

'Time has run out. Call me Tom when you've been to Woodbridge. Take care, love. 'Bye.'

Chapter 27
England

Tom felt ill. He hadn't cried so much since he was a boy. He glanced at the clock. It was five thirty and Sally would be home from work by now. He decided to take Mary's advice and drive down to Greenwich before he turned to the bottle of single malt for support.

Sally wasn't surprised to see him. In fact she was expecting him.

'Come in Tom. Oh dear. I just don't know what to say. What terrible news,' she said giving him a friendly hug. When he clung to her and began to cry, she gently pushed him towards the bathroom door.

'I'll leave you to have a quiet moment, Tom, while I serve up William's supper. His father is taking him to a football match in half-an-hour.' Sally rushed into the kitchen. Tom washed his face and hands and sat on the edge of the bath, staring at a gaunt image of himself in the mirror opposite. He had lost weight recently and had not been sleeping well. The pressure at work was increasing too, as the term got nearer to Christmas. What was the point of all this? Everything he had done had been for Mary and for their future together. He heard voices in the hall and then the click of the front door closing.

'Tom, are you okay in there? William has gone. Come and have a drink and some supper with me. I've made some 'spag–bol' and there's plenty.'

Tom was calmer after a hot meal and a glass or two of red wine.

'Did you ever suspect that your father might have had a mysterious past? Did you know much about his family background?' Sally asked.

'The answer is no, to both of those questions. Dad came from a village in South Wales originally and according to him, he made his money by buying and selling property. I had no idea that he had been in Canada for years before he met my mother. I'm sure that she doesn't know either.'

'What about his Welsh family?'

'He told us that his parents were both dead and that he and his brother didn't talk anymore. It was something to do with the family inheritance apparently. He always said that we were his family.'

Tom let out a deep sigh, ran his fingers through his hair and hung his head. Sally handed him a large whisky and sat next to him on the settee.

'What are you going to do now?' She asked quietly.

'That's it. I don't know what to do, about any of this. I want to fly to Whitehorse tomorrow to be with Mary, but there's my job, and also Mary needs me to confront my parents with this. She says she needs confirmation that Dad really is her grandfather, the father of her mother, Jeannie James. This news will tear them apart. It could even destroy their marriage and what about our marriage?

Will Mary and I still be free to marry? I'm her uncle for God's sake. It's all horrible!'

Sally thought back to that night in Whitehorse when Mary confided in her about Jake. Sally had said, at the time, that Mary should be more up front about her feelings for Jake. It will be too big a shock for poor Tom now, on top of everything else. Sally's heart went out to Tom. He just didn't deserve all of this. She let him talk. He talked about everything that was in his mind and in his heart. He had needed to do this for weeks now.

William arrived home just before nine o'clock and Sally was keen to get him to bed. Their team had won 2-1 and William was excited. He rambled on about it even whilst brushing his teeth. Sally sat with him until he dozed off to sleep. When she came downstairs, Tom's empty glass was on the coffee table and he was sound asleep on the settee. She put a pillow under his head and threw a blanket over him. He didn't even stir.

As she handed Tom a mug of tea early the next morning, Sally shared an idea with him.

'Tom, if you can possibly live with this news until Saturday, I'll come with you to Suffolk. William is with his father this weekend and you might need some moral support on the journey home. I wouldn't intrude upon your time with your parents of course. Would you like some company? I'm happy to drive too so that you can have a drink afterwards. I know it's not going to be easy.'

'Thanks. I'd really appreciate that, Sally. It'll give me time to make a decision. Should I share this with Dad or should I talk to both of them?' Tom gave her a quick hug.

He worried about this dilemma all week. He went to bed thinking about it and it was the first thing he thought of when he woke up in the morning. He couldn't decide how to orchestrate this. If he told his parents together it would no doubt shatter their marriage and if he challenged his father, without his mother present, he might set up another wall of secrecy. Also, it would look as though he was colluding with a criminal because, after all, his father had stolen thousands of dollars and was still wanted by the R.C.M.P. in Canada.

Sally was standing at the front gate when Tom arrived. William and his father had just left. She grabbed her bag and her coat and locked the front door.

'Hello Tom. You're very prompt. I suggest you come into my parking space as I vacate it. We've all got our own little parking spot in this road.'

Tom did as he was directed and then jumped in next to Sally.

'Are you sure you don't want me to drive us there and you drive back?'

'Ok. Yes it's a good idea to share the driving,' she said, getting out of the car.

They set off across the heath and headed towards the M25. The roads were busy and full of hesitant weekend drivers. They chatted about Tom's visit most of the time, that and Mary's Yukon family.

'What if I don't reveal Dad's true identity? What then?' Tom asked.

'You'll have to reveal this to your parents, because Mary and her sister might want to communicate with their grandfather. They have every right to do so.' said Sally.

Sally was quiet as they drove through the Suffolk countryside. She studied the cottages and the farms and tried to imagine living there. She was a city girl and was used to a faster pace.

'It must seem really dark out here at night, Tom. Did you like growing up in the country?

'As a young boy I really enjoyed it, but there was very little for teenagers to do unless you were into sport like me. Rugby, swimming and horse-riding took up most of my life in those days and my mother was like a permanent taxi-driver. She moaned about it all the time. I couldn't wait to get my own little car. This is our drive,' announced Tom as he drove up to the gates of his parents' estate.

'Gosh! It looks like a stately home. Why don't you leave the car with me, here, and walk up to the house. Tell me how to get to Woodbridge and I'll have a look around the shops,' suggested Sally.

'You're welcome to come and have a coffee with us and then you could make some excuse that you want to visit a friend in Woodbridge or something.' Tom was beginning to feel nervous.

Charlotte was standing by the open door as they approached the house. She was waving and smiling and then her expression changed to one of annoyance when she saw Sally.

'Hello mother. This is Mary's best friend Sally Davies. She has someone she has to visit in Woodbridge, so I suggested that she have coffee with us first. Hope that's okay?'

'I'm pleased to meet you Sally,' said an intrigued Charlotte shaking Sally's hand and looking at Tom. 'Have you got another car darling? This one is very small.' She sneered at Sally's Peugeot 206.

'It's *my* car actually. My son and I only need something small in Greenwich, as parking is a big problem,' said Sally ignoring her rudeness.

As they sipped coffee out of bone china cups in the drawing room Charlotte dominated the conversation as always. Most of her questions were directed at Sally. Tom had heard this line of questioning before. It was as though his mother was assessing one of his new girl friends. Sally looked very uncomfortable. She stood up and was about to leave when David came into the room.

'Oh darling you can't come in here in those awful trousers. We've got a visitor. Go and change them at once,' ordered Charlotte.

David winked at Tom and Sally and left the room. He re-appeared a few minutes later wearing his best plus-fours and came over to greet them, turning his back on his wife as he did so.

'Sally has just been up to the Yukon with Mary for two weeks and has brought back lots of news for me. We've had a really good chat. I almost feel as though I've been with Mary myself,' said Tom.

'Did you like it up there?' asked David.

Tom studied his father's face carefully as he discussed this with Sally.

'I loved it. What a beautiful place. I enjoyed Whitehorse and I really liked the village of Carcross. Mary's friend has a log house right on the edge of a huge glacial lake.' Sally enthused.

Charlotte didn't appear to be taking any interest in this talk of the Yukon. Instead she had got up and was arranging some flowers over by the window. This time Sally stood up and walked towards her hostess. She looked at her watch. It was time to go.

'Well, it was good to meet you both and thank you for the coffee, but I've arranged to meet a friend in Woodbridge in half an hour.'

'How will you get there?' David asked.

'In my car. We've bought my Peugeot today as Tom's is in the garage being serviced,' she said. How easy it is to lie, mused Tom. He raised his eyebrows and smiled at Sally.

Charlotte remained in her corner of the room and made no effort to say 'goodbye' properly. Sally turned to David who shook Sally's hand warmly and smiled.

'Good to meet you Sally,' he said. 'Mary is lucky to have a friend like you.'

'I'm sorry about my mother's rudeness Sally. I don't know what else to say,' said Tom as he walked Sally to the car. 'I'll see you in a couple of hours. Just sound the horn and I'll meet you by the main gate. I think I'll need to make a quick get-a-way.' Tom walked back to his parents with a heavy heart.

'She seemed nice,' said David. 'Fancy her going all the way to the Yukon. No-one goes up there.'

'What does she do for a living?' Charlotte always judged people by their qualifications and their place of work.

It made Tom really angry.

'She's an Occupational Therapist at the Greenwich Hospital,' said Tom.

'So she has a degree does she? Why couldn't you find someone like her to go out with? Does she have a husband or is her child illegitimate?'

'She's divorced and her son is with his father this weekend. It's really none of your business what Sally does. Why can't you enjoy people instead of dissecting them all the time? I suggest you both sit down because I have something to tell you and you won't like it.'

'Well if it's that bad I suggest you pour us all something stronger than tea,' said Charlotte. David glared at Tom and then walked over to the cocktail cabinet.

'I spoke to Mary on the phone earlier this week and she talked a lot about her family as usual. Mary was given a photograph, by one of the nuns, when we visited the convent at the beginning of this year. It was in Mary's anorak pocket when she first came over here from Canada apparently.' Tom turned to his father. 'The photo is of a piano player in a hotel bar.'

The colour had drained from his father's face. He held up the flat of his hand towards Tom and shouted, 'Tom, don't do this. I beg of you. Please don't do this!'

'I have to Dad. There are at least four members of your Yukon family who need to know who you are and where you are, and quite possibly a lot more than four.'

Charlotte looked shocked and, for once, was speechless. She stared at her husband's haunted expression and went to sit next to him on the settee. David covered his face with his hands as Tom told the story of his deception. Tom included every little detail about the theft, his work in Dawson City, his long affair with Mary's First Nations grandmother, his mysterious disappearance from the Yukon and his connection to the man who brought Mary to England.

'This appalling discovery means that I am related to my fiancée and that I have been living in sin with my niece for the past six years. How could you do this to me? How could you let this happen? Some father you turned out to be!' Much to his annoyance, Tom's eyes filled with tears.

Charlotte was screaming hysterically. She turned to David and started to hit him. David covered his head and simply let her do it.

'Aah! My husband's a thief and a liar and a pub pianist. How could you - two children and with a native woman – ugh! Twenty years in that ghastly place and you never said a word about it. I suppose you married me for my money and my name. God, I've been blind – blind and stupid.' She screamed and hit him again. 'Don't just sit there like a frightened child. Speak up for yourself.'

'Something you seem to have overlooked is the fact that Dad is still wanted for theft by the police in the Yukon. Also, what about me? Doesn't anyone care that you have completely ruined my life and Mary's life? We can't possibly get married now. How can we – we're related.'

'Actually you're not.' David looked up and spoke for the first time.

'Shut up David! Don't spoil everything. The only good thing that's come out of this is that Tom can't now marry that awful half-caste girl.'

'That 'awful girl' is my grand-daughter if you don't mind, and the love of Tom's life. I told you we should have explained this to Tom years ago, when he was a boy. Tom, you are our adopted son,' he said.

'You told me lots of things – all of them now lies it seems.' Charlotte stormed out of the room.

Tom fell silent for a moment and stared, in disbelief, at his father.

'Adopted? You wait until I'm nearly thirty to tell me something as important as that? Christ, is there no end to these secrets? Was Mandy adopted too? This is crazy. Mary now knows who her family is but I suddenly don't know anything about mine.' Tom's voice turned into a high-pitched squeal.

'No, Mandy wasn't adopted. She was a surprise.

Charlotte thought she was unable to have any children, which is why we adopted you,' said David sheepishly.

'Do you actually know who my natural parents are or where they're from?'

'No. We never knew anything about your parents. We only knew that that they weren't able to care for you. You can apply to find them though, if you want to. I still have the paperwork.' He spoke in a whisper as though he'd had all his energy knocked out of him.

'And that's supposed to make it alright is it? I just don't know what to say to you Dad. You've broken my heart. Even if Mary and I are able to marry, she and I will share the same family thanks to you. It's a mess. Nothing will ever be the same again, and what about all that money you stole? Are you going to finally own up to what you've done? Do you think mother will stay with you after this? Somehow I don't think so.' Tom started to pace up and down. 'So where do we go from here – eh Dad?'

'I'm so sorry son. I've no idea what's going to happen.' David held his head in his hands.

'Sorry just isn't enough and I'm not your son!' Tom was near to tears. 'I'm taking the dogs for a walk. I'm tired of talking. I need some fresh air.'

Tom went to the back of the house to the covered enclosure where his father's two border collies lived. They jumped up excitedly as Tom approached, knowing that either food or some exercise was about to happen. Tom put them both on a leash and took them out the back way to the path that led across the fields. The fresh, cool breeze felt good and he breathed deeply to try to calm himself a little. This was his home. This contained all of his childhood memories. He had known nothing else for nearly thirty years. Nothing will ever be the same again, he thought. Dad will probably be thrown off the estate that he has nurtured and renovated for nearly half of his life. He might even end up in prison somewhere. My mother won't be able to manage all of this on her own so she will want me to take over the estate. Meanwhile I might be living in the Yukon with Mary, which I'm not sure I want to do ... with Mary yes, but not in the Yukon. All of these thoughts ran through Tom's mind as he watched the dogs race each other and sniff for rabbits. It was like a living nightmare. He desperately needed to join Mary as soon as possible. His father hadn't even asked about his Yukon children or about Sara. Oh well, he will know soon enough. Tom checked his watch; time to go. He called the dogs back with a piercing whistle and returned them to their enclosure, giving them food and water before he left. As he went in to wash his hands he saw that his mother was waiting for him.

'What are you going to do now?' Charlotte asked. 'You can stay for lunch. We've all got to eat.'

'No thanks. I'm meeting Sally for lunch and then we'll head back to London. You've got rather a lot of sorting out to do with Dad, I'd have thought, or are you just going to kick him out without any discussion?' Tom had lost all patience where his mother was concerned.

'You're being unkind to the victim here,' said Charlotte. 'What would you do in my position? Your father is a criminal and a liar. All this time he's had another life and another family.'

'No he hasn't. He gave up his life and his family to build a future with you,' said Tom.

'So that he could hide away you mean. Oh darling, don't turn against me. I couldn't bear it.'

Charlotte began to cry. Tom had had enough. He needed a drink and just at that moment the car horn sounded right on cue.

'I've gotta go. I'll ring you in a couple of days. Now go and talk to Dad.' Tom rushed out.

Tom ran down the drive. Never was he so delighted to see anything than to see Sally's car parked by the gates. He sat in the passenger seat and sighed deeply. Sally put her hand on his arm and gave it a gentle squeeze.

'Was it awful, Tom?' She started the car and drove away from the estate and stopped further down the lane in a small lay-by. The view across the fields was restful and the only sound was the occasional skylark. She listened attentively whilst Tom described the scene at the house. She smiled in her mind at the thought of Tom's arrogant mother discovering her husband's past life in the Yukon. She was shocked to hear about the adoption though and she was upset for Tom.

'You must feel as though you don't know who you are anymore?' She said. 'What do you think will happen now?'

'I don't know. All I know is that I need to go to Whitehorse. I need to be with Mary.' Tom had said this so many times just recently. 'There's one thing I must do before I do that, though. I have to confront Bob James with all of this. Do you realise that he is my step brother? Christ, what an awful thought. What a mess!'

'Would you like to do that, Tom, after we've had some lunch? We've got lots of time. Maybe you should get all of these difficult confrontations out of the way rather than prolong them,' said Sally.

'I don't know whether I have the strength or the energy to deal with any more of this today,' said Tom. 'Come on, let's go. I'm gasping for a pint.'

Tom felt much better after an excellent roast dinner and a pint of local ale. He asked Sally if she could cope with any more family trauma.

'Let's do it Tom. Then you can go back to London and leave this behind you for a few days. You need to do something different tomorrow, like a game of rugby,' she said with a smile.

Tom was impressed that Sally always seemed to understand exactly what was needed. He guessed that it was to do with her job and her training.

'We must try to catch Rob unawares. If he sees us drive up, he'll hide from us like he did before. If you drop me somewhere a couple of hundred metres away then I can try to approach their house without being seen,' suggested Tom.

'Is this going to be a physical confrontation like your meeting in the forest? Would you like me to come with you? I can always stay hidden somewhere and read the new book I bought in Woodbridge.'

'You're quite the little Miss Marple aren't you?' Tom laughed at Sally's idea. 'Mind you, you never know, that could prove to be a useful plan, I suppose.' They set off towards the A14.

When they got to Rob and Wendy's lane Sally parked the car in a lay-by not far from the house. It was a mild, dry day for November, so Sally grabbed her book and a rug from the back seat. They walked down the lane together and as they came in sight of the front drive, they could see Rob outside working on his Land Rover.

'This is perfect,' said Tom quietly. 'I don't even have to try to find him. What are you going to do now?'

'I'm going to free-wheel the car down the hill to this spot and have a front-row seat,' said Sally. Tom's face broke into a smile.

'Thanks Sally. Somehow you've managed to lighten this whole episode for me.' Tom crept nearer to the drive and the moment Rob turned his back towards him, he raced forward and took him by surprise. Rob could have run off but there didn't seem much point. Tom would simply have chased him again.

'Well, well, well, if it isn't my step-brother?' said Tom. 'I assume that you've heard from your mother by now?' Rob said nothing which told Tom that he had heard the news.

'What do you want? I've got nothing to say to you. Get off my property.' Rob walked around to the far side of his vehicle.

'You mean to say that you've found your father, who is also my father, after all this time and you have nothing to say? I thought you'd been searching for him for the past twenty five years?'

'That's just it. You're too late. It's all too long ago. I don't care anymore.' Rob turned towards his vehicle and carried on working.

'But you've got a family here in Suffolk now; a father, a niece and a step-brother. Doesn't that mean anything to you? Mind you, you've got a lot of making-up to do with Mary. She may never want to see you again after all that you've done. That shouldn't stop you seeing your father though, surely?'

'I can't be bothered to make up with anyone. What's done is done. I don't want a family. I don't want any of you. Wendy and my dogs are my family. I don't need anything else.' Rob was becoming aggressive. 'Get out of my way! I'm trying to work here.'

'What about my Dad? Also your mother is probably desperate to see you again. You're being bloody selfish if you ask me.'

Rob spun around and faced Tom.

'Well, I didn't ask you. Your father made his own choice. Now get the hell out of here!' Rob pushed Tom hard in his chest and without even thinking what he was doing Tom hit Rob squarely across his jaw, knocking him to the ground. Rob jumped up and went for Tom and the two men ended up rolling around on the ground like a couple of teenagers.

Sally had watched the whole scene from her car. She ran down the lane, across the drive and rang the doorbell. She went over to Tom and shouted at him: 'For goodness sake, stop it you two! This is insane. Tom – that's enough.'

Wendy appeared at the door and immediately raced over to Rob, who was holding his bleeding nose. Tom rubbed a badly bruised hand.

'What's going on? Rob, what's happened?'

'Yeah, go on *Bob*. Tell your wife all about it. It's time she knew what a bastard you really are.'

Sally grabbed Tom's arm and led him back to the road. She said nothing until they were back in the car.

'What on earth did he say to deserve that?' Sally couldn't believe what she had just witnessed.

'That's the first time I've ever hit anyone. I'm so sorry you had to see that and I'm ashamed of myself. I don't know what got into me. Something just snapped. This has all been too much. Do you realise that I've probably helped to wreck two marriages today?'

'No marriage can survive for ever if it's based on lies and deception. You know that,' said Sally.

A feeling of intense relief suddenly washed over him.

That's one skeleton that's gone from the cupboard forever, he thought. Mary would be relieved too.

As they turned into Earlswood Street, in Greenwich, two hours later Tom reached for his wallet.

'Sally thanks a lot for today. I couldn't have got through it all without you. Here, let me pay for your petrol.' He handed Sally some money, but Sally shook her head.

'Oh Tom, that's good of you, but really I've been glad to help. I enjoyed our pub lunch today too. We must do it again sometime. What are you going to do now?' she said as they got out of the car.

'I'm going to take your advice and play rugby tomorrow and beyond that I'm not sure. I'll call Mary tonight and see if she'll be home for Christmas. If not, I suppose I'll book my flight to Whitehorse.'

'It won't be an easy trip for you Tom, knowing that Mary's family is also your father's family. Why don't you book a session with Mary's counsellor before you go? She might be able to offer you a coping strategy of some kind.'

'I'll think about it. Thanks again for today. Must go ...'

Tom walked to his car like a convict walking to the

guillotine. His life, as he knew it, was over.

'Keep me posted Tom. You know where I am if you need anything. Bye.' Sally parked her car quickly before anyone else nipped into her space.

Chapter 28

Tom spent most of the first day of his Christmas holiday in the jewellers' shops. He would have liked to have bought Mary an engagement ring for Christmas, but as their future was still uncertain he settled for a gold bracelet instead. He had it engraved: 'To Mary, with all my love, Tom.' He had bought his airline ticket to Whitehorse. Only two days to go. He was longing to see Mary again. The past two months had seemed like two years. It was torture not knowing whether he and Mary would be able to marry or not. He had telephoned Karen when he first heard the news about his father. She seemed fairly certain that their marriage would be legal because Tom was adopted as a baby and was raised separately from Mary. She promised to try to find out the legal situation in Britain for them. Whether or not it would be the same in Canada, she didn't know, of course. Tom couldn't imagine his life without Mary by his side and he couldn't bear the thought of being nothing more than a friend either.

He booked a deluxe room for the two of them at the High Country Inn. They would have two whole weeks to really plan their future together - that's if they had a future together.

Much to Tom's surprise, his parents had decided to stay together for the time being. Charlotte didn't want to spend Christmas with just Mandy for company and David wanted to stay put for as long as possible. The final decision to move out would have to go hand in hand with his confession to the police. If Charlotte threw him out, she would report him instantly. Tom spoke to them on the phone and told them of his trip to the Yukon, but he had no desire to see them right now. He ignored all of his mother's protestations. He needed to see Mary before visiting his parents, although he might go to see Mandy and take her a Christmas gift. She was always so excited about Christmas and he hadn't seen her for a while.

Sally returned the favour and took Tom to the airport. William went along too. He had never been to Heathrow before and he was hoping to go up to the observation deck to watch Tom's jumbo jet take off. Tom talked about Mary and about how much he had missed her. He showed Sally the bracelet he had bought for her and told her, with pride, about the fresh flowers that he had ordered for their room at the hotel. He said nothing about the First Nations family he was about to meet. Sally's heart sank at all that she was hearing. She knew exactly how hard this trip was going to be for Tom.

Mary felt very nervous as she waited in front of the double doors at the Whitehorse Airport. She wished now that she'd told Tom about Jake before. She knew that it would break his heart, on top of everything else. It would cast a huge shadow over his visit too. She felt a rush of affection for him when she saw his excited smile as he rushed towards her. He swept her up in his arms and twirled her around, kissing her passionately. Mary almost lost her balance when he put her down.

'Goodness me, you must be pleased to see me,' laughed Mary.

'It's wonderful to see you darling. I've missed you so much. Have you missed me?' Tom stood at the carousel with his arm around Mary. 'I don't ever want to let you go again.'

'Of course I've missed you,' said Mary. She had missed him. She had missed her best friend, but she hadn't longed for him in the way she did for Jake.

'I've booked us a King size room at the High Country Inn. I know you're living with your friends, but I thought this would give us time to really be together and to sort out our future. What do you think darling?'

Tom put his luggage in the back of Mary's car. It was a relief to be out of the cold wind. It was dark, and so Tom's final descent into the airport hadn't told him much about the Yukon, compared to Mary's first flight, at the end of August, in glorious sunshine.

'How was your flight? You'll have seen more of Vancouver than you have of the Yukon. I warned you that there wouldn't be much daylight here in December. There's even less up in Dawson City,' said Mary, sounding like a local and purposely ignoring Tom's question.

'The flight was fine. Not much leg room though in the domestic flight to Whitehorse.' Tom studied the lights of the city before him, as they drove down the Two Mile Hill. Nearly three months worth of frozen snow lay alongside the highway.

'The pilot said the temperature would drop to minus 38 degrees Celsius tonight. I've never experienced that temperature before. What's it like? I see you're wearing a new parka,' said Tom.

'You get used to it. I don't spend any time outside when it's as cold as this. Mostly you just go from heated car to heated building. Annie says that everyone gets 'cabin fever' by late February. I do miss the sunshine.' Mary surprised herself. She hadn't realised how quickly she'd adjusted to all these changes.

'What stops the cars from freezing up? Does everyone have a garage?'

'Not everyone. If you leave your vehicle outside for any length of time, you have to plug it into a roadside socket. I'm lucky with this car because I have Jake's space in the garage during the week while he's at work in Carcross.' She suddenly realised that she hadn't mentioned Jake to Tom before.

'I'm surprised to see you driving. You never want to drive at home; not even in Suffolk,' said Tom. 'Who's Jake? Is that Annie's son?' Mary nodded.

'Yes. There's so little traffic on the roads here. Mind you, I'd rather drive in daylight. Well, this is the hotel,' she said as she entered the guests' car park.

'Thanks. Let's find our room and then I think I'm ready for a drink. You'll need to go and get your things won't you?' Tom had slipped into the role of the organiser.

'Let's find the room first,' said Mary, delaying the moment of confrontation. Tom led her into the room. His flowers had been delivered.

'Wow! What beautiful flowers. Did they come with the room?' Mary asked innocently.

'No. I ordered them especially for you, as a surprise,' said Tom looking pleased.

'They're a surprise alright. They're lovely. Thank you,' she said reading the card. 'Tom, before we go any further, I need to talk to you about everything. I can sense that you're here to bring me home to London and I can see that you're still thinking about our future together. I need to tell you that I've made a decision in the past three months. I want to stay here in the Yukon. I don't want to return to London to live. I've found my family after all these years and they all need me, or at least, my father and my sister do. I can't explain it, but I feel I belong here. I've never really felt that anywhere before.'

'Not even in London with me?' Tom asked, looking hurt. 'Are you saying that you want me to live with you up here in the Yukon or are you leaving me?'

'I don't think you'll want to stay with me when you've heard the whole story. We might not be able to stay together, anyway. Have you asked anyone about that Tom?'

'Karen is looking into it for us. She said she'd let us know as soon as possible. What do you mean, when I've heard the whole story - not more bad news surely?'

'This news of your father has shaken me. My grandmother was his wife and my mother was his daughter. If I marry you Tom, I'll be raising children with my uncle. It's a terrible mess. I'd never feel that we were doing the right thing. I'd always feel as though we were living in sin, and anyway...'Mary stopped suddenly.

Tom waited but Mary didn't continue. He could see that her eyes were full of tears and her hand was shaking as she clutched the card from the bouquet of flowers.

'And anyway what ... ? You did say the whole story. I don't know whether I can take much more but you might as well hit me with all of it.'

'I've been seeing someone from here. He's part First Nations like me, but from a different part of the Yukon. It's Annie's son Jake – Jake Hughes. There, I've said it.' Mary felt a sense of release.

Tom sat on the bed with his shoulders slumped and his face was ashen. He looked as though he was in a state of collapse.

'Oh Tom I'm so sorry. I didn't want to tell you over the phone and yet now I think I should have done.' She had avoided Tom's eyes as she spoke but now she could see the pain in them. She leaned over and held his hand, but he pulled it away.

'Please don't Mary,' he said and began to cry. 'This is the last straw. First my father, then the adoption, then Rob, and now you – the one person I thought would *never* leave me.'

'But it's quite possible that we won't be able to stay together anymore, anyway. Don't you feel uncomfortable about us being related?' Mary felt distraught seeing Tom like this.

'Of course I do, but this is just an easy let-out for you isn't it? You probably had your first night with this Jake fellow weeks ago?' Mary chose not to reply to that. Instead she went over to the mini-bar and took out a miniature of brandy. She handed this, together with a glass, to Tom, hoping it would calm him a little. What happened next took her breath away. Tom took the glass and hurled it at the opposite wall. An anguished silence followed. Mary felt helpless. This was a man she had never seen before. They sat at opposite ends of the room and said nothing. Finally, Mary broke the unbearable silence.

'Tell me truthfully, Tom, would you like to live and work up here, 9,000 miles away from everything you're used to? Wait 'til you meet my family. My father lives in the bush in a cabin that has turf on the roof. The culture and the way of life of my family in Carmacks is a world away from London and Suffolk. I'll get used to this. I have to, I belong here. I need to help my family get back together again. They are lost souls at the moment. Jake feels as I do. He's passionate about the future of the First Nations people too.'

'I can see why you want to stay. I've secretly feared this for months now. I'm also aware that our relationship might be considered illegal. The worst thing of all is the thought of you in the arms of someone else when I've been missing you so much. It hurts like hell.' Tom wiped his eyes and carefully placed the empty brandy bottle on the bedside table. The brandy had helped. He seemed calmer.

'We're keeping apart from one another right now. Jake is like you. He's a perfect gentleman. His mother and his uncle disapprove of us. They feel my loyalty is to you. They are good people. I really want you to meet Annie and Uncle Albie when you feel that the time is right.' Mary could see that this was going to be hard. The thing she wanted most was to keep and protect her friendship with Tom. She moved to sit next to him on the bed and reached out for his hand again. This time he didn't pull it away.

'This is all my fault. I've handled this really badly Tom, and I've hurt you so much. I should have told you about Jake straight away. Tom, I do love you. I think I'll always love you. You are the most supportive and loving person I've ever known. I'd be nothing now if I hadn't met you when I did. But I've fallen in love with Jake. His people have the same history as mine. He understands me in a way that you would not be able to, because you've always lived in such a privileged world. Tom, I never want to lose our friendship. You and Sally are my best friends, my only friends. Shout at me, blame me for everything, call me any name you wish, but please don't turn your back on me love. I couldn't bear it.'

Mary and Tom faced each other. Tom's earlier outburst had frightened her. She held her breath, wondering what he would decide to do next. The atmosphere in the room was heavy and oppressive.

Tom reached across and hugged her. He held her close but said nothing. She kissed him on the cheek and sat back from him, still holding his hand. Tom pulled away from her and stood up.

'Why don't we have some dinner together and then

you must get back to your friend's house.'

'In fact I should call her anyway and let her know that you've arrived.' Mary smiled fondly at him. 'Maybe you'd like to meet Annie tomorrow and possibly Josie if she's up to it?'

'Annie and your sister yes, but not Jake. I can't cope with that. You'll have to give me time.' He sounded weary. He was weary. It had been a very long day. 'I'll ring reception about the broken glass.'

Tom got a little drunk as the evening progressed and Mary let him. The drink was relaxing him and he seemed brighter. Mary helped him up to his room and removed his shoes and his tie. She waited until he was sleeping soundly and she left a note for him on his suitcase.

'Sleep well, love. I'll see you after breakfast, at around 10.00,' love Mary x.

When Mary got back to Porter Creek, Annie was waiting up for her, something she had not done before. Jake had gone to bed and it was obvious that Annie needed to hear Mary's news. Mary sighed. She felt as though she was in an emotional whirlpool. She couldn't cope with an inquisition tonight. Annie smiled as Mary walked in.

'You look tired. Would you like a drink?' said Annie. Mary shook her head. 'By the way, your father called. I told him that you and Tom were going to visit him on Monday. I hope that was okay?'

'Good. Thank you. I was wondering how we'd get in touch with him,' said Mary.

'So, how did it all go?'

Mary explained the events of the evening, while Annie clutched her mug of hot chocolate and listened intently.

'The thing is I know I'm being selfish, but I don't want to lose Tom's friendship,' said Mary.

'Did you ask him how he would feel about living up here in the Yukon?'

'Yes. Tom would find it hard to adjust, I think; besides which, we don't know yet whether our relationship is legal or not. My counsellor at home is trying to find out for us.'

'What about Jake? Did you mention him to Tom?' There was still disapproval in her voice.

'Yes. He was heart-broken. We were both upset. It was awful, just like I knew it would be. I was afraid that Tom might take the next flight out of here but he said he would like to meet you tomorrow, Annie, and Josie as well. Obviously I want him to meet Dad but I don't think he'll want to see Sara's family. He'll need time before he can face Jake too, of course. I'll talk to Jake about this in the morning. I've just realised that it's Christmas Day on Tuesday. What are you and the family doing, to celebrate?' Mary asked.

'Julie arrives from Vancouver tomorrow, and then the three of us will go to Carcross and spend Christmas with George's family, like we always do. What about you?'

'I'd like us to spend Christmas Day with Dad and Josie. I'll take Tom to meet Josie tomorrow and then to Carmacks to see Dad on Monday. Josie is due to return to Carmacks so I could take her with us. Maybe we can arrange something? They might not want to do this of course, and it could be difficult. Dad won't be able to stay off the booze just because Josie is there. Also Josie will want to see her son.'

Mary wondered what Tom would think of Jack's cabin. At least he had four chairs now and four mugs.

'You're welcome to have them here for two days if you'd like to. No smoking in the house though,' said

Annie. 'It would be lovely for you to be with your family, although everyone will miss you in Carcross, especially Julie.'

'Thanks Annie. That's so generous of you. I'll see what everyone says. Right now, though, I must go to bed. I'm exhausted.' Mary yawned and rubbed her right eye.

Annie discreetly left Mary and Jake to have breakfast together. Julie wasn't due until mid-day, but Annie went into town first to stock up on food supplies for Carcross.

Mary explained to Jake all that had happened the previous day. Jake sensed that she was upset. He led her over to the sofa and sat with his arm around her, studying her face as she talked.

'Jake, I'm so sorry but I won't be able to see much of you whilst Tom is here. Sadly, we can't join you all in Carcross. Tom would find it difficult and anyway I'd like us to spend some time with my family. I'm going to see if I can get Jack and Josie together after all these years. Dad would be thrilled. You do understand, don't you love?' Jake kissed her and stroked her face tenderly.

'Of course I understand. This is a tough time for you. You've been anxious about it for weeks. I'll miss you in Carcross, we all will, but you and I have the rest of our lives to be together. I must say, I'd like to meet this man who has been in love with you for the past six years, but right now he must feel like punching me,' said Jake. 'I'm sure I would if it was the other way around.'

'No. He doesn't feel that. He's just very hurt and is distraught that we can't now marry. I want us to remain friends. He's done so much for me. Tom was everything to me. I mustn't ever forget that.'

'Was he hoping to live up here with you do you think?' Jake asked.

'I don't think so. Tom is very English and he is used

to the culture and the buzz of London. He'd hate the harsh winters in the Yukon and the continual darkness at this time of the year.' Mary glanced at the kitchen clock and jumped up suddenly.

'Gosh it's nine-thirty. I said I'd meet Tom at ten o'clock. Jake, I must go. Happy Christmas, my love!' Mary put her arms around his neck and ran her fingers through his soft black hair which hung loose half-way down his back. 'I'll try to call you all at Aunt Amy's on Christmas Day.'

'I've a special gift for you but I haven't put it under the tree,' said Jake. 'We'll find a moment to be together very soon.' He gave her a long passionate kiss. 'Now get out of here or you'll be late.' He smiled at Mary as she grabbed her things and turned towards the garage door.

As she drove along Second Avenue, Mary thought about the events of the past twenty four hours. How lucky she was to have found two such sensitive and caring men as Jake and Tom! Jake had taken her by surprise just now. His words had been almost like a proposal. 'We have the rest of our lives to be together,' he had said. She stored this line in her heart as she went to meet Tom.

Chapter 29

Mary led Tom through the front doors of the main Crossroads building. Standing with her arm through his she could feel his body stiffen. His eyes darted about him as though he was expecting a crisis to occur any minute. The world of drug and alcohol abuse was not something that Tom had ever experienced in his safe and comfortable life. Even at university it seemed to have escaped him. She tried to reassure him that it was peaceful there most of the time and that Josie had had lots of 'good days' just recently. As they walked towards the office Mary could see Don chatting to the secretary. She waved.

'Hi Mary. How's it going? Have you come to collect Josie?' Don asked when he saw her in the doorway.

'Why? Will the centre be closed over Christmas then? Josie never mentioned it.' Mary was surprised.

'Hell, no! This place is overloaded at this time of the year what with the weather and the Christmas/New Year celebrations. Josie feels that she's now ready to return to Carmacks. She'll still need regular visits from her support worker of course. I think she's looking forward to seeing a lot more of you and also of her son. How long are you staying up here?' Don asked.

'I plan to stay permanently,' said Mary, 'although I'll have to make a trip to England, to collect my things and to see my friends. This is my home now. My family is here.' Mary looked sideways at Tom as she said this. She hadn't announced her decision publicly before. Tom stared straight ahead to avoid showing any emotion.

'She'll have her medication with her. Just try to keep her away from the booze if you can; an impossible task over Christmas, I know. Excuse me ...' Don was called away to answer the phone, so Mary and Tom made their way downstairs.

'What a place. Poor Josie,' said Tom.

'It's a lot more comfortable than some of the places she's stayed in. There's warmth and food here, and the counselling support. Here we are,' said Mary, noticing the 'Peace' sign on her door. Just like last time, Mary could hear Josie singing. She put her hand on Tom's arm.

'Listen. That's Josie,' said Mary proudly to Tom. 'She sings when she's unhappy like I used to do. I expect she's nervous about going home.' 'She sings just like you, too,' said Tom.

Josie was sitting cross-legged on her bed with her back against the wall. She stopped singing and smiled when she saw Mary and Tom walk in. Mary gave her a hug and introduced Tom.

'So, you're Mary's boyfriend from England?' Josie said, staring up at Tom. 'Shit, you look a hell of a yuppy.'

'Josie, be nice. Tom's come a long way just to meet you.' Mary blushed with embarrassment. Tom turned the comment into a joke and laughed.

'Hi Josie. It's good to meet you too.' Fortunately this made Josie smile too. She liked people who didn't shock too easily. They talked comfortably for over an hour. Tom studied the two sisters each in turn. He was fascinated by the similarities between them - their eyes, smile, voice and simple mannerisms. Mary explained, to Josie, that she was going to take Tom up to Carmacks to meet the family and that they could take her up with them if she would like that. She also invited her to spend Christmas Day with Tom, Jack and herself in Whitehorse.

'It would be really special,' said Mary, 'and I know that Dad would be thrilled. It would be my first Christmas with my very own family.'

'I don't do Christmas. I hate Christmas,' said Josie.

'Anyway there'll be too much booze around. I should go straight back to Grandpa Tommy and stay out of trouble. He don't drink – never has done.' She directed this at Tom. 'I want to see Mikey though.'

Tom could sense Mary's disappointment. Her excited smile had disappeared instantly so he intervened at this point and made a suggestion.

'What about this for a plan? We'll all go to Carmacks today and visit Jack together. Mary and I will call in on Sara, while you go to Grandpa Tommy's. You girls can stay overnight with your Grandpa and I'll get a room at the hotel. We'll all return to Whitehorse and spend Christmas together.'

'Great idea,' enthused Mary, 'and don't forget that Mikey will only be three blocks away from us because Annie has offered us her house for two nights in Porter Creek. You can spend some time with Mikey and then we'll take you both back to Carmacks when you're ready to go.'

'Don't you two sleep together?' Josie's directness took Mary by surprise. She studied Tom's face to see if it had hurt Tom, but instead, he was smiling at them both.

'It's complicated and anyway it'll be fun for you two to be together,' he said.

Josie asked the secretary to call Betty in Porter Creek so that she could make arrangements to see Mikey on Christmas Day. Betty invited her to join them for their Christmas dinner around two o'clock. Josie was very pleased.

'She's never done that before,' said Josie. 'She must trust me this time.'

'Josie you'd better get your things and we must go. The morning is nearly over,' said Mary.

Tom was astonished that Mary had managed to find Jack's cabin so easily in the dusk. The light was fading and, to Tom, every bend in the road looked the same as the one before.

'Josie you mustn't worry. Dad will be really pleased to see you, you'll be surprised. He's trying so hard at the moment. He's been buying things for the cabin and keeping it tidy,' said Mary.

'Good God!' Tom couldn't believe his eyes. 'Your father lives in there in temperatures like this? How come he hasn't died of exposure?'

'You'll find out in a minute.' Mary smiled as she knocked on the door and shouted out to him. Jack came to the door. He had trimmed his shaggy beard and was wearing clean clothes.

'Come in and warm yourselves.' He hugged Mary and then his eyes went straight to Josie. His face broke into a broad smile. He took her hand and gently pulled her towards him.

'Josie, this is a wonderful surprise. My two beautiful girls have come to see me. Holy Jesus, I can't believe it.' The tears ran down his cheeks and he put an arm around them both. 'I never thought I'd ever see this day. It's a miracle, so it is,' he said, sounding very Irish all of a sudden.

'Hi Dad. It's good to see you.' Josie wasn't used to all this sudden rush of affection from her father, but she was obviously making a big effort too. Mary's smile was the happiest that Tom had seen for a long time. He had stood by the door all this time and was moved by the scene that lay before him, a family reunited. He could see why Mary needed to stay here.

These two people really loved her. For a brief moment he felt like some sort of guardian angel smiling down on them all.

'Dad, do you remember the story about the rugby tackle? Well this is Tom. He arrived from London yesterday for a holiday in the dark.' Mary laughed as Tom stepped forward to shake Jacks' hand.

'I can see you're a rugby player. Welcome to the Yukon.' Jack rubbed his hand to revive it after Tom's firm grip and he looked frail. In fact so did Josie.

Seeing the two of them looking so thin and undernourished, as they stood next to Tom, Mary realised just what their hard lives had done to them both. She made a promise to herself that she would help them as much as possible, from now on, to make up for lost time.

They sat around the table together and drank coffee. Josie was quiet. Mary kept the conversation flowing. She told Jack how well Josie was doing at Crossroads and how she had been encouraged to return home to see how things would work out.

'I am here you know,' she said to both of them.

'Sorry,' said Jack. 'Tell me, how's Tommy doing, Josie? Is that where you stay when you come back here? I often wondered why I never saw you in the village. I always hoped I would. You two always did get on well together. Tommy was probably the father that I should have been.'

'He's good. He never changes. He's ninety four now; still chops his own wood and fishes for the whole community. He and Granny were always kind to me, especially when I was pregnant with Mikey. I'd be dead now without them. I'm going up to see him before we go back.'

'Your success at the A.A. has inspired me Josie. I

must do something about the booze in the New Year. Do you like a drink?' He asked Tom.

'I only drink socially. All rugby players do as you no doubt remember; whether they win or lose,' said Tom. Jack laughed.

'Can we drop this subject please? Dad, we have an invitation for you,' said Mary, before everyone got the taste for alcohol. 'We'd like you to come to Whitehorse with us for two nights so that we can all spend Christmas together. Annie has offered us her house while they are all in Carcross. Our first Christmas as a family – what do you think?'

'I haven't celebrated Christmas for many years. I don't know. I'm used to being on my own so I wouldn't be good company. You haven't invited Sara have you? I couldn't cope with her giving me the evil eye all the time.'

'No. It'll just be the four of us. In fact Josie is going to have Christmas dinner with her son and his foster family. So it'll be three of us for dinner.' Mary glowed with excitement.

'So, is that a 'Yes' Dad? Please say you'll come.'

'I don't know. You go and visit the rest of the family while I think about it.'

'Jack, before we go, would you like me to bring some more logs in for you? I see you're running a bit low. I like this cabin. It must be great fun living here in the summer. Do you do much fishing?' Tom asked. Mary thought he looked surprisingly at home and smiled at his enthusiasm.

'Everyone fishes and most people up here hunt too, although there are lots of rules about hunting now.' Jack picked up his rifle. 'Can't live here without one of these,' he said, polishing it lovingly.

'My Dad has one of those. It belonged to my greatgrandfather. It's been in the family for generations.'

Tom stopped suddenly and looked across at Mary.

'Dad we must go. We're staying over, so we'll come and pick you up in the morning. Don't forget to pack an overnight bag. You'll need a toothbrush, some clean socks and something to sleep in. You can't wear boots or sleep in your clothes in Annie's house,' Mary teased him and gave him a hug. Jack hugged both his girls and stood at the door waving to them.

Mary drove across the bridge and followed the narrow track up to Grandpa Tommy's with Josie acting as navigator. She didn't need light to find her way home. She knew every little landmark.

Now it was Josie's turn to be in charge. She rushed up to Tommy when she saw him. He looked surprised to see the two of them together. He said something to Josie in his language.

'What did he say?' Mary asked Josie.

'He said – 'my babies' – meaning you and me.' Josie grinned.

The visit with Tommy was a joy for everyone. Josie was happy and relaxed. Tom got along really well with the old man and went out to meet his huskies. He showed Tom some of his carvings and they disappeared out the back together while Mary and Josie made some tea and sandwiches. It was a normal domestic scene and Mary was thrilled.

'What sort of meat is this?' Mary asked as she put the last of the sandwiches on the plate.

'Moose meat. Most families come away from their fish camps in the summer with a hunk of moose for the freezer.

They kill the moose, then skin it and divide it up before bringing it back to camp. It's a tradition that has gone on for thousands of years and meant survival for everyone. I used to enjoy the family fish camp in July, but then I was banned by Grandma Sara because I couldn't control my drinking. I guess I was around fifteen or sixteen,' Josie chatted on. 'Grandpa and Granny were real angry about that at the time.'

While they were alone, Mary told Josie about the dilemma of Grandpa Davey James, and the fact that she and Tom might be related. Josie was shocked. She wanted to know what her grandfather was like. Mary also explained about Jake and Jake's family in Carcross.

'I've only just told Tom about Jake. Tom was devastated. This trip is really difficult for him and he's trying so hard to fit in with everyone. He's a very special person. I really hope we can stay friends.'

'The cops up here will want to know that Grandpa Davey has been found. Are you gonna tell them? He's a thief for Christ's sake. He stole a fortune. He needs to do his time. What about Tom's mother?'

'I reckon she's the one that will tell the police. She's a real snob. She hates me.' said Mary.

Tom came into the kitchen. 'No-one hates you darling. What are you telling Josie?'

'Actually, Josie was asking about Grandpa Davey. So I told her what's just happened. Is anyone hungry? Come on, let's eat.' Mary was becoming very skilled at avoiding people's awkward questions.

'Mary, I hope you don't mind but I'm going to stay here with Tommy and Josie while you visit Sara,' said Tom quietly. 'In the circumstances I don't think I want to meet her. I'd feel very uncomfortable. Anyway, Tommy has offered to let me have a go at wood carving and I'd love to do that. Some of his stuff is fantastic.'

'I don't blame you,' said Josie. 'She's a hard faced cow! I don't want to see her either. She's ruined all our lives when you think about it.'

'Only up until now,' said Mary. 'Okay. I'll go on my

319

own. I've got a Christmas present for her.'

'Will you be alright on your own in the dark? Come back soon won't you?' Tom gave her a hug.

When Mary arrived at Sara's house she parked next to Sylvia's truck. She knocked on the door and walked in cautiously. Sara seemed to be cleaning a cut above Sylvia's left eye. Mary could hardly believe it was Sara. She was being so gentle and caring. She obviously loved her niece. A month ago Sylvia would have hidden her face from Mary but this time neither of them moved.

'Hello Grandma, or should I say Nurse Sara? What's happened to you?' she asked Sylvia.

'Her old man's a drunk,' said Sara. 'I tell her she should leave and live with me. She says he's good when he's sober. They all say it.'

'Well he is,' said Sylvia, 'and anyway, he'd only come and drag me back home.'

Mary laid her Christmas presents on the table.

'These gifts are for you both. They're only small, but it's the thought that counts, isn't it? My holiday savings have almost gone. Shall I make us all a cup of tea?'

'Thank you,' said Sara. 'You know where everything is. Where's that boyfriend of yours?'

'Tom sends his apologies. Grandpa Tommy is helping him to do a woodcarving. I couldn't tear him away. He's really keen. What's everyone doing for Christmas by the way? Do you usually have a family gathering?'

'Not since Granny Edith died. No-one bothers. Auntie and I'll probably go up to Grandpa's for the day like we do every Sunday. It'll be a normal day for us. What are you doing?' Sara put a band aid across the cut on Sylvia's forehead. 'There,' she said.

'We're celebrating it with Jack and Josie in Whitehorse. We're staying in Annie's house for two nights while they're in Carcross. A family Christmas. I'm quite excited about it,' said Mary.

'Jack in someone's smart house? You'd better hose him down first.' Sylvia said coldly.

'You should see him. He's taking more care of himself lately. He's even tidied his cabin and bought some new things. Tom really got on well with him,' said Mary pointedly. Sylvia's comment had hurt.

'Grandma, I've come to wish you both a Merry Christmas, but also to tell you that I'll be going back to England with Tom on the 2 January, just for two or three weeks, and then I'll be back in Whitehorse for good. Josie and I are talking about sharing an apartment together and looking for jobs. Josie is doing really well at the moment.' Sara said nothing.

'What about your boyfriend?' Sylvia had been looking forward to meeting him.

'Thanks to Grandpa Davey, Tom and I are now connected by marriage and anyway, Tom wouldn't want to live here. He would miss his rugby, and the English pubs,' laughed Mary.

'Well well much has happened since you came last time,' said Sara with a weak smile. Mary gave them both a quick hug and said she would see them sometime in January.

'Tell Davey to get back here and do his time or I'll tell the cops myself,' said Sara. Mary felt sure that Charlotte would beat her to it.

'Merry Christmas Mary and thanks for the gift. 'Bye,' said Sylvia.

The next morning Mary felt quite sad saying goodbye to her Grandpa. It had been fun, staying there with Josie. She felt as though they were recapturing a little of their lost childhood. They talked long into the night so Mary hoped that Tom would drive them back to Whitehorse.

They collected Tom from the hotel and went to get Jack.

'Come in if you know me, go away if you don't,' called Jack as Mary gave three knocks. He sounded as though he was in a good mood. As Mary walked in, Jack was washing up in a large enamel bowl which he'd placed in the middle of the table. Some soap and a small cracked mirror lay to one side. He'll probably feel lost in Annie's big house, thought Mary.

'Morning Dad. Are you nearly ready? We thought we'd make an early start; lots of shopping to do before we get to Annie's,' said Mary. She grabbed a cloth and helped him to put everything back in its place. She noticed a basket full of empty beer cans on the floor by the stove.

'I hope you had a proper meal last night, Dad.' Jack grunted, and gave Mary a re-assuring hug.

'Are the others still in the car? Bring them in. They'll freeze to death out there,' he said.

'Tom is driving and he's left the engine running, so hurry up.' Jack grabbed a tattered day-sack, turned out the new lamps and put the padlock on the front door.

Once out on the highway, Mary, Josie and Jack exchanged stories in the dark. Everyone's guard was down and the visit to Carmacks had been good. Sara didn't know what she was missing, thought Mary. When she told Mary that she had no interest in Christmas get-togethers, Mary felt sad for her. She'd either lost members of the family or she'd driven them away. Maybe next year would be different.

Once in Whitehorse, Mary suggested that Tom and Jack go off and have lunch somewhere, whilst she and Josie did some grocery shopping. Mary also wanted to buy Jack a new parka. His old one was falling apart. She'd already bought Tom and Josie a present, and also a new transformer toy for Mikey.

She was now relying totally upon her American Express credit card.

'I haven't bought presents for anyone except Mikey,' said Josie. 'I bet Jack hasn't either.'

'Don't worry love.' Mary put her arm around her. 'That's not what tomorrow is all about. It's about all of us being together. You know I was thinking Josie – wouldn't it be great if you and I could share an apartment together in Whitehorse, when I get back from the U.K.? What do you think?'

'Share an apartment, what with? I haven't got no money. Either you live in a dream world or you have a secret fortune stashed away somewhere.' Josie looked sad.

'We could get jobs. Annie said there might be a vacancy for a special support assistant in February, in a school in Porter Creek. Someone she knows is going on maternity leave. That's the job I've been doing in London for the past five years. My principal would give me a good reference. We could manage on my earnings until you decide what you want to do. Think about it while I'm away.'

'When are you and Tom leaving?' she asked.

'Our flight is on January 2nd. Tom has to be back in school on January 5th for a training day. I'll definitely be back here by the end of January, if not before.'

'Poor Tom,' said Josie. It was Mary's turn to look sad.

Mary let them in through the garage and Tom parked the car. Jack took his boots off by the door and headed straight for George Hughes' lazy-boy chair in front of the T.V.

'Now isn't this just what I need,' he said and promptly fell asleep.

'He had quite a few beers at lunchtime,' said Tom.

'We went to the Edgewater, his local bar, he told me.'

'Also, he doesn't have the luxury of a chair like this very often. Bless him,' said Mary. 'Tom, are you going back to the hotel tonight or are you staying here? Annie has put clean sheets in Julie's room for you if you'd like to stay with us for two nights. Dad is in Jake's room and Josie is sharing with me. Maybe you should call the hotel though, in case they think you've checked out.' Mary saw the pain in his face and her heart ached for him. 'Oh Tom, I'm so sorry. You're being wonderful, with all of us and I can see that you're hurting.'

'Don't say anymore Mary. It doesn't help,' said Tom.

'Now where's this room? I hope it's not all pink and fluffy, like Mandy's bedroom.' He grinned at Josie as he carried his overnight bag and Jack's day-sack upstairs.

Christmas Day was a huge success and the tension surrounding the alcohol worked out well. Jack drank when Josie was in bed or with Mikey, but not when she was with them. Mary and Tom did the same. Josie would have made her counsellor and her support worker proud. They had a big Christmas breakfast with Christmas crackers so that Josie could be part of it all. Jack gave a little speech which made Mary cry and everyone raised their glass of orange juice. Each one opened their Christmas present and Mary was overwhelmed when she saw the gold bracelet from Tom. She had bought him a black leather travel wallet with his name printed on it in gold. Everyone clapped when Jack tried on his new coat. Josie said very little when she saw the silver locket and chain from Mary, but Mary could see she was pleased. Also, Mary had copied the photo that Sara had lent her, of Josie and herself as babies.

Mary and Tom cooked the Christmas dinner together while Jack dozed in front of the T.V. with a couple of bottles of Yukon Gold.

When Josie got back from seeing her son, she was happy and relaxed. Mary felt like singing, something she hadn't done since the barbeque in Carcross.

'Tom, is there a guitar in Julie's room?' Mary asked.

'Yes there is. I tuned it last night before I went to bed.'

'You can play a few chords, Tom, so let's have a singsong and Josie can sing some of her own songs to us.'

'Great, I'll go first,' said Jack, much to the surprise of everyone, and he began to sing his version of 'The Wild Rover', an Irish folksong that Mary had sung many times in the folk club in Greenwich. She and Tom joined in the chorus.

This has been the best day of my life, thought Mary ... and then she thought of Jake.

<u>Chapter 30</u>

Once back at the hotel Tom sat back in the armchair in his room and dialled Sally's number. She had left him a message to call her. He was tired. The strain of meeting new people and being in party mood, when he was nursing a broken heart, was beginning to show. Sally's message was a welcome surprise and a chat with her was just what he needed right now.

'Hi Sally. Sorry I missed you yesterday. We were up in Carmacks with Mary's family. We've been backwards and forwards from there all week.'

'Hello Tom. How's it going? How was your Christmas?' She sounded tired too.

'It was surprisingly harmonious. Mary had her first family Christmas. Her father and her sister joined us and it worked out fine. It's been hard to keep smiling though. Sally, did you know that Mary has been seeing a local man called Jake Hughes and that she's decided to stay here permanently in the Yukon?' Tom asked.

'Yes. Mary told me when I visited her in October. I've been thinking of you since you left, Tom. You poor love. What's the news in connection with your father?'

'I've just had a message from Karen to say that if Mary and I intend to marry then our marriage will be legal, as I was adopted as a baby and we were both raised separately, just as she said it would be. Well, it doesn't matter now as I've lost her anyway.' Tom felt a lump in his throat and his voice cracked.

'Come for dinner when you get home. We'll have a

good long talk. What's the date and time of your arrival?
My parents will still be with us so I'm free to meet you if
you like?'

'Mary is coming back with me. She's changed the date
of her return flight. There's a lot for her to sort out. She'll
need a new dual passport for a start. I'm not looking
forward to any of it. It'll simply be prolonging the agony
as far as I'm concerned. I'll have to take a rain check on
that dinner I'm afraid.'

'Oh well. It'll be lovely to see you both.' Sally didn't
really know what to say, so she didn't say anything.
'What time shall I meet you – is it still January 3rd?'

'How about - in the Terminal 3 arrivals hall around
11.00am? Thanks Sally. It's really good of you. I'll tell
Mary when I meet her for lunch later. How was your
Christmas by the way?'

'Oh fine. We went to church on Christmas morning
and then I cooked for the four of us this year, to give
Mum a break. William went to his father's for Boxing
Day. The rest of us went for a walk in Greenwich Park
and had a drink by the river. You know, the usual. I'm
not due back at work until Monday January 7th.'

'I wonder what my parents' Christmas was like. I've
tried not to think about it. Anyway, I must go. I'm
meeting Mary in half an hour. Thanks again Sally. See
you on Wednesday. 'Bye.'

There was a long queue at the Whitehorse airport.
Everyone had chosen the same day to return home after
the holiday. Mary and Tom had spent the last two days
saying 'goodbye' to Mary's family and friends –
everyone except Jake. Tom was relieved that he had kept
well out of the way. He assumed that Jake and Mary had
had some private time together back at Annie's. Mary
hadn't said anything. She seemed sad and was very quiet.
Whatever Tom said to her, her mind seemed to be

elsewhere. God, this line-up is slow, thought Tom. Mary suddenly jumped up and waved. She could see Jake running past the check-in counters. He stopped when he saw her. Mary turned to Tom,

'Tom, excuse me for a minute. I can't leave without saying 'goodbye' to Jake. Sorry.'

Tom watched as Mary hurried down to meet him and winced when she hurled herself into his arms. He turned his back on them, cursing that the scene would stay in his memory forever now. He was almost at the conveyor belt when Mary ran back, panting heavily.

'I'm so sorry Tom.' She said again. She clutched a tiny gift and was flushed with excitement.

It was a quiet and rather morose journey home. Luckily it was a night flight so Tom watched a movie and then slept for a few hours after two large whiskies and some red wine with their meal. Mary had curled up with her head on his shoulder to sleep. It felt so like old times ... but those times had gone.

'Wake up Mary, we'll be there soon,' he said.

'Thank you Tom. I hope I haven't missed breakfast.'

'Oh, I think a roll and a coffee or something similar is on its way.' Tom sighed. They had nothing to say to each other.

Seeing Sally rushing towards them soon lifted their spirits. Tom felt surprisingly pleased to see her and realised he had missed her during the past two weeks. Mary sat in the front of the car with Sally and told her every little detail of her family get-togethers. Tom was relieved as it meant that he could catch up on some sleep most of the way home. Mary was too excited to sleep.

'One of the things I have to sort out is my passport,

now that I know that I was born in Canada.' Tom heard her telling Sally. 'As Dad is from Ireland, I should be eligible for a dual passport.'

'I can't get used to hearing you talk about 'Dad', all the time, after all these years?' Sally smiled.

'It's wonderful isn't it? Sally, while Tom is sleeping,' she lowered her voice, 'could I possibly stay with you and Will once your parents go home? I don't think it'll be fair on Tom to carry on living with him. He's suffering enough as it is, without me sleeping in the next room. I'll pay my way.'

'Of course you can. It must have been really hard for Tom up in the Yukon with you. Some men would have got on the next plane home.' Sally's words were like a slap and Mary hung her head.

Tom heard every word, but kept his eyes closed. He felt comforted by Sally's words of support.

When they got back to Greenwich, Sally's mother was busy preparing a roast lamb dinner for them all. Tom thought it smelled wonderful and instantly his heart felt lighter. Sally had bought them a bag of groceries as their fridge would be empty. She had even included a six pack of lager and there was a present for both of them under her tree.

'You are so thoughtful Sally. You think of everything. Thanks a lot,' said Tom. 'Where on earth did Mary find you?'

'At the Playgroup,' laughed Sally.

The next morning Tom looked across the breakfast table at Mary and knew that living with her for more than a couple of days would be impossible. She wanted to talk about her plans and her future, but he didn't want to hear about any of it. He'd offered to help where necessary but he was grieving for the fiancée he no longer had. Mary didn't seem to notice sometimes; her head and her heart were in the Yukon. They hadn't even talked about his father – Mary's grandfather.

'Mary, what do you want to do about my father? Do you want to see him, as his grand-daughter, or would you rather forget all about him? I'll have to visit him at the weekend, that's if mother hasn't already reported him to the police. If she hasn't, I want to try to persuade him to do the honest thing and own up, although I can't decide which would be worse, a convict for a father or a thief. What do you think about it all?' Tom spoke without emotion. The tears had already been shed.

'I can't decide either. The main reason I'd want to see him is to hear stories about my mother. Grandma Sara gave me those two photos but she hasn't said much about her. He's not likely to want to sit and reminisce with his mind full of all of this is he? I wish he wasn't wanted by the police. I've always liked your Dad, but I don't see how I can keep in touch with him now. I think you'd better go on your own, Tom. Anyway, your mother certainly won't want to see me.' Mary was looking through the telephone directory for the number of the Canadian High Commission. An unfamiliar silence fell between them as they each withdrew into their own thoughts. Tom picked up the local newspaper.

'As he flicked through the Classified Ads., a private advertisement jumped out at him from the 'motoring' section. He couldn't believe what he was reading:

FOR SALE : '1974 Triumph Stag V8
convertible with hard top. 4 seats,new engine,
fully restored. Burgundy, with biscuit interior.'

'Hey, look at this, Mary, the very car I've dreamed about for years. The phone number is local so maybe it's a collector of classic cars. Do you reckon I could talk my mother into lending me the money? I feel I need a spot of luxury right now. I'm going into school today, just to meet up with everyone and to collect my timetable. I think I'll go and have a look at this car first. Do you want to come with me?'

'Sorry Tom. I've got so much sorting out to do here and also I have to find out about this new passport. But you go ahead. It's a great idea. You've searched for this car ever since I've known you,' said Mary.

Tom dialled the number, excitedly, and rushed out, leaving Mary to sort through her things and clear out all her rubbish. She'd lived with him for nearly six years. He couldn't believe how much rubbish she'd accumulated. He'd been instructed to find a large, strong box, as most of her clothes would have to be sent on ahead. This is all so final, he thought, and to think that this time last year they were planning a holiday together in Ireland.

As he climbed into his old Peugeot, he pictured himself behind the wheel of his dream car. It won't remove the pain I'm feeling, but it'll help, he thought, smiling to himself.

This was one trip that Tom did not want to do but it couldn't be avoided. He really did not know what he would find on arrival. His mother had said very little on the phone, just that she had to drive to Bury for an appointment in the morning but hoped to see him in the afternoon. She said she would think about the money for the car as she hadn't bought him a Christmas present yet, but she would need to see it, of course. In fact she had said –'If it's that luxurious, you can drive me back to Woodbridge in it. I'll wear my fur coat.'

Tom was relieved. It would be easier without her at the house. He would have a good heart to heart with his

Dad and try to talk some sense into him.

As he turned the corner into the lane that ran past his parents' estate, he could see three police cars parked in front of their gates. His heart sank. He parked his car and walked over to the officer in charge who was giving instructions on his walkie-talkie.

'Good morning. My name is Tom Selby-James and my parents live in that house,' he said. 'What's happened, although I think I can guess? Did you receive a phone call from my mother by any chance?'

'No. We had a tip-off from the R.C.M.P in Canada to say a wanted thief by the name of David James could be traced to this address in Woodbridge. Actually, they just said 'a big classy house near Woodbridge', so my men called here to talk to your father,' he said.

Tom was surprised. Mary had told him of Sara's threat and Sara had kept to her word. He really hadn't expected this.

'Why so many cars? My Dad's an old man. He's seventy five years old and he's in there on his own. My mother is out for the morning. Are you arresting him?' Tom asked.

'We will when he puts his gun down,' the officer said. 'He sounds very upset and his rifle is clearly visible. The house is now surrounded by my men. He's been up there for over an hour now and all the entrances to the building are locked. We'd prefer that he came peacefully.'

'I'll go and talk to him. He won't shoot. He really is not a violent man. Anyway, I doubt very much whether there's any ammunition in his old rifle.' Tom walked down the drive, straining his eyes to try to see where his father was hiding.

As he approached the edge of the forecourt he could see the barrel of a rifle jutting out from the study window.

'Dad – what the hell are you doing? It's me, Tom. Put

that gun down. I need to talk to you.'

'Keep out of this son. Don't get involved. This is nothing to do with you,' David called down to him. 'This is Mary's fault. We were doing fine before she spoilt it all.'

Tom spoke to one of the police officers and explained that he needed to talk to his father. They spoke to their chief and then agreed to let him have half an hour with him.

'Dad, I'm coming round the back, to the dogs, so let me in through the kitchen door,' he yelled.

The door clicked open and then was immediately locked again. David looked ill. His grey hair was ruffled where he'd run his fingers through it a hundred times, he hadn't shaved, and he had a mad look in his eyes. He clutched his gun to his chest and stared at Tom.

'You'll have a heart attack if you carry on like this Dad.

What do you think you're doing? There are police everywhere outside. They're looking for a thief not a homicidal maniac. Oh Dad. Look at you.' He gave his father a hug.

'I'm an old man. I don't want to die in prison.' He was trembling and was near to tears. 'Charlotte had agreed to say nothing about it so we could carry on as we are. I might be dead soon, anyway.' Tom led him into the drawing room by the fire and poured him a large brandy.

'But Dad, could you live with yourself, knowing that we have all heard the details of what happened thirty odd years ago? How do you think I felt hearing that my father, who I love, had embezzled thousands of dollars from a bar and had hidden under an assumed name in England all these years? You've got to face this. How much was it anyway?'

'About ten grand or thereabouts, I think. I don't know. It was a long time ago.'

'Ten grand? You and Mum could pay that back between you, surely? Also the Courts would take into account that you've led a good and honest life since you settled here with us. You never know, they might be lenient and let you off with a fine. It depends how they feel about your John Wayne showdown. Come on Dad. Let's face this together.'

Meanwhile Charlotte had arrived home and was trying her best to persuade the police to let her go into the house to talk to her husband.

'I know he has a gun Officer, but the gun is not loaded. It belonged to my grandfather and has been locked away in the games room for years. Please let me talk to him. He's an old man, much older than me, of course. He has a weak heart and is probably very frightened. You've let my son go in.'

The policeman finally relented and told his men to let her through. Very few people ever lost a battle with Charlotte.

'Oh God! That's the front door.' David lifted his rifle into position and came close to hitting Charlotte, who had just rushed into the room.

'Put that thing down, you silly old fool. You could hurt yourself, not to mention Tom and me. I leave the house for four hours and this is what happens. Tom did you do this – did you phone the police?'

'No of course I didn't. The mother of his children did. She contacted the R.C.M.P.'

'I suppose that wretched girl told her where we lived. I knew all along she'd be trouble.'

Tom went to the front door and begged the police for more time. He reassured them that the gun was now safely behind lock and key in the games room. He poured his mother a drink and the three of them tried to discuss the situation rationally. It was difficult. Everyone was upset and his father looked exhausted.

'You'll probably be released on bail, so you can go to bed as soon as you get back from the station. We'll go with you, won't we Mother?' He topped up his father's glass.

Tom took Charlotte to one side and told her quietly to pack a little overnight bag for him just in case. She rushed out of the room in tears.

The three of them walked out together and were met by the officer in charge and two other policemen. He read out the charges and checked David's pockets. Charlotte was still tearful.

Tom asked where they were taking him.

'I'll follow you,' said Tom. 'I have to make a phone call. Don't worry. I'll lock up behind me.' Tom watched the car disappear out of sight and then rang Mary. She was upset, of course.

'Fancy Sara reporting him. She must have loads of anger stored up inside her to go to all that trouble,' said Mary. 'I do hope he gets a fine rather than a prison sentence. I'm glad I didn't come with you. By the sounds of it, I'd have made things a lot worse. Are you alright Tom?'

'As well as can be expected after the year I've just had,' sighed Tom. 'I'll see you tomorrow.'

'Sally and William are coming over for Sunday lunch tomorrow and then we're going to feed the ducks in Greenwich Park if you want to get back in time to join us,' said Mary. 'I'll leave it up to you.'

The visit to the police station was distressing for all of them and to make things worse, Charlotte had forgotten to bring the Warfarin pills for David. They all had to give

separate statements, and they kept asking the same
questions over and over again. Tom reminded them that
his father was seventy five and had a weak heart. He also
stressed that he'd been a pillar of the community for over
thirty years and was highly respected at the rugby club
and his local church. Charlotte was surprisingly quiet.
Tom assumed that she didn't want to make things any
worse for his Dad. He saw her in a new light. She
obviously loved him. It showed. After an exhausting two
or three hours it was finally agreed that David could be
released on bail, pending further investigation.

'This case might have to be handed back to the
Canadian police,' said the Inspector. So don't try to leave
the country. We'll need your passport; and make sure you
remain at your home address for the time being. I suggest
you get yourself a solicitor, someone who knows you
well.'

'Come on Dad – let's go home.' Tom led his
traumatised parents out to his car.

'I don't suppose this is a good time to mention my
new car?' Tom asked tentatively. Silence from the back
seat was the only answer he needed.

'I guess that's a 'No' then.' Yet another of his dreams
had been shattered.

Tom had specifically asked Mary to move out of their
flat while he was there. She knew it would be more
painful that way, but Mary had agreed. She would have
felt as though she was creeping out from behind his back
if she'd left while he was at work. He'd helped her so
much to organize her departure. Her clothes and
mementoes had been sent to Whitehorse already, her new
passport was being processed and her two flights were
booked. He had even offered to lend her some money
until she found a job.

'You've been so lucky Mary,' said Sally. 'I've never known anyone quite like him – ever.'

Chapter 31
February 1991

The snow was falling thick and fast across the country. Some flights to North America had been cancelled. Mary stayed close to the radio and the television. Sally had offered to drive her to the airport, but Mary was worried that she might get stuck in traffic jams on the motorway. It was a nightmare. Jake telephoned from Whitehorse to check on her plans and Tom said he would drive her to Heathrow Airport if she needed him to. His Peugeot was bigger and more roadworthy in the snow than Sally's car.

'I don't think it'll be fair to expect Tom to see me off this time,' said Mary. 'We'll both get upset and I'll worry about him as he makes his way home alone in all this bad weather.'

'I could travel with you both so that Tom has company driving home. William could go to his friend's house for the day, I'm sure,' offered Sally.

'Then I would worry about both of you. Oh God! I don't know what to do for the best.' Mary wanted her decision to be right for everyone. 'Maybe I should just go down to London by bus.'

'You've got a whole week yet. The weather could change completely by next Saturday. Let's not panic. Let's wait and see.'

'How am I going to manage without you to keep me calm?' Mary said, giving Sally a hug. 'We'll always remain friends, won't we?'

'Of course we will. Don't forget that there'll always be a bed for you here if you want to come back for a visit; for either you on your own or with Jake.'

'Thanks Sal and I hope you bring William to Whitehorse one day. Mikey would like that. Sally you must promise that you'll keep an eye on Tom for me, especially in the next few months. He's pretending to be so strong at the moment and I know he's a lot more upset than he makes out. It's been a year of hell for him what with one thing and another. First me, then his father and he didn't even get his dream car. I'll ring from time to time, to see how you're both doing and I'll write as often as I can.'

It was wonderful staying with Sally again. It was quite like old times. Mary cooked dinner every night during the working week. She really enjoyed it. Annie had done all the cooking in Whitehorse, and Tom often preferred to be in charge of the kitchen at home. He did most of the shopping too.

Mary visited the staff and the pupils at school, before the holiday, and said her farewells. Roy had asked her to come in for an Assembly and he presented her with a new flight bag and a school photograph from the staff. She told them that she hoped to be working in a Canadian school very soon, up north in the Yukon. Mary's last week in London happened to be the half-term week so she was able to have lots of time with Sally and William. She and Sally had a day in the city. They shopped in Oxford Street, had lunch at Garfunkels, giggled like teenagers as they had their photos taken in a booth in Woolworths and watched a movie in the afternoon. They both realised that they hadn't done this kind of thing often enough in the past and they relished every moment.

Also, Mary spent an afternoon with Karen and brought

her up-to-date with all the news. They lit candles and meditated together. Karen asked if she could visit Mary in the Yukon sometime. She said she would love to talk to the local First Nations people about their spiritual beliefs and would also like to meet Grandpa Tommy after listening to Mary's wonderful description of him. Mary took the opportunity to enjoy Blackheath and Greenwich one last time although she felt sure that she'd be back for visits. They had been her home for nearly ten years and the memories, both good and bad, that they held for her would be forever imprinted on her heart.

Tom went to Woodbridge at the end of the week and reported that the roads were much clearer. His father was still waiting for the date of his trial. The weather had certainly improved and the final decision was that Tom and Sally would both go to the airport with Mary. William didn't want to go.

'I've been before,' he said. 'The car journey's too long. It's boring.'

The snow had cleared and early signs of spring helped to lift the grey days of winter. The nights were cold still and black ice was a problem, even on the major roads to and from London. Mary's night flight to Vancouver left at 17.15, so they planned a leisurely drive to Heathrow.

Mary woke up early on the Saturday morning. It was still dark and as she lay in bed listening to the early morning traffic in Greenwich she tried to imagine what her life would become in the months ahead. She was feeling very emotional about this last trip with Tom, and had even awoken in the middle of a bad dream in the early hours, something she hadn't done for a long time. It seemed so final this time and yet she was sure that Tom and Sally would all keep in touch with her. Leaving Tom behind at the airport would be like leaving part of her soul behind. She knew that Jake would have to be patient with her for a while. Jake had said, in his last phone call, that he had a surprise waiting for her in Vancouver, but he wouldn't say any more.

'Wouldn't it be wonderful if Jake was there to meet me off the plane in Vancouver?' Mary confided in Sally, as they ate breakfast together, 'especially as I have to stay overnight before going to Whitehorse. Maybe he's booked a room for us in a hotel nearby? I won't be able to sleep on the plane. I'll be too excited just thinking about it.'

'Be careful,' said Sally. 'You know what you're like. The surprise might be totally different and then you'll be terribly disappointed.'

The drive to Heathrow was easy. Tom had allowed time for road-works or accidents on the M25, but there weren't any. Mary sat in the front with Tom but however hard they tried there was tension between them. Sally chatted on from the back seat and tried to keep the conversation light and casual. She talked about her son and also about her determination to find a lovely man this year.

'I've been on my own long enough,' said Sally. 'There must be someone out there who's waiting for me to come along. William could do with a male role model too. He's getting to that difficult age.'

Mary wanted to tease her about Tom, but she felt that he wouldn't appreciate the joke today.

Once in Terminal 3, Mary checked in her luggage and then all three of them went in search of a cafe or a bar for a final drink together. Sally had arranged with Tom that she would drive them home. She'd also said that she would leave him to finally see Mary off on his own, so she said her goodbyes in the cafe. With tears in her eyes, she held her arms out to Mary.

'Sal, I don't want to say 'Goodbye', because it's too final. You'll always be the best friend that anyone could ever have and I'll miss you loads. Don't forget to write. I'll be desperate for all the gossip,' said Mary. Both of them were in tears.

'Take care of yourself Mary and don't forget what I said – our spare room is yours if ever you need it. I hope all works out well with your family. Keep me informed won't you?'

The two of them clung to one another and finally Sally gently pushed Mary away and told her to get going in case she missed the plane. She stood and waved as Tom led Mary towards the departure gate.

Strangely enough, when the moment came, Mary found it easier to part from Tom than from Sally. Officially, they had separated in the High Country Inn in Whitehorse weeks ago, and the tears had already been shed. Tom gave her a hug and one last kiss and Mary promised to always keep in touch.

'Take care of yourself, darling,' was all he said, as she joined the queue.

'And you Tom ... thanks for everything. Have a safe journey home. 'Bye.' And she was gone.

When Tom got back to the cafe, Sally was in the pub next door waving at him. She had bought him a large whisky. She looked up and smiled.

'Cheers Tom,' she said, raising her glass of Coca Cola. 'I suggest that I ring my friend to see if she'll have William overnight and then we could go out for a nice dinner somewhere. What do you think?'

'Thank goodness it's Saturday, otherwise we'd be just in time for the rush-hour,' said Tom. 'Dinner somewhere sounds a good idea. Let's gets off the main motorway at some point and find a country pub with a log fire.' They found exactly that, about an hour later, in Surrey.

They chose a table facing the fire and lit the candle. Tom's mind had become preoccupied as he sat watching the traffic on the motorway. It suddenly struck him what an unsure future now stretched before him. Mary had gone from his life, his father might have to go to prison and might even be sent back to Canada, his mother wouldn't be able to run the estate on her own, and he'd be back to the bachelor life after all these years. Maybe he would apply to teach abroad for a while.

'A penny for them,' said Sally, breaking the silence between them. 'There's something about an open fire isn't there? It's the flames. They seem to give flight to your thoughts and to your memories don't they?'

'I'm sorry Sally. I'm not good company for you today. I was thinking about the uncertainty of my future and what I'll do with myself now that I'm single again.'

'I suggest that you don't plan anything for a while. You never know what's likely to be around the corner and it tends not to appear if you try too hard. I've tested that one out myself. Don't forget Tom if you ever need some female company, I'm only at the bottom of Maze Hill,' said Sally.

'I know. Thanks. You've been great.'

After their meal, they sat either side of the fire with their coffee for a while until Sally began to relax just a little too much. The warmth was making her feel a little drowsy. It was time to go.

By the time they reached the A2 to Blackheath, they were both feeling tired; in fact Tom was asleep. Even Sally's C.Ds hadn't kept him awake. Just as she turned off on to the slip road that led across the heath, the car hit a patch of black ice and spun across the left hand lane. A driver in a large black car appeared from nowhere it seemed. He tried to overtake her on the left, just as her car skidded. Sally had indicated that they were turning left but it was too late. There was a horrid sound of crunching metal and breaking glass and Tom was screaming. The car had smashed straight into the passenger side door of Tom's Peugeot and he was lying across the dashboard at an awkward angle. His face was lying in broken glass. The driver of the offending vehicle backed up and then screeched ahead to the roundabout leaving them in a crumpled heap at the side of the road. Sally appeared to be unhurt, and Tom had passed out.

'Oh my God!' cried Sally. 'Oh Tom, please don't be dead. I couldn't bear it.' The tears were streaming down her cheeks. She jumped, as a loud knock on her window brought her back to her senses.

'Are you alright Miss? I saw the whole thing and I took that guy's number. I'm a cab driver and I was right behind you. Selfish bastard! He didn't even stop.' The man was staring across at Tom.

'I *seem* to be alright, but my friend isn't. He screamed when it happened and then he fainted; at least I hope he fainted. Can you help us?' Sally asked, shaking with shock.

'He needs an ambulance. I'll call my office and ask them to get one for you. Don't worry. I haven't got a passenger, so I'll wait with you until the ambulance comes. I'll just put my cab off the road. Here's the registration number of the idiot who crashed into you. My name's Charlie, by the way. Blimey Miss, you're shaking. I'll get a blanket for you.'

'Thank you. You're being very kind.'

Sally stroked Tom's back gently, wishing him to wake up. She felt so helpless.

'Describe the impact to me Miss,' said the paramedic

to Mary, twenty minutes later.

'I saw the whole thing,' said Charlie. 'This idiot in a BMW tried to overtake the lady's car on the left whilst she was going into the left lane and he hit the passenger door head on. He could see that she was indicating. He was going at quite a speed. Too fast on these icy roads.'

'The impact has bent the door inwards and appears to be dangerously close to your husband's side Miss. It's impossible to really see his injuries at the moment. I think we'll have to get the fire brigade to cut off the roof and lift him out that way. Better call the police too.'

'Someone already has,' said Charlie as he saw the lights and heard the sirens approaching.

'I suggest that you sit in your friend's vehicle over there, while we do this,' said a kindly fireman. It's rather a dramatic operation and it looks worse than it is.'

'Come on Miss,' said Charlie, helping Sally out of the car. 'I'll put some music on to drown the noise.' He wrapped the blanket around her shoulders.

'Tell me when he's been lifted out. I can't bear to look.' Sally closed her eyes and prayed.

She eventually stepped out of Charlie's taxi, and Tom was in the ambulance. When she saw the tangled mass of his car and noticed his blood-soaked passenger seat, she cried out and then promptly fainted.

As soon as Tom was in the safe hands of the staff in the Accident and Emergency department, Sally rang Charlotte and David to let them know what had happened. She assured them that she would stay at Tom's side during the night and would give them a progress report in the morning. She also rang the friend who was looking after William, to see if she could keep him until late afternoon on Sunday, or at least until Tom's parents arrived.

Waiting alone in the waiting room for news of Tom was like being in the midst of a nightmare. Sally had thought he was dead and she realised she was still shaking. Where was the doctor? She was desperate to know the extent of Tom's injuries. She sipped some hot, sweet tea that one of the nurses had given her and stared at the clock on the wall – 9.40pm. Finally a doctor arrived to talk to her. Sally held her breath.

'Your friend is a very lucky chap. It could have been a lot worse by all accounts. Tom has a deep tear in the upper left thigh and he has lost quite a lot of blood. The x-ray showed that he has three broken ribs and his left hip was dislocated, but fortunately, not broken. He also has whiplash and minor lacerations to the face and neck. He is now in theatre having repairs to his thigh as there has been some muscle damage. Overall though, he'll be fine. Is there anyone we should call?' He patted Sally's hand.

'I've already rung Tom's parents. They live in Suffolk, so they'll visit him tomorrow. Can I see Tom when he is out of the theatre?' Sally asked feeling relieved that Tom's injuries were not life-threatening.

'Of course. The staff nurse will take you to him. Has anyone seen to you? I gather that you were driving when the accident happened?' He smiled at Sally.

'Yes, thank you. I'm still a little shaken. I'll feel better when I've seen Tom,' said Sally.

'Please excuse me, I must go.' The doctor's 'bleeper' had called him away.

The next morning, Sally managed to eat some breakfast in the restaurant while the nurses were seeing to Tom. He had slept through most of the night and Sally had tried to doze in the armchair at the side of his bed. When she returned to the ward, Tom was sitting propped up against the pillows. He looked a sorry sight, unshaved with a mosaic of cuts all over his face and his neck encased in a support collar.

'Oh Tom. I feel awful that I didn't manage to steer you away from all that. You poor love. How are you feeling?'

'It hurts to breathe. Don't make me laugh whatever you do. I've got morphine for the surgery on my leg and I can use it whenever I need it.' He said pointing to the control button that was lying in his lap. 'Please don't apologise Sally. We hit an icy patch. You did a damn good job controlling the car the way you did. It was that idiot who crashed into us. What exactly happened?'

Sally described the accident to Tom and explained what had happened to his Peugeot. She mentioned the kindly cab driver and the fact that he managed to get the registration number of the offending BMW.

'My poor old car! So it was taken to the dump in pieces, was it? Thank goodness we weren't in the Triumph Stag. I'd probably have been driving and you would be lying here instead,' he sighed. 'I've got thirty staples holding my thigh together. Imagine that. Have you got a mirror? I want to see what my face looks like.' Sally searched through her handbag. She had everything but a mirror.

'Don't worry. We've got a visitor,' said Tom as he watched his mother enter the ward.

'Oh my poor darling,' she gushed. 'You look absolutely frightful. What happened to your face? You haven't broken your neck have you?'

'No mother. They are just little cuts from the broken glass and this collar means I have whiplash. I've had surgery on the slash in my thigh and I've broken three ribs. Apart from that, I'm fine. Mother, you remember Sally don't you?' Tom re-introduced Sally, while Charlotte pulled an armchair across from the patient in the next bed, ignoring the look of surprise on the old man's face.

'Oh yes. Hello dear. Tell me, were you driving Tom's car?' There was an accusing tone in her voice as she said this.

'We had just seen Mary off from Heathrow Airport and I was upset, so Sally kindly offered to drive me back. She handled the car brilliantly in those icy conditions. It was the fault of the driver of the BMW. He was going far too fast on the slip road,' said Tom. 'We have a witness, a taxi driver. He saw the whole thing and got the man's car registration number, so I'll be able to claim from his insurance. My old car has been taken to the dump. They had to cut me out through the roof.'

'Oh how ghastly. He might be dead now if he'd been in your little car,' Charlotte said to Sally.

'Where's Dad?' Tom asked, at the same time mouthing 'sorry' to Sally. 'Isn't he allowed to come this far with you?'

'No. He has to stay in Suffolk. He's spending the day with Amanda. She'll be upset. You know how she worries about you at the best of times.'

By the end of the third day, Tom was asking if he could go home. His mother had stayed in a nearby hotel for two nights but she proved to be more of a hindrance than a help. On the Monday Sally spent most of the day with him, as it was her day off, and she had lunch with Charlotte - just the two of them. Without an audience, Charlotte almost managed to be pleasant company. She asked Sally about her parents and about her son. She talked a little about her own daughter's disability and how good Tom was with her.

'Amanda will want to see Tom as soon as possible now that she knows he has been involved in an accident, but I don't know how we will do this. Tom won't be driving for a while and Amanda won't cope with a two hour car journey to London,' said Charlotte.

Sally could see that Charlotte was asking for her help in a roundabout way. 'William and I could bring Tom to Suffolk so that he can see his sister. I'd be happy to help. Of course, Tom will want to buy a new car once he's able to drive again. He'll miss his independence any day now.'

'I have a surprise for him dear. Actually, I have two surprises. Let's go and tell him. I have to go back to Suffolk this afternoon. I can see that I am leaving him in good hands though.' Charlotte smiled at Sally and gave her a sideways hug. Sally couldn't quite believe what was happening.

As they walked into the ward, Tom was sitting in the armchair fully dressed. He was wearing a tracksuit that Charlotte had collected from his flat, as neither his trousers nor his jeans would fit over the dressing on his leg. He looked a lot more cheerful.

'Hello darling. You look more human today. Are you feeling better? Amanda and your father send their love. Amanda wants to see you as soon as Sally can bring you to Suffolk. You know how she worries. We haven't told her about your father's troubles. She would be distraught,' said Charlotte.

'What's happening with Dad? Has he seen a solicitor yet or heard from the Courts?'

'The solicitor feels that they will take your father's age, health and otherwise clean record, into consideration. The Court hearing will be on April 11th, so not long to wait now. He will, of course, be able to pay back the money he owes, although whether they will add interest to that, we don't know yet.'

'Sally has offered to have me stay with them until I can drive again. My school has told me to take as much time as I need. I'll have physiotherapy as soon as all the broken bits are mended, to get my muscles working again. Hopefully it won't take too long and then I have to get another car.' Tom winked at Sally.

'You already have a new car darling. I've just put a large deposit down on that Triumph you wanted. Your father and I went to have a look at it. It's very classy. You'll need a garage for this car though.' Charlotte beamed when she saw Tom's face.

'Mother, that's fantastic news; the best news for a long time. Thanks a lot. What do you think Sally? It's a sports car with four seats and so they'll be room for all of us.' His face glowed with excitement.

'That's great, Tom. I'm really pleased for you. I think this might be a good year for you after all. As Mary would say, 'the signs are there.'

Chapter 32
Yukon 1991

Mary's heart was beating fast as she stood in line at the passport control in Vancouver. She pictured Jake's anxious face searching for her as she walked through customs. Please let him be there, she said quietly to herself. She touched the beautiful gold ring, on her right hand; the Christmas gift that Jake had given her at the airport in Whitehorse three weeks ago. She hadn't wanted to wear it in England. She loved it – a round black diamond set in a band of tiny gold nuggets. It was special, a real Yukon ring, and it fitted her perfectly. She had ordered Jake his very own Tlingit drum for Christmas which was currently still being made for him. She hoped he'd be pleased.

'How long do you plan to stay in Canada?' asked a young man as he studied her new dual passport. Mary jumped. She had been miles away.

'I plan to stay permanently, from now onwards. I was born in the Yukon and I'm returning to Whitehorse tomorrow,' said Mary with pride. 'I can't wait to get there.'

She saw him as soon as she entered the arrivals hall. Jake stood slightly apart from the main crowd with his arms outstretched. Mary felt eighteen again. She ran towards him, pushed her trolley to one side and leapt into his arms. They were both so excited that people around them watched and smiled.

'Welcome back darlin'. It feels like you've been away

for months. I've missed you loads. But you're here now.'
He lifted her off her feet and showered her with kisses.

'Oh Jake. I was hoping and hoping that you'd be here
to meet me. The cloud has lifted Jake. I'm free and I'm
going back home.' Mary laughed and hugged him some
more. Jake led her to the taxi-rank outside the airport.

'Where are we going, or is that a surprise too?' Mary
asked.

'We're going to downtown Vancouver. A friend of my
Dad's has an apartment there on Nelson Street. I asked
him if we could stay with him. He said he'd be away so
we've got the place to ourselves.' Jake looked really
pleased with himself. 'I stayed there last night. It's great
down there.'

They had a fun time together. It was cold, but not as
cold as it would be in Whitehorse. Jake wasn't used to the
big city and he was like a child in Disney Land. They had
dinner in a Vietnamese restaurant, walked down to
English Bay and enjoyed the lights. They laughed, they
held hands and they revelled in just being a couple for the
world to see. Mary felt a huge sense of relief, being able
to show her love for Jake so openly. No more silence. No
more secrets. There had been so many of them
surrounding her life and the Yukon had released them all.
She said this to Jake, as they sat drinking coffee and
eating chocolate muffins, the next morning. Much to her
surprise he quoted a poem to her:

'It's the great, big, broad land 'way up yonder,
    It's the forests where silence has lease;
It's the beauty that thrills me with wonder,
    It's the stillness that fills me with peace.'

'Jake that's beautiful. I didn't know you liked poetry.

Where is it from?' Mary felt quite moved. This poem echoed her thoughts exactly. It could have been written for her.

'It's from a Robert Service poem called 'The Spell of the Yukon'. We learnt it at school. He lived in Dawson City about a hundred years ago, and he wrote about the characters of the Gold Rush mainly.'

'Well, you lovely man, you're full of surprises. There's so much about you that I don't know yet.' Mary leaned over and kissed him. 'Jake, did you manage to visit Josie at all while I was away?'

'Yeah. I drove up to Carmacks a couple of times and I met her in Whitehorse whenever we were both in town. She's okay. We get on real well. She gets angry sometimes. Mind you she has every right to. She and I share the same passion. We want to do our bit to help the First Nations people.'

'You must teach me, Jake. You must teach me their history, their traditions and their beliefs. I want to help too.'

'Then you must talk to the Elders and listen to their stories. That is how we all learn. Get your Grandpa Tommy talking. What a great guy he is. Did you know he still fishes for the people in his community? He was a champion dog racer you know. He's famous. I'd heard of him from Uncle Albie.' Mary loved to watch Jake when he felt passionate about something. He was on fire.

'Yes, I know. I love him and so does Josie,' said Mary. 'There's so much to look forward to. I could listen to you for hours love, but we have a plane to catch.' Mary suddenly felt eager to get back to Whitehorse and to see her family. 'Now, let's get cleared up and go to the airport. The Yukon is calling us.' They both laughed.

Mary gazed out of the window at the breath-taking

view over the snow capped peaks of the Coastal Mountains. She thought about her very first trip just six months ago. She had no idea at the time what she would find, if anything, in the Yukon. What a lot had happened in her life in those few months.

'Will your Mom meet us at the airport do you think?' Mary asked as the plane made its descent into Whitehorse.

'She said she would. I bet she'll be there,' said Jake. 'In fact I think there might be another surprise waiting for you.' He grinned.

Josie stood next to Annie, looking a little self-conscious. She hadn't been up to the airport for years and wasn't used to all these emotional gatherings. She smiled broadly when she saw Mary and Jake though.

'How are things my love?' Mary hugged her sister. 'Are you still with Grandpa Tommy?'

'Yeah. I'm good. Sylvia brought me in to town so that I could see Mikey and she said she'd take me back to Carmacks later. Do you wanna come with us?'

'I'm quite tired tonight Jose. It's been a hectic couple of days. Annie, could Josie share with me just for tonight please?' Mary asked. 'I'll take her back to Carmacks tomorrow.'

'Sure,' said Annie with a smile.

'I'd better let Sylvia know, I guess. She said she'd meet me outside White Pass,' said Josie.

'I've taken Friday and Monday off work so I could drive you up there if you like,' offered Jake.

'Mary, I've got an application form for you from the school I was telling you about. The teaching assistant from the special class goes on maternity leave in two weeks time and I told the Principal about you. You'd better do this tomorrow. He wants it back as soon as possible,' said Annie.

'Thanks Annie. You think of everything. The sooner I get a job, the sooner Josie and I can look for somewhere to live.'

'I thought this young man would try to persuade you to go to Carcross with him,' said Annie.

'He did, but I've told him he has to be patient,' laughed Mary, as she snuggled up between Jake and Josie on the back seat of the suburban. 'I need to get to know my new family for a while first.'

Mary reckoned she had just enough money to last until the middle of next month. She hadn't told anyone that she'd accepted the offer of a loan from Tom, not even Sally. She had hated doing it, but her own savings had run out and she felt there wasn't anyone else she could turn to – not for money anyway.

The next morning she rented a car for a couple of weeks and she managed to get the same little car she had rented before. It was sitting there waiting for her.

'This is a good sign,' she said to Jake. 'No-one wants my car. They've left it for me.'

They decided to drive to Carmacks in two vehicles so that Jake could keep on the highway and drive straight back to Carcross that evening. But first, Mary stopped at the local school and handed in her application form. She had called Roy who was happy to give her a good reference. The secretary took her form and was very welcoming.

'Keep your fingers crossed,' Mary said to Josie. 'The job looks perfect for me.'

'I might see if they've got a job going in Tim Horton's until I can get on a counselling course. They take on First Nations people. I've seen them in there,' said Josie.

'Every place should take on everyone, surely? It's the law now,' said Mary.

'But they don't. Some folks say that we're not reliable. They can stuff their stupid jobs. I wouldn't wanna work for them anyway.' Josie scowled. She caught Mary smiling at her and she laughed.

Mary studied every lake and every stand of trees with pride as they journeyed towards Carmacks. This was her home now, the place of her birth. She hadn't known her mother, but she had her photograph now. The fact that she looked very like her brought her comfort and a sense of belonging. The history of the First Nations people was a part of her and in time she knew that her life in England would seem like a collection of distant dreams. She and Josie and Jake had lots of plans for the future but, at the moment, she had no idea what her life would become. She just knew that she was home.

As they drove down to the river in Carmacks and out towards Jack's place Josie gazed across the frozen Yukon River. It was about twenty degrees below zero but a watery sun lit up the horizon.

'Look Mary! There's Grandpa away out there. He's fishing,' said Josie. 'Let's park the car and walk across to him. You've never walked across the river before have you Mary? Have you got some good boots?'

'Yes, I have. Are you sure it'll be safe?' Mary asked.

'Sure it's safe. We could drive the truck across this river.' Jake parked behind them.

'What's up? Have you run out of gas?' He teased her.

'It's Grandpa. He's fishing and we're gonna see if he's struck lucky,' said Josie excitedly. 'Come on you two.'
As the sun faded, Mary, Josie and Jake walked arm in arm across the river to the community fishing hole, where ninety-four year old Tommy Black waited patiently for the next bite.

ACKNOWLEDGEMENTS

My sincere thanks to everyone who read and commented on early drafts of 'Where Silence has Lease', particularly to Christine Page and Joey Peake; to Eleanor Millard for her proof-reading and her invaluable help when researching the Yukon history and background to the story; to Gill Thomas for the beautiful design of the book cover; to Sally Leich and Ali Koops of 'Forstal Kennels' for giving me the experience of a husky training session; to Heather, Ida, Mark, Eileen and all those at the C.T.F.N. in Carcross, to Amy Ekins and May Roberts of Carmacks for sharing their stories, and my special thanks to Millie Jones and her family for their knowledge, inspiration and encouragement. Without Millie, this book would never have been written.

ABOUT THE AUTHOR

I majored in English when at college in the 1960s and I have always enjoyed writing. I have written poetry and short stories, but 'Where Silence has Lease' is my first novel. In 1968 I emigrated to Canada and although I now live in Suffolk, Canada has become my second home. I visit friends and family there almost every year and I lived in the Yukon for three months in 2010 to research material for this book. The characters and events in my story are fictional, but the places - with the exception of the convent, the name of which has been changed - are drawn from real life.

Printed in Great Britain
by Amazon.co.uk, Ltd.,
Marston Gate.